Clare Connelly was raised in small-town Australia among a family of avid readers. She spent much of her childhood up a tree, Mills & Boon book in hand. Clare is married to her own real-life hero, and they live in a bungalow near the sea with their two children. She is frequently found staring into space—a surefire sign that she's in the world of her characters. She has a penchant for French food and ice-cold champagne, and Mills & Boon novels continue to be her favourite ever books. Writing for Modern is a long-held dream. Clare can be contacted via clareconnelly.com or at her Facebook page.

After spending three years as a die-hard New Yorker, **Kate Hewitt** now lives in a small village in the English Lake District, with her husband, their five children and a golden retriever. In addition to writing intensely emotional stories, she loves reading, baking and playing chess with her son—she has yet to win against him, but she continues to try. Learn more about Kate at kate-hewitt.com.

THE SICILIAN'S DEAL FOR "I DO"

CLARE CONNELLY

PREGNANCY CLAUSE IN THEIR PAPER MARRIAGE

KATE HEWITT

MILLS & BOON

First published in Great Britain 2024
by Mills & Boon, an imprint of HarperCollins*Publishers* Ltd,
1 London Bridge Street, London, SE1 9GF

www.harpercollins.co.uk

HarperCollins*Publishers*, Macken House, 39/40 Mayor Street Upper, Dublin 1, D01 C9W8, Ireland

ISBN: 978-0-263-31995-8

02/24

THE SICILIAN'S DEAL FOR "I DO"

CLARE CONNELLY

MILLS & BOON

PROLOGUE

Twelve months earlier

BENEATH THE CHAPEL WINDOW, in the small square tucked deep in the ancient heart of Palermo, the world kept turning. Children ran by, gelatos in hand, sun on their chubby cheeks, parents walking behind them arm in arm, smiling, doting, adoring.

Mia watched as a boy of about nine tucked behind a wall, grinning, waiting until his sister, perhaps six, walked near to him, when he jumped out and shouted something. Though the chapel glass was thin and rippled by age, Mia couldn't hear through it, but she guessed it was something like, 'Boo!' The girl jumped, then both keeled over, laughing.

Despite the anxiety building inside Mia's gut over her own situation, she smiled. A weak, distracted smile, before she turned her back on the outside world with deep reluctance.

'Surely he's just been delayed.'

She caught sight of herself in an ancient mirror. Like the windows, it too was damaged by the passage of time, so it distorted her slightly, but that didn't matter. The ludicrousness of this was all too apparent, even without a clear reflection.

Had she really thought this would happen?

That today would be her wedding day?

That Luca Cavallaro would *actually* marry her?

Flashes of their brief, whirlwind courtship ran before her eyes. Her bewilderment at the idea of marriage, her parents' explanation that it was best for the family, for the business, and then, meeting Luca, who had swept her away with a single look, a brooding, fulminating glance that had turned her blood to lava and made her wonder if she'd ever really existed before knowing him.

Every time they'd been together, she'd felt that same zing. When they'd touched—even just the lightest brushing of hands—it had been like fireworks igniting in her bloodstream, and their kiss, that one, wild kiss, had left Mia with the certainty that she was born to be held by him.

The hot sting of tears threatened but Mia sucked in a calming breath, refusing to give into the temptation to weep. Not here, not now, certainly not in front of her parents, who were staring at Mia with expressions of abject disappointment, and, worse, a lack of surprise. As if they had almost expected this, for her to fail them.

'What did you say to him?' Jennifer Marini pushed, arms crossed over her svelte frame. 'You were alone with him, by the car the other night. What happened?'

Unlike Mia, Jennifer was tall and willow thin—a difference Jennifer never failed to highlight. Instead of growing into a stunning, svelte woman, like Jennifer, Mia had stopped growing a little over five feet, and had developed lush, generous curves. *Just like your mother*, Jennifer had never failed to condemn, as if bearing a resemblance to the woman who'd birthed Mia was a sin.

Reluctantly, Mia's eyes were drawn back to her own reflection. To the frothy white dress and ridiculous hairstyle.

She'd been primped and preened and pulled in a thousand directions since first light. An army of women had worked on getting her 'bride ready'. She thought of the waxing with heated cheeks and blinked again quickly now.

Despite their efforts, Mia couldn't help thinking how far this was from her best look. She was under no illusions as to her beauty. She was pretty enough, she supposed, in the right light and to the right person, and as long as she could remember her biological mother's eyes and smile, Mia felt glad that they lived on in her own face. But she liked pasta far too much and disliked sweating generally, which ruled out a vast array of cardio exercises. She was never going to be reed thin like her adoptive mother, nor did she want to be. There was a sternness to Jennifer, and a general lack of *joie de vivre* that Mia had always associated with her restrictive diet: far better to eat the pasta— and the gelato and the focaccia and the mozzarella—and be happy, Mia always thought.

'I—nothing,' she said, quickly, even though memories of those snatched moments were making her pulse rush now.

'I did everything I could for you,' Jennifer said with a ticking of her finger to her palm, the harsh red of her manicure catching Mia's eye. 'I did everything I could to pave the way for this marriage. You must have said something.'

'I haven't spoken to him in a week,' Mia denied. Perhaps it was strange not to talk to your fiancé for so long, but then, this was far from a normal marriage, and her situation was far from normal. Marriage to Luca Cavallaro wasn't a love match. Not for him, anyway. She frowned, and her heart began to beat faster, to race, as she remembered their first meeting. The way their eyes had locked, and something had shifted inside her, a part of Mia she hadn't known existed, the part of her she'd always wondered about.

Whatever physical beauty she lacked, he made up for, with abundance.

Like a specimen from a gallery or a famous actor or a pristine example of what the male species *should* be. Tall, sculpted, muscular without being bulky, strong, and when he'd looked at her, she'd felt this giddy sense of disbelief that *he* was actually going to be her husband.

They'd only seen each other a handful of times after that, always with Mia's parents until that last night, and the conversations had revolved around the businesses. The sale of Mia's father's old family corporation to Luca Cavallaro and his newly minted multibillion-dollar fortune. Just what the world needed: another beyond handsome, alpha-male billionaire!

But then there'd been *that* kiss, when he'd been leaving one evening and Jennifer had hastily told Mia to walk him out. The moon had been high in the sky above her parents' estate in the countryside surrounding Palermo, the sound of the ocean drowned out by the rushing of her blood as he'd pulled her into his arms, stared down at her, frowned for a moment and then, he'd simply kissed her, as though it were the most natural thing in the world.

Perhaps it was. They'd spent hours in each other's company over the course of their engagement—maybe he'd expected more kissing, more of everything? Mia didn't know. That night, he'd taken matters into his own hands... She'd expected it would turn out like a movie, a three-second kiss, maximum, but his lips had lingered, and the world had slowed right down along with it. She'd moaned, because he'd smelled so good but tasted better; the kiss was by far the best thing she'd ever felt. Like coming home—

except, Mia had never really felt at home anywhere since her parents had died.

And then his arms had tightened around her back, melding her curvy body to his, and he'd deepened the kiss, his passionate inspection of her mouth leaving her shaking, writhing wantonly against him, until he'd pulled away and stared down at her once more. Was that surprise in his features? At the time, Mia had thought so, but, like all memories, it shifted and morphed so she couldn't have said with any confidence the next morning that it hadn't been boredom. Or worse, disgust. After all, Mia had very limited experience with kissing men.

That had been one week before their wedding. They hadn't seen nor spoken to one another afterwards, but she'd had no reason to doubt him.

No reason to doubt this would come to pass. If anything, the kiss had cemented his intentions for Mia. How could he make her feel like that and then walk away?

She could have wept when she thought of her childish fantasies, the dreams that had kept her awake at night and stirred her body to a fever pitch of wanting.

When her parents had first told her about the wedding, she'd been unsure about the idea. They'd wanted to know a Marini would still work in the family business, and also that Mia would be taken care of once they'd sold off such a valuable asset. But it didn't take long for Mia to warm to the idea.

Of no longer being a Marini, which, in some ways, she'd never really felt herself to be.

Of no longer being alone.

Of being a wife, married—and to someone like Luca. Putting aside his physical beauty, he was rich and powerful and she was sure she'd be able to lead her own life while living under his roof, that he wouldn't trouble himself with her comings and goings. But also, there would be children, and that thought alone had made her a very willing accomplice to the whole scheme. Children, a family of her own, something she'd so desperately wanted since losing her parents and the sense of security that came from knowing she was loved.

Though she was outwardly compliant with her adoptive parents, a streak of rebellion had been growing inside Mia, and marrying Luca Cavallaro seemed like a brilliant way to exercise her independence, finally.

'He's probably just late,' Mia murmured, trying to reassure herself.

'To his own wedding?' Jennifer demanded, moving one of the red-taloned hands to her hips. 'He is supposed to be out there, waiting for you, Mia. That's the way it works.'

'He's a very busy and important man,' Mia pointed out. 'That's why we're here, isn't it?'

Gianni Marini shook his head, his rounded face showing obvious impatience. 'All you had to do was sit in the corner and smile from time to time.'

Something sparked in Mia's chest. Had she done something wrong? Had she been the one to ruin this? Had the kiss been so bad? She spun away again quickly, trying to find the same family with the brother and sister playing hide and seek, but they were gone. The light danced off the large tree in the centre of the square. Mia had always loved the light of Palermo. She'd hated leaving it to go to milky grey England, but Jennifer had insisted that her daughter attend her alma mater, so boarding school it had been. How she'd missed the sunshine and sea salt.

'Oh, God.' Jennifer's voice crackled in the air. Mia closed her eyes without turning around. She'd been holding onto hope, remembering Luca's eyes, absolutely certain that someone with such beautiful eyes and the ability to truly look at someone and *see* them could never do anything quite so callous as this. But then, she also knew. Even as the hairdressers had worked and the make-up artist had glued false lashes in place and her nails had been painted and made hot beneath a UV light, Mia had somehow *known* it would all come to nothing.

'What is it?' Gianni asked loudly.

'He's not coming.'

'How do you know?'

'The whole world knows,' Jennifer snapped. 'Look.' Mia kept her eyes shut, back to the room, breath silenced despite the heaviness of her heart.

Gianni read aloud, quickly, '*"Runaway Groom"*—that's the headline. *"It appears Luca Cavallaro preferred the idea of an airport runway to that of a wedding aisle after all. The billionaire bachelor was spotted leaving Italy last night despite his planned wedding, which was to take place today, to Mia Marini, daughter of steel magnate Gianni Marini. Trouble in corporate merger paradise? Watch this space."*'

Mia groaned, the last sentence almost the hardest to hear of all, because she realised that the whole world knew their marriage was just a corporate merger. And it was. But was it so implausible to think a man like Luca might actually want to marry Mia for herself?

A single tear slid down her cheek.

'He left last night!' Jennifer barked, her voice trembling with rage. 'And didn't have the decency to tell us. All of this, all of this trouble, and not even a chance to save face. How could he do this to us, Gianni?'

To you? Mia wanted to scream. She was the one in the

ridiculous dress with awful hair and over-the-top make-up. Suddenly, she was claustrophobic and couldn't breathe. Could barely stand up. Stars danced behind her eyes and she spun wildly, staring at her parents without seeing them, then locating the door to the small room.

'I have to go.'

'Go where, Mia?' Jennifer asked sharply.

'Outside. Anywhere. I don't care. I just—I can't breathe.'

'Mia, don't,' her mother warned, but too late. Mia burst into the chapel, to a packed room of people, all there for the spectacle of this. Most were on their phones, but when she appeared, they looked up, almost as one, some with pity, others with a delighted sense of *schadenfreude*. Mia barely noticed any of it. She scrambled along the back of the church, past the guests who'd not been able to find seats, ignoring their words, their voices, throwing open the heavy, old timber doors so the beautiful Palermo light bathed her. She closed her eyes and let it make her strong for a moment, then ran down the stairs and across the square, right into a child who smeared strawberry gelato against the horrible white dress.

And all Mia could do was stand still, in the middle of the square, hands on her hips, head tilted to the sky, and laugh. There was nothing else for it.

CHAPTER ONE

NOT A SINGLE day went past between then and now in which Luca Cavallaro wasn't convinced he did the right thing. He couldn't think of the Marini family without a sense of ruthless anger and disgust.

They'd lied to him.

They'd tried to sell him a worthless business with clever accounting and incomplete statements. And to tie him up in marriage to their daughter. Worse, Luca had come damned close to going along with it. Luca Cavallaro, who'd known from almost as long as he could walk and talk that he never wanted to marry, never wanted to love. Not after seeing what love could do to a person.

Then again, this hadn't been about love, so much as a necessary term to secure a company that had come to mean a lot to Luca. His hand formed a fist at his side as he remembered how he'd felt when he'd first heard that Marini Enterprises was available...the company his father had coveted but failed to secure. Luca would stop at nothing to make it his. Not because he cared about earning his father's approval, but because he was driven to win, at all costs, and if he could beat his father, so much the better.

So he'd accepted the marriage deal as part of the merger, had even started to relish the idea of marriage to Mia Marini. It wouldn't be a real marriage, after all, just a convenient union—but there would have been some definite perks. In fact, he'd started to look forward to having Mia in his home, and his bed. That wasn't the same as marrying for love—there had been no risk to either of them.

But then, he'd learned the truth: that the Marinis were trying to swindle him. The company his own father had fought tooth and nail to buy ten years earlier had become practically worthless. Did the older Marini really think Luca was so stupid? That he wouldn't undertake more due diligence than the average person?

His team of forensic accountants had been raking over Marini corporate documents for more than a month and finally found evidence of Gianni's deception, of the true state of Marini Enterprises. It was almost bankrupt. Using an admittedly clever scheme of shadow companies and trusts, he'd been able to make it look profitable and successful in order to lure a buyer, but it was all a façade.

Just like Mia.

Outrage had filled every cell of his body. It wasn't just the money, it was that they'd taken him for a fool who would believe their lies. It wasn't as if Luca craved anyone's approval, least of all his father's, but in the back of his mind there'd been the knowledge that Carrick Stone was waiting for Luca to fail, to come back to Australia with his tail between his legs. The Marini family wouldn't have ruined him—Luca was too wealthy—but he would have been mortified for the truth to come out, and for his father to know. And so he'd left, without a backwards glance.

And yet…

In the warm, afternoon sun, standing near the edge of his infinity pool, Luca reached for his phone once more, his eyes landing immediately on the article, to the photo of Mia standing, smiling sweetly, beside a man Luca had met on a handful of occasions. Lorenzo di Angelo had inherited the responsibility of running his family's textile business, based out of Milano, but in the last few years he'd been launching an impressive move into the south, and wider across Europe. Luca had been watching with interest—he watched all business expansion with interest, having an almost savant-like ability to track the landscape of corporate movements across the world.

So, Gianni had found another investor.

And Mia was going along with it, just like before, a willing lure to the next mark.

Mia Marini engaged—again!

Even though he didn't regret walking away from their deal, something about the headline left a stain of discomfort in his chest, and he couldn't say why. Mia had gone along with her parents' scheme. She worked for the business; she was undoubtedly complicit in their lies. And yet, the media coverage of their failed wedding had all focused on her. Jilted. Ditched. The photo of her in the square, the dress covered in ice cream, a child staring at her with wonder as she'd looked at the sky, face scrunched, lips parted.

Shame had been a blade at his side, even when he knew he'd done the right thing, even when he knew she deserved it. He'd ignored calls from his father—as if Carrick had any right to lecture Luca about any damned thing—and his half-brother, Max. Though that was much harder to do, given the affection and respect he felt for Max Stone. But he hadn't wanted to answer questions about the marriage, nor about the Marini business, and the fact he'd left Mia to clean up the mess after he'd discovered the truth.

And hadn't she deserved that?

She'd gone along with it all. She could have told him the truth, especially on that night, by the car, but she hadn't.

That kiss... He closed his eyes as he remembered, as pleasure vibrated through his body in a way that still had the power to shake him. What had he thought? That a kiss like that was somehow an unlocking of her soul? That she would be honest with him because of the desire that exploded between them?

There was too much at stake for honesty.

She'd been a willing piece in the whole scam, had even been willing to sell herself into the deal, to marry a man she didn't know, to get him to shore up a worthless company.

That made her almost the guiltiest of all.

After the wedding of the century that wasn't, Mia Marini is trying again, this time with the oldest son of the di Angelos, bringing together two of Italy's most established families.

Well, good for Mia. She'd duped another guy into the scheme.

He placed his phone down on the table, moving to the edge of the pool and staring now at the crystal-clear water that led all the way to the tiled edge, and beyond it, to the immaculate Sicilian waters.

She'd been an irrelevancy at first.

And then, she'd kissed him—or he'd kissed her—and a spark of desire had ignited into something far more powerful.

She'd been his fiancée.

He could have taken her if he'd wanted, and suddenly, he had wanted. He'd wanted to fold her into the back of the car and drive away from her parents and their estate, drive anywhere there was a big, comfortable bed, and make love to her, to hear her moan a little more like she had, to have her cry out his name.

CLARE CONNELLY

He didn't need to go back to his phone, to loo. .. the photo. He could see Mia in his mind, as she'd been that night beneath the milky moonlight, and as she was in the picture, with di Angelo. He dived into the water as a resolution formed firmly in his mind. Less a resolution, he thought with powerful strokes, but a need to possess what was, at one time, his. Or should have been.

He'd walked away that night because he'd been angry with her, angry that she'd lied to him, angry she'd tried to dupe him, then kissing him like that.

He was still angry.

But the Sicilian blood ran hot in his veins and it demanded something of Luca that he could no longer deny: before Mia married anyone else, before she willingly sold herself to another man for the sake of her family's crumbling empire, she would be his.

All his, just as she'd pledged to him when they'd become engaged, and as her body had promised that night when they'd kissed beneath the moonlight. Something had been ignited between them, something urgent and intense. He'd been able to ignore it until now, until reading that Mia was about to marry someone else, and he would lose the ability to act on this desire once and for all. With a new sense of resolve, he cut through the water, temptation finally something he intended to obey.

Ostensibly, the ball was a way to honour her parents. Each year, the Marini family hosted this event, a fundraiser for her parents' charity, but for Mia, it simply drew attention to how alone she was. Despite her newly announced engagement, despite her parents' professed love for her—it all felt like an elaborate lie! She was marrying a man she barely knew and certainly didn't love, who'd made it clear he intended to be a free agent right up until they signed on the dotted line—which was fine by Mia, she was under no illusion as to the kind of marriage they'd have.

But on top of that, she'd been raised by parents who'd taken her in out of a duty to her biological mother—her adoptive mother's oldest friend—and who'd found themselves steadily disappointed by Mia as she'd grown. Somewhere deep down, Mia was sure they did love her, in their own way, and certain that they wanted the best for her, but it hadn't been a happy childhood and even now the shadows of those years reached into her life and dulled her view of things.

Nights like this made it worse, because she was forced to remember what life had been like before. With her parents.

She'd only been young when they'd died but core memories of their happiness and love were imprinted on her soul. Was it any wonder her greatest fantasy in life was of having a family of her own? Of having children she could adore and spoil, and pour all of her love into, finally?

'I thought they'd be here,' her mother hissed through clenched teeth, eyes darting to Gianni's face, skin pale. 'Where are they?'

Standing beside them in the crowded bar, Mia leaned closer to hear.

'A scheduling conflict. Don't worry, Jennifer. This wedding—and merger—will go ahead. This time, it's different.'

Mia's eyes briefly swept shut. The di Angelos. Her gut twisted with doubts and uncertainties, at the idea that her second attempt at marriage might be as ill-fated as the first, but then, no. It wasn't possible. Lorenzo was nothing like Luca. Where there was something dangerous about Luca's brilliant genius and ruthless determination, and certainly about his unfettered sex appeal, Lorenzo was calm, methodical and not at all sexually attracted to Mia, which put her at ease. They'd calmly discussed the merger, their reason for marrying, his intention to continue to date discreetly until they were officially married. Which was just how Mia wanted it.

'They know how important this night is to us. The media will be wondering—'

'The media does not matter,' he interrupted sharply. 'Now stop worrying and smile. People are looking.'

Sure enough, some people were looking in their direction, or were they? Eyes that were pointed their way were, on closer inspection, focused ever so slightly beyond them, so Mia threw a glance over her shoulder and then shivered, for no reason she could think of.

'Excuse me,' she murmured to her parents, nonetheless unnerved and deciding she needed a sip of champagne and a quiet moment.

'Where are you going?'

'To mingle,' she lied, flashing a smile at her father. 'I won't be long.'

Disapproval flattened Jennifer's lips but Mia had long since given up trying to guess what she'd done to upset her adoptive mother. She turned her back and disappeared into the crowd before Jennifer could invent a reason for her to stay.

Whether the di Angelos were there or not, the night was a success. Mia could tell by how many guests were in attendance, and by the calibre of celebrities. The event had drawn a host of well-heeled, monied glitterati and that meant the charity would benefit. She was glad, though no one observing Mia would have realised it, if they'd looked at her serious expression.

At the bar, she waited in line, and finally, at the front, ordered a glass of champagne, gripped it with relief and began to cut through the crowd once more, nodding politely when she saw an acquaintance or someone her parents knew, until she reached the doors that led to the rooftop garden. The night was warm, and so there wasn't as much privacy out here as Mia had craved, but she remembered a small corner that offered a little more seclusion and she moved there, glad to find it unoccupied. She could sit on one of the chairs and remove her painfully high heels, reaching down to massage the ligaments of her ankles with relief. Above her, fairy lights had been strung from edge to edge of the rooftop garden, giving it a magical feel, interspersed as they were with potted plants. The sound of happy conversations swirled around her from the elegant guests, giving Mia a sense of anonymity—compounded by the two enormous ferns that shielded her from view.

When her champagne was half empty, she wondered how much longer she could reasonably hide out here for. Would anyone be missing her?

A wry smile tipped her lips.

Her parents' initial impatience with her disappearance would have dissipated in the face of the success of the event, and Jennifer was no doubt in there enjoying the attention of her well-heeled friends. Which meant Mia had at least the rest of her champagne glass to go...

She leaned back a little in the chair, closed her eyes, breathed deeply and tried to relax, to tell herself that she was making the right decisions in life, even when doubts often chased her. If her parents had lived, what would they say about this marriage?

Her smile turned into a grimace and then a sigh as she sipped her champagne.

If her parents had lived, she'd have never been in this situation—forced to seek an escape from adoptive parents who both loved and resented her, who showed their love by being way too protective and controlling, and for whom Mia had been conditioned to have such a high level of gratitude that she could never countermand them.

The rational part of Mia's brain knew how stupid that was, wondered why she didn't just tell them that she didn't want to work in the family business, that she didn't want to marry a stranger just to retain an interest in Marini Enterprises. But the little girl who'd been rescued from foster care was told over and over again how lucky she was to have them, couldn't defy their wishes. So the best she could do was try to make her own wishes accord with theirs.

And in Lorenzo, perhaps she'd succeeded?

She sighed again, lifted her champagne flute to her lips, then glanced left when a sudden motion caught her eye.

And felt as though every cell in her body had reverberated to fever pitch then stopped altogether.

She jerked to standing, spilling champagne on the tiled ground in a dramatic splashing motion, shock rendering her body capable of only staccato movements.

'Luca?' She blinked rapidly, sure her eyes were deceiving her.

But then his lips curled in that smile she remembered so well, half cynicism, half seduction, and her stomach rolled so hard she thought it might fly out of her body.

'What are you doing here?' she demanded, unable to resist wiping a hand across her eyes in case this was a fantasy.

'It is a charity event. I bought a ticket.'

'You bought a ticket,' she parroted, eyes huge. 'Erm, why?'

He shrugged indolently. 'Why not? I have the money.'

'But this is my *parents'* charity,' she said quickly, lifting her champagne glass and draining it completely.

'So it is.'

Her lips parted with indignation. 'You shouldn't be here.'

He watched her with such a look of relaxation that she was sure it was fake. Either that, or he truly didn't care about the way he'd humiliated her and upended her life, not to mention the pain he'd caused her parents. The gall of him to appear like this, wearing a tuxedo and looking so damned gorgeous. How dared he? Next minute, he'd tell her he was here with some supermodel or something. Grinding her teeth, she flashed him a look that was pure resentment.

'I mean it, Luca. You need to leave.'

Instead, he took a step closer. Mia braced. Waves of heat seemed to rush towards her, radiating from his body, reminding her of when they'd first met and she'd been so completely overwhelmed by him and her desire for him. She squeezed her champagne glass more tightly, wishing it had magical refilling capabilities.

'Why?'

She was at a loss for words. Shaking her head, she finally said, 'Isn't that obvious?'

'Not to me.'

'You…you…you left me on our wedding day!' she spluttered, then quickly looked around to make sure no one had witnessed her outburst. She lifted her fingertips to her forehead, tried to remember that it had been a year ago, that she was different now, that her whole life was different. Not only that, his treatment of Mia had made her stronger, smarter, had forced her to really take control of her life. To an outsider, it might appear that nothing had changed—after all, she was entering into another arranged marriage—but her eyes were wide open this time. She was nobody's fool. This marriage would be all on her terms.

'Yes,' he agreed, taking another step towards her. Why wouldn't Mia's feet work to draw her backwards? 'But that does not mean I haven't thought about you.'

Her lips parted, the statement striking her in the chest like a bolt of lightning. It was a lie. It had to be a lie. She placed her champagne flute down on the nearby table with unnecessary force.

'Oh? Thinking what a first-rate bastard you were?'

His eyes narrowed imperceptibly. 'Of opportunities wasted.' He moved closer still, so close she could smell his aftershave and feel his warmth, and her insides jerked accordingly. 'I have been thinking of that night.'

'What night?' she asked in a strangled voice, taking a step back until she connected with the stone wall behind her. She was grateful for the support at first, but then Luca moved forward and effectively trapped her, his frame so much larger than hers, so it was impossible to imagine how she could escape. Only—she could. If she told him to go away, firmly, she was pretty sure he would.

So why didn't she?

Why didn't she stamp on his foot, for good measure, then tell him to get lost?

Her mouth was dry. The simple act of swallowing seemed to require a monumental effort.

'Do you need a reminder?'

His gaze dropped to her lips and Mia's heart felt as though it might leap out of her chest, ribs be damned. 'No,' she said quickly. 'That's fine.'

His smirk showed scepticism. 'Are you sure?'

Her lips parted, forming a perfect 'oh', and she stared up at him, so close now, his body locking hers to the wall, so she couldn't think straight, couldn't do anything other than feel. The air between them reverberated with tension and need—she could taste adrenaline in her mouth.

'Or would you like me to kiss you, Mia?'

Her blood screamed in her ears. What was happening? Was this a dream? Why on earth would he be here, offering this? And now? She tried to think straight, tried to put logical thought in front of logical thought, but her mind wouldn't cooperate.

'You can't,' she groaned. Something was pushing its way into the forefront of her brain. Something important she needed to grab hold of. She lifted a hand to his chest, to hold him right where he was, and then she saw it. Her engagement ring.

She was getting married.

Okay, it wasn't a love match either. In fact, she barely knew her husband and had no expectation that he was honouring any kind of old-fashioned celibacy arrangement in the lead-up to their wedding. And she didn't much care. This wasn't to be a normal wedding, nor a normal marriage, and Mia found the idea of that quite thrilling. She was charting her own course, plotting a life for herself— finally—that would best suit her. Without her parents' over-the-top meddling at every turn.

Nonetheless, here at this event, tucked away in a corner of the rooftop, the threat of discovery made her blood curdle.

'*I* can't,' she clarified, infusing her voice with a certainty she didn't feel. 'I'm getting married, Luca. For real this time.'

His eyes bored into hers, something in their depths she couldn't understand.

'But you are not married yet, are you?'

She tried to swallow again, past a throat that was thick and raw.

'I—what do you want?'

'An interesting question. Are you sure you would like the answer?'

She squeezed her eyes shut on a wave of feeling, then shook her head a little. Luca's finger beneath her chin had her tilting her face to his. 'I have a proposition for you.'

Her heart slammed into her throat.

'If I'm honest, I'm still reeling from the last proposition we entered into.'

A quick, cynical smile flooded her and was replaced with warmth. She focused over his shoulder. 'I want you to come home with me.'

The floor seemed to open up and swallow Mia whole. 'What?'

'One night.'

She scanned his face, looking for evidence of a joke, but he wasn't smiling now, and there was such a look of intense hunger in his eyes that she gasped, because it was exactly how he'd looked at her that night, by the car.

Desire was a fever pitch in her bloodstream.

'I can't,' she said, desperate to believe that. Luca was the opposite of what she wanted in every way except one—physical. But he was dangerous. Far too dangerous for Mia, who'd experienced more than enough hurt and humiliation in one lifetime. Now she was all about control. Measured, calm, unemotional control.

'Not even for old time's sake,' he prompted with a softness she hadn't expected. In anyone else, that soft tone might have spoken of uncertainty but in Luca it was dangerous.

'There were no old times,' Mia hissed, furious. 'There was a stupid arrangement and one quick, forgettable moment by a car.'

But for a man like Luca, who was all alpha-male pride, her insult appeared to sail right into its mark. His lips twisted in an approximation of a smile but she saw something else in the depths of his eyes, something darker. 'Forgettable?' He dipped his head forward just as she realised she'd wanted him to, as she'd been goading him to. Oh, what kind of fool was she? 'Let's see if this next kiss is any more memorable then.'

He stared at Mia, challenging her, waiting for her to say or do something, to fight back, but instead, to Mia's shock and despair, anger had her pushing up onto the tips of her toes and seeking his mouth with her own, as if to prove to him how far she'd come in the past year, to show him that she wasn't the same stupid, ignorant girl who'd gone blindly into a marriage arrangement with this man.

But how quickly her control was sapped by the desire that instantly flared between them, as his body pressed hers to the wall, holding her immobile, as he then demanded—and received—her total surrender, the tables utterly turned. The kiss she'd initiated to prove a silly point had become an ultimate surrender.

It had been over a year, and, despite what she'd just said, Mia had never forgotten the power of his mouth. She'd dreamed of this, had longed for it, even when she hated him, and thought him the very worst man on earth. How was it possible that her head and heart could exist in such conflict?

His tongue lashed hers, his body still at first and then

moving, a knee moving between her legs then lifting higher, separating her thighs, one arm pressing to the wall at her side, the other curving around her waist, stroking her, holding her, as if he couldn't let her go. But it was all a ruse. A lie. A game.

A game?

Yes. That seemed appropriate. For whatever reason, he'd played Mia. She couldn't understand it, because there had been so much in their arrangement for him to benefit from: the business had seemed so important to him—he'd spent hours with her father, going over the corporate structure, hinting at plans he'd developed to turn Marini Enterprises into a global powerhouse. He'd seemed fully invested, as though buying Marini Enterprises was the most important thing in his world. And then he'd disappeared into thin air.

But these were logical thoughts, and Mia was well beyond the ability to be logical. Her brain was mush, rendered that way by the power of his nearness, the chemistry that sparked between them like a match being struck. She felt its heat and flame ignite inside her body, as though her veins were flooded by pure rocket fuel.

'Luca,' she groaned his name, liked the taste of it, the feel of it, the weight of it against her tongue, the way they rolled together, a tsunami of feelings, but there was terror too, because this was all too much. By the car that night it had been powerful, but like an electrical shock, sharp and succinct, splitting her world in two, then it was over. This was long, growing, a spreading heat that was gripping Mia, changing her, making her want things she couldn't understand, things that were powerful and overwhelming and *necessary*.

She was a woman, damn it. At twenty-three, she was old enough to understand enough about her body and yet she had no experience. While in theory she knew what was going on, the reality of these sensations was totally overwhelming and daunting.

His hand moved to her waist, to the silk shirt she wore, lifting it slightly, just an inch, separating it from the waistband of her full, ballgown skirt so his fingertips brushed her bare skin and she trembled, goosebumps covering her flesh, responding to the possessive glide of his fingers, and all the while a pulse began to beat between her legs, overheating her body. This had to stop, this had to stop, a little voice tried desperately to drag her back to a place of reason, but feelings were drowning it out, the rushing of her blood too loud to allow for any thought.

His fingers crept higher, beneath her shirt, all the way to the underside of her bra, touching her there, as if they were so much more than this. As if he hadn't treated her like dirt. It was too much. Everything was overwhelming to Mia; she couldn't breathe, and yet she needed to. She needed space. In the midst of passion, she clung to that one fact: he'd treated her—and her parents—so badly, in a way she could never, ever forgive. She hated him, with all her soul. Luca Cavallaro was not a man to be trusted.

With a guttural, soul-destroying cry, she pushed at his chest, anger making her strong, her breath wrenched from her body as she tried to regain her footing, staring at him across air that sparked with a strange, cosmic energy.

What was happening?

Luca showed no emotion. His face was carefully muted of it, but in the depths of his eyes she saw something, *felt* something. Too quickly, he concealed that, too.

'Forgettable?' he prompted, the derision in his voice showing how easy it was to see through her lie. Damn it! She'd tried to hurt his pride, to dent his ego, to prove how much she'd grown, but why bother when he could so eas-ily scatter her resolve?

'Yes,' she spat, anger vibrating through her, the lie one she clung to even when he'd just proved it to be exactly that: a lie. 'You say you've thought about me, Luca? Well, I haven't thought about you at all, except to reflect on how glad I am I didn't end up married to such a heart-less bastard!'

Again, his eyes shuttered, hiding something from her, but Mia was too incensed to care. 'How dare you come here and think you can…you can…'

'You kissed me,' he reminded her quietly.

'Yes, but only because you—'

'Because you wanted to,' he interrupted, so close she could feel his breath. 'Don't lie to me again, Mia.'

She frowned. 'When have *I* lied to you?'

His brows shot up with evident surprise. 'I didn't come here to litigate the past.'

'Good, because I have no interest in talking to you.'

He spoke as though she hadn't. 'I am offering you one night, Mia. One night that we should have shared then, that I think we both still want. Our engagement was a mistake, our marriage would have been doomed to fail from the start, but *this*—' he gestured between them '—is undeniable.'

'What the actual hell?' she shouted, spurred to raise her voice by the tide of feelings threatening to engulf her. He pressed a finger to her lips, reminding her where they were, and that they were far from alone.

'Come home with me. Stay the night.'

The words were the most seductive she'd ever heard, rendered that way by the sexual awareness he'd awoken within her over a year ago.

'Why on earth would I do something as stupid as that, Luca Cavallaro?' She was pleased with the derisive anger in her words, with the way her brain was asserting itself over her libido, even if her voice did shake a little.

'Because you want to,' he prompted, eyes holding hers with the force of a thousand suns. 'As much as I want you to.' His finger lifted to the corner of her lips, brushing her soft flesh. 'Come to me, Mia.'

It made no sense. He was the one who'd walked out on their marriage. 'You left me on our wedding day.'

'And I don't regret that,' he responded sharply.

She glared at him. 'I seriously hate you.'

His eyes narrowed. 'This isn't about hate, or love, or a wedding. It's about one thing, and one thing only. So ask yourself, do you want me enough to forget the past, Mia?'

How on earth could she admit to that? Even when he was right, she hated herself for being willing to ignore the way he'd treated her and go home with him! She clung to defiant anger with difficulty. 'Pigs will fly before I'd ever do anything quite so stupid.'

Their eyes locked and it was a silent, angry war of attrition, a fierce battle. But before she could stalk away, he caught her hand, her wrist, his thumb padding over her flesh. 'We'll see, *cara*.'

And with that, he turned on his heel and disappeared around the corner, his dark head joining the crowd. She watched him until he was absorbed by the milling guests. Mia collapsed into the seat, a maelstrom of feelings and uncertainty.

CHAPTER TWO

MIA DIDN'T GO to him that night. How could she? He'd torn her pride into tatters, but she'd worked hard to rebuild it in the intervening twelve months. She'd rebuilt herself.

Not to mention, she was technically engaged.

Okay, her engagement was definitely not normal. She wasn't in a relationship with Lorenzo and they both understood that. Their marriage would be barely more than a business partnership, only they intended to live together afterwards. Lorenzo was free to see whomever he wished until they were married and he'd made it abundantly clear that he expected her to do the same.

She couldn't hang her resistance on the idea of infidelity—it was so much more complicated.

She was afraid.

Afraid of how much she wanted Luca. Of how she turned to sun-warmed butter in his arms. Of how he made her forget the past: her anger, her hurt, the bitterness of betrayal. Of how easily he made her forget that he was untrustworthy and despicable.

Of how, when she was in his arms, she wasn't capable of rational thought.

But what would happen if she went to his home?

She groaned audibly, in the safety of her bedroom long

after the charity event had concluded, staring at her reflection in the floor-to-ceiling mirror her mother had had installed. 'If one can see oneself often, one is less inclined to have the second biscuit, darling.'

Mia was getting married in two months, and she was a virgin. Not by design, but because her parents were strict and protective, and Mia had never been given the freedom to date. Or was there another reason Jennifer had been so controlling in that regard? Any time a man had so much as looked at Mia, Jennifer had been sure to intervene, to tell Mia she was imagining it or that he couldn't be trusted. Mia had taken those messages to heart—was it any wonder she had very little confidence with the opposite sex?

She was getting married with the sole purpose of having children. For her father, it was about the business, for her husband-to-be, it was also about the business, but for Mia, it began and ended with family—the family she had craved since she'd been a little girl and her parents had died, and she'd known the strange no-man's-land of a care home before Gianni and Jennifer had adopted her.

She wanted a family of her own, and Lorenzo could provide that.

But she wasn't an idiot. In order to have children, she'd first need to have sex, and wouldn't it be nice—preferable, anyway—to have some experience before surrendering to her marital bed? Lorenzo left her cold. She didn't desire him at all, and she was pretty sure that was mutual, whereas Luca had the ability to turn her blood to lava with a single look.

Only Luca couldn't be trusted. Not again.

Was there a way to have her cake and eat it too?

Mia stood up straighter, her eyes narrowing, thinking of how much had changed for her in the past twelve months.

Back then, Mia had been vulnerable, too eager to please everyone, so she didn't question, didn't negotiate, didn't do anything except allow herself to be bowled over by desire for Luca. But now? She knew what he was like. She wouldn't be lied to, she wouldn't be hurt, she wouldn't be tricked.

Could she even play him at his own game, and win?

The idea sent sparks of anticipation through her.

What if she were to go to him and take exactly what she wanted, then walk away without a backwards glance, just as he had? What if she were to go to him and *demand* answers for what he'd done? All year, she'd wondered *why*. Over and over, the single word had rattled through her brain, tormenting her, because she couldn't understand how any person could be so evil as to no-show their own wedding.

If she went to him, could she take what she wanted—indulge her desire *and* get the answers she desperately wanted—and emerge unscathed?

Of course you can, a voice from deep in Mia's soul chided, and she wanted to believe that voice, that promise.

Mia's heart began to rush, and her fingers trembled with the possibilities before her.

She would never have chased him down, but having this opportunity laid out before her, wouldn't she be a fool not to take it up? It would be one night, in which he was completely fair game, and then she'd disappear, never seeing him again, the whole matter put to rest behind her, once and for all. Allowing her to marry with a clean slate?

'Argh!' she cried into the room, for surely even contemplating this was madness! And yet she found the idea impossible to dismiss, impossible to let go of. And so, the next night, having said goodnight to her parents and walked up to her bedroom, in the time-honoured tradition of overprotected children everywhere, she silently crept out of her window, climbed down the trellis and walked quickly to the street to wait for a ride-share, adrenaline making her blood roar.

He'd expected her to come.

He'd wanted her.

But it was only when Mia didn't arrive at his home that Luca realised just how much he'd been looking forward to possessing her after all. She'd lit a fire of need in his belly that night by his car, a year ago, and no one else had extinguished it since. It was her innocence, and the vulnerability he sensed within her, that stirred something up in his chest. But those feelings were at odds with his anger towards her and her family for the scam they'd been running.

Innocent? Hardly.

She played the part, but Mia Marini had been all too willing to con him into a billion-dollar hole. Oh, Luca could have afforded it, but that wasn't the point. He was nobody's fool. He'd worked hard and considered at every turn that it was his pride and reputation on the line—the reputation he'd built as a tribute to his late mother, and to make his father eat crow. He wasn't about to buy a worthless company and have the world—his father, particularly—laugh at his stupidity.

Nonetheless, his anger towards Mia now had as much to do with his disappointment that she hadn't arrived at his home as it did with her original betrayal.

His body was alive and waiting, ready, desperately hungry for her. Yet she didn't show up. He cursed her for yet another sin, even as he dreamed of that kiss at the rooftop bar, and craved more, so, so much more.

* * *

She passed six churches in the two blocks before reaching his inner-city villa, and, as the car pulled up, she wondered if there'd been a sign there for her to stop, reconsider what she was doing. To go and worship at an actual altar rather than the altar of Luca's physical perfection and the possibility of sexual satisfaction. But Mia was feeling reckless. A storm was brewing, more powerful than any cyclone, and she wouldn't—couldn't—run away from it.

Doubts, however, rolled like thunder through her belly as she stepped out and looked around, awed by the beauty of this street, with ancient cobblestones and beautiful trees, growing lush and green towards the historic façades of these homes. She moved quickly, unwilling to be seen. Sicilia was surprisingly small, and her parents were well known, an old and powerful family. It would be just her luck for some cousin of her father's to see Mia and mention it in passing. It was one of the reasons her gilded cage was so effective. There were not many places Mia could go without meeting someone who knew her parents and would report back. That was just how it worked around here.

And so she had to move quickly; there was no time for regrets.

She took the steps with haste, reached the doorbell and hesitated for the briefest of moments before pressing it, keeping her head bent, lest someone walk past and spot her.

Heart rushing, blood pounding, she stood waiting, nervous, hungry, but not for food: anxiety and tension of the best possible kind were making her body hum and zip.

She pressed the doorbell again, jabbing her finger against it, other emotions beginning to rush through her now, like panic and doubt—but those emotions belonged to the old Mia, to the version of herself she'd been before Luca had, inadvertently, forced her to wake up and start taking control of her life. Before she could act on those unwanted feelings, the big old timber door creaked a little, moved, opened, and Luca was standing on the other side.

He wore suit trousers and a collared shirt with the sleeves pushed up to reveal his tanned forearms. He looked as though he was still working, perhaps. Or maybe entertaining? The thought hadn't even occurred to Mia, but Luca had invited her for the previous night. Perhaps he was busy this evening? Mia considered all of these options in the space of a couple of very fraught seconds, and then the static noise in her brain became overwhelming as her eyes lifted to Luca's and pleasure made every part of her, even her toes, tingle.

'I shouldn't have come,' she murmured, without attempting to leave.

He stared at her for a beat. 'Do you want to go?'

She pressed her teeth into her lower lip, eyes huge in her face, and slowly shook her head.

For a moment, relief flashed in his eyes, then he reached out, a simple gesture, one that Mia had always thought embodied trust, because he was asking her to put her hand in his, to walk with him. It was somehow both simple and far too intimate and yet she needed to get off the street, so she lifted her hand and brushed her fingers against his, trembling at the moment of connection, eyes jerking to his with surprise. How could a simple glance of flesh be so incendiary? Then again, hadn't it been like this before? Wasn't that part of why she'd been so overwhelmed by the idea of marrying him?

She exhaled a breath of relief when the door closed, glad that she'd crossed the first hurdle, glad that at least she was away from the risk of discovery by someone her parents might know.

She paled at the enormity of this, but then Luca pulled her, through the enormous entrance foyer towards a glass-fronted living room with elegant leather sofas, glass and steel coffee tables and bronze lamps, so the impression was immediately both comfortable and architectural. There was a half-finished glass of something on the coffee table. Whisky? Despite the fact Mia never drank, she disentangled her fingers from his, walked to the glass and took a sip, closing her eyes as the liquid fired courage into her veins.

When she opened her eyes, it was to find Luca staring at her, appraising her, as if weighing her up somehow, working out just what to do with her.

But the whisky had worked, and Mia's courage was returning in spades. This was about her—what she wanted and needed. For far too long she'd been pushed around and manoeuvred to suit other people. She'd been sent away from Sicilia, from the home she loved, from the light she loved, to a cold, dark boarding school in England because it was her mother's wish. She'd come home after making friends and a life in England, because it was her parents' wish. She'd stayed living at home even when she'd found an apartment she could rent, because it was her parents' wish. She'd turned down job offers because her father had insisted she work in the family business—that was her destiny. She'd agreed to marry Luca Cavallaro before she'd even met him, because her parents had convinced her that it was wise and necessary. Her entire life had been a procession of 'yes, yes, yes', from Mia and, just this once, she wanted to take something all for herself, to hell with the consequences.

Besides, there would be no consequences.

Luca Cavallaro wasn't in her life, by his own choosing. He was nothing to her and she was nothing to him, except, perhaps, unfinished business. And if she could exploit that connection, so what?

'Take me to bed, Luca. I don't have all night.'

His eyes sparked with something like surprise, briefly, but then he covered it, his features neutral and impassive, his handsome, symmetrical face captivating and compelling—she couldn't look away.

'What about your fiancé?' he growled, and with good reason: Mia had held Lorenzo up like a shield the last time they'd spoken.

Her eyes met Luca's head-on and she forced herself to be brutally honest, because it was important to her honour that Luca should know she wasn't someone who would ever cheat. 'He's a free agent until we're married, and so am I.'

His eyes narrowed with a speculative power that made her knees knock and he prowled towards her, stopping just short of touching. 'Are you sure?'

'What, have you suddenly developed a conscience, Luca?' she scoffed. 'You're the one who propositioned me.'

He lifted her chin, tilting her face to his. 'I am simply interested.'

'Yes,' she admitted after a beat, the air rushing out of her lungs in a single whoosh. 'I'm sure. We discussed our expectations. We're not a couple and there's no point pretending. As long as we're both discreet, we can do what we want until the wedding.'

It was evidently enough for Luca. He paused only to lift the whisky and take a drink, his eyes holding hers, and she trembled at the intimacy of that too, of sharing a glass with him. His Adam's apple shifted as he swallowed and then he held out the glass to her lips. 'Open.'

Wordlessly, she did exactly that.

He tipped a little more of the alcohol in and then placed the glass on the table, watching as she drank, as a tiny drop of the amber-coloured liquid escaped from the corner of her mouth. An invitation, evidently, because he leaned down and chased it with his tongue, and then captured her lips, tilting her head back with the force of his kiss, his fingers weaving into her pale hair, holding her steady when she might otherwise have slumped to the ground, rendered quite weak by the rush of pleasure.

All doubts fled.

She was doing this.

It was right.

It felt right. And when he lifted her and carried her against his chest, kissing her as he strode through the beautiful apartment, it was just perfect.

She was slimmer than a year ago, those curves that had had the frustrating habit of appearing in his mind at the least convenient times were smaller, but she was still stunning and voluptuous, and so natural. A testament to womanly beauty, from her generous breasts to her tapered-in waist and wide hips, rounded bottom, he wanted to lose himself exploring her valleys and peaks—and he would.

I don't have all night.

Well, nor did he. At least, he didn't have the patience to last the night. But he had now, this moment, and he wanted Mia. Because she could have been his?

Or because she was different from the women he usually dated?

It was strange to want someone you knew to be capable

of such a deception, and yet he did want her. This was an aberration for a man famed for his vice-like grip of self-control, but it was just one night. Then he'd never think of her again.

As if to underscore to himself the purely physical nature of this, he placed her on the ground just inside his bedroom and began to remove her clothing, piece by piece, not slowly, not even particularly sensually, more as if he needed to see her naked and tick that box. His fantasies had been filled with what he'd *imagined* she looked like, surely the reality would be disappointing.

He stripped away her cotton shirt and simple bra, revealing her breasts, pale with dusky pink tips, better than he'd fantasised about. His gut tightened. Her arms were slim, tanned, her decolletage delicate and fascinating, with a pulse point that was rushing beneath his languid inspection. She stood perfectly still, eyes wide, as if she hadn't expected this, as if she hadn't come here for it.

Perhaps she'd thought it would be different. More foreplay. More touching. But hell, Luca wanted Mia *now*. Keeping a grip, barely, he moved his hands down her waist, squeezing at her hips a little before sliding down her skirt. It was elasticated at the waist and went easily. She stood in just a scrap of cotton. He wanted to kneel before her and reverently remove it, but he was still angry with her for the lie of a year ago, and even angrier because he wanted her despite her betrayal. What kind of fool did that make him?

Her breath snagged as he slid his fingers into the elastic of her underpants and began to push them lower, so he felt it against his forehead, warm and sweet smelling.

She stepped out of her underpants and kicked off her shoes, losing a vital inch in height, so he towered over her.

He hadn't noticed how dramatic their height difference was before—then again, she'd only ever worn shoes around him, and always heels. Was she self-conscious about her petite stature?

She was delightfully short and curved, the stuff men dreamed about, so womanly and soft, her skin like rose petals.

'Please stop,' she whispered, so Luca's chest thudded. Stop? Now? His eyes jerked to hers, searching.

'You're staring at me,' she explained, gesturing to her body.

'Yes.'

Her cheeks flooded with pink. 'I—don't like to be looked at.'

He frowned, wondering at her meaning.

'Would you prefer I touch, *cara*?'

She trembled, her nipples growing taut, her body swaying a little, so he took her physical response as confirmation, moving closer, close enough to feel her warmth, before wrapping his arm around her waist and drawing her forward, hard against his body, so he could indeed touch her, all of her, from the sweet curves of her bottom to the beautiful roundness of her breasts. He cupped her rear, pressing her against him, his arousal hard through the inconvenient barrier of his own clothing. She made a muffled groaning noise, tilting her head back, giving him access to the swan-like neck, so graceful, and he took full advantage, pressing his lips to her pulse point first, flicking it with his tongue before suckling, taking pleasure in the idea of her getting a mark from his ministrations, hoping to leave an imprint on her flesh of where she'd been— and what she'd been doing.

Her responsiveness was his undoing. He moved his

mouth to hers and she writhed against him, just like that night near the car, so desperate and hungry and he couldn't resist touching her all over now, moving one hand to her breast, cupping it, fondling it, feeling the weight in his hand until he was taut with need, then driving it lower, over the swell of her hip, between her legs, parting her thighs and finding her womanhood, her warm, sweet, feminine core and pressing a finger inside, her moist, slick heat breaking the last of his self-control, so he kissed her as he undressed himself, so hungry and desperate for her, so overcome with needs that he barely had time to grab protection—an essential for Luca, who never intended to have children, and particularly not accidentally. Having lived with the consequences of being an unwanted child himself, he had no intention of inflicting that pain on another living soul.

His arousal was so tight it hurt to extend the rubber over his length; it hurt even more because it required him moving away from Mia to his bedside table, and taking a few seconds to perform the miraculous act. But once sheathed, he spun back to her, wild, like a caged animal with a glimpse of escape, and all the emotions this woman brought out in him rode to the fore. Anger. Frustration. Betrayal. Need.

'Come here,' he barked, the words short because he couldn't help but resent the effect she had on him.

Her eyes widened, her tongue darted out and she moved, unsteadily, across to him, her body so beautifully perfect, he couldn't tear his eyes off her as she sat down on the edge of the bed and stared at him, lips parted and breasts heaving with each rushed breath.

He prowled towards Mia, intentional and determined, standing above her, naked, hard, ready, eyes finding hers, cynicism unknowingly written across his face as he brought himself down, one hand on either side of her head, pressed to the bed, his body over hers.

'I am glad you decided to come to me,' he admitted gruffly.

She didn't say anything. Her eyes were huge in her face, beautiful and mesmerising and awash with feelings he couldn't decipher and didn't want to know about. He couldn't allow himself to care about Mia. It was bad enough that her body had haunted his thoughts without his consent for this long year, but he wouldn't allow her humanity to seep into him. Better to stick to the bare facts of who she was, and all the reasons he couldn't trust her.

But that didn't mean they couldn't enjoy each other's bodies.

He didn't want to think about the betrayal of her parents now. He nudged her thighs apart with his knee, wishing he wanted her less so he could play with her more, but instead, he held himself over her, contenting himself with watching her face as he drove into her, hard and fast, he was filled with urgency, then still, because she froze, and he realised that the tightness around his length spoke of absolute inexperience, that the woman beneath him, around him, was a virgin.

His usually sharp mind could barely make sense of it.

Mia Marini had been going to marry him.

And she was a virgin.

He couldn't say why but those two statements felt incongruent. He pushed up, staring at her, looking for answers in her face, but she was already recovering, moving her hips, drawing him deeper, and, while questions were launching through his mind, he was still driven by his body's needs, by urges that made it impossible to see clearly through the forest. Thankfully, he knew enough to pause, to demand, roughly, 'Are you okay?'

She nodded, quickly. 'Oh, yes,' she groaned, twisting beneath him, her muscles squeezing his length, so he pushed aside chivalric duty and any concerns of decency and focused on what she'd come here for. There'd be time to interrogate and analyse. Later.

Pushing back up to watch her properly, he moved gently, slowly, then he gave up on studying her because he needed to kiss her, to taste her, his mouth hungrily seeking hers, his tongue emulating his body's rhythms, his hands greedily running over her, finding her breasts, weighing them, running fingers across her nipples until she was crying out, exploding, her orgasm sharp and explosive, almost robbing him of his own control, but Luca refused to finish yet, refused for this to be over. He waited—barely—for her to come back to earth, for her breathing to slow, and then he was moving again, faster and harder this time, the sound of their flesh slapping together driving him almost over the edge, so he gritted his teeth, waited, watched, listened for Mia's own cries to grow sharp and desperate and only then did he let go of his control and join her in the sublime ecstasy of post-orgasm euphoria.

He rolled off Mia, onto his back, staring at the ceiling, taking a second to regain his wits, trying to order his thoughts, but her breathing was so rushed, her body so close, that it was impossible. He needed proper space from her. He needed to move away from her fragrance, her nearness, from the temptation to reach out and touch her.

'Give me a moment,' he muttered, standing, prowling from his room and into the adjoining bathroom, bracing his palms on the edge of the sink, staring at his reflection, waiting for the world to start making sense again.

Luca was very rarely surprised.

He generally considered himself to be a good judge of people, and yet he hadn't expected this. He'd thought Mia's quivering innocence to be an act. He'd thought her a very, very good liar.

Because when she'd kissed him, out by the car, her body had instinctively responded to his—she hadn't seemed like a virgin then. She'd been a siren, calling to him, inviting him, begging him…and he'd wanted to listen. He'd been so angry that night. So angry with her, her parents, for the discovery his team had just informed him of. If he'd slept with her then, it would have been to punish her, and, while Luca knew he had a dark side, he wasn't, he hoped, quite so messed up to resort to using sex for anything other than giving and taking pleasure…

He bit back a curse, because whatever tonight had been, it had gone in a different direction from what he'd anticipated.

He took his time. He needed to. Removing and disposing of the condom, he then had a quick shower, hoping the water would bring clarity, so he could go back out there and calmly ask Mia just what the hell she was thinking not to at least *tell him* that she'd never been with a man before.

But much to Luca's disgust, whenever he contemplated that, all he could focus on was the fact that he was her first, and a primal, ancient thrill made him grow hard again.

It was ten long, disjointed minutes before Luca felt he could join Mia, and when he stalked into his room, he did so with a command: 'Okay, Mia Marini, explain yourself, right now.'

But there was no answer, because there was no Mia. She'd disappeared into thin air.

* * *

'G'day.'

Max Stone's broad Australian accent boomed down the phone line. Luca, in a foul temper, furrowed his brow. He could practically hear the sunshine and salt water in Max's tone, and imagined him somewhere near one of their pearl farms, happy, relaxed, the exact opposite of how Luca was feeling.

'Max. What's up?'

'Just checking in. Did you have a look at the prospectus I sent you?'

Luca ground his teeth. His father had been trying to get Luca interested in the Stone family business for years—he took a direct approach and Luca enjoyed giving a direct answer: no. But Max was more skilled. He waved things beneath Luca's nose that would be almost impossible to ignore.

'I glanced at it,' Luca lied. The figures for opening a new flagship Stone store in Tulsa were persuasive, and Max knew it as well as Luca. What Max was really asking was for Luca to weigh in on some of the trickier decisions, such as location and size.

These were matters Luca had no intention of discussing, even though he'd immediately formed some thoughts.

'And?'

He dragged a hand through his hair. 'And, to be completely honest, the Stone stores are the last things on my mind right now.'

Silence crackled, and Luca grimaced, because he'd made an uncharacteristic error. When talking with Max, he had to keep his wits about him—his brother was too insightful and could read Luca like a book. If Luca even got close to intimating that he'd been obsessively thinking about the woman he slept with last night, Max would push for more details and before Luca knew it he'd be revealing that he'd seduced the woman he'd been supposed to marry a year ago.

It wasn't as if he kept secrets from Max. He'd never needed to. But the whole business with the Marini family was something Luca didn't want to discuss.

And he definitely didn't see the need to go into last night.

Luca was a man who liked to be in control, and things with Mia had spiralled way, way out of his comfort zone. She was different from what he'd expected, and her virginity had caught him totally off guard. So too her disappearing act.

With a tightening of his jaw, he stared straight ahead, eyes sweeping the view without really seeing it.

'Come on. I'd love your input.'

Luca let out a harsh laugh. 'You'd love me to sign my life away on the bottom line.'

'Don't be so dramatic.' Luca could hear his brother's grin. 'Besides, would it really be so bad to join the family business?'

Luca gripped his phone tighter, that simple, throwaway phrase one Max used without thinking, without any idea how it goaded Luca.

'It's your family business, not mine.'

'You don't like him, you don't respect him, but, however you may *feel* about the man, Carrick Stone *is* your father, we are your family.'

'Yes. You are.' Luca ground his teeth. 'But that doesn't mean I have any interest in working for him.'

'With him, Luc. Not for him. You'd be equal to me, to him.'

'Does it occur to you that I cannot be equal to him? That I cannot—it's too much.' Luca sighed heavily. 'You know why I feel this way.'

Max was quiet a moment longer. After all, he did know. He'd been there when Luca had arrived at their home in Sydney, grieving the sudden death of his mother, reeling from the discovery of his famous, wealthy father, simmering with resentments at having been ignored and unwanted. Then, there'd been the sense of competitiveness Carrick Stone had tried to instil in both boys, an almost gladiatorial fight for supremacy that, thankfully, they'd both grown out of. Luca and Max both had a lot of reasons to despise their father.

Max sighed heavily. 'I get it, Luca. Carrick is—you know we're on the same page about his lifestyle, his decisions, his attitudes.'

Luca closed his eyes. His father had treated women like dirt, and his own mother had paid the ultimate price, because she'd fallen in love with him and been destroyed by that love. Carrick had lived and left a trail of destruction in his wake because he'd never really loved or cared for anyone—even his sons. He was the lowest of the low.

'But almost for as long as I've known you, I've thought it would be great to do this together. You hated coming to live with us, but, for me, I suddenly wasn't alone. I had a brother, and someone to do all this with.'

For the second time in twenty-four hours, Luca felt a pang of regret. He'd walked out on Carrick as soon as he could, but he'd also walked out on Max. Was he being selfish, just like Carrick, to avoid his responsibilities to the family business? None of this was Max's fault...

'I'll look at the prospectus again,' Luca conceded with

a grimace. After all, that wasn't too much to ask. 'And send you an email with my thoughts.'

Luca disconnected the call with a sense of misgiving, but whatever headspace he had to think about his father's business evaporated pretty quickly. He closed his eyes and there she was: Mia Marini, taking up all his thoughts, driving him crazy even when she was nowhere to be seen, and Luca had the unpleasant realisation that he'd been utterly and completely wrong: one night hadn't been enough. He wanted more, he wanted answers, he wanted Mia.

CHAPTER THREE

ALL MIA COULD think of as she stared at her reflection in the large mirrors of the bridal shop was that it was next-level inappropriate to be trying on a wedding gown the day after having sex with someone other than your fiancé. It didn't matter how many times she told herself that it wasn't cheating, that she and Lorenzo had no expectations of their relationship being anything like a normal marriage, it still felt the complete opposite of the fairy tale Mia had, at one point, desperately hoped for.

Well, if she wasn't to have the fairy-tale marriage, at least this time her dress wasn't going to be such a disaster.

She'd deliberately chosen something that was dramatically different to before. Not a hint of lace or tulle, the gown was instead simple and elegant. Cream silk, cut on the bias, the dress somehow flattered the curves Mia liked and played down those that she didn't. Her mother would hate it; Mia didn't care. She'd seen the image of herself covered in ice cream, staring at the sky, so many times: she never wanted to wear a puffy, tulle dress ever again.

The fact this was close to white was a miracle.

If she had her way, though, Mia would elope. There'd be no wedding, as such. Just a signing of the certificate, to mark the fact the wedding was, essentially, a business deal.

'All okay, *signorina*?'

Mia's body felt different. How could people look at her and not see how she'd spent the night? Heat coloured her cheeks as she remembered the way it had felt to have Luca drive into her, so strong and hard, to have her mind blown with pleasure again and again.

'Fine.' She nodded quickly, her voice hoarse. 'I like it.'

'I will trim the hem to this length, to allow for the heels you showed me.'

'Great.' Mia smiled over-brightly. She didn't want to think about Luca again.

She'd done what she'd set out to do. She'd lost her virginity, gained experience and walked out on him while his back was turned. Okay, it wasn't anywhere near as hurtful as what he'd done to her—ditching her on her wedding day—but there'd been a petty sense of satisfaction in disappearing from his home while he showered.

Then again, he'd probably been glad.

As for Mia, she'd wished, the whole drive home, that she hadn't left, and not just because she'd also intended to get answers from him, to find out why he'd ditched her on their wedding day. But mostly, she'd wished, more than anything, that she was back in that bed with Luca: naked, strong, powerful, skilled, showing her all the things her body could feel, teaching her about sex, mastering her so cleverly, as he'd already done.

Instead, she'd quickly dressed and slipped out of the front door, onto the quiet midnight streets, and disappeared into the dark—and from his life, for good.

She emerged from the bridal store distracted, head dipped, so at first she didn't notice the shiny grey car with jet-black tinted windows parked in a no standing zone outside the shop. But when a car drove past and beeped at the offending vehicle, Mia looked up and did a double take.

Luca.

Here.

The coincidence was uncanny. But *of course* it wasn't a coincidence. He was waiting for her.

With a heart that wouldn't stop jolting, she changed course, moving towards him as if drawn by magnetic force, stopping a metre away, staring. Her insides leapt, the recognition overwhelming. 'What are you doing here?' Had she forgotten something? She did a quick mental catalogue of what she'd taken to his house—purse, phone, keys. She definitely had all those. Something else? 'How did you know where I was?'

His eyes flashed to hers. 'Get in the car, Mia.' The command made her pulse shiver.

'Thank you for the kind invitation, but I think I'll choose to decline.'

He ground his teeth, his jaw visibly moving with the effort. 'Get. In.'

'It is a free country, isn't it? Or are you proposing to kidnap me?'

'If that's what it takes.' He moved closer, and a thrill of anticipation rushed through her. Mia knew she should have been annoyed at his heavy-handed, dictatorial manner but, in truth, she found it exciting. The thought of being kidnapped by Luca conjured all sorts of strange, unacknowledged fantasies. Mia remembered how it had felt to be carried by him last night, as though she weighed little more than a feather. She wanted to feel that again. Her determination was slipping.

Looking in one direction and then the other, she jerked her attention back to Luca. 'Only because I don't want anyone my parents or fiancé know to see me talking to you. Of all people!' She was pleased at how withering her voice sounded.

'Heaven forbid.' His own was scathing. 'Now.' He wrenched open the door and gestured impatiently for her to take her seat.

Mia shot him one last fulminating glare then moved to the car, careful to give him a wide berth. It was a futile manoeuvre, because if she'd hoped to avoid being close to him, inhaling his intoxicating fragrance, she was just about to step into the lion's den. The moment she was inside the car, sliding across the plush back seat to the far side, he joined her, folding his far larger frame into the seat then leaning forward and pressing a button that lowered the screen between himself and the driver.

'Leave us. I'll call when I'm ready.'

'Yes, sir.'

The driver left and then Luca turned to Mia, eyes swirling with dark emotions. 'What happened last night?'

She blinked at him, deliberately avoiding the question. 'You need me to explain it to you? I would have thought you understood the biology...'

His expression showed he wasn't amused. 'You disappeared.'

She tucked her hands together on her lap. 'No, I left after we finished.'

His eyes probed hers, as if looking for something, she didn't know what.

'And you think that's okay?'

She stared at him, genuinely dumbfounded. 'I'm sorry, what?'

'You left without even having a conversation with me? Without explaining your virginity? Without telling me— anything?'

Anger was a whip, stirring Mia to a fever pitch. 'Isn't that a little like the pot calling the kettle black?' she demanded fiercely. 'You left me standing in a church in a ridiculous wedding dress with three hundred people watching! You seriously think *I* owe *you* an explanation?'

'So what does that mean?' he snapped. 'That last night was payback?'

'Is that your way of saying sex with me was a punishment? Gee, thanks,' she muttered, reaching for the door.

His hand came across, grabbing her wrist, and sparks ignited beneath her skin.

'You know that's not what I meant.' His voice was a sensual rumble, and he was closer now, his body framing hers, big and strong. She shrank back into the seat, afraid of how her desires might overtake everything else.

'Yeah, well, I don't care. You can think whatever the hell you want. It happened. We had sex. Isn't that why you invited me over?'

'Yes.' His answer came without delay and Mia tried to ignore the strange sinking feeling in her chest cavity. 'But I didn't realise you were totally inexperienced.'

Mia glared at him. 'Does it make a difference?'

His frown was instinctive. 'Yes,' he said after a beat. 'You should have mentioned it.'

'And you should have mentioned that you weren't planning to marry me.'

He moved closer, his body magnetic and strong. She licked her lower lip. 'Do you really want to open that Pandora's box, *cara*?' He drawled the term of endearment with a hint of cynicism, so she shivered, despite the attraction sparking in the atmosphere.

'What's that supposed to mean?'

'You were not honest with me either.'

About being a virgin? Why should she have mentioned that? 'It would have come up,' she said with a shake of her head. 'After our wedding.'

'By then, it would have been too late. But you didn't care. You didn't care that every part of our marriage deal was based on a lie.'

'I—' She couldn't unravel what he was saying. Was her virginity really such a big deal? Big enough for him to say everything else was a lie, too? 'I never lied to you,' she denied.

'Selective truth telling,' he corrected with obvious disgust. 'It is just as bad.'

She frowned. Really? 'I would have thought someone with your experience would have been able to tell…'

'Yes, I could,' he agreed after a dangerous, silky beat. 'Which is why I decided not to marry you, in the end. Why I decided to walk away from you and your family. It was the right decision.'

She flinched, the harshness of his decree cutting her to the bone.

'Fine, good to know,' Mia responded when she could trust herself to speak. 'If you're done, I would like to get on with my day.'

'We're not finished,' he responded, so close the words seemed to reverberate inside her.

'We are *so* finished,' she corrected, lifting a hand to push him away, but he pressed his own over the top, holding it there, his eyes widening as he moved his head closer. 'We're finished,' she repeated, more feebly. 'We were finished the day you left me in that church.' To her frustration, her voice wobbled and she felt the awful sting of tears in the back of her throat, threatening to moisten her eyes. 'I hate you.'

'Not last night,' he reminded her, moving his other hand to her thigh, then lower, to the hem of her dress.

'Yes, I hated you, even last night.'

'So it was revenge. To sleep with me and then run away?'

Heat coloured her cheeks, but whatever she was about to say scattered from her mind as his fingers slid up her inner thigh, towards her sex.

'Did it feel good, Mia? Did you have enough revenge?' He moved his mouth to hers, brushed it lightly then pulled away, so he could look into her eyes. 'Or do you need to punish me some more?'

Say no. Leave. Get out of his car. This man is quicksand and you're falling, falling into a danger you have no skill to navigate.

'I hate you,' was all she said, and she really, really did, but oh, how she wanted him.

His eyes narrowed. 'But do you blame me, Mia? Do you really blame me for not going through with our wedding?'

Her heart dropped to her toes. Hurt lashed her. She knew she couldn't hold a candle to the women he usually dated, she knew she wasn't a show-stopping beauty, or slim like her mother, or confident and worldly, but she had qualities that people might consider more than made up for those shortcomings. She didn't need him to hit her over the head with his lucky escape from marriage to a wallflower like Mia.

'Then why proposition me?' she asked quietly, her desire and anger evaporating in a wave of shock, because his words had been so hurtful.

'Why do you think?' he asked, and then his hand moved higher, all the way to the fabric of her underpants, which he slid aside, his fingers brushing her most sensitive cluster of nerves until she bucked against the back seat of the car, and then he was kissing her, swallowing the groans she offered up to the heavens, losing herself in this moment even when she knew she should tell him to go to hell. It was somehow much more tempting for Mia to be carried to heaven, anyway.

She didn't know what game he was playing—but surely it was a game. She was a toy to him, and he was deriving some kind of pleasure from the push and pull of this, whereas Mia felt as though she were blindly navigating an awful storm.

'Come home with me…again,' he said against the side of her mouth.

Mia had enough wits about her to shake her head, somewhat unconvincingly. 'No way. Never.'

'Careful, Mia. There's nothing I like more than a challenge.'

His words barely penetrated the thick fog of her brain, and any hope she had of thinking rationally evaporated when he lifted her easily and settled her on his lap, kissing her as he fumbled to push up her skirt and unbutton his trousers so his arousal was shielded only by the flimsy cotton of his boxers. He pushed himself against her sex, and desire exploded through her. Mia rocked on her haunches, wanting, desperate to feel him, as he kissed her and felt her breasts in his palms, delighting in the different sensations that were changing her body chemistry completely.

'Do you still hate me?' he asked with a mocking smile.

'Yes,' she whimpered as he reached around into his back pocket.

'But you want me anyway?' he prompted, and she moaned, because she hated herself for feeling that way, and hated him even more for making her admit it.

She bit down on her lip as he removed his arousal and curved his palm around the base; all she could do was stare, marvel, hunger.

'Say that you want me,' he demanded, the words harsh, hissed from between his teeth. With the effort of self-control.

'Screw you,' she muttered, those stinging tears forming on her lashes.

He arched a brow, then slid the condom into place. 'That can be arranged.'

It was Mia who moved, sinking down over his length, tilting her back, crying out into the limousine at this new sense of fullness, of perfect, heart-stopping completion. The relief was terrifying.

She rocked up and down, moving as she needed to, pleasure building, waves speeding up, growing in intensity, until she lifted her hands and pressed them to the top of the car, arched fully, so his mouth came down on her breast through the fabric of her shirt and sucked, then bit her nipple lightly, then sucked some more, so all she wanted was to be completely naked.

'Luca,' she groaned as pleasure built to a fever pitch. 'Please.'

Luca took over, gripping her bottom and moving her up and down his length, thrusting his hips off the seat, so powerful and commanding, so demanding. Mia called his name into the air. She was everywhere in the world all at once, a thousand fragments of herself scattered on the wind. She wasn't sure she'd ever be able to go back together again—not in the same way.

He was playing a dangerous game. Dangerous because he no longer understood the rules, he knew only that having sex with Mia was the most compelling and addictive experience he'd had in a long time. Luca had been bored for years. Even his business successes were less exhilarating these days, because there was no longer the risk. He was too talented at what he did.

But with Mia, there was a charge of something that made adrenaline flood his body and he wasn't capable of thinking and planning, he simply acted on instinct. And every instinct had been shouting at him, since he'd emerged to find her gone last night, to finish what they'd started.

But he still wasn't finished, even as his own orgasm receded, and the world began to make sense again.

This wouldn't be their last time together. He wouldn't allow that. He refused to question his motives. He didn't want to analyse why he felt this sudden need to possess the woman he'd turned his back on without regret a year earlier. Was it simply because she was about to marry another man, and some primal jealousy had reared its head? Yet he'd had other lovers who'd married, and it had never bothered Luca. Not an ounce. So maybe it all came down to unfinished business. To the fact he'd wanted Mia that night, and he'd never had her. To the fact they'd been engaged, both intending to marry when they'd made that arrangement, and yet they hadn't. Their story deserved some completion. Was that it?

Mia, perhaps, did not agree.

She shifted, not meeting his eyes, lifting up from him and moving to the far side of the car, with a surprising amount of grace given the space constraints.

He could sense her prevarication, her doubts returning, so he did the only thing he could and pulled his phone from his pocket, firing off a quick text to his driver.

'That shouldn't have happened,' Mia said, anger directed towards herself. 'Damn you, Luca. You can't just approach me on the street—' A frown changed her features, pulling him back in, fascinating him all over again. He'd thought her beautiful last year—distractingly so—but he'd fought hard to keep his focus where it had belonged: on the business. Until that kiss, when he'd no longer been able to ignore the searing attraction he felt towards her, but by that point, he was already filled with so much anger about her family's lies, he hadn't been able to act on desire.

He looked at Mia now and saw so many different emotions flitting through her expressive eyes. They told a thousand stories; he could see how easy it would be to become enthralled by those eyes, and, much like the king in Scheherazade's tale, to sit and listen each night, waiting for more.

Luca would never be so stupid, of course.

He knew what Mia was capable of, what her parents had embroiled her in.

'Do you have any idea what this wedding means to me?'

'I know what it means to your parents,' he responded swiftly.

She narrowed her eyes. 'To *me*.' She pressed her fingers between her full, rounded breasts.

His eyes dropped and held. He couldn't look away. He was acting like some inexperienced teenager.

Pull yourself together.

'I need to marry him. Anyone could have seen us just now, could have been waiting…this can't keep happening.'

'Why do you need to marry him?' he demanded, curiosity warring with some other, sharper emotion. 'Can you really be so mercenary as to commit yourself to a man you don't know for the sake of your family's business?'

The driver's door closed and Mia startled, annoyed. But before she could put two and two together, the engine had started and the car pulled out into traffic, the screen between driver and passengers going up as the car moved.

'Wait! What's happening?'

'We're driving, Mia, what did you think?'

She gripped the car door. 'No way. Let me out.'

'Answer my question,' he demanded bullishly. 'Why are you so determined to marry him?'

Her features took on a mutinous set as she glared first at him and then beyond him, through the heavily tinted windows. 'Where are we going?'

'Why did you agree to marry me?' he pushed.

Her eyes flew back to Luca's then she turned away from him completely, crossing her arms and staring out of the window. Without answering.

Despite the dark emotions that were threatening to undo his self-control, Luca felt a strange lick of amusement— and a double dose of admiration—for the tactic. But she was seriously underestimating him if she thought he'd let it go.

'Are you so desperate to help your parents, Mia?' A thought occurred to him, one he didn't like but needed to test. 'Or was the whole thing your idea?'

'What are you talking about?' she demanded hotly, turning back to face him and puffing out a breath to move a pale clutch of silk hair that had drifted in front of her lips. It danced an inch off her face then fell down again. He reached for it, his fingers gentle, guiding it behind her ear and lingering there. Their eyes held, hers troubled, confused, his own, he hoped, devoid of any telltale emotion.

'Your being included to sweeten the deal,' he said

darkly. 'Did you volunteer yourself? Or did your parents suggest it?'

Her lips formed a perfect, voluptuous circle. He dug his fingers into the leather seat to stave off the temptation to kiss her again—because a kiss would lead to more and they needed to talk.

'I don't think my inclusion was intended as an inducement,' she said after a beat, her lips pulling to one side, a troubled expression on her face as she once again turned away from him. He hated that. Her many-storied eyes were his to read. Or he wanted them to be.

'Then why?'

But Mia didn't want to have this conversation. 'Tell your driver to let me out.'

'No.'

She shook her head angrily. 'Are you actually intending to kidnap me?'

The decision was instant. 'Yes.'

That got her attention. She pivoted to face him, chest moving with the force of her breathing. 'Luca Cavallaro, you stop the car this damned minute. Or else I'll—I'll—'

He waited with the appearance of calm when, inside, something was ticking faster than was healthy, making him question the wisdom of this on so many levels.

'You'll…?' he prompted, when silence fell. Her expression was mutinous.

'I haven't made up my mind yet.'

'Well, you have over an hour to think about it. Let me know what my punishment will be.' He leaned closer, deliberately provoking her. 'I like your style of punishment, Mia. Please, do keep it coming.'

CHAPTER FOUR

As a GIRL, Mia had visited San Vito Lo Capo on vacations. Jennifer had loved the crystal-clear ocean and white sandy beaches, the extra-salty water making for buoyant swimming. They'd always brought a yacht around, and Mia had jumped off the edge, knees bundled to her chest, feeling sublimely contented until pre-adolescence, when Jennifer had begun to make comments about Mia's bikini not being appropriate given Mia's size, or pinching Mia's hips and remarking that Mia should really try the watermelon diet Jennifer was a die-hard fan of.

Somehow, it had soured the beachside town for Mia. She'd started to loathe their trips here and, eventually, managed to get out of coming altogether. So while she could appreciate the beauty of the coastline as Luca's car swept around the corner and produced a breathtaking view of the sea, she couldn't look at this familiar aspect without a curdling sense of anxiety gripping her.

'Tell me we're not stopping here.'

'You do not like it?' he prompted, gesturing to the stunning aquamarine sea.

She clamped her lips together, angled her face away and harumphed.

On the drive from Palermo to the coast, she'd made a thousand resolutions to deal with his apparent kidnapping.

One of them was to stop making conversation with him as though they had anything in common.

As though she'd forgiven and forgotten what he'd done to her—the embarrassment and shame his rejection had caused. Last night hadn't been about forgiveness, it had been about…closure. Revenge? Or at least taking back the narrative, taking control, because in the last year, she'd learned the importance of asserting herself, and she wasn't going to forget those lessons.

Luca's laugh was so quiet it was almost inaudible but to Mia, whose nerves were stretched tight, it not only reached her ears but seemed to wrap around her, so she ground her teeth together, wishing there were some way she could inoculate herself against his masculine charms. Hating him apparently wasn't going to cut it.

'Relax, Mia. It's just one night. Perhaps two.'

'Two?' Disbelief rang through the word. 'I can't stay with you for two nights. Listen to me, Luca, my parents will have kittens if I'm not home after work.'

'Your parents will survive.'

She narrowed her gaze, connecting the dots. 'Did you kidnap me…to hurt them?' She frowned. It didn't make sense. It was Luca who'd let her family down. Her parents were the ones who had every right to be angry, not the other way around.

'Why do you hate us so much, Luca?'

He scanned her face, as if trying to comprehend something, then leaned forward. 'I cannot tell if this is an act, or real.'

'What?'

He reached out, smudging his thumb over her lower lip. As if he could wipe away whatever was making it difficult to read her and see more clearly.

'You don't think I have a right to despise them? And even you, a little, Mia? Perhaps you, most of all.'

Her heart twisted.

'You were willing to go further than either of them.'

'I don't know what you're talking about.'

'You were willing to sell yourself, and your virginity, to the highest bidder, to cover up their scam. How exactly should I feel about you?'

She flinched, his words making absolutely no sense. Scam? Her parents had a lot of faults, but they were hardly grifters. 'You're delusional.'

He moved closer, eyes flecked with brown and caramel. 'Did you really think I wouldn't find out?'

'Find out what?' she asked with urgency. She needed to understand what he was accusing them of, even when she knew it couldn't be true.

'Perhaps another buyer might not, but I am always cautious when I invest. Did you think our marriage would be enough of an inducement to make me look the other way?'

'Please stop talking in riddles,' she demanded haltingly, 'and tell me what you're accusing us of.'

He was very quiet, and the engine idled, then cut altogether. A moment later, Pietro, Luca's driver, was at the door, opening Luca's side. He immediately resented the intrusion but concealed that from his long-time staffer.

Luca took the briefest possible moment to give some instructions to Pietro then came around to Mia's side, opening the car door and waiting for her to step out. She glared up at him, heart pounding, tempted to refuse to move, but she had no doubt he'd simply reach down and lift her from the car—which had every possibility of leading to the kind of passion they'd just shared. Fighting made them spark.

Something about them was instantly combustible.

Or, maybe sex was always like this? She hoped so.

Because, no matter what was happening between her and Luca, she had no intention of walking away from her engagement, and her marriage. Her heart gave a painful lurch, because she needed to remember what was fantasy and what was real—and nothing about Luca was real. This was a dangerous game they were playing, dangerous because there were no rules and no clear path to victory for either of them.

Despite her misgivings about this place, she couldn't help but admire the villa at which they'd arrived. A wide gravel drive led to a turning circle with a pale yellow fountain at its centre. Four ancient statues of robe-draped women formed an elegant pyramid that led to a dolphin spouting water over their breasts and down into the water below. The sound was beautiful and relaxing. The driveway was surrounded on one side by a grove of citrus trees, fragrant with blossoms at this time of year, and on the other by a garden that might have been quite formal at one time but that was now delightfully overgrown. Wisteria ran rampant over the arbour, and half of the house, and a stone bench seat was covered in lichen and ivy.

The air hummed with bees and the smell of sweet flowers.

She hardened her heart. Against the beauty, and the seductive temptation of this.

The doors to the villa had ornate brass hinges, very old, she guessed, and the doors themselves were wide, timber and painted a lovely turquoise colour that perfectly complemented the glistening ocean beyond the house. The sound of the gently lapping waves called to Mia, but she heard her mother's voice, as clear as a bell, and knew she wouldn't indulge her childish desire to sprint down to the hot sand and into the refreshing ocean.

'You have to take me home,' she said, moving to Luca and pulling on his sleeve.

'Why?' he demanded, looking completely untouchable. In fact, it was impossible to recognise the passionate man she'd just made love to with the determined glittering in his dark eyes. 'So your parents can raffle you off to the next highest bidder? So you can simper and smile across the table, all wide-eyed innocence, for your next target?'

'Stop saying that,' she shouted with rich anger. 'You have no right to speak to me so disdainfully. I entered into our engagement in good faith.' Her hand lifted, finger jabbing his chest. 'You're the one who broke the deal. You're the one who left me...who left me...' Emotions welled inside her. This place had haunted her and was taunting her now, flooding her with memories that weakened her. 'Who left me on our wedding day,' she finished anticlimactically, staring at a point past his shoulder. 'How dare you try to pin any blame on me?'

'On you? Who would have had me sink a billion dollars into a worthless company? Who thought a single kiss might tempt me to ignore common sense and go ahead with the deal anyway?'

She shook her head, to dispel his words, the implication buried in them. She knew the value of their family business because she worked in it—and what was more, she'd seen her parents' lifestyle first-hand for years. 'A worthless company?' She rolled her eyes, hoping her derision would dismiss the very idea from his head.

'You are very beautiful, Mia, and I'm not going to say I wasn't tempted, but I am not stupid enough to gamble my fortune on a woman, no matter how nicely she kisses.'

Mia's fingers tingled with a need to slap him but that would be far too demure. Instead, she shoved him hard

in the chest, hard enough to fell someone else, but Luca
stood perfectly still, head tilted down at her, almost as if
he'd been expecting it. But that wasn't it: it was simply
that Luca was always poised for a fight.

'This is all—lies,' she said, pushing him again. 'To what
end? Perhaps to assuage your guilty conscience?'

'I have no guilt, Mia.' His calm voice only aggravated
her further.

'No guilt,' she repeated, dropping her hands to her sides
and staring at him with disbelief. 'You handed me, without
a doubt, the worst day of my life—and, believe me, that's
saying something. You feel no compunction about that?'

'Did you hear what I said?' he demanded, after the
smallest of pauses. 'You were a part of a plan to con me
out of more than a billion dollars—that's tantamount to
theft. As far as I'm concerned, you forfeited the right for
any consideration.'

Her lips parted.

'I feel very sorry for you, Luca. To be so cynical at such
a young age.' She shook her head. 'No one in my family
intended to con you into anything. I don't know what you
think you "discovered", but you're wrong. This was a business deal, pure and simple. We are a respectable family
and you—you are nothing. *Niente!*' She slashed her hand
through the air. 'No, you're worse. You are a bastard, and I
can't stand the sight of you.' She pulled away and began to
run, with no idea of where she was going, only absolutely
certain that she needed to get away from him.

She had taken a path through the citrus grove, and towards the beach, but Luca hadn't followed immediately.
He'd been frozen. With shock, but also with the emotions

he'd thought he'd conquered as a young boy, when the children in his village called him *bastardo* as a running joke.

Bastardo. Bastard. The illegitimate son of a poor, struggling housekeeper, and no idea who for a father. The bullying had followed him all through primary school, until his mother had died and his father had come from the woodwork to claim him. But by then, the damage was done. Luca, rejected and ignored by his father, raised by a mother who couldn't look at him without seeing Carrick Stone and feeling the pain of his betrayal, and taunted by his contemporaries, Luca's heart had hardened a long time ago. And yet that single word, issued by Mia, cut him in a way he was truly surprised to feel.

He clenched his jaw and stared after Mia's retreating figure until she was no longer in sight.

She hadn't meant the word in the traditional sense. She'd intended it purely as an insult, as she might have chosen 'jackass' or any other not particularly flattering term to describe him and his behaviour.

And she wouldn't be one hundred per cent wrong.

Oh, he hadn't changed his opinion of her, nor her parents, but he wished he hadn't been drawn into that argument.

He didn't want to argue with Mia—there was no point. Arguments were useful to clarify disagreements, in the spirit of seeking a more harmonious relationship, but Luca didn't intend to have a relationship with Mia beyond a few nights in bed together. It was very obvious to him that they both needed to work this out of their systems, and he presumed time here at the villa would be sufficient.

But once they returned to Palermo, that would be the end of it.

He might even leave the country again, to be sure.

A visit to Singapore was always nice—he had an office there and could lose himself in operations for a while. Even Sydney, at a pinch. He'd avoid his father, see his brother. Perfect.

By the time his anger had simmered down and the wound from her insult had faded, Mia was long gone.

Discarding his jacket on the front steps of the house, he began to stride through the groves, instinctively heading to the beach. It was as good a place to check as any.

He found her there, but far away, her figure small as she walked too far, too fast, in the afternoon heat. He quickened his own step, easily outstripping hers, until he was close enough to reach for her.

He grabbed her wrist, a hint of his anger returning, spun her around and then froze.

Because Mia Marini was *crying*. Actual tears. Her cheeks were wet with them.

It pulled at something in his gut, something he hadn't felt in a long time, something he really didn't like. He knew, with absolute certainty, how angry his mother would have been with him, for having made Mia cry. No matter what sins Mia had committed, Luca should have been better.

Don't stoop to their level, Luca amore.

Mia had been a part of a plan to effectively steal from him, but that didn't mean he needed to debase himself by hurtling insults at her feet.

'Just don't,' she groaned, pulling at her hand. He didn't let go. He couldn't. It was as if they were welded together.

'I don't want to fight with you,' he said, simply, frowning because it was absolutely true. 'That's not why I brought you here. The past is, as far as I am concerned, in the past.'

She shook her head. 'But we share a past, with very different opinions on it. That's important.'

'Not to me,' he said, pulling her to him. 'You made a mistake. I don't care any longer. I didn't marry you. I didn't buy the company. No harm was done. We have both moved on. Let's not discuss it again.'

She opened her mouth but he didn't want to hear it. It suddenly became very important to Luca that Mia not use those stunning lips to issue any more lies, and definitely no more defences of her parents. That was what bothered him most of all. That she'd been embroiled in the deception, and that she was attempting to excuse it now. Or worse, to still treat him like a fool, by refusing to admit the truth.

'But I haven't moved on,' she said, quietly. 'Not really, and you can't say that no harm was done, because it was. That day, when you didn't show up...'

He refused to react, but how could he not feel? Just a hint of compunction at that decision now, when faced with the obvious impact it had had on Mia?

Her eyes narrowed, tears still falling. 'When did you decide you wouldn't buy the company?'

His eyes roamed her face. 'It doesn't matter.'

'When?' She lifted a hand to his chest, imploring him to answer.

'I had just discovered the truth the last time I saw you. Earlier that day.'

'Truth,' she spat, then her eyes swept shut, shielding her thoughts and stories from him. 'You knew even then that you wouldn't marry me, didn't you?'

He didn't answer.

She blinked up at him, anguish in her features. 'You came to our house that night knowing you weren't going to go through with it?'

'I gave your father a chance to prove me wrong. He couldn't.'

She shook her head, frowning, so it was obvious to Luca that she didn't really accept the premise of that statement. 'And in the six days between that night and our wedding day, it didn't occur to you to tell me?'

He was very still. The world seemed strange.

At the time, he'd taken pleasure in simply walking away. They'd been a single team of people who'd conspired to trick him, to make a fool of Luca. Why give them the courtesy of civility? Luca had achieved what he'd achieved in life precisely by being ruthless in his approach to all things. Fair, ethical, but once wronged, he showed no mercy. That approach had served him well.

But now, standing opposite Mia, close to her, being forced to relive that day through her eyes, he had the very unpleasant experience of realising he'd taken it too far. It was one thing to defend your interests, another to wilfully harm another person.

And he had harmed Mia.

But didn't she deserve it? a voice in the back of his mind argued. Didn't her decision to get involved in the scam sale of the business negate any right to his compassion?

Evidently not, because he felt it now in abundance.

'I didn't think you would be hurt.'

More tears fell.

'I presumed your father must have told you about the business, that you would likely know what was coming.'

She shook her head. 'Did you see the photos of me?'

'Yes.' He'd been in the air at the time, flying from New York to San Francisco. His brother had emailed him.

'I was in a wedding dress. Waiting for you. And you just…you didn't arrive. You'd left the country the night before without so much as a goodbye text. I find it impossible to believe you just didn't think how your departure would affect me.' She sucked in a shaking breath. 'You *wanted* to hurt me. You wanted to inflict the most pain possible for whatever imagined wrong you felt had been done against you.' She blinked up at him, and those eyes stared into his, so layered with feeling that he took a step back, as though she'd pushed him again.

'I was very angry, Mia. You have to understand what my business means to me. I built this from scratch. I worked very hard to create my fortune and my success—it's more than money, it's more than that. Your parents wanted to take it all away from me—you did, too.'

'Tell me why you say that,' she pleaded. 'As far as I know, my father simply wants to sell the business because he is looking to retire. And he wants me to be a part of that, because I'm a Marini. At least, I am on paper,' she added with a shaking voice.

'You work in the business,' he said, needing to cling to what he had, for a year, considered to be the truth. Her working deep in the trenches of Marini Enterprises was further evidence of her involvement in the whole sordid scheme.

'So?' She lifted her shoulders. 'That's no guarantee that any new owner would keep me in the role—it's important to my father that a Marini remains in the company. Besides, it's about more than the business.' She frowned, trailing off, not answering his question.

She'd misunderstood him anyway, but he was glad, because he didn't want to put any more blame at her feet. He wasn't in the mood.

'I meant what I said, Mia.' He moved closer to her again, pulling her against his body, linking his hands in the small of her back. 'I didn't bring you here to argue over what happened then. As far as I'm concerned, that was then, this is now, and now, this, is what I'm interested in.'

She swallowed, her throat shifting. 'You mean sex?'

His eyes bored into hers. He didn't particularly like her description and yet, wasn't it the most accurate?

'Sure. Sex. Why not?'

'Because I'm engaged?'

He hadn't forgotten about Lorenzo, exactly, but Mia's fiancé was a thousand miles away from what Luca wanted to contemplate. When she lifted her hand to show him the sparkling diamond ring she wore, something strange filtered through him. He didn't want to see it. He knew she was planning to marry another man, someone else she didn't know, and didn't care for, but, for some reason, he didn't want it thrown in his face.

'And is marrying Lorenzo di Angelo really what you want with your life?'

She blinked up at him as though he'd sprouted three heads, and then she made a strange noise, dropping her head into her hands and laughing silently for a moment. Luca's heart squeezed tight.

'What I want doesn't matter. It's what has to happen,' she said, but through a sad, awful smile that pulled at his insides and made them hurt. She knew how bad their finances were, despite what she was trying to claim to him, that much was abundantly clear. Why else would she feel such a sense of obligation? This was the only way to save her parents from destitution.

'You are a free woman, Mia. You can do what you want.'

She lifted a brow. 'Says the man who kidnapped me?'

He ignored her accusation and the accompanying jab

of guilt. 'Why must you marry him? This is the twenty-first century.'

'Yes, and I'm the overprotected only child of a very old, proud Sicilian family.' She shook her head. 'You couldn't possibly understand.'

A muscle jerked in his jaw as he tried not to let her throwaway rejoinder dig beneath his skin. 'Because of how I was raised?'

She furrowed her brow, shaking her head, looking confused, so he'd clearly read too much into her comment. 'No. Because you're not me. You don't know what it's like growing up as I did.' She bit down on her lip. 'My duty—and obligation—is to make them happy. It's the least I can do. Marrying Lorenzo will do that.' Her eyes were swirling with angst. He analysed her words, her statement—she would do anything her parents asked of her. Lie for them? Con him? 'It will fix everything that broke on our wedding day. I have to do this.'

The world tilted sideways, and his brain power, all of it, homed in on her final statement. He'd had no idea the ramifications of his rejection would be so intense for Mia. He'd thought her very much a part of the scheme to dupe him, but what if she hadn't been? What if she'd been innocently, blithely going along with her parents' plans and when those plans had fallen through, she'd been blamed?

'They cannot have thought it was your fault.'

Her eyes swept shut. She was pushing him away. His hands were clasped behind her back, he pulled them now, jerking her against him, demanding with his body that she face him, and this, head-on.

'They never said as much,' she admitted. 'But I felt it. I know how devastated they were, how completely blindsided we all were. Whatever you may think, my dad clearly had no idea you wouldn't go through with the wedding.'

'Then he's a fool.'

She blinked at him with consternation. Belatedly, he remembered what he'd said, about not discussing the past. He tried to pull the censure back from his tone, to focus on the present, and the future, but, in the back of his mind, how could he not dissect what she'd said? Mia had been a part of the deal he'd resented at first, but he'd wanted the company enough to go along with it. But then, as they'd spent time together, he'd been struck by how much he wanted her, by how drugging her company was. Which had made him even angrier when he'd learned the truth. If they'd shared no chemistry, if he hadn't been prepared to ignore his usual caution with relationships and jump into bed—and marriage—with her, maybe he would have cared less? But Mia had wronged him and he'd hated that. It had all seemed so right at the time but now he wasn't so sure, and Luca hated being uncertain about anything, least of all his decisions.

'So you're marrying Lorenzo to redeem yourself, in their eyes?'

'People get married for all sorts of reasons,' she said with quiet pride.

'Love is generally the most common.'

'This *is* about love,' she murmured, and he was very still, because that changed everything. Was he wrong about their relationship? Had she fallen in love with the other man? Were they actually a couple? Infidelity was not something Luca had any interest in, being, as he was, the by-product of a messy affair. 'Love for my parents,' she continued unevenly, eyes not meeting his. 'They're far from perfect, I know that, but they chose to adopt me, to raise me as their own, to give me every advantage they could in life. They're not perfect, but I care about them, I'm grateful to them, and I want—'

She broke off, eyes troubled when they lifted to his. She was nervous, not sure how to finish what she wanted to say, but he needed to hear it, because it seemed important, and he wanted to hear all her secrets, even when he could guess the conclusion to that. She loved her parents enough to do anything for them. Even commit criminal fraud. It hardened his voice, just a little. 'Yes?'

'I want them to be proud of me,' she finished softly, closing her eyes again, and then his heart seemed to split in two. He went from sitting in judgement of her to pitying her and hating her parents more than he already did. That they weren't already proud of her made him despise her parents more than previously, which was saying something.

'But it's more than that.' Her voice continued, and there was renewed strength in it, determination. 'I want freedom from them, too. My parents show love by exerting control. I'm twenty-three and they treat me like I'm a teenager. When I'm married, I'll move out. I'll have my own home, my own life, my own family.' She shrugged. 'Those seem like pretty good reasons to get married—even to someone I barely know. Don't you think?'

CHAPTER FIVE

MIA KNEW THAT, no matter what she might say to Luca, she was willing to go along with this the minute she sent the text message to her mother.

Have gone to Rome to meet with a potential buyer, I'll be back tomorrow.

It was a little white lie, a courtesy to Jennifer because if Mia simply didn't arrive home, Jennifer and Gianni would worry—and it was only a slight bending of the truth anyway, as Mia had indeed held an online meeting with a buyer in Rome that morning.

She tilted her face to the sun, the warmth almost unbearable. She had no spare clothes, and the outfit she'd worn to work that morning didn't exactly scream 'relaxing by the pool', but maybe that was a good thing? She didn't want Luca to know how readily she'd acceded to his heavy-handed plans. Perhaps her corporate clothes could be seen as a form of silent protest? Only, it really was very hot, and so, with a sigh, she finally gave in and removed her jacket, placing it over the back of one of the loungers. But that was as far as she intended to go in a concession to comfort!

'It's a private pool. A private beach.' He gestured behind them, and her eyes followed his hand, her heart tripping at the beauty of it all. 'You do not need bathers, *cara*.'

Her stomach swirled. This man had seen her naked. He'd worshipped her curves—not once had she felt as though he wished she were skinnier. But when she looked at him, in just a pair of black boxer briefs, so toned and tanned, she became self-conscious again, her mother's repeated barbs hitting their mark, even now, years later.

'I'm fine,' she said, prim-sounding. 'You go ahead.' She crossed her arms over her chest, seeking refuge in irritation rather than allowing herself to relax into this paradise.

'Suit yourself.' He shrugged before diving into the water, his dark head sleek when he emerged at the other end a moment later, his powerful body mesmerising as it tore through the water. He was built like a swimmer, she realised, with those broad shoulders and a slim, tapered waist, powerful legs, all lean and muscular. He looked completely at home in the water, like Poseidon, Greek God of the Sea. And Earthquakes, if she was remembering her ancient myths correctly. Which made a lot of sense, given how unstable the ground felt whenever she was near him.

Prevaricating a moment, she kicked off her shoes and placed them neatly beneath the lounger, then walked to the edge of the pool, choosing a part that wasn't splashed with water and sitting down, dangling her feet and calves in. It was divine. The perfect balm to such a warm day.

You've been kidnapped, her brain tried to remind her.

But there was a small part of Mia that wondered if maybe she hadn't actually been saved. For a moment, she rested back on her palms, face tilted to the sky, and pictured herself as some kind of modern-day Rapunzel, brought down from the tower and carried away on a horse.

But Luca was no knight in shining armour, and she wasn't a damsel in distress. She was determined not to be. Mia was taking control of her own life and destiny. Marrying Lorenzo would be her ticket to freedom. She was going to make sure of it.

His hands around her calves jolted Mia out of her thoughts. She looked down at Luca and her heart skipped a beat. For one perfect moment, she let herself imagine that this was real.

That her other life had been a dream. An awful nightmare.

She imagined that Luca hadn't left her on their wedding day. That they'd married and lived here, just the two of them, in this picturesque paradise, far from her parents, from anything and anyone. She imagined that instead of marrying Lorenzo, she was already married to Luca. It was an illusion, a balloon she had to burst, and so she spoke quickly, needing to drag herself—even if inwardly kicking and screaming—back to reality.

'Where did you go anyway?'

His sexy smile made her blood pound. 'When?'

'The night before our wedding.'

His smile dropped. His face was thunder. He didn't want to answer.

'It's a straightforward question.'

His jaw was clenched. Perhaps he disagreed, but after a beat, he spoke. 'It's no secret. I went to America.'

'Why?'

'I have an office in New York.'

She furrowed her brow. 'And you suddenly needed to be there?'

'Is that so hard to believe?'

She tilted her lips to the side. 'Well, so far as I knew,

you were planning to marry me.' A thought occurred to her, one that made ice trickle down her spine. 'You were going to marry me at some point, weren't you? You didn't set out from the beginning to humiliate me like that?'

'No, Mia, no. Up until I uncovered your father's…disingenuity, I believed you and I would marry. It was part of the deal.'

She nodded slowly. It should have mollified her, but hearing him describe their marriage as part of the deal— even when that was a very accurate assessment—made her insides hurt. 'But you didn't *want* to marry me.'

His eyes didn't quite meet hers. 'Before your father suggested it, I never intended to marry anyone.'

'So why agree to that term?'

'At the time, I wanted your father's business.'

'Enough to marry me?'

He moved between her legs, and now, when their eyes locked, sparks flooded her blood. 'I wanted his business more than almost anything in the world.'

Her eyes swept shut. 'I see. So what changed?'

He didn't answer the question. 'About ten years earlier, my father had tried to purchase it,' he admitted, voice rough. 'He failed. Your father wouldn't sell. My father was…displeased. He takes all corporate losses seriously. I enjoyed the prospect of succeeding where he'd failed.' He confessed the truth without a hint of apology.

Mia considered that carefully. 'You don't get on with your father?'

Luca's lips twisted into that now-familiar mocking smile. 'No.'

She shivered involuntarily but before she could probe further, Luca changed the subject. 'Prior to your father proposing the term, I had no intention of marrying, Mia. I have never wanted a wife.'

'So why did you agree to it?'

He eyed her carefully, probing, and then shrugged his broad shoulders. 'Because I met you,' he answered after a beat. Her heart stammered. Was this the truth?

'And I was intrigued.'

He lifted a hand, trailed water over her thigh. She shivered. 'Do you remember that evening?'

She bit into her lip. 'Dinner with my parents? Of course I do.' She remembered everything about it, from Luca's late arrival, his arrogant features, but then...he'd looked at her and time had seemed to stand still. When he'd held out his hand to shake hers, Mia had felt as though everything was falling into place. She was no longer afraid of the proposed wedding. She was no longer anxious about the future. There was something about him she'd instantly trusted and liked. And the desire that had overheated her insides hadn't hurt.

Had he felt it too?

'You were so beautiful, and so enigmatic. Your mother spoke all evening. Even when I asked you a question, she answered, so I found myself quite desperate to get you alone.'

Mia made a sound of surprise.

'But I couldn't; not then. I felt as though they were keeping me away from you on purpose, to make me mad with desire, so that I would agree to almost anything to marry you.'

'As if,' she said with a roll of her eyes. 'No one in my family has that inflated view of my abilities to appeal.'

His brow lifted cynically. 'I have spent the last year believing you played your part to perfection, but now...'

'Now?' she asked, breathlessly, leaning forward unconsciously.

'I think I was wrong. About you,' he clarified quickly, letting his fingers drop to her skin above her knee, then lower, to her calf.

Pleasure swirled inside her, but Mia tried not to let it alter her resolve. Whatever he'd felt, he'd had no right to simply disappear from their wedding day.

'What did you imagine our marriage would have been like, Mia?'

She hesitated a moment. 'I—I'm not sure.' She didn't want to admit to the fantasies she'd allowed to run rampant through her mind. 'I didn't really think about that.'

'You agreed to marry me,' he pointed out quietly. 'So what would you have *wanted* that marriage to look like?'

'I've told you what I wanted,' she murmured. 'To make my parents proud. To escape. To gain a degree of independence.'

'And from your husband? Simply a roof over your head?'

She still wouldn't look at him, and Luca, using those powerful arms, pulled out of the water to sit beside her, dripping wet. He'd placed himself directly in her line of sight, his face only an inch from hers. The water droplets beaded across his face. She ached to reach out and lick them.

It made her mouth dry and her cheeks heat.

'Mia?' He caught her chin, lifting her face, holding her gaze locked to his.

'What I want—what I've always wanted—is a family of my own. I never expected...for a long time, my parents have spoken about finding me a suitable husband, someone of whom they approved, who my biological parents would have approved of too.' Her brow crinkled, and, in the back of her mind, she wondered when she'd become okay with that. 'It wasn't like I had dreams of growing up and falling in love. But I always knew I wanted children of my own. Lots of children.' Her lips were twisted in a strange smile. 'I would have settled for two, though. A boy and a girl, if I could prescribe such things.'

He was very still, watchful, his eyes probing hers, and when he spoke, his voice had a strange, heavy resonance. 'Then it's just as well we didn't marry, Mia, because I have always known, since I was a boy, that I would not have children.'

Her heart stammered and her stomach rolled like the motion of a dolphin dipping beneath the ocean. 'You can't?'

'No. Not can't. I won't.'

'Why not?' It made no sense to Mia. She couldn't fathom his feelings; not even a little.

'Why do you want children?'

She toyed with her fingers. *Because I'm an only child. Because I was adopted. Because I desperately wanted siblings. Because I want actual unconditional love.* There were any number of reasons she could have chosen, but instead, she lifted her shoulders. 'I just know I want them.'

'Just as I know I don't.'

He was right, then, she realised with a leaden feeling. It was for the best that they hadn't married. But it felt like the slamming shut of a door she realised she still wanted open. Ridiculous. Their 'marriage' hadn't happened. He'd humiliated her, made her a laughing stock. And now she was marrying someone else. Someone kind and gentle who didn't intimidate her at all, who she suspected she could twist around her little finger. Most importantly, she was marrying someone who came from a big family and had willingly agreed to Mia's stipulation that they would have children. Not straight away, but within a couple of years, when she was ready.

Why hadn't she thought to make such a stipulation with Luca?

Had she been so swept up in the idea of becoming his wife that she'd been happy to leave such things to chance? Or had she just presumed that he'd feel as she did? Had she taken it for granted that everyone must have such strong feelings on family?

'Then I guess it all worked out for the best,' she said, wondering if her voice sounded as brittle to him as it did to her. 'I could never have been happily married to you.'

Silence fell. A strange, weighted silence.

'And Lorenzo?' he prompted.

She forced a smile, hoped it seemed genuine. 'He wants children, too.'

'You've discussed it?'

'Yes.'

A frown flickered on Luca's brow, like lightning, quick but obvious. 'How well do you know him?'

She shrugged again. 'We've met a few times. I learned from our engagement.' She gestured towards Luca. 'I wanted to know—'

Luca stared at her, silent. Somehow that silence was deafening.

She sighed. 'I wanted to be sure he wouldn't…'

She didn't finish the sentence, but she didn't need to. He seemed to understand anyway. Luca tilted her chin once more, bringing their faces together. 'I had no intention of hurting you.'

Her lips pulled to the side. 'I think you did,' she said softly, slowly. 'I think you believed I deserved it, though.'

His eyes narrowed and Mia's heart twisted. She was so confused. When she was with Luca, she wanted to slam shut the door on the rest of the world and exist purely in this space, purely with him. But she couldn't forget how he'd treated her, and her parents, how he'd hurt her. She'd gone to him last night with the intention of hurting him back. Of giving him a taste of his own medicine. And instead, she'd fallen more under his spell than ever. What else could explain her willingness to sit beside him and calmly discuss their almost-wedding day?

'Yes.' His response was quiet. 'I did.'

Her eyes lifted to his, sadness in their depths. 'And now?'

He captured her face with his hands, holding her cheeks, moving closer, brushing her lips with his. 'The past is immaterial,' he said, except it wasn't.

'Not to me.' She pulled back, just a fraction, so she could say what was on her mind. 'That day changed me, Luca. You changed me. When you walked out on our wedding and left me like that, it fundamentally altered who I am. Probably for the better,' she added after a beat. 'I'm less trusting, less gullible, more careful to look after myself. That's *not* immaterial.'

'Mia.' He said her name on a groan, then pulled her back to him, kissing her hard, fast, hungrily, perhaps to silence her? To stop her enumeration of all the ways his behaviour had affected her?

It suddenly became imperative to Mia to make him understand how she felt—what she knew to be the truth. 'You're not safe, Luca,' she said quickly, against his lips. 'You're not good for me. When we go back to Palermo, I can't see you again. I'm getting married. This has to be the end of us.'

His response was to bring his wet, beautiful body over hers and kiss her senseless, until white-hot need drove them inside, to his bedroom, and the essential supply of contraceptives he kept there. But Mia, by then, was too saturated in pleasure to care.

'You're not safe, Luca. You're not good for me.'

Her words played over and over in his mind like an awful song he couldn't switch off. Back at home in Palermo, he heard her voice, the sad yet determined tone, and wanted to reach out and kiss her again, to kiss away that pain and, indeed, the entire sentiment.

Luca had no fantasy of being any woman's saviour. He'd assiduously avoided relationships, rarely got involved with the opposite sex. He dated, from time to time, but he was always careful to manage expectations. His mother had driven that lesson into him. Not by anything she'd said directly, but whenever she'd refer to his father, it was always with that wistful, lovelorn look in her eyes, so Luca had grown up understanding the truth: she'd loved Luca's father, he hadn't loved her back. He hadn't wanted any part of their family, because he'd already had a family of his own. A family who could never know the truth. And so Luca's mother had moved them down to Sicily, where she had family, in an attempt to hide Luca away, and Luca had grown up understanding more than any little boy should ever have to.

While he had no fantasy of becoming Mia's knight in shining armour, nor did he want to be her villain.

Somewhere along the way, he'd promised himself he would never be like his father, leaving a string of broken hearts in his wake. He'd promised himself he would act according to his strict moral code, a black and white system of right and wrong, and he had. Even his departure from Italy had, at the time, met that criteria: *an eye for an eye*.

He had no doubt Mia's parents had been scamming him. The business figures were fraudulent. They'd lied to make Marini Enterprises appear far more profitable than it was, and perhaps they'd been hoping he'd be so fascinated by the silent, enigmatic, beautiful Mia that he wouldn't notice—or care. He'd naturally presumed she'd been a part of the deception.

And if she hadn't?

Not *if*. He knew she hadn't.

Mia just wasn't capable of that kind of deceit. She was all that was decent and good. Which meant her parents had used her, too. Perhaps out of love, out of a desire to see her taken care of, as she'd said. Or maybe it was more sinister?

Either way, on the eve of his wedding, he'd taken great satisfaction in leaving the country without an explanation. But now, a year later, her words were a form of torture because they forced him to reckon with the fact he'd made a mistake. He'd acted out of his unfailing black and white morality but he'd been wrong. Whatever trouble her parents' business was in, whatever means they were using in order to sell it without disclosing the true financial situation, Mia wasn't complicit in that and never had been. She'd agreed to marry first him and now Lorenzo out of a sense of love for her parents, and a duty to them that was completely unreasonable, and he'd only made everything worse for her.

But could he see her again—as he desperately wanted to—without hurting her? Could he do this and protect her? Luca knew he had nothing to offer Mia long term.

He wasn't interested in a real relationship, and marriage wasn't on his radar. Children were unequivocally off the table. So in going to Mia, he had to make sure he didn't do anything that would jeopardise her plans, that would make life more difficult for her than it already was. What she did with herself next wasn't Luca's concern—he wanted her in the here and now, but Mia's future was her own to plan for.

'You can't be here.' It was one of those instances where her words were at complete odds with her feelings. She was scandalised and terrified, but also exhilarated. Luca appearing in her office was both incredibly stupid and… everything she'd been wanting, since coming back from San Vito Lo Capo two days earlier, feeling as though she were missing a limb.

'You left me no choice,' he responded with a sardonic drawl.

Heat bloomed in Mia's cheeks as she moved quickly to the door of her office and closed it, swooshing down the venetian blinds. Everything felt smaller with him in this space. He stood with feet planted wide apart, so he was like a statue made of stone in the centre of the room, and she was torn between wanting to run towards him to embrace him, or to push him over.

Her fingers shook as adrenaline rushed through her body.

'This is my office. My father works two doors down. He could have *seen* you.'

'I waited until he left,' Luca said, arms crossed over his chest.

She gaped. 'Luca—'

His nostrils flared. 'What we do with our time is our business.'

'How do you do that?'

'Do what?'

'Make it all sound so easy,' she said, pressing her fingertips to her forehead and then, as if it were a talisman, holding her hand towards him, displaying the large engagement ring she wore. 'I'm getting married.'

Luca's expression didn't alter, his appearance didn't change. 'To a man you barely know and don't care about.'

She let out a deranged half-laugh. 'Yes. That's true. But I am *getting married* and you know why. And you're—'

He moved closer, putting his hands on her cheeks, just like at the beach, so she felt safe and valued and calm even as a storm raged in her chest. 'What am I?'

'I am so angry at you,' she said honestly, because she needed to cling to that. 'For what you did a year ago. I can't forgive it.'

His eyes held hers but they were impossible to read, despite the strength of their connection. 'I'm not asking for your forgiveness.'

Of course he wasn't. Luca wasn't a man who cared for the good opinion of others. What did it matter to Luca Cavallaro how Mia felt about him? His sense of self was far too assured for her feelings to have any impact.

'Then what are you asking for? What do you want from me?' She lifted a hand to his chest. 'What do you want from me?' she repeated, groaning, because she'd been going crazy with wanting him and suddenly, she didn't care about anything except the fact he was here and seemed to need her as she needed him.

'One week.' He pushed her backwards, pressing his body to her, so she was caught between the edge of her desk and his strong thighs, and her world began to crumble and tumble and roll, her eyes filled with stars and fireworks and flame. 'Give me one week of your time, Mia. Let me have you, just for one week.'

'And then what? You've had me already for two days. Was that not enough?' She needed to know.

'I'll go away again. I'll stay away.'

She swallowed, trembling, tortured and delighted in equal measure. He was offering something so simple. A week. A week out of time, to enjoy him and this and then return to normal. With a set-in-stone end point to their fling, surely that would limit any potential harm.

He moved his mouth to the corner of hers, kissing her there lightly, making it hard to think clearly.

'Nobody can ever know.' She tried to cling to sense, to hold onto rational thought for long enough to negotiate this in a meaningful way, to make the kinds of stipulations she should have made in the first instance, way back when they were engaged. But in the last year, Mia had grown, and she'd changed, and that meant being more determined to stand up for herself and what she wanted.

'I am not intending to take out an advertisement.'

'I mean it, Luca.' She pulled back to stare into his eyes. 'You pulled my life apart once—you can't do it again. You have to play by the rules. *My* rules.'

His eyes narrowed slightly. 'And what are they?'

Given the opportunity to enumerate a list, she found her mind becoming blank. But she waded through the flotsam and forced herself to focus. 'We have to keep this secret. No being seen together in public, no turning up at my office,' she added quickly. 'No following me to bridal-dress fittings. No going out for dinners, nothing like that. My parents know everybody in Sicilia, just about, and those they don't, Lorenzo's family will know. Nowhere is safe.'

'Except my home,' he pointed out.

A thrill of excitement exploded inside Mia's chest. 'Yes,' she conceded carefully.

'Any other rules?'

'One week,' she said emphatically, because she needed to cement that in her own mind. 'Nothing beyond it. This is an aberration. I want to focus on my new life and I can't do that when you're here. So after a week, you'll go, just like you said.'

He nodded curtly. 'I've already agreed to this.'

'You also agreed to marry me,' she reminded him, then winced, because she was sick of dragging up the past, of remembering that hurt. 'But we both know it's a good thing you didn't.'

Silence sparked in the air. 'Now, it's my turn.'

'For what?'

'Rules. I will do everything I can to ensure no one learns about this,' he promised. 'But you are completely and utterly mine for the next week. Do or say whatever you need, but you will be in my bed, at my home, for the next seven days.'

Her eyes widened and her mouth parted. Terror and delight were tangling in her belly. It sounded so wonderful, so heavenly, but it wasn't reality. 'I can't…'

He pressed a finger to her lips. 'We have one week. You *can*.'

She thought of some options, desperation making her like a descendent of Machiavelli suddenly. 'I'll try,' she said with a nod, thinking of her best friend, the one friend of Mia's who her parents actually approved of. Mia had mentioned a desire to travel to London to spend some time with Caroline—she could fib and say she was going, spur of the moment, next week. Excitement pounded in her chest.

'Anything else?' She was breathless.

He lifted up, eyes sparking with hers. 'No.' He ground his hips against her and she whimpered, because he was hard and she was desperately hungry for him after two days of not seeing him. 'My car will collect you on the corner. Don't keep me waiting too long, Mia.'

'I won't.'

'Promise?'

Everything slowed down until the world stopped spinning. Standing on a precipice, Mia knew she should hesitate, that doubts should be flooding her, but the truth was, everything suddenly seemed so simple and *right*. 'I promise,' she agreed huskily, and she really, really did.

CHAPTER SIX

Mia had expected the car to take them to Luca's Palermo town house but instead, within ten minutes of leaving the office, they were on their way down a familiar road, out of the city, towards San Vito Lo Capo, and Mia was glad. Glad because Palermo felt risky even within the confines of his home, and because what they were doing was such a slice out of time that it felt better to be also out of space, out of her familiar geographical locations.

'I have no clothes except these,' she said with a tilt of her lips.

'You will not need clothes,' he drawled, reaching across and wrapping his hand over her thigh.

Anticipation flooded Mia's veins. 'Luca…' Her breath hitched. What had she wanted to say?

'I have arranged everything. Trust me.'

Her eyes flicked to his and then away again, a frown tugging at her lips.

He was the stuff of fantasies, but surely not a man to be trusted after what happened a year ago, and Mia needed to remember that. She had to keep her wits about her, to limit what they were doing to the incredible, mind-blowing sex, and nothing more. This wasn't her real life.

They arrived at the villa as the sun was dipping low in the sky and it was the most stunningly picturesque view, the gradients quite mesmerising. She stood on the front step, staring outwards, towards the mountains that were welcoming the sun with open arms for a night's rest, and sighed.

The future was murky, but, right now, everything was just as it needed to be. Recognising that unlocked a part of her to fully enjoy this. She couldn't marry Lorenzo without getting Luca fully out of her system. It wouldn't have been fair to Lorenzo or herself to bring this kind of desire for another man into their marriage. So she'd enjoy this week with Luca and happily farewell him at the end of it, ready to move on with her life and put Luca where he belonged: properly in the past. But rather than thinking of him and feeling a sense of rejection and hurt, she'd look back at what they'd shared as the birth of something within Mia—her sensual awakening, her self-confidence as a woman. These were aspects of Mia that had been totally neglected.

She would always be grateful to Luca for drawing them into the light.

'Ready?' He reached down and linked their fingers. She stared at the sky a moment longer, thinking about sunsets and endings and the promise of new beginnings, and then turned, blinked up at him as if seeing Luca for the first time, because if she was completely his for the next week then he was also completely hers.

'Yes,' came the breathy response.

'Good. Because I know just what I want to do with you first.'

Her heart was pounding as he led her through the beautiful old villa, but rather than guiding Mia to the bedroom they'd shared a few nights ago, he showed her out onto the terrace, to the stunning infinity pool with views towards the orange-hued sky, and darkening ocean.

'Turn around.' His voice was thick, hoarse.

She did as he said, her heart pounding. His fingers caught the zip at the top of her back and drew it down, loosening the dress she wore, until it fell away from her body altogether, leaving her exposed in just her underwear. She was outside, visible to the world, and yet the world couldn't see into the villa—it was, as Luca had told her, a completely private stretch of beach, there was no need to feel embarrassed, and yet usually Mia would have been riddled with self-consciousness. Only something about Luca, and the way he responded to her, was empowering and intoxicating and for the first time in her adult life she revelled in her nakedness, in being naked for him.

There was a rustle of clothing and then Luca's naked body was at her back, holding her, arms around her waist a moment, chin pressed to her shoulder. She trembled, knees weak. He removed her bra and underpants and Mia felt a thrill of power.

'You are beautiful,' he said with wonder, turning her to face him, eyes hooded. 'So beautiful. And all mine.'

'For one week,' she reminded him firmly, warmth spreading through her. When he called her beautiful, she really believed it. Years of conditioning by her mother seemed to ebb away.

His eyes flared and then he lifted her, holding her against his chest, carrying her towards the pool and stepping in. He was so strong. Not once did he appear to struggle, to stumble, but rather stepped easily, down, and down again, until Mia was enveloped by the delightfully warm water and sensations flooded her from head to toe—his nakedness, so close, his warmth, the water, it was all utterly mind-blowing.

And when he kissed her, she was already at a fever

pitch, the whirlpool of longing having begun to swirl from the moment he walked into her office, and it hadn't stopped all afternoon. When he kissed her, she felt beautiful, she felt warm all over, she felt like the most precious, fragile yet strong person in the world, and she never wanted it to stop—not now, and deep down, Mia admitted only to her most secret self, not even in a week.

Their hands were laced on the top of the table as the older woman brought out a platter of risotto, scampi and salad.

'My housekeeper,' Luca had said on Mia's last visit, when the sound of the door closing had alerted them to someone else being in their space and Mia had panicked. 'When I am at the villa, she comes for two hours each night. She can be trusted, Mia. She's worked for me a long time, and before that she was a friend of my mother's. She will not tell a soul that you are here.'

There was that word again: *trust*.

Mia smiled at the older woman as she bustled about with a wine bottle and then, when they were alone once more on the starlit terrace, the smell of night-flowering jasmine and honeysuckle heavy in the air, Mia pulled her hand back, flexing her fingers a little to remove the tingling effect of Luca's touch, and fixed him with a level stare.

'Do *you* trust her?'

His eyes locked to Mia's, then he reached for his wine glass, taking a sip of the crisp, white liquid before responding. 'Catarina? With my life.'

Mia frowned.

'You weren't expecting that answer?'

'No.' She speared a scampi and tasted it. Delicious.

'Because…' he prompted, when Mia didn't respond.

Her lips tugged to one side. 'You don't strike me as a

man who trusts anyone.' She thought about that a little more. 'Or who lets people get close.'

'You're close. Look.' He reached out and touched her under the table.

Mia smiled but rolled her eyes. 'You know that's not what I mean.'

He sipped his wine, said nothing more.

'So?' she asked, leaning forward, elbows on the table, no longer interested in the food, though it was absolutely spectacular.

'What do you want to know?' There was a guardedness to his voice, a wariness about what she might ask him, and how he might answer.

Mia didn't back down.

She had a limited time to get this man out of her system and that meant coming to understand him, because she didn't want to find herself thinking about him in six months' time, wondering what made him tick, what made him a certain way.

'Why?'

'Why?' He let out a sound of exasperated amusement. 'That's unquantifiable. A thousand things happen in a person's life that cause them to behave or feel a certain way, it's rarely just one.'

'And I'm asking about yours.'

'Why?'

'Well, because I'm here for a week and we can't be in bed the entire time,' she pointed out, cheeks blushing.

'Is that a challenge?'

She dipped her gaze to the table. 'I want to understand you, Luca.'

He reached over and lifted her chin. Mia's eyes hooked

to his and her heart lurched in her chest. 'That wasn't part of the deal.'

Did he really mean to keep her at arm's length emotionally while physically exploiting all of their chemistry?

'Is this what you do with women?' She changed tack. 'Have sex but refuse to talk?'

'I'm happy to talk.'

'About things that matter.'

His eyes were hooded, no longer easy for Mia to comprehend, but they were darkened by emotion, so she wished she had the key to understanding. She wished she knew him better.

'I don't have serious relationships.' He removed his hand, returned it to his wine glass, sipped, swallowed, his Adam's apple drawing her attention to his throat. 'It wouldn't be fair.'

'No?' She was glad that he'd at least expanded a little on his answer.

'Why date when you have no intention of marriage?'

'You aren't unique in that respect, Luca. I'm sure there are lots of women who would be happy to spend time with you without wanting more.' Even as she said it, she suspected that was false. Of course that wasn't the case. Even women who might have felt they were anti-marriage or long-term commitment couldn't fail to be tempted by Luca. *And you?* a voice inside Mia jeered. After all, what insurance policy did Mia have against wanting more from him? More than this week?

Her eyes dropped to her engagement ring and she stared at it with a rush of relief. That was her insurance policy, her real life. Her duty. Her obligation. Even if she decided she wanted more from Luca, she couldn't have it, because she *needed* to marry Lorenzo. She'd promised her parents, and they had stressed to her how important the wedding was, as well as the sale of the business. Her father was desperate to retire, desperate enough to sell the family business, but only if Mia was a part of the deal, so that she would retain an interest in the ongoing success of the company her great-grandparents had built from nothing. She reminded herself it wasn't a love match. And Lorenzo knew that too. It was a mutually beneficial marriage on paper.

Something fuzzed at the edges of her mind, something dark and ominous that tightened her stomach into knots, but she couldn't quite grab hold of it. Her father had been stressed lately. Was it any wonder? After the debacle of the last would-be sale and wedding, he probably had the same form of stress echoes that Mia did.

'I have a policy of not stringing women along. I see women, when it suits me, but I don't date often, and I am always careful not to make any promises of more than I intend to offer.' He replaced the wine glass carefully. 'Personal conversation isn't…necessary.'

She frowned. 'So you'll sleep with them but not talk?'

'It works for me.'

She angled her face towards the dark sky over the shimmering, black ocean. 'I don't know why, but that makes me feel kind of sad for you.'

He didn't respond immediately. 'There's no need. My life is just how I like it.'

She nodded, because of course that was true. Just because Mia would find his type of intimacy hollowing, didn't mean he felt the same way.

They were different creatures, and it barely seemed to matter, because after this week, they'd cease to know one another at all.

* * *

Mia slept late the next day, which was hardly a surprise, given that she hadn't actually fallen asleep until well into the early hours of the morning.

Their agreement had unleashed something within them—a new sense of urgency, because they'd defined what they were and delineated how long they'd be this for. Both knew an end point was looming and seemed determined not to waste a moment.

It was exhaustion that had finally drawn Mia into sleep, when her eyes had grown too heavy and her body, her over-sensitised body, had felt unnaturally heavy, and Luca had gently pulled her to his chest, one big, strong arm clamped around her shoulders, and held her there, so the last thing she was aware of as she fell asleep was the beating of his heart.

He swam from one side of the cove to the other, as he did most mornings while at the villa, the workout and seawater a perfect way to energise his body for the day ahead. Usually, he then had a light breakfast and went to work in his study, so he could have been anywhere in the world— his Milan office, New York, Singapore, Sydney. They all had the same décor, the same equipment, to avoid the jarring sense of being out of routine.

But he didn't feel like working today.

He wanted Mia.

He swam harder, anger fuelling his strokes because he'd spent hours pleasuring her and surrendering to the pleasure she gave last night and it was almost unnatural that his body should still yearn for her with this blinding intensity, and yet it was all he could think of, all he wanted.

Mia was an anchor, drawing on him, even as he swam.

In line with the house, he stopped, stood against the sandy bottom of the ocean with hands on his hips and stared at the building, trying to picture her, wondering what she was doing, imagining her naked body, those beautiful curves against the black silk of his sheets, her honey-coloured limbs tangled in the fabric, her hands wandering, exploring, touching herself because she'd awoken hungry for him, too.

Grinding his teeth, he began to stride from the ocean, intent on reaching the house by the shortest means available and, as quickly as possible thereafter, Mia. In the back of his mind, he had a virtual whiteboard and on it was written, in big red letters, six more nights.

He had no intention of wasting them.

The boat was everything she might have expected someone like Luca to possess—luxurious, fast, glistening white and chrome with very black windows and a sleek frame, and he drove the thing with expert ease, wearing just a pair of navy-blue shorts, so Mia found herself trying to focus on the beautiful coastline and, instead, unable to tear her eyes from his body.

Strange how these waters had once been a place of deep self-loathing and dread for Mia, and now, as Luca navigated through them, she felt an unbending need to ask him to stop the boat and let her off, to dive deep beneath the calm, crystalline surface, to be engulfed by this bay, its healing powers making her see herself as Luca claimed to. To feel truly beautiful. To erase all of the insults her mother had gently and cleverly woven into Mia's being, over all the years of her life.

They were far from land, far enough that she could see it as a postcard, all the tiny homes and the streets that lined the seafront, with their brightly coloured shops, restaurants with umbrellas, gelaterias bustling with queues of people in this midday heat. She sighed, reclined on her bed and reached for the lemon water Luca had brought her, a half-smile on her lips.

'You're lost in thought.'

Her eyes flicked to his. 'I suppose I am.'

'About?' There was a seriousness to his voice, as though he wasn't sure he'd like the answer.

She turned back to the water, the stunning turquoise ocean, and ran her fingers lightly over the arm of her daybed. 'I was reflecting on how different it is being back here with you, from when I used to come as a girl. I mean, obviously it's different.' Her cheeks blushed. 'But how I feel… I feel…happy.'

He frowned. 'You weren't happy then?'

Her lips pulled to the side. 'I thought you didn't do serious conversations.'

He hesitated a moment. 'Would you prefer not to talk about it?'

She laughed softly. 'I don't want to drag you into unfamiliar waters,' she said with a shake of her head. 'Forget it. It doesn't matter.'

Silence fell between them, and Mia presumed the conversation was closed, but then Luca reached out and squeezed her hand. 'I want to know. Tell me what you're thinking.'

It was nothing. Perhaps he was just being polite? But to Mia, something in her chest exploded and she couldn't say why.

She blinked away from him, staring at the crystal-clear waters.

'It would be a good idea for you to skip breakfasts for a while, Mia. Particularly those heavy English cooked ones.'

'We used to come here on summer vacations, to this exact place,' she said, softly, her words barely carrying to him in the afternoon sunshine. 'I loved it. As a girl, I would lose myself in the water for hours, emerging only when my skin was wrinkled like a prune and my eyes bleary from a combination of sunscreen and salt water.'

He squeezed her hand. 'And then, when I was about eleven, it started to change. I got heavier. Awkward. I'd come back from school and Mum would weigh me, frown, shake her head, tell me she was going to call the dorm mistress to speak about my diet.' Mia's voice was thick with emotion; she didn't look at Luca, didn't see the way his eyes sparked with a mix of anger and surprise.

'Swimming became a form of hell. She'd criticise my body as soon as I emerged from my room. I felt so self-conscious. I mean, your body's starting to change at that age and that's hard to get used to, but to have Mum draw my attention to it, as well as whoever else happened to be on the boat, it was excruciating. I stopped wanting to swim. I stopped wearing anything that showed skin. Eventually, I got out of coming on these trips altogether. But that didn't matter. Whether it was here or at home, Mum never let me forget what a disappointment I was because I wasn't like her.'

Luca stood, prowling to the edge of the boat, staring out at the sea, his back turned and ramrod straight, his shoulders taut. She found it easier to talk to his back, anyway.

'My mother is very beautiful and fashion is her favourite hobby. She would bemoan how unfortunate it was that none of her clothes would ever fit me, that they couldn't be passed down. She'd hoped to have a daughter she could share a wardrobe with, but instead she adopted me, and I was short and round.' Mia mimicked her mother's voice then closed her eyes, mortified to be revealing this much to Luca.

He spun around sharply, staring at Mia, his jaw clenched. 'Mia, you are beautiful. I say that not as a man who's become obsessed by your body, obsessed with making love to you, but as an objective stranger. When I first met you, I couldn't get you out of my head. You *know* that.'

She shook her head, struggling to accept that he'd felt as crazy with lust as she had. And yet, didn't she have more than enough evidence of that? Everything about his behaviour in the past week demonstrated that his own infatuation was at a fever-pitch level, like hers.

'It's hard to explain,' she said after a beat. 'It's not about whether her remarks had any basis in reality, but how they made me feel.'

'I can imagine,' he grunted. 'What kind of bitch goes out of her way to destroy a vulnerable teenager's self-esteem?'

She lifted her shoulders.

'I honestly think she meant well. She wanted to encourage me to lose weight—I'm not like her, so much as my biological mother, which makes a lot of sense, really.'

His eyes narrowed. 'Why the hell should weight loss be any kind of goal?'

She swallowed, and the academic part of her brain knew that he was right, that it was her mother who had been wrong to criticise and undermine Mia. 'Beauty is important to her.'

'Mia, listen to me. Let's set aside for a moment the indisputable fact that you are very beautiful and focus on something else. Would you like to know what I think happened?'

Mia nodded her head once, and Luca came to sit beside

her, on the lounger, his body so close she felt his warmth wrapping around her. 'I believe you went away one year as a little girl and then came back showing the woman you'd become, and your mother was jealous. Because you're young and gorgeous and suddenly she realised she'd have competition. I have known women like her, who can't bear to be outshone, even by their own family members. That's her sickness, not yours. Don't take on her wounds and make them your own.'

She stared at him as if he were divining a lightning rod, right into her soul. Could this be true? Was her mother actually jealous of Mia?

'Not only are you beautiful, you shine from the inside out.' He pressed a hand to her chest. 'You shimmer with life. Happiness, joy, light and kindness, qualities that your mother could never experience as you do. Do not give her opinions any more room in your head, *cara*. You deserve better.'

When he said it, she found it so easy to believe. She felt as though a weight she'd been carrying for a million years were lifting off her, as if she could breathe properly for the first time in for ever.

'It's not like I care about looks,' she said, brow scrunching, because she wanted him to understand her. 'It's not a question of vanity. It's—a question of value. Self-worth.'

'You've lost weight,' he said slowly, as if the words were dredged from deep in his chest. 'Since our wedding.'

'There was no wedding.' She pulled her hand away, the memory of that day incongruous with the warmth and contentment he'd just poured through her. 'And it wasn't intentional.'

'I would hate to think you have been suffering under the

misapprehension that what happened that day had anything to do with your appearance, and my lack of desire for you.'

She blanched, shaking her head. 'Can we really, please, seriously not talk about this?'

'Mia, it's important.'

'It really isn't,' she pleaded. 'In the scheme of things, what I think about this, how I feel, it just doesn't matter.'

'To me, it does.'

'Why?' she challenged with an urgency that came right from the very middle of her chest. 'Why do you even care, Luca?' She stood up, frustrated, pacing to the other side of the deck, staring out at the familiar view, hands clenched around the railing. 'You're the one who told me you don't do serious conversations. So why are you pushing this? Why can't you just let it go?' Her voice cracked. 'Please, would you just let it go?'

'I will.' He was speaking to her so softly, gently, as though she were a child. She compressed her lips, frustration making her nerve-endings reverberate. 'When you've explained this to me, I will never speak of it again.'

Her eyes glimmered with mutinous annoyance. 'That hardly sounds like a victory for me.'

'Why won't you discuss it?'

'Because it's in the past and because it hurts. Why dredge up something painful?'

'If it is pain that I caused, then I have a right to know about it.'

'God, Luca! What do you want me to say? That you not showing up for our wedding didn't impact me at all? That there were no negative consequences from that day?' She shook her head to dispel both sentiments. 'It was a disaster. You humiliated me. Worse, you confirmed every negative feeling I had about myself, every sentiment my

mother had ever expressed to me. I felt worthless and unwanted and laughable. A total joke. Is it any wonder I'm
a different person now? And I don't mean physically, I
mean all of me.'

She tilted her chin with outraged defiance, hoping he
could see the strength and determination that fired from
her eyes. 'I fully believe you had no intention of hurting
me, that you didn't even think about me as an individual,
so much as a part of a business deal you no longer wanted
any part of, but your actions that day broke me. I swore I'd
never admit that to you,' she muttered. 'I swore I'd never
let you know...'

'Don't.' He moved across the boat, drawing her into his
arms. 'Don't lie to me any more, don't hide from me. I deserve to know what happened.' He drew in a deep breath,
eyes swirling with feeling as they stared at each other.
'You're right,' he admitted gruffly, after a beat. 'I didn't
think of you as an individual. Not really. But I didn't walk
away because I didn't desire you, Mia. It had nothing to do
with that. If anything, how I felt about you, how attracted
I was to you, scared the hell out of me. It still does.'

He pressed a finger to her chin and she trembled, his
words making no sense and all the sense in the world because this was *terrifying*. 'I walked out on our wedding
because of your parents' actions. Not yours.'

She closed her eyes, hating their past, hating how much
she wanted him, how complicated everything was.

'I worked hard to build my fortune, my life, to get out of
the slums of Sicily, to prove to my father that I was more
than he'd ever thought, more than the boy he spent twelve
years ignoring. It's never been about money. It's so much
more than that. The idea of someone trying to cheat me
out of what I've achieved—I was enraged. You bore the

brunt of that.' A frown marred his handsome, symmetrical features. 'I'm sorry. I wish you had not ended up as collateral damage. If I could undo it, I would. But, Mia? You are beautiful. Now. Then. Always. I'm sorry that your mother's treatment gave you cause to doubt that, and that my own actions inadvertently—and incorrectly—reinforced her behaviour.'

A tear slid down her cheek as she shook her head, hearing his words but refusing to heed them. Self-preservation was an instinct that died, oh, so hard. But when he kissed her, she let him, and she relaxed into it, because it was just a kiss, it was just sex, it was just physical. Mia's heart was as locked as ever, and Luca's was too. This was safe, this was okay, because they knew when they'd stop seeing each other, and go back to their normal lives. Everything was going to be just fine.

'Mia? How's England?'

Her skin paled as her dad's voice came down the phone line. The lie felt heavy in her gut. But then her eyes drifted across the dazzling white sand beach, following Luca's figure as he ran parallel to the coastline. 'Oh, fine. Yeah, fine.'

'Doing pre-wedding shopping?'

Mia clamped her hands together in her lap. The wedding, which she knew to be inevitable, now loomed as a terrifying drop right off the edge of the earth. Certainty about what she was doing, and why, had begun to recede. She knew the wedding mattered to her parents, the company did too, but what about Mia? She wanted freedom from her parents' oppressive type of love, but was there only one way to obtain that freedom?

'Dad, I wanted to ask you something,' she said without answering. 'Do you have a minute?'

'I have precisely two minutes before my meeting arrives.'

'Great, this won't take long.' The quicker the better in fact, like ripping off a plaster. She furrowed her brow, tummy in knots. 'It's about Luca Cavallaro.'

Silence stretched between them. Saying his name aloud sent a rush of something through Mia—she realised she hadn't done as much since the wedding day.

'Bastard of a man. What about him?'

Mia's cheeks coloured. 'Did you have any idea, before that day, that he was having…doubts?'

More silence but, this time, Mia was sure she heard it crackle down the phone line. 'What kind of question is that?' Gianni spluttered eventually, either truly indignant or doing an excellent job of feigning it.

'I'm just curious.'

'Mia, as far as I was concerned, the wedding was going to happen.'

She sighed, frustrated. Someone was lying to her, and as she watched Luca running, she knew who she believed. Luca had hurt her, but he was ruthlessly honest. He wouldn't say he'd had a conversation with Gianni if it hadn't taken place. Was it possible her father had misunderstood? Her frown deepened.

'What is all this about, Mia?' Gianni asked sharply. 'That bastard is in the past. Lorenzo is a good man. His family is rich and powerful, the business will be in good hands.'

'As will I?' she asked, ice in her veins. How much of this was about the business, rather than Mia?

'Yes, yes, of course. Now, is that everything?'

CHAPTER SEVEN

WHAT WAS HE DOING? He felt a slip in the side of the road, a precarious tumble, not only likely but almost happening in that moment. Things with Mia were different from anything he'd experienced, different from what he'd anticipated they'd be. She was like a diamond in one of his father's stores, with dazzlingly bright eyes and many, many facets. Every time he thought he understood her, she revealed something else about herself. He didn't think a lifetime would be long enough to properly know her.

But that was for her husband to find out.

Luca tightened his jaw, trying not to think of how that could have been him, if he'd been willing to let the Marini family con him into a worthless business partnership.

He closed his eyes a moment, trying to grab hold of the anchor points in his life, the touchstone moments that informed the man he'd become. The difficulties of his childhood. His mother's poverty despite her hard work—that had taught him a determination to never be hungry again, to never know the discomfort of a winter without electricity. It had taught him a fierce desire to be so rich money became almost inconsequential. His mother's death—sudden and abrupt—and whatever trials he'd had before then had seemed ludicrous, because suddenly the carpet had been ripped from beneath his feet, his whole world tumbled and shattered and unrecognisable without the woman who'd been a bookend to his days for as long as he could remember. She was not a demonstratively loving mother. Perhaps the hurts his father had heaped upon her had closed shut her heart, but, despite a lack of obvious affection, she'd been there for him, even when she was exhausted.

He'd missed her like a limb.

And then, his world had changed again, when a lawyer had arrived in a smart grey suit, with an even fancier grey car, and bundled Luca into the sweet-smelling interior—lollies and air freshener—and taken him to the airport, where he'd boarded a large jet and been flown to the unfamiliar, sticky and hot landscape of Sydney, Australia.

He'd hated his father immediately.

He'd hated him even more when he came to realise that he had a brother just three months older. At twelve, Luca was mature enough to understand what that meant. He'd been conceived while his father's wife was pregnant with Max. His father had cheated—on his mother, and also Max's mother.

Was it any wonder the marriage dissolved? But not simply and quietly, as the word 'dissolved' might have implied. It was a wreck. A total implosion, with sparks and flames and detritus and collateral damage in the form of two young boys who were forced to watch on and listen to it all, who would be shaped for ever by the visage of two grown-ups going out of their way to be as hurtful and angry with one another as they possibly could be.

All of these moments had shaped Luca, had informed his outlook on life, family, relationships. His trust was hard won, but Max had earned it.

Their early relationship had been difficult. Naturally. It didn't help that their father had almost seemed to delight in setting the boys against one another, in fuelling a competition between them. But competition had somehow turned to mutual respect, then to the realisation that they had far more in common than they didn't, and that their differences could, if used in tandem, unite them, strengthen them.

Somewhere along the way, they became a pair.

Except in one vital way: Luca swore he would never touch one cent of the Stone fortune, and he hadn't. To this day, his wealth was a by-product of his own work, his sweat, strength, daring, guile and genius. He'd worked harder than anyone he knew to rise to the top, to prove to his father that he didn't need him. Or perhaps that he shouldn't have ignored him, for the first twelve years of Luca's life. A deeply buried sense of worthlessness, of having been unwanted by his father, was hard to shake, and Luca had learned the best way to conquer that vulnerability was to never need anyone again.

He couldn't be hurt if he stood completely on his own, a pillar of autonomy and strength, a man utterly untouched by concern for another.

But Mia…

He dragged a hand through his hair, eyes blinking open and landing immediately on her, where she lay on the sun lounger, body a deep caramel, hair like gossamer silk so his fingers itched to reach out and touch her.

Mia was not his concern, he reminded himself emphatically. This week was an aberration, a rare moment of indulgence that he'd get out of his system and be done with. He didn't need her. He didn't need anyone.

But that didn't mean he didn't want to fix something

inside her that he suspected he'd helped break. Moving quickly, he reached for his phone and placed a couple of calls, a sense of something like pleasure building in his gut as he imagined her reaction, when she realised what he'd done.

'What is all this?' Mia stared at the bags and bags and bags with a knotty feeling in her stomach.

'You didn't have time to pack clothes,' he reminded her, gesturing to the bags as if it were nothing.

But Mia read the labels and knew that the island of things on her bed constituted an investment of tens of thousands of dollars, probably more like hundreds of thousands. Particularly when her eyes alighted on a small burgundy bag at the front with gold swirling writing that said *Stone*. His family's jewellery stores were amongst the most prestigious in the world. And the most expensive.

'Luca...' Her voice faltered as she turned to face him, ambivalence on her delicate features. 'This is too much.'

'It's just fabric.'

That was so like him, to simplify this gesture down to the nuts and bolts.

'I hate shopping,' she said with a shake of her head.

'This isn't shopping. Someone else has done that for you.'

'Who?'

'Does it matter?'

'I'm interested.' She moved to the bags out of idle curiosity, pressing one apart with her fingertips.

'An assistant.'

'You had your assistant buy me clothes?'

'Why not?'

'I just—' She furrowed her brow. 'I'm just confused. I don't understand why you'd do this.'

'Am I not allowed to gift you something?'

'This isn't something. It's many somethings, and it's extravagant and...' She shook her head. 'I don't know. I'll feel strange keeping them after this week.'

His eyes narrowed before his face was quickly wiped of emotion. 'Then don't keep them. Donate them. For now, let me have the pleasure of seeing you try some on.'

It would be ungrateful and churlish to refuse, though Mia also hated trying clothes on. However, she discovered that the clothing Luca's clever assistant had selected was so beautiful that, rather than feeling her usual revulsion at the activity, she actually enjoyed slipping into the silky fabrics, the delicate skirts and bottom-hugging jeans.

'They're beautiful,' she admitted after a third outfit change.

'Not the clothes.' He came towards her, linking his hands behind her waist. 'You are beautiful, Mia.'

Her heart fluttered; this time, she absolutely believed him.

'And now, this one.'

He reached for the burgundy bag and her heart began to thump. 'What is it?'

His smile was knowing as he reached into the bag and removed a small velvet box. 'Something I wanted you to have.'

She bit down on her lip, butterflies bursting through her.

The box shape was all wrong for a ring, and she was glad. A ring from Luca would remind her of the last ring he'd given her. No, she corrected swiftly. He hadn't ever given her a ring. One had been couriered over with the contracts, to Mia's father, who'd given it to Mia unceremoniously, except for a throwaway remark on his having presumed Luca Cavallaro might have sprung for a large diamond.

'A larger diamond would have made your fingers look so much slimmer, Mia. What a shame!' Jennifer had chimed in.

For her part, Mia had loved it. The ring had been small and delicate, a fine gold band with a single gemstone in the centre. Not a diamond, but an emerald, it had caught the light and refracted it into the room.

She'd had it sent back to Luca by her assistant the week after their non-wedding.

She couldn't have borne the thought of having it in her home.

With fingers that weren't quite steady, she opened the box, her breath catching in her throat at the sight of the necklace within. Her father would have been delighted, for surely this necklace was both exquisitely beautiful and also very valuable.

Her finger ran over the chain—platinum gold with a round diamond set in each inch or so, leading to a teardrop diamond with three solitaires on either side. It was incredibly beautiful. Despite the double-digit carats, it was still, somehow, delicate and wearable.

It was far more valuable than anything Mia owned, and yet she could immediately see herself in it.

He'd chosen well.

But perhaps this hadn't been Luca's choice, so much as the clever work of an assistant.

'May I?'

Her lips pulled to one side and she nodded jerkily, turning and catching her hair over one shoulder, stomach swooping as she waited for him to fasten it behind her neck. His fingers brushed her flesh there and she jumped, her cells flooding with awareness and need. She lifted her hand and felt the diamonds, then turned a little so she could catch her reflection in the mirror.

Her breath burned in her lungs.

It wasn't just the necklace. It wasn't just the clothes. It wasn't just the man standing behind her, so rugged and addictively attractive. It was *everything*, a whole combination of these things. It was standing in this room of Luca's house, in a town he'd brought back to life for her, it was seeing herself like this, that made Mia fully realise this was a reality she could have been living.

If the forks in the road of life hadn't driven him away, if, instead, he'd been waiting at the church for her, dressed in a tuxedo and standing up at the front, those dark eyes watching her, waiting for her, she would now be Mrs Luca Cavallaro.

And then what? a voice in the back of her head demanded. You'd be desperate for the children he'd never give you. Desperate for the love he'd never give you.

And she knew then that her innermost doubts were accurate.

If she'd married Luca, she would have fallen completely head over heels in love with him. If she'd married Luca, she'd have wanted far more than he could ever give her, and Mia's life, despite the trappings, would have been a misery.

All of this was an illusion.

Despite the way he made her feel, despite the happiness spreading through her, threatening to make her forget, Mia knew the most important thing she could do this week was keep a firm hold of reality. Because none of this was real. None of this would exist by the end of the week.

She wanted to keep things casual, to be relaxed and light-hearted, but something was pulling at Mia, a desperate need to understand the one thing that didn't make sense.

'Why?' She met his eyes in the reflection, her heart lurching in a now-familiar response to looking directly at him—and being seen.

'Because it suits you.'

'I mean, why all of this?' Her hand gestured towards the bed. 'You didn't have to—'

'I wanted to.'

'Okay, but why?'

'So many questions.'

'One question, that you haven't answered.'

His lips compressed, showing, momentarily, his impatience, but then he gave a nonchalant shrug and put his hands on her hips, turning her to face him properly. 'Because you deserve this. And because I am sorry. I have spent the last year convinced you were as bad as your parents, that you were as guilty as they, and now—'

'Now?' she whispered.

'I know that's not the case.'

She frowned. 'Why?'

'Another question?'

She nodded once.

'I can tell. I was wrong about you. I treated you badly, and I regret it. Please, accept my apology.'

So the necklace was a guilt gift? She didn't want it to take the shine off things, but it did, even when, on her fateful non-wedding day, she would have given anything for Luca to acknowledge his fault, to actually apologise to her.

'Why do you hate them? Why did you disappear like that?'

'That's more questions,' he said quietly.

'Don't I deserve to know, Luca? It's part of the same history you were so desperate to understand, after all.'

'Perhaps the greater question is how you don't hate them,' he said after a moment. 'The things you've told me about your mother, even the fact they're willing to trade you away with the company...'

'It's really not like that,' she said defensively.

'Isn't it? Why not?'

'The marriage thing is, I know, hard to understand. It's the twenty-first century and I'm in my twenties. It must seem absurd to you.'

He dipped his head. 'I had never heard of something like this, when your father mentioned it.'

'Arranged marriages aren't actually that uncommon,' she said with a lift of her shoulders. 'But nor are they regular. For my parents, this is one of the ways they show love.'

He lifted a brow.

'They worry about me.' She toyed with her fingers. 'They tried to have kids for years. They couldn't. Then, when my parents died—they were old friends—they knew they had to take me, to raise me. I had been sent to foster care, which I hated, and then Jennifer and Gianni appeared and took me in. They loved me so much, when I needed it most.'

He listened silently, but she felt the judgement emanating from him. 'I was only a child and the gratitude I felt to them for saving me from foster care, at a time when I was grieving my parents, made me feel...makes me feel... indebted to them for life.'

'That is not how adoption is meant to work.'

'Perhaps not, but for me, that's how it was. Is. I know they're not perfect,' she said on a sigh. 'And our relationship is complicated. But they do love me, Luca.'

He compressed his lips.

She tried again. 'People aren't just good, or just bad. Good people can make bad decisions, and vice versa, but when you love someone, you have to accept them, all parts of them, and I do. I see them as they are: imperfect, well-meaning people. My parents.' She shrugged again. 'I love them.'

'And if your father has made very bad decisions?'

She narrowed her gaze. 'Has it ever occurred to you that you're wrong about them? That you made a mistake?'

His nostrils flared.

'You've already admitted that you were wrong about me,' she pointed out, gesturing to the bed, laden with gifts. 'So what if you were wrong about them, too?'

So much hung on his acceptance of that.

'I wasn't.'

She shook her head. 'I gather you think Dad lied to you about the company's worth. You've accused him of attempting to scam you. But how can that be? An independent auditor verified the value prior to agreeing to sell it to you. I know my father was very stressed about ensuring all of the financial reports were done accurately.'

'Or perhaps he was stressed for reasons beyond your comprehension?'

She shook her head slowly, wanting to immediately dismiss Luca's insinuation even when she had to acknowledge there was a small possibility she'd misunderstood the behind-the-scenes dealings of her father. After all, Gianni had made a point of keeping Mia away from the financial operations of the business. She was not a signatory on any of the corporate accounts, her role was confined to business development.

'Tell me what you believe he did,' she said quietly, her

finger lifting to the largest diamond and pressing to it, remembering the strength and simplicity of gemstones such as this, trying to build that inside her.

He looked torn, as though he wanted to tell her but also didn't. She lifted her hand to his arm, squeezed. 'I'm stronger than you think. I can handle it.'

'I believe you're strong. I just don't know if it's your burden to carry.'

'You don't get to make that determination.'

'With respect, I do.' He took a step backwards, dislodging her hand. 'I know what it's like to lose a parent—I don't mean to death, but to lose respect for them. Your relationship with your father is your own to navigate—and you seem to be doing a good job. You are far better at accepting nuance and imperfection than I am, Mia.'

'But you're keeping something from me that has to do with the company. The value of the company and the sale he's about to make to Lorenzo. Something that will affect my marriage to him?'

A muscle jerked in Luca's jaw. 'It's not my place to get involved, *cara*. Please, leave it at that.'

God, but how he wanted to. He knew he'd done the right thing, to let Mia work it out for herself, to ask questions not of Luca but rather of her father and get the answers that would help her understand why Luca had walked away. And if the old man didn't speak the truth? If he continued to lie to Mia, for the sake of the business deal and the marriage? Desperate people did desperate things and the company's financial status was dire. It was a miracle they'd managed to hobble along throughout this year.

But that didn't mean Luca could be the one to tear it all down for Mia.

How would she feel to realise everything was built on a house of cards? That her father's prosperity was an illusion, that her marriage was destined to fail—at least, that was likely, if Lorenzo was currently blind to the truth of things.

So the alternative was not to tell her. To let her marry a man who might come to resent and hate her, as he would her parents, once he realised that Marini Enterprises was accumulating losses faster than children did sweets.

With a groan, he flicked off the shower, stared at the wall, his body tensed, his mind running three steps ahead. He wanted Mia to be happy. She deserved that. Would Lorenzo be the answer? She seemed to think so. So why did that bother Luca?

He reached for his towel, frustration making his movements brusque.

None of this was his problem.

He was a man who'd sworn off emotional involvement, who was a lone wolf and always would be. What Mia did with her life after this, quite simply, wasn't his concern.

Mia couldn't believe how adept she was becoming at compartmentalising her feelings into different boxes. On the most superficial of levels, the easiest to understand was how Luca made her feel physically. That was a no-brainer. When they were together, they sparked, they buzzed, electricity arced in the air between them and they acted on instinct alone. It was sublime and irresistible.

But when they were apart, for even the smallest amount of time, Mia's thoughts began to spin and twist and turn, and doubts grew, heavy and insistent, so a sense of foreboding was her companion, every minute of those moments, until Luca reappeared and rational, logical thinking was well out of her reach.

'This place is like heaven on earth,' she murmured, on the edge of the pool, staring out at the ocean.

It really was.

But in the back of her mind, there was the beating of a drum, because they'd been here six nights. Tomorrow, they'd leave this paradise, this exemption from reality, and return to Palermo, where her life, her parents, her impending wedding, would all be waiting for her.

And without the answers she desperately wanted.

'I'm glad you like it.'

'I do.' She forced herself to be brave, to confront reality head-on. 'It's hard to believe I won't see it again.' Damn it, her voice cracked ever so slightly.

Was she imagining the way he stiffened at her side? Of course she was. A quick glance at Luca showed him to be the picture of sexy, tousled relaxation. As always, just the sight of him made her pulse thunder. She looked away again quickly.

One more night.

'You can come back any time, *cara*.'

She took the throwaway comment as civility, nothing more. They'd made an agreement that this one week would be the end of their relationship—Mia wasn't going to go back on her word, and she knew he wouldn't either. Too much was at stake to be so foolish.

If she were to back out of her arrangement with Lorenzo, she'd have two failed engagements behind her. And for what? A man who, by his own admission, didn't do serious relationships and didn't want children. And who hated her parents, to boot.

But, that annoying little voice pressured, *isn't it better to be ecstatically happy for a short time than mildly contented for ever?*

And was it really the right thing, to marry Lorenzo? A fortnight ago, she would have said yes, unequivocally, but everything was different now, including Mia, and what Mia wanted from life, and the path forward was no longer a path so much as a mess of sand and grit that she had no concept of how to navigate.

Mia knew two things for certain: she didn't want to consider a life without Luca, but she couldn't consider a life with him in it either. It would never work. So she forced herself to remember that, over and over and over again.

And as the night slipped towards dawn, and their time came close to running out, she had almost convinced herself that she was ready for this. Goodbyes, though, were never easy, even the ones that were utterly necessary.

CHAPTER EIGHT

'HE'S SICK.' LUCA APPRECIATED the fact Max cut right to the chase. And his older brother didn't need to go into further detail. Luca knew that 'he' was their father, and that by 'sick' Max must have meant seriously ill, because he'd have never called in the middle of the night if the old man had a trifling cold. Not that Luca had been sleeping, anyway.

Having dropped Mia at her office earlier that day, he'd found himself ravaged by a vicious, internal war.

On the one hand, he knew there was wisdom in never seeing her again.

It wasn't only wise, it was *right*. Mia had chosen what she wanted in life and her priorities didn't—couldn't—accord with his own.

The fact they hadn't married a year ago was, as it turned out, a blessing in disguise. Why hadn't it occurred to him that the issue of children might prove controversial?

Because he was selfish.

The answer blinked right in front of his eyes, bringing him little pleasure. Her supposition—that children would, at some point, follow marriage—was the more natural of the two.

He knew his strong desire to never put down roots was unusual. How arrogant of him not to have given her any explanation on that score. He hadn't treated her like a person, but, rather, a commodity. He couldn't look back on that time in his life without a deep sense of shame. It was as though he were a different person altogether.

'Luca?'

He drew himself back to the conversation with Max with effort. *'Sì?'*

'He's known for a while.'

Luca grunted. That was so like their father—to conceal something important. 'And?'

'Bottom line? He's probably got weeks, not months.'

Something shifted inside Luca. Though he wasn't close to his father, it was yet another touchstone in his life being eroded away, leaving him with flint in his chest. 'I see.'

'He wants to see you.'

Luca stared at the wall across the room for a long time without speaking. He didn't know what to say. Of course, the norm would have been to immediately assure his brother that he would come home, but Luca hadn't thought of Australia as home for a long time—if ever. It was this foothold of Italy, where his mother had chosen to raise him, where he saw himself in the features of the people he passed on the street and in the rugged landscape that abounded in these parts.

Australia was just where he'd spent his adolescence.

'I'd like to see you, too. There are some things to discuss.'

A sixth sense had the hairs on the back of Luca's neck bristling. 'Oh?'

'I've seen his will.'

Luca moved to his desk chair and sat down, legs wide, elbows braced atop his thighs. 'I don't care about his will.'

'I figured you'd say that.' Max half laughed, but it was a sound without humour.

'And yet you are saying it anyway?'

'Half his business is left to you.'

Luca sat straighter, rubbed his jaw. 'What?'

'Yeah.'

'I told him—'

'I know. But it's your legacy. Look, it's not up to me to speak for the old man, but I wouldn't be surprised if contemplating his own mortality hasn't given him some insight into the past, into things he would change if he could. Maybe it's not enough for you, but I think you'll regret it if you don't come and see him. Listen to him. If you don't like what he has to say, you can leave again.'

'Thank you for your permission,' Luca drawled, then cringed, because Max was his brother, and Luca not only loved him, he respected him, and his opinions. 'I am grateful for your insight,' he tried again, more sincerely. 'But I need to think about it.'

Max was silent and Luca knew him well enough to picture his brother's face, so like his own, with those symmetrical features, angular jaw and chiselled cheekbones. His expression would be one of discontent, but Luca wasn't about to offer more than some consideration.

'Think fast, Luc. I have a bad feeling about this.'

Luca disconnected the call and reached for his Scotch glass in one swift movement, mulling over the news he'd just received, trying to disentangle his feelings from his duties, to weigh up whether he had any duties towards his father or if his father's treatment of the boys, and of Luca's mother, absolved Luca completely. And all the while, Mia's sweetly spoken words ran through his mind. People were neither wholly good nor bad. Had he overlooked the nuance of his father's personality? Good people could make bad decisions, and vice versa.

He let out a gruff noise of frustration.

It wasn't as if he hadn't tried to resolve this.

When he was seventeen, a year before leaving Australia, he'd confronted his dad and given him a chance to offer something, anything, by way of explanation. Apology. Justification. *Anything* that would help Luca understand. But his father had simply shrugged and told him he couldn't change the past and if Luca had an issue with it, that was exactly what it was: Luca's issue. In fact, he'd told his son he needed to toughen up if he ever wanted to amount to anything in this world.

And so the day he turned eighteen, Luca had left, and not looked back.

With each corporate victory, he'd remembered his father's words, the implication that Luca would never be good enough. The biggest delight in his life came from proving his father wrong.

But Luca had also sworn to himself that he'd be different from his father. That he wouldn't make the same mistakes and treat people as expendable. That he wouldn't hurt someone the way his father had hurt his mother, and Max's mother.

So how could he accept what he'd done to Mia? Who, as it turned out, hadn't deserved even a hint of his anger. Mia, who'd been innocent in every goddamned way.

Luca raked his fingers through his hair, spiking it at odd angles. Suddenly, all he wanted was to see her, to speak to her, to bare his soul to her about his father, to ask her advice. So he poured another Scotch and paced the room, because needing someone was a mistake Luca didn't ever intend to make. Particularly not someone engaged to another man.

* * *

'You can't be here.' It was history repeating itself, Luca arriving at her office—though, mercifully, he'd come late in the day again, when most of the staff had left. And her body's response, predictably hectic and flushed, desire pooling between her legs. She was wearing one of the dresses he'd bought for her—as if she could ever donate such a beautiful item that reminded her of him—but now she wished she weren't. It made her feelings for him too obvious.

'I needed to see you.'

Oh, how she needed that too. Her heart lurched and her blood pounded in her veins but she held her ground, standing behind her desk, hoping she looked something like impassive. But how could she? It had been three days since they'd returned from his beach house, and she'd been waiting, hoping, wishing to see him even when she was glad each night that she hadn't weakened.

She was getting married.

Her parents had met with Lorenzo's parents only the day before, for a long, family lunch. The expectation was set. The business merger was happening. Grandchildren were being planned.

Strange how, a few weeks ago, Mia would have said she wanted children more than anything on earth, and now the thought left her strangely hollow. Because when she closed her eyes and imagined swelling with new life, holding her baby in her arms, it was Luca's eyes that stared back at her, a son or daughter of his to love and hold and raise and care for.

'You can't be here,' she repeated, to remind herself of all the reasons this was wrong.

'Why?' He prowled towards her but stopped on the other side of the desk, a strange echo of a time in their lives when their businesses had been destined to merge. Her heart crackled. How different it should have been...

'Because we had an agreement.'

'Agreements can be changed.'

She shook her head angrily—angry with herself for being secretly glad to see him, angry with him for arriving like this and skittling her common sense. 'You promised me.'

'So? I'm breaking it.' Then, with an angry sigh, 'Apparently that is a skill of mine.'

She flinched, because she didn't like to hear him speaking that way about himself, and because she hated the truth of his words. She tried to remind herself that she had also thought she couldn't trust him—wouldn't trust him.

Her heart stammered, because even as she thought that, on a soul-deep level, her trust for him was intrinsic. Perhaps his being here showed why she *could* rely on him.

'I need to see you.'

Need.

Yes, it was need. He needed her as she needed him. But it was lunacy. This thing with Luca had no future, they needed to end it.

'We had a deal,' she reminded him through gritted teeth. And then, as if to remind them both: 'I'm getting married.' She lifted her hand between them, showing the ring she wore, a ring she'd come to feel was unnaturally heavy.

'Don't.' His eyes whipped from the ring to her face, his lips were tight. 'I don't want to talk about your wedding right now.'

She stared at him, completely lost. 'Well, what do you want to talk about?'

He paced away from her then, towards the office, bracing an arm against the window and staring out at the setting sun.

She took advantage of his distraction to study him, to drink in the sight of him, because she'd been missing him with all of her soul. She was so weary. So exhausted.

It felt to Mia as though she'd boarded an express train to the wrong destination and there was no way to get off it, no way to stop. She'd made a commitment—to Lorenzo, to his family, to her parents. She couldn't back out.

Oh, none of them was pretending this was a romantic connection. They all knew it to be a business deal. But that didn't mean they weren't taking it seriously, that they didn't have their hearts set on the union.

Two powerful, prosperous families uniting was the epitome of her parents' hopes for Mia, and Lorenzo's for him.

'My father is dying.'

It was the last thing she'd expected him to say.

Luca had made an artform of evading her questions.

She knew a little about his family empire—the Stone jewellery stores were famous the world over, so too was the fortune attached to the business, but Luca's own business concerns were distinct, based largely outside Australia, his prosperity his own creation. Luca had never discussed his father or brother with Mia. She pressed her palms to her desk.

'My father is dying,' he repeated, turning back to Mia, frowning, staring at her as if trying to make sense of something she couldn't understand. 'And all I could think, when I heard this news, was that I had to see you. I have spent the last two days fighting the urge to come to you,' he explained with urgency, and she felt it—how hard he'd fought, how annoyed he was that he'd lost that fight. 'I know what we agreed, what I promised. But I need you. I need your help. Is that selfish of me?'

Was it? She didn't know. Needing someone and being

able to admit that seemed like a watershed moment, but for what? Mia couldn't answer, she knew only that she felt something forging between them, interlocking, something important, and she knew that she was glad. He needed her, and she wanted to be there for him. His father was dying, and he'd come to her.

Something rose inside her chest and it wasn't until she heard the noise that Mia realised it was a sob.

She smothered her mouth with her hand and came around her desk, striding quickly to Luca and standing in front of him.

'I'm sorry,' she whispered, lifting up onto the tips of her toes and kissing him, salty tears in her mouth as she wrapped her arms around his neck and held herself there, breathing in his scent, hoping that her closeness would give him strength and whatever else it was he needed from her.

'Will you give me tonight?'

'Just tonight?' she asked, softly, pulling back so her eyes could read his face. When would it ever be enough with them? She was drowning in the middle of the ocean, and she wasn't even sure she cared.

Emotions flickered in his eyes and then, to her immense relief, he shook his head once. 'I won't make that promise again.' The words were virtually growled from him. 'Give me tonight, Mia. We'll negotiate what comes next…later.'

Her heart twisted and her stomach churned. She knew the smart thing would be to say no. To tell him he could stay in her office for a while, to talk to her from a safe distance, but that then he should go, and let her go, and that would be the end of it.

But Luca was standing there with his heart on his sleeve—a heart she hadn't really even known he possessed—and Mia couldn't walk away from this. Danger

swirled all around her. She knew what she was jeopardis-
ing, and she knew that Luca would never be what she
wanted long term, but right now, in this moment, he was
her everything, and she couldn't step away from that.

'Yes,' she said quietly, terrified. 'But you must leave
now. Go. I'll follow when I can.'

His expression was impossible to interpret. Relief, but
there was something else too, like a whip, that cracked
between them.

'I can wait for you.'

'No.' She was adamant. 'We can't leave here together,
and you know it. You shouldn't come here. You can't come
here again.' She pressed a finger to his lips, silencing whatever response he might have been poised to make. 'I'm
glad you reached out to me, though.' She lifted onto her
tiptoes and replaced her finger with her mouth, just a light
quick kiss, a down payment of what would come next.

He stalked out of her office with a face like thunder, head
bent, moving quickly towards the narrow bank of elevators, almost willing her father to appear, to see him, to
speculate and wonder. Selfishly, he wanted that. To throw
the cat well amongst the pigeons and leave them in no
doubt of what was going on. Of how much he wanted Mia
after all. Of the fact she was *his*. Clearly that explained
why he had come here not once, but twice. On some level,
he welcomed discovery. In the hopes it would lead to the
cancellation of her wedding? And then what?

Frustration gnawed at his gut. How could she go
through with this? Mia was too beautiful and full of love
to enter into a marriage of convenience. A business deal,
and nothing more. And when he thought of another man

calling himself Mia's husband, touching her, making love to her, Luca felt as though a vein in his head might explode.

Yes, he welcomed the idea of discovery, but for Mia's sake, he was as incognito as possible anyway, because he knew she'd be devastated if anyone found out about them. Fate smiled upon her, and the lift doors opened immediately, shepherding him away from the risk of discovery, for now.

Mia arrived at his home an hour later and slipped in the front door with the key he'd given her. Having a key to his place did something strange to her belly. As she inserted it into the lock, she had the weirdest sense of coming home, of truly coming home, and again she felt that jarring fantasy take over—what it would have been like if they were married, this were their house and she were simply coming back from a day's work.

The clawing feeling of tears made her throat ache. How could she yearn so much for something she'd never known? But then, tonight wasn't about her, and their failed engagement. Luca needed Mia. He'd come to her because he needed her help, and she would give him that.

Mia took a moment, composed herself, then stepped fully inside, closing the door and stepping deeper into his home. The lights were dimmed, and he'd lit candles— long tapered ones that had been burning for long enough that wax had formed streaky puddles down their sides and onto the base of the candle holders. Soft, jazzy music played. She sighed as she entered his lounge room fully, looking around, eyes landing on Luca at the grand piano, head bent, fingers pressed to the keys without any noise coming out.

She padded over to him silently and wrapped her arms

around him from behind, pressed her head to his shoulder and just held him, hoping, as she had in her office, that some physical strength and certainty would pass from her to him with that small gesture.

They stayed like that for a long time, just the softly shifting glow of candles to alert them to the passage of time, but eventually, Mia stood, then came to sit beside him on the stool.

'Do you play?' he asked, turning to face her, eyes roaming her face almost as if he'd never seen her before.

She shook her head. 'I took lessons for a few years but "Three Blind Mice" is about all I remember.'

One side of his lips lifted in soft acknowledgement of that.

'And you?'

A muscle jerked in his jaw. 'My mother taught me.'

'I didn't realise that.' Then again, why would she?

'She learned as a little girl. She was very good. She lost a lot over the course of her lifetime—her parents threw her out when they discovered she was pregnant with me and, after that, her life was hardly comfortable. She moved down here, to Sicily, where she had a cousin she was close to. She got my mother a job, and I believe they treated her well.' His voice showed restrained anger. 'At the hotel she worked at, there was a piano in the lobby. The manager would let her play, early in the mornings, before it got busy. So a few times a week, she would take me in to learn as well.' He pressed his fingers lightly to the keys. 'She was a hard teacher.'

Mia's smile was soft, involuntary. 'In what way?'

'Completely intolerant of mistakes, even when I was a beginner. My mother spoke music like a second language. It just came naturally to her. She found my errors jarring.

We couldn't afford a piano, but one day, our neighbours had a piece of furniture delivered and I saved the box it came in. I measured out the pieces with a black pencil and drew a keyboard on top, so that I could practise finger placement at home.'

Mia's heart flipped over at the very idea of the earnest little boy he'd been. 'You wanted to make your mother proud.'

He dipped his head once in what Mia took to be silent acknowledgement of that. 'I was fascinated by the piano, and the way she could coax such beautiful music out of something otherwise inanimate. I wanted to speak the language too.'

'Show me.'

His gaze locked to hers, the air between them sparking and growing warm, so Mia felt the hairs on her arms lift and the cells in her body tingle. Then, he turned away, so his face was in profile, and his hands pressed to the keys, picking up in time with the music that was playing, echoing it perfectly, so it was a form of surround sound, but so much better, because when Luca played, he added a richness and emotion to the music that Mia hadn't been aware of before. His fingers moved skilfully and fast over the keyboard. She watched them for a few moments but then his face drew her attention back, because it was so fascinating, lost in concentration not, she suspected, on the piece he was playing, but rather on the situation with his father. She wriggled closer, because suddenly it wasn't enough to sit beside him, she wanted to feel him, to touch him, and to know he could also feel her.

He pulled his fingers away from the piano. The song had ended. But another song picked up, on the album he was playing—this time, Luca didn't accompany it.

Shifting a little, he turned to face her.

'She must have been thrilled with how well you learned.'

His brows flexed. 'My mother was not given to lavish praise,' he said with a hint of humour that Mia took for deflection. How that must have hurt a young boy who'd worked so hard to impress her.

'You play beautifully,' she said. Surely he knew that. He didn't need Mia to tell him. But it was possible Luca had never been told before, and she couldn't bear the thought of that.

It was such a strange thought, a silly aberration. As if Luca lacked self-esteem! He was naturally the best and the brightest, a king amongst men, the kind of person who could walk into any room and take control. He didn't need Mia praising his piano-playing abilities, of all things.

'How old were you when she died?' Mia prompted. In the past, he'd evaded her questions, but tonight, he'd come to her, acknowledging that he needed help, and something vital had shifted between them. Mia didn't understand it, but she felt the rhythms of their relationship shift and wasn't afraid this time that he might not answer.

He pressed his fingers to the keys; the noise now a little jarring. 'Twelve.'

She shook her head sadly. 'Still just a boy.'

'I didn't feel it.' He put a hand on her thigh, staring down at his tanned fingers against the silk fabric of the dress he'd bought her. 'She died and I was alone. I'd known, all my life, that my father wasn't a part of our life. He didn't want me. He didn't want her.' His jaw tightened.

'And had she wanted him?' Mia pushed softly.

'She never really spoke about their relationship.' Then, a heavy, angry exhalation of breath. 'But yes. She was in love with him. Even after the way he treated her, she loved him—I could tell. And I hated her for that, but I hated him more.'

'Why would you hate her?' Mia pushed, surprised.

'What a weakness! To love and want a person who rejected you as he had her. I hated the power she gave to him, the way she worshipped him even when he'd thrown her life into such abject poverty.'

'When he'd refused to acknowledge you,' Mia murmured, because naturally a child would take that view, would feel hurt and rejected, and would want their mother to share that viewpoint.

'I never knew him. But she did. She knew and loved him and pined for him. She let him ruin her life. I saw how vulnerable and weak that love made her.'

'And swore you'd never be in that position,' she murmured, feeling as though a door had opened, showing her a side of Luca that was important and vital, a door that helped her understand who he was.

His eyes seemed to pierce Mia's soul. 'No one should be in that position.'

Her lips tilted to the side. 'Your mother was unlucky to fall in love with someone who didn't love her back.' Something clanged inside Mia. A realisation, or a slow-spreading dawn, but she couldn't quite see her way to understanding it. She knew only that something was shifting, that she was shifting and changing.

'Tell me about your father.' She pressed her fingers to the keys lightly, her lips bending into a half-smile. 'You don't talk about him at all.'

'No.' His Adam's apple shifted.

'Why not?'

'My mother had an expression. If you cannot say anything nice—'

'Don't say anything at all.' She moved her hand to his, lacing their fingers together. The music in the background was slow, gentle. It threaded through Mia, pulling at her emotions. 'Is there nothing nice you can say about him?'

'He's a competent businessman.'

She arched a brow, her smile involuntary, softened with disbelief. 'Competent?'

'Not brilliant.'

'Not brilliant like you?'

Luca's nostrils flared. 'Perhaps not as motivated as I am. Being born into immense wealth has that effect on people, in my experience.'

'Your brother?'

Luca considered that. 'Max is different. We are half-brothers, but so alike, though he feels more of a connection to the Stone family businesses. He grew up knowing, from birth, that it was his destiny to inherit them, to take over from our father. Our grandfather drilled that into him from a young age. Max had little choice.'

'Do you think he might have chosen to do something else?'

'Who can say?' Luca lifted his shoulders. 'I believe he's happy. He oversees the pearl-farming operations.'

'What a fascinating thing to do.' Mia shook her head. 'I mean, of course I know pearls come from the sea, but I never really think of them being farmed, growing, being harvested.'

'It's an impressive process.' He was quiet. She wondered if he was thinking what she was: that she'd have loved to see the pearl farm. With him.

'You weren't interested in moving into that line of work?'

'No.'

'Luca, why don't you use their last name?'

'I was a Cavallaro first. I lost my mother, there was no way I'd give away her name.'

Mia could understand that. 'Did it bother your father?'

His smile was bitter. 'Immensely. In fact, he would often introduce me as Luca Stone. I corrected him, every time.'

Mia could imagine the determined teenager he'd been. She pressed her cheek to his shoulder, resting her head there, enjoying his nearness and warmth.

'When did you last see your father?'

'He flew to Rome for my twenty-first birthday.'

Mia shook her head sadly. 'So long ago. Did something happen?'

Luca lifted a hand, cupping her cheek. 'Why? Do you want to fix it, Mia?'

She frowned, hating how easily he understood her. 'You asked me for help,' she couldn't help reminding him.

'So I did.'

'Was that not in the hope I could fix this?'

'I'm a pragmatist. Some things are beyond fixing.'

'But not beyond trying.' She tilted her face into his hand, her heart swelling and squeezing. 'You fixed me, Luca. You fixed what you did, with our wedding.'

His eyes swept shut a moment, as if her words were too hard to fathom.

'You have a more forgiving temperament than I do, re-member? You see the good in people, even through their faults.' He pressed a hand to her chest. 'You are a beauti-ful woman, with the kindest heart in the world.'

Mia swallowed past a lump in her throat, but she wouldn't let the praise—no matter how ground-break-ing—distract her from this conversation. 'Tell me what he did, Luca. Tell me why you can't forgive him.'

CHAPTER NINE

MIA HAD ALWAYS loved mornings. As corny as it sounded, there was something exciting about the breaking of a fresh day, filled with promise and newness, of memories not yet made. She'd been a firm subscriber to the belief that all things looked better with the dawn.

But this morning, when she woke, it was with a strange heaviness in her chest, a sense of dread that she couldn't immediately comprehend.

And then she remembered. Her fantasy. Her secret game of make-believe, that this was all real. That waking up in Luca's bed was normal. That he was really hers, not in this mad, passionate, temporary way, but in a forever and ever kind of way.

She stared across his room at the light breaking through in a fine beam and her stomach dropped to her toes.

It wasn't real, and she needed to go.

But how could she leave him?

Memories of last night played through her mind. She shifted a little, rolling over so she could see him. His beautiful face, so fascinating and strong, so filled with detail and emotion, restful now, in contrast to how he'd been last night, when he'd told her, in short, unwilling snatches at first, and then longer, reflective monologues, about his life.

His whole life.

His upbringing. The mother he loved and respected but had never felt a warm affectionate love from. The shock of her death. The resilience he'd showed in facing that head-on. The courage in moving to Australia. The despair at breaking up a family, of knowing himself—indirectly—to be the cause of it. His very existence was the death knell to his father's marriage and his brother's family.

As for his father, Mia knew she shouldn't stand in judgement of someone she'd never met, but it was natural to have developed a dislike for the man who'd treated Luca so badly. Oh, Luca didn't say as much. He spoke sparingly, the details given almost unwillingly, but he'd said enough for Mia to glean a pretty clear picture.

She understood Luca so much better now.

And that was dangerous, because understanding him brought her two steps closer to forgiveness, to true forgiveness, and, without the resentment that she'd become used to, she was terrified of what her feelings might morph into. Suddenly, the simplicity of her life, her future, the plans she'd calmly laid in place for everything she wanted seemed like a house of cards.

Her marriage to Lorenzo was the smart choice. Maybe it wasn't even really a choice any more? Plans were in motion, guests had been invited, her parents were excited. And, more importantly, the business contracts were being signed, the merger too important to her parents to jeopardise.

For every answer she'd received last night, dozens of questions proliferated through her now, as she looked at her future with the exact opposite of clarity. She could barely see two steps in front of herself, but when she thought of marrying Lorenzo, she felt only a deep, terrifying sense of panic.

And yet, at the same time, she had to acknowledge that whatever feelings she had for Luca, he would never be her future.

He was a lone wolf. Not born that way, but shaped into it by life, and by a self-preservation mechanism that meant he wouldn't change easily.

Even for her?

She heard the question and squeezed her eyes shut against the dangerous bloom of hope.

This couldn't go on.

They couldn't keep doing this.

Because Mia wasn't an automaton. When she'd first met Luca, there'd been the most overwhelming sense of recognition, as if, here he was, the person she hadn't even known she'd been waiting for all her life. She'd dismissed those feelings then as a stupid infatuation—he was beautiful and she was totally inexperienced and in awe of his larger-than-life charisma.

She knew him now. She was no longer mesmerised nor intimidated by him. But the sense that he was a complementary part of her wouldn't shift. With a growing surge of panic, because everything was getting way too out of hand, she crept carefully from his bed and tiptoed out of the room, taking one last peek at his sleeping frame, closing her eyes and trying to steel herself against the gargantuan task ahead.

In his kitchen, she found a notepad and ran her finger over the top—the embossed logo for his company. Even that made her heart beat faster, and love squeezed her insides into a different shape. Because it *was* love.

Love for him, his personality, temperament, his strength, determination, intelligence, all the parts of him. Just as he'd said. She loved. Her heart was his. She saw his complexity, his perfections and failings, and loved *all* of them.

'Oh, God,' she groaned softly, picking up a pen and writing quickly, ignoring the tears that were threatening.

> *Dear Luca,*
>   *I hope last night helped. I think you know, deep down, what you need to do.*
>   *I'll be thinking of you in Australia, wishing you all the best.*
>   *Goodbye.*
>   *Love, Mia*

She signed it with love because it was true, and because, though she'd never be stupid enough to tell him how she felt, nor to place that burden upon him, it felt like a small victory, a cheating, to be able to put in writing the honesty of her feelings.

But the 'goodbye' above it almost hurt her to write.

She stepped out onto the kerb in the early morning sunshine and walked quickly to her car, head bent, determined not to look back. A single glance, a moment's pause, and she'd lose her will. She had to do this—there was no alternative.

She didn't consciously make the decision then and there, but by the time Mia arrived at her office, it was with the grim understanding that she absolutely could not marry Lorenzo di Angelo. In fact, she was appalled that she'd ever agreed to go along with the plan. It was as though loving Luca had woken her up to what she deserved in life, to what she'd be denying herself in marrying someone she barely knew and didn't love, didn't desire. And

she was asking Lorenzo to make the same sacrifice, all
for the sake of their family businesses! What a silly, short-
sighted decision to make.

Though that explanation gave the thought process a ve-
neer of rationality that wasn't really behind Mia's decision.
The truth was, when she thought of marrying Lorenzo,
of marrying anyone other than Luca, she felt a visceral,
stomach-rolling sense of despair.

There were many times in Mia's life when she'd ignored
her instincts and deferred to her parents, but this was not a
time for that. She would not marry Lorenzo di Angelo, no
matter how embarrassing it was to extricate herself from
the situation now. She'd been able to go along with it, just,
when she'd thought things with Luca were meaningless
and purely physical—though had she ever really believed
that? But now that she understood her heart, it would be
wrong on every level to marry Lorenzo.

With the decision made, she walked past her own office door and approached her father's. Her stomach loop-
ing in knots as she braced for what was going to be one
of the most difficult conversations of her life. She loved
Luca Cavallaro, and while she wasn't foolish enough to
hope he might love her back, nor that there was any future for her, that love still deserved better than for Mia's
marriage to another man. And with that in mind, she held
Luca in her heart like a talisman, a strength she needed
more than anything in this moment.

'Do you have a second to talk?'

Gianni was staring at his computer screen, a frown
etched into his face, so Mia's own lips tilted downwards.
He slammed the laptop shut, gestured to his seat. 'Of
course. What is it?'

Mia's stomach rolled. Now that she'd reached the moment of truth, she struggled to know exactly how to say what she wanted to say. 'It's about Lorenzo.'

His eyes narrowed imperceptibly. 'Is something wrong? Has he contacted you?'

Mia shook her head. 'No. No. Nothing like that. I mean, yes. Something is wrong.' She made a sound of exasperation, stood up, paced towards the windows and tried to take solace from the familiar view. 'I can't go through with it.'

Gianni jackknifed out of his chair. 'What?'

'The wedding.' She twisted her fingers together. 'I need to cancel it. I can't marry him.' She felt as though she were suffocating. 'I don't love him. I'll never love him. I can't marry him.'

'I don't believe this. You are supposed to be getting married in a matter of weeks…'

'I know. It's not ideal. I know I promised him, you, his family. I get it. I'm letting everyone down. But I can't go through with it. I'm sorry.'

'Sorry?' he repeated, dragging a hand through his hair. 'Mia, I don't think you understand what you're saying.'

'But I do. For the first time in a long time, I understand myself, my words, my wants, perfectly. I will not marry Lorenzo di Angelo. The company will have to be sold without the marriage as a part of the deal.'

Gianni's face drained of all colour. 'It's not possible.'

'Of course it's possible,' she said firmly, refusing to allow her resolve to be weakened. 'Companies change hands every day without some feudal marriage deal.'

'This is different.'

'Why? Because I'm me? Why do you think I need to marry Lorenzo di Angelo? Do you honestly not think I can stand on my own two feet?'

He stared at her, eyes boring through her, then collapsed

back in his chair, as though the weight of the world were pressing down on him.

'I need you to marry him, *principessa*.'

The childhood name was like an arrow through Mia's heart. She walked slowly across the room, alarm bells blaring now. Her father was crumpled; destroyed.

'What is it?' she asked, the tone of her voice carefully wiped of her anxieties. But she *knew* that he'd been lying to her. She knew that Luca had told the truth. Even when he'd been careful not to tell her too much, he'd said enough for Mia to understand that her father's business was in a bad way.

'Oh, God,' she whispered, coming to crouch at his side. 'Tell me the truth, Dad. Tell me everything: how bad is it?'

It was bad.

As her father finally, slowly, spelled out the truth: that the business had been running on air for eighteen months—which was the sole reason he'd looked for a buyer in the first place—Mia realised just how heavy his burden had been. But the older man had looked for solutions in all the worst ways.

'Do you have any idea what you've done?' she asked, lifting fingers to her lips, numb from the revelation she'd just listened to.

'I had no choice!'

She shook her head. 'This is *illegal*, Dad. You cannot falsify corporate figures for the purpose of enticing someone to buy the company. You cannot seriously have thought this wouldn't be found out?'

'But by then, you would be married, perhaps even pregnant. They would not be able to press charges.'

'Of course they could have. It would have been a sham

marriage, not a real one. There's no love between Lorenzo and me!'

'It is still a marriage,' he insisted.

'So I would have been, what? Insurance? You've turned me into an accomplice.' She thought of the guilt Luca had laid at her feet when he'd learned the truth, naturally presuming she was a part of the deception. 'Damn it, Dad, you've made me guilty by association.'

'But you are not. And anyone who knows you will see that.'

'You cannot do this.'

'Nor can I let the company go, our family fall into bankruptcy.'

'Is it really so bad?' She shook her head. 'It can't be. I'd *know.*'

'I have been able to make things work—just barely—but it's all borrowed, Mia. Everything. My debts are—profound.'

Her heart shattered. 'Oh, Papa.' Tears filled her eyes then and she hugged her dad. Nothing mattered more than helping him find a way through this. Judgement was irrelevant. 'This is what Luca knew, isn't it? It's why he walked out on the wedding.'

Gianni's eyes were like flint for a moment and then he slumped forward. 'Yes. He knew. I don't know how...'

Mia let out a deranged half-laugh. 'Because he's ridiculously intelligent and thorough. He came to you about this, didn't he?'

Gianni nodded and Mia felt as though she'd been stabbed through the heart. She'd known one man was lying to her, but not both. They'd both known the truth, all this time, and neither had loved nor respected her enough to be honest. She pressed her fingernails into her palm, heart stammering. 'So a week before the wedding, you knew he wouldn't go through with it—'

'I thought he still would. I honestly believed—'

'No, you hoped,' she contradicted fiercely. 'Because you were desperate. You threw me to the wolves rather than face the reality of the situation. You let him do that to me.'

'When I didn't hear from him again, I presumed he had calmed down. I knew how much he wanted the business...'

'Not enough,' she whispered, 'to tie himself to our family after such a blatant deception.' She squeezed her eyes shut, because her world was crumbling down around her shoulders and Mia didn't want to bear witness to that destruction.

A million emotions throttled through Mia as she left the office that night. Anger, disbelief, incredulity, panic and despair. She felt a million things and sought refuge in one emotion that was satisfying and for which there was an easy outlet.

Anger.

Anger at Luca.

Who *had* known the truth, and refused to tell her, time and time again, even when she'd begged him. And he'd tried to make that sound noble!

Anger at the man who'd made love to her, who'd treated her so gently, who'd acted as though he were protecting her by keeping this secret, rather than taking the coward's way out, and all the benevolent, loving feelings he'd stirred the night before evaporated, leaving only waspish rage in their place.

Perhaps it wasn't fair to blame Luca. What did he owe her, after all? But the fact of the matter was that her love made her want more from him, made her expect more of him, and he'd failed her. It hurt. It hurt more than his abandonment on their wedding day ever had, because she *loved* him, and he'd let her down. He had left her to fail, rather than being with her, united, a team.

A sob was wrenched from Mia's chest. They *weren't* a team. They never would be.

Rather than give into the desperate sadness that realisation brought, she focused on her anger—a safe emotion, one that would serve her well.

Before she'd even realised what she was doing, Mia had started the engine of her little red Fiat and was turning it away from her home and, instead, towards Luca's, her ears roaring with the sound of her thundering blood the whole drive, so she heard nothing and saw almost as little.

Relief flooded him when she arrived. This was not the first time she'd asked him to leave her alone, but it was the first time he'd truly intended to at least try to listen. It was the only thing he could do. They both knew there was no future here.

But when Mia arrived at his front door and used the key she still possessed to let herself in, an unfamiliar emotion surged in his chest. He wanted to run to her, to wrap his arms around her, to laugh with giddy relief because he'd *missed* her, but he did none of those things.

He was Luca Cavallaro, a man of no emotions, and he wouldn't further complicate the situation by doing anything that might undermine that opinion of him.

'Damn you,' she said quietly, slamming the door then holding her ground, shaking all over, like a beautiful, delicate leaf. 'Damn you to hell, Luca Cavallaro, I hate you. I really, really hate you.'

It was the last thing he expected her to say.

He was glad then that he hadn't moved to her, because it was easier, somehow, to maintain a neutral expression when he was across the room, to conceal the surprise and, yes, hurt—a feeling he didn't know he was capable of— flooding his body, by standing completely still, hands in pockets, eyes fixed on her. Then again, when he'd read that note this morning, hadn't he hated her too? Just a little? For leaving him, for mentioning her marriage, for not being there when he woke up after the night they'd shared, the things he'd told her?

Rage emanated from her frame like waves vibrating through the room. 'I do not know what has happened, but I suggest you tell me why you are so upset.'

'Seriously?'

He waited, watching her, with the strangest feeling in the pit of his stomach. It was as if they were one person. Whatever Mia was feeling, Luca felt too. His insides churned while he stood, impatient but not rushing her.

Mia sucked in a deep breath, her eyes spitting fire. 'You *knew.*'

The penny dropped but before he could speak, Mia continued.

'You knew what he was going through and you didn't tell me. You knew how bad it was, and you said *nothing,* even when you had the opportunity, even when I begged you. How dare you keep this from me? After everything, *everything,* we've shared?'

Her words landed with a thud against his chest but he refused to let her accusation stand. He could see her anger, acknowledge her grief, but he wouldn't take the blame for that. While he hated the idea of Mia thinking the worst of him, the businesslike part of Luca's brain took control, calmly wading through her accusation to find a logical thread. 'These are your father's errors, not mine.'

'How can you be so callous? How can you stand there and apportion blame?'

'Isn't that what you are doing?' Why was he allowing them to argue? It was clear that Mia was upset, that she was spoiling for a fight, but why was Luca fanning the flames of her anger? Why didn't he go to her to offer comfort? Why did he allow her to glare at him and simply stare back, as if his heart were cold, his emotions incapable of being stirred even now, when the opposite was true?

'With good reason,' she roared, stalking towards him then stopping, turning around, shaking her head. 'You are to blame.'

'For your father's ineptitude and dishonesty? Really? How so?'

She spun back, eyes wild, fury unleashed—and hell, he deserved that. It was an utterly insensitive thing to have said. But he was angry—and for no reason he could easily identify, so he sought refuge in the kind of wide-nozzle spray of anger that was immediately satisfying, even if he feared it would turn out to be a mistake.

'Are you mocking him?'

He had—finally—the good sense to slam his lips together.

'You are a pig!' She thrust her hands onto her hips, standing right there, feet wide apart, body tense, ready to fight.

'How could you keep this from me?' she demanded again, lips white-rimmed.

'Your father should have told you. It is him you are angry with, not me.'

'I'm angry with him, yes, but I'm angrier with you.'

Something buzzed in the back of his brain. A realisation. An understanding. But it flitted away again as quickly as it had appeared.

'Do you have any idea what he's done? This is very likely criminal, Luca. As in, illegal. If Lorenzo's parents were to find out, and decided to press charges, not only would he be ruined, he'd go to jail. I could go to jail too, if they suspect, as you did, that I'm involved in this. How could you know this, and not tell me?'

The bottom of his world fell away in a spectacular fashion and an awful heat began to burn Luca's insides. He hadn't even contemplated, for one second, that Mia would pay the price for her father's crimes. But she was right. He'd easily jumped to the conclusion that she was a part of the deception. What if a court thought the same thing? Evidence might exonerate her, but not necessarily. It was easy to allude to a person's involvement and raise a conviction against the odds.

His hands shook. His control was slipping. He turned away from her on the pretence of getting a drink from the bar. A Scotch. God knew he needed it. He threw it back in one harsh motion, then turned to her, slowly, focusing all of himself on containing his emotions.

'I will not allow that to happen.'

'You think you have the power to stop it? You think you're some kind of god?'

A tear slid from the corner of her eye and he stared at her, unable to look away, even when the sight of her was tearing him into pieces.

'It's all so misguided,' she groaned with a shake of her head. 'I cannot understand what he was thinking. It's like the stress temporarily deprived him of sanity. Do you think that might work in his favour? Luca, he's a good man. You have to believe me, this isn't like him.' Tears were falling freely now, and his body physically ached with the need to cross his living room and pull her into his arms.

God, but he wanted her. All parts of her. He wanted Mia for himself. He didn't know how long he'd feel this way, but he wasn't ready to walk away from her, and she clearly still needed him, if even just to sort this out.

And out of nowhere, like the most perfect blade of lightning, Luca saw it. A solution.

An answer to his problems, and to Mia's too.

'I can fix this.'

'You can't,' she sobbed. 'It's gone too far. Oh, why didn't he tell me?'

Luca didn't have time to analyse his idea. He was used to acting on instinct, to taking gambles that almost always paid off, and that had emboldened him, so even when he acknowledged this was a risk, he didn't feel overly worried, because there was, finally, light at the end of the tunnel.

There were limits to what he and Mia could be. They wanted different things. Mia deserved better than him long term. But in the short term, their common goals could be met.

'Agree to be mine, and I will fix everything, Mia.'

She shook her head again. 'I don't understand.'

A strange lurching sensation tipped through him. He ignored it. 'Yes, you do. Agree to stay here with me. Do not marry Lorenzo. Forget about him. Be mine, and I will fix this.'

She bit down on her lower lip, eyes huge in that face that haunted his dreams. He felt euphoric. Victory was within reach. Here was a way to have Mia in his life, his bed, without the guilt, the ticking time bomb of a countdown to her wedding, without the need for secrecy and the hovering certainty that within weeks she'd become someone else's wife. She would be his.

'Your father's business is in a parlous state, but I spent twelve months looking at strategies to strengthen it, twelve months understanding it, inside and out. I will honour the original terms of our deal and become his partner.'

'Do you mean—are you saying you want to marry me?'

It was like a grenade blowing up in his face. Strange that before, when their marriage had simply been part of a business deal, he'd been able to blithely accept the necessity of the albeit odd term of the contracts. But now that he knew Mia so well, now that he'd made love to her over and over, marriage was utterly unimaginable.

Before, there'd been no feelings, and so the idea of a businesslike arrangement had been entirely feasible. Now, it would never be the case. His emotions were dangerously close to the surface with her.

There could be no marriage.

'No. I'm not suggesting we marry, only that you call off your wedding to Lorenzo.' He spoke pragmatically, with no concept of how the words affected her. If he'd been paying attention, he might have seen the way she shrank down into herself, but Luca was fixated on the nearing victory. He could make everything okay for her—and they could get what they wanted too: more time together.

'There's no need for us to do anything stupid. We're adults, it's the twenty-first century, and I'm telling you now, I will bail out your father. I will pay off his debts, ensure the company remains liquid and then set about rebuilding it fully. God knows I need a challenge, particularly now. It's partly what attracted me to the purchase in the first place. I can see the potential in Marini Enterprises, just as my father did before me.'

She flinched, and that, finally, he did see.

But she nodded, slowly. By way of acceptance?

'And I would stay here, with you.'

'Yes.' He breathed out, relief making his body feel light, his feet barely on the ground.

'Until?'

A hard note entered her voice.

'I don't have a crystal ball. Until we agree it's no longer working.'

'How lovely and simple,' she murmured, wrapping her arms across her chest, the phrase at odds with the tension in her body.

He began to tread with care, aware that perhaps victory was not so assured as he was hoping. 'Every bit as simple—if not more so—than our marriage would have been.'

'But you're missing one important thing,' she said, eyes narrowing as they met his.

'I don't believe I am.' He ignored the blinking light in the back of his brain. 'You want to keep seeing me, yes?' He didn't wait for an answer. 'And your father needs to be bailed out, or it's likely he'll face charges in the future. So? Stay here with me, terminate your engagement and I will immediately release the funds needed for his business to remain solvent.'

Her tears began to fall again. Tears of relief? Not joy, he noted, going by the stern pull of her lips.

'I don't want to stay with you like that.'

He stood very still. There were rejoinders at the forefront of his mind, but he didn't speak them. It was better to let her speak, so he would have an idea of how to reply. Because he would win her over. He would convince her this was for the best. Luca knew it would work out—he could have his cake, and eat it, too. Unlike his father, he would be completely upfront with what he wanted, what he expected and how much of himself he was willing to give. Mia wouldn't be hurt the way his mother was hurt, because he was being completely transparent.

'What you're offering isn't enough.'

Her words hit him like a sledgehammer. It was the fear at the very heart of his worst fears, the core damage inflicted on him by a lifetime of having been let down by those he dared let himself love—and hope to be loved back by.

He wasn't enough.

He'd offered her more than he'd ever offered another woman, and it wasn't enough.

'And yet *he's* enough?'

She tilted her chin, glaring at him. 'Lorenzo has nothing to do with this.'

'How can you say that? He's your alternative, isn't he? You want to marry him and just hope for the best?' He couldn't help himself now. He stalked towards her, his hands wrapping around her arms, drawing her to his chest. 'To go to bed with him and pray you conceive a baby, so that he's less likely to prosecute your father? Is that really what you want with your life, Mia?'

'Damn you,' she shouted, lifting her palm and slapping it to his chest. 'Goddamn it, none of this is what I wanted. None of it. To feel this way about you, to have let myself get involved with you, it's all wrong. Everything is wrong.'

'No, it's not,' he responded quickly, moving his body, trapping her between his large, strong frame and the flat, white wall. 'You know that staying is right. You want to hate me for suggesting it, you want to hate me for the offer, but, deep down, you know it's the answer. At least I'm being honest with you. I'm telling you how I feel, what I want, so you don't expect more from me.'

He let his explanation sink in, then pushed another point. 'You don't really want to marry him, and you don't want to stop seeing me. So stay. I'm giving you the perfect solution. You just have to say yes, and I will do everything else, *cara.*'

She was silent and he fervently hoped that was a good sign.

She simply stared up at him, her expression unreadable, save for the grief in her eyes.

'You are mine, Mia. All mine. Do you understand?' And he kissed her, with the furious, passionate possession that was exploding inside his veins.

CHAPTER TEN

IN THEORY, ONE PERSON couldn't belong to another. Mia knew that to be the case. And yet, on the other hand, hadn't she been Luca's from almost the first moment they'd met?

His demanding, hotly asked question rang through her ears and she ached, yearned to agree, to submit to him, but rational thought was like a tentacle wrapped around her brain, pulsing and refusing to quit, so she knew she couldn't subjugate herself to him like this. For money.

And if he'd cared about her at all, if he'd felt even a brief shadow of anything remotely like love for her, he wouldn't have dared suggest it.

Luca didn't do love, though.

He did business and power plays and acquisitions and, ultimately, fierce self-preservation, which meant refusing to love with his dying breath, because love equalled vulnerability. Mia had become just another commodity to acquire, for as long as it suited him to possess her, at which point he'd let her leave, like some stock he no longer had any use for.

And Mia would be damaged.

Beyond repair.

Because every day with Luca, every day of his holding her and saying things like 'you're mine', would make her heart more and more in lockstep with his, would make her forget the temporary nature of what they were doing, would make her want so much more than he could give.

And what of children?

Even if there were the slightest possibility Luca might one day care for her enough to ask her to be his not for a small window of time but for ever, it was impossible to imagine him changing his mind about children.

He'd been adamant, irrefutably absolute.

'I can't,' she whispered, groaning, because just standing like this was drugging her, making her forget all the sensible reasons she'd mentally enumerated.

'Yes, you can. I will fix this, Mia. I will fix this.'

If you stay.

She heard the condition, even though he didn't say it again.

It was her fault. She'd told him, just last night, that he'd fixed her, had suggested he could fix anything, and it had gone to his head, but in all the wrong ways. This wasn't what she'd meant.

She tried to find ways to articulate that, but then he was kissing her, his mouth parting hers, his tongue slipping inside, tangling with her tongue, his dominance never in doubt, her submission sadly also a *fait accompli*, because when he touched her she ignited and flame could not be brought to order easily. Not by Mia. She was raging out of control, all heat and explosive need, all fiery, desperate hunger, and a deep, desperate desire to believe that he *could* make everything okay.

But what if the biggest problem she faced was Luca?

Everything he was suggesting was terrifying, because Mia knew she wouldn't be able to agree to this without losing herself to him.

And knowing that he'd bought her? For a ridiculously large sum of money? She'd love him, but she'd hate him too, and she'd hate herself.

Many things in life were nuanced. She no longer believed in black and white, good and bad. In most instances, there were shades of grey. Except for this. There was clearly a right and a wrong and she had to do what was right, or she'd never be able to live with herself.

With a final, wrenching sob, she jerked herself away, glaring at him as though he'd just stabbed her, chest moving with fast, rapid movements as she breathed in and out and her lungs burned with the effort.

'Don't.' She shivered. She trembled. She searched for more words, but 'don't' was the only one she could quickly wrap her tongue around and it tripped from her mouth, over and over. 'Don't touch me. Don't ask this of me. Please, don't say it again.'

When he took a step towards her, she lifted a hand in the air and said it again. 'Don't.'

This time, he listened, eyes sparking with hers, but body still.

She struggled for breath, for thought, but finally, words came to her. 'What my father has done is stupid and wrong. I cannot fathom how he got into this mess. But I will not agree to your offer.'

'Why not?'

She shook her head, furious. 'Do you really not see, Luca? Do you not see how cheap this makes us seem? How demeaning it is to what we've shared? You are the only man I've ever made love to, the only man who's ever touched me, and now, all my memories of you, this thing, will be tainted by what you've said tonight, by what you clearly think of me.'

She stopped, waiting for him to react to that, to say something, to demur, but he didn't, so she pushed on, her voice wobbling a little. 'Do you really think you can buy me? And for what? Some more time? A few more weeks? A month perhaps? And what do I do when it ends? When you decide you are bored of me and leave? How do I pick up my life and go on, knowing that I sold myself to you to save my father's skin?'

She could see that her words were hitting their mark. His skin paled and his eyes seemed to widen, just a fraction.

'I am not for sale,' she reiterated, finally, tilting her chin and glaring at him for the last time.

She'd come here furious and she was leaving devastated—but Mia was just glad she was leaving at all. Another moment of being kissed by Luca and she feared she would have been unable to find the strength to go. It was now or never.

But Luca was not a man to be walked out on. Not ever, and not by Mia. He wouldn't let her leave. Not without resolving this. Not without…what? He couldn't force her to stay. He'd offered her more of himself than he'd thought he'd ever freely give another person. For Mia, it turned out, he was prepared to go further out on a limb than he'd even known existed a month ago.

And he'd tried to offer a solution to her pretty significant problem.

What good could come from chasing her?

Perhaps none, but his legs carried him anyway, out of the lounge room and then his front door, onto the street, where the afternoon sun was still bright, the heat of the day powerful.

'Mia, stop.' His voice was commanding and strong. Mia's steps faltered for a moment, but then she pushed on, reaching into her bag as she went, shoulders determinedly square as she dug for her keys.

He went for her car instead, easily identifiable in his street.

'Stop.' He almost cursed. Frustration was simmering through him. He couldn't understand why she was leaving.

'No.' Her eyes zipped around the street and belatedly he recalled her fear of being seen with him, of one of her father's friends spotting them. Well, wasn't that the point of his suggestion? That they could come out of the shadows?

'Come back inside,' he said quietly. 'It's hot, and you're angry. Come and have a drink. A swim. Think about what I'm proposing.'

Her eyes jerked to his, a frown tugging at her lips, and then she shook her head, moving to the driver door of her car. 'I could think and think and think and never change my mind. It's not enough, I told you.'

'Then what is? What do you want, Mia? More money? More clothes? What?'

She stared at him with abject confusion, then paced back to stand right in front of him, her eyes narrowed as she looked up into his face. 'Please tell me, at what point in time have I ever seemed like the kind of woman who could be bought? Do you believe, for even one moment, that financial considerations would lead me to give myself to you?'

This was coming out all wrong. It wasn't what he'd meant. Of course their relationship existed separately from any financial deal he made with her father. He simply wanted her to stay.

'I saw my mother destroyed by a man who wasn't honest with her.' His voice was raw. 'I'm just...trying to tell you what I can give you, so we both know where we stand.'

'I know where I stand,' she muttered. 'And right now, it's directly opposite an A-grade jackass.'

Pulling on her handbag strap, she looked down the street as an older couple began to promenade the length.

She stiffened, turned her attention back to Luca. 'I'm leaving now. Don't follow me. Don't call me. Don't... Just let me go.'

Letting her go was important. After all, she couldn't be any clearer about what she wanted, so what choice did he have? It ran contrary to every fibre of his being, though, and as he watched her drive away, he felt as though he was missing something important, something that he could have said or done to change her mind. But Luca Cavallaro, with all the events that had shaped him into the man he was now, was incapable of recognising the one gift he possessed that Mia wanted—the one thing he could have offered her that would have convinced her to stay. Not for a month, but for the rest of her life.

'You came.'

Luca had expected Carrick Stone to be frail, but he hadn't been prepared for just how tiny his father would seem, huddled in the large hospital bed, those sharp eyes following Luca across the room.

'You sound almost as surprised as I feel.'

Luca was rewarded by the hint of his father's smile. As a teenager, he'd wanted to impress his father, for a time, until he'd realised it was almost impossible.

'I am glad.'

Luca nodded once. A thousand feelings were bubbling inside him and yet there was a pervasive numbness too, a lack of feeling he'd been navigating ever since Mia had walked out of his life. Because if he let himself feel anything, it would overwhelm him. He knew that. Self-preservation had kicked in. He didn't think about her, he didn't talk about her, he sure as hell didn't think about her impending marriage to Lorenzo di Angelo, because that thought made him want to set the world on fire.

'Sit.'

Even now, Carrick's voice was commanding. Luca lifted a single brow, contemplated refusing, then bowed to his better nature, moving to the leather chair near the top of Carrick's bed.

'How are you?' Luca asked, even when the answer was a foregone conclusion.

'Brilliant. Fit as a fiddle,' Carrick said, eyes sparking with his dry sense of humour, so now it was Luca who found a vague smile tightening his mouth. 'Max told you about the state of my affairs?'

Luca dipped his head once, so he didn't see Carrick's hand reach out, wasn't aware of the gesture until his long, pale fingers curved around Luca's forearm.

'I want you to have it. I want you to be a part of the business.' He hesitated. 'I've wanted that for a long time, son. I just didn't know how to explain.'

'You've told me,' Luca said quietly, the touch on his arm strangely soothing.

'That is not the same as explaining.' Carrick paused to cough. Luca waited, his heart tightening at his father's evident pain. 'When you walked out on me, on us, I was so angry, Luca. I was angry and hurt. My pride was hurt. You were my son and I had offered you everything I possessed, but you didn't want it.'

Luca's jaw tightened. There was such familiarity in that sentence, such an overlap with how Luca had been feeling lately, that he couldn't help but sit up straighter. Perhaps Carrick mistook that for a gesture of withdrawal because he pulled his hand back, settled it in his lap.

'It took me a long time to realise that it was my fault. Blaming you was easier.' He laughed softly, shook his head, but there was sadness in his face. 'But I was wrong. I didn't know how to be with you. I never did. You're different from Max. Max I held as a baby, watched learn to walk. I know I messed up there, too, but I was never afraid of him like I was you.'

'Afraid of me?' Luca repeated.

'You arrived so angry. So sad and angry. You blamed me for everything.'

Luca bit back his rejoinder: that Carrick had deserved it. And out of nowhere, he heard Mia's words, her voice so soft against his ear but so loud inside his heart that he started.

'People aren't just good, or just bad.'

Luca had simplified things to a fault by casting his father as a villain. As a teenager, he'd seen only his father's errors, but hadn't extended compassion to the toll circumstances must have taken on Carrick. He'd never shown it to the boys, but that didn't mean he hadn't felt it.

Luca reached out, put a hand on his father's and shivered, because for a moment he felt as though Mia were with him, guiding his hand, filling him with compassion and understanding. Her wisdom had changed him. She had changed him, in so many fundamental ways.

Something clogged his throat. He looked away, angling his face until he had a better grip on his emotions.

'I know I have no right to ask.' The words were gruff.

'And I know you have your own business.' A sound, a gar-bled noise. 'I am very proud of you, Luca. I have tried to tell you that so many times over the years but pride always held me back. I am glad I got to say it before—the end.'

Luca's eyes felt sore. He ran a hand over them.

'If you do not want your share of the company, sign it over to Max. He knows there is a possibility of that. But I hope—we both hope—you will consider stepping into your birthright. It would mean…everything to me.'

The emotions that were strangling Luca were too pro-found to unravel. He simply nodded, because he didn't trust his voice to speak.

Allegedly, it was winter in the northern tip of Australia, but it felt nothing like it, and Luca was glad. The last thing he needed was that the weather should emulate his grey mood. Sydney had been sunny too, though Luca had only stayed in the city for a few hours. Long enough to see Car-rick, to have some of his most fundamental life views al-tered by the older man. And despite the healing that had begun—and it was indeed a healing, of such long-held wounds Luca hadn't even realised they existed: they were simply a part of him—he couldn't shake the foul mood that was heavy upon him.

His father's ill health had rattled him more than he'd expected but it was more than that.

Some of Carrick's words had dug deep into Luca and resonated with his own feelings. Pride had stopped Car-rick from being honest about his feelings. What if pride had stopped Luca from understanding, let alone convey-ing, what he really wanted from Mia?

But what was that?

And did it even matter? She was going to marry another

man, despite what he'd offered. But what had he offered that could possibly tempt her to stay with Luca? She was right. He'd cheapened everything, had created the impression that there was something transactional about their relationship, instead of... Here, he floundered, because describing what he shared with Mia was overwhelmingly difficult.

'Drink?' Max strode onto the wrap-around balcony of the old timber house holding two beers, one extended further, for Luca.

He took it with a nod of thanks, cracked the lid and leaned forward, forearms against the railings.

'What do you think?'

Luca didn't want to tell his brother what he thought. In the days since arriving, he'd managed to avoid mentioning Mia, even though she was at the forefront of his mind constantly. Even his sleep was filled with her, his dreams flooded by Mia, so waking was always the nightmare, because she wasn't there when he reached for her.

But she could have been.

If she'd agreed to his proposition, she could have been at his side here in Australia, seeing this strange, exotic place with its unrivalled natural beauty, the outback and the bush and then this tropical paradise on the coastal fringe, with an ocean as startlingly clear as those of the Mediterranean, and huge, prehistoric-seeming trees in all directions.

Instead, she was on the other side of the globe, likely losing sleep over her father's financial mismanagement and her marriage into the di Angelo family.

'Luca?'

He grunted.

'Okay, that's it.' Max's tone was sharp. Luca had generally only heard him employ this voice when chastising his daughter, Amanda—and even then, only occasionally. 'I've had enough. What the hell is going on with you?'

Luca turned his gaze on his brother, heart racing.

'At first, I cut you some slack, because I know how seeing the old man gets to you. But not like this. This is different. So? Mind telling me why you're acting like a bear with a sore head?' He paused. 'Even more so than usual.'

Luca grunted again.

'I've never seen you like this.'

Luca took a long draw of his beer, turned his gaze back to the ocean. He wouldn't talk to Max about her. He couldn't. Not only did Luca lack the emotional experience to explain what he was feeling, he had no experience with the words needed to adequately convey his despair, and an insufficient understanding of the situation to elucidate, in any event.

'Let's start with something small.' Max swapped to a cajoling tone. 'Tell me where you were last weekend.'

Out of nowhere, Luca's mind was flooded with images. Mia. His beach. His pool. His bedroom. His kitchen. Sitting on the edge of the table eating sun-warmed strawberries. Lying on her stomach on the tiles of the pool, reading a novel. Laughing as he drove them, her tanned legs always catching his attention, and also her easy smile. Mia's eyes—happy, shining with the force of a thousand suns, and stormy, sad, as they'd been at his home in Palermo, the last time he'd seen her. Mia, sitting beside him as he'd played the piano, listening to him talk about his family, his father, offering gentle, wise counsel. Mia, acting as though she would always be there for him.

'Luca? Answer the damned question.'

'I was in San Vito Lo Capo.'

'And were you there alone?'

Luca dropped his head forward, grief finally cracking him apart, so he felt as though he'd been drawn an awful, almighty blow to the chest. 'No.' His gut hurt. 'I was with someone.' And suddenly, he was desperate to say her name, despite everything he'd been doing to avoid this conversation. He needed to say it, like an incantation. To get her out of his head, finally. 'Mia.'

And then, despite all the reasons for his inability to explain, he found the words tumbling out of him, the whole story. Their engagement, what he'd discovered, what he'd thought a year ago when he'd gleefully avoided the wedding, how wrong he'd been, how he'd wanted her only because she was suddenly someone he couldn't have, at least, that was what he'd thought, at first. But he'd been wrong about that, too. He'd wanted Mia all for herself, for the woman she was, the woman he'd met a year ago, who'd worked her way into his mind and stayed there. But she'd worked herself into more than his mind: she was everywhere inside him, a part of his genetic make-up now.

And finally, he relayed the offer he'd made, his suggestion that he would help her father, because he'd been so desperate to keep her in his life. So desperate not to let her go off and marry another man.

'I see,' was all Max said, some time later as the sun dipped lower in the sky. From inside the house, Amanda's voice came to them.

'Daddy? Zio?'

Luca's heart clutched. *Zio.* Uncle. He'd never wanted children of his own, but his niece was an incredible person. He couldn't imagine life without her.

'I have to get Amanda's dinner.'

'Wait.' Luca held the now-empty beer bottle in both hands. 'You haven't told me what you think.'

Max considered his brother for a long time. 'Do you really want my advice?'

That was a strange question. Luca wasn't in the business of asking anyone for their opinion. But he nodded, slowly.

'You do realise I'm hardly an expert in the relationship stakes?' Max pointed out with a grimace. After all, Max's marriage to Amanda's mother had been a trainwreck from day one. Luca had urged his brother to rethink the whole idea, because clearly marriage was a fool's errand unless there was a very specific business purpose behind it, but Max had been adamant. To him, the fact a baby was on the way had meant marriage was the only option.

But they'd made each other miserable. Amanda's mother, Lauren, had drunk too much, partied too hard, and eventually died while out partying.

Luca, though, was just desperate enough to throw himself on his brother's mercy regardless, because he could see no possible option to fix a damned thing—and nor could he understand if he even wanted to fix things. After all, to what end? 'Tell me what I can do. Tell me. Anything. God, anything.'

Max stared at his brother long and hard and, finally, laughed, tilting his head back and letting the sound crack into the evening air. 'You really don't know?'

Luca hated asking for advice almost as much as he despised being laughed at. He scowled at Max.

'Forget about it. Forget I asked.'

'You didn't ask.' Max sobered. 'I offered. So let me state what is patently obvious. Mia was upset that you propositioned her. What she wanted was a proposal. A real one, this time, not because of her father's business, but because you're in love with her.'

Luca shook his head, dismissing the appraisal immediately. 'Ridiculous. You of all people know me better than that.'

'I know you have always avoided relationships that have the potential to get serious. I know you hate the idea of loving anyone, because it means you need them, and it exposes you to a loss and rejection you've felt before. When your mother died, you were still a kid, Luca. You had everything pulled out from under you, and you never really recovered, so you push everyone away, all the time. Except...' He hesitated, shook his head. 'You've let Mia in, and now, it's done. You're in love. And so's she. It's stupid and needlessly cruel to both of you to continue pushing her away.'

Luca was very still, staring at the ocean, as Max's words threaded through his consciousness. If he was in any doubt regarding his own feelings, then the unmistakable burst of euphoria he felt accompanied by the swift blast of fear convinced him.

'How do you know?'

'Because if she didn't love you, she wouldn't have been so infuriated by your offer. Which was really, really stupid, by the way. Totally beneath you. Another clear sign that you'd lost your mind to love.'

Luca ground his teeth, wanting to deny the charge, to point out how fanciful the entire idea was, but Max had a very annoying habit of being able to put things into perspective for Luca. Until recently, he'd been the only person on earth who Luca had listened to, whose opinion he truly valued. And now, there was also Mia.

'I've royally messed up, haven't I?'

'Yes.'

Luca cursed into the night air.

'*Zio!*' A scandalised Amanda stood behind them, looking stern and cranky, and then her little face broke into a broad smile. 'Put a dollar in the swear jar!'

Max grinned at his daughter. 'Honey, would you go and call Reg?'

'Uh-huh. What for?'

'Tell him Luca's going to need a ride to the airstrip.'

'Oh, no, already?' Amanda's face fell.

'Yes, already.' Max's voice was adamant. 'But with any luck, he'll be back soon.' He grinned. 'And he might even bring a friend.'

Except, it wasn't that simple. The entire flight back to Italy, Luca tried to work out what to say, how to say it, how best to achieve what he wanted, and every time he drew a complete blank, because understanding how he felt, why he'd said what he'd said, put a completely different spin on things.

So too did the knowledge that he loved her, and he might have made her hate him, for real, and for good.

As the flight came in to land, and his eyes traced the familiar outline of his beloved country, he realised that there was one place he could start, a small way he could *show* Mia that he hadn't meant a word of the bargain he'd tried to make.

'You cannot be serious.' Gianni Marini stared at Luca as though he'd sprouted two additional heads, one with a tail coming out of the top. He shoved the cheque back across the table. 'I will not accept it.'

Luca marvelled at the other man's pride, in the face of clearly impending destitution. Then again, hadn't he recently had a crash course in pride and the mistakes it could lead a person to make? 'Yes, you will, and we both know it.' Luca prowled to the windows, frowning as he looked down on the garden, imagining Mia here, all the years of her life since moving to Italy. His heart skipped a beat. 'It's not a gift.'

'Then what is it?'

'A year ago, I saw the potential of your company, and I still see it.'

'You also saw the ruinous state of it,' Gianni said, sitting down in his chair, head in hands. 'I don't know what to do.'

Luca felt something like pity roll through him. The older man's desperation was hard to miss, and in that moment he saw Gianni Marini as Mia did. Imperfect, but not all bad. Just misguided. But his mistakes had been formed out of love—for Mia, and a company that was part of a rich family legacy.

Even good people make bad decisions.

'But I do.'

'What?'

'I have a full business proposal to discuss with you, but now isn't the time.'

'You know what the company's worth. If you wait a month, you can get it in a fire sale. I'm going to declare bankruptcy.'

Luca stiffened.

'What?'

'The di Angelo merger is off.'

Luca's brain was pulsing so hard he felt that his head might explode. His next question was heavy with the weight of all his hopes. 'And the marriage?'

'Another failure. It was a failure from the start. What did I do to deserve this?'

Luca thrust his hands onto his hips, hearing the older man's question and disregarding it. Didn't he realise that this was turning into one of the best days of Luca's life? It was imperative now that he find Mia. He needed to speak to her, immediately. If there was any chance this was because of him...

But of course it wasn't.

Far more likely, Gianni had come to his senses and pulled out of the merger, and, as a result, the wedding had been called off.

'What happened?'

Gianni's eyes met Luca's, then shifted away. 'Mia happened.'

Luca's heart thudded. 'Explain it to me, carefully.'

And the older man did. He told Luca that Mia had come to him, even before she knew about the state of the company's finances, to tell him she couldn't go through with the marriage. 'I don't love him.'

Luca dropped his head forward. 'When?'

'A long time ago. Weeks.'

Before she'd come to Luca that night, so furious. 'And you told her about the business's dire situation?'

Gianni paled. 'I wanted to change her mind. It was selfish of me. So selfish.'

Desperate people do desperate things.

Luca had reflected on that himself, when in a more compassionate mood.

So even that night, she'd known she wouldn't marry di Angelo, and that her father's business would crumble, and still she hadn't thought twice about accepting his offer. Because she loved him too much? Was it possible that Max was right? She would have sooner seen her father go bankrupt than agree to Luca's terms.

Luca felt as though he were drowning and the only way he knew how to grab a life raft was to focus on his purpose for coming here today. 'I'm taking over Marini Enterprises,' he said with a determined nod. 'And when I ask you this next question, you're going to understand why it makes crystal-clear sense for me to do so.' After all, it was a family business, and Luca had every intention of becoming just that: a family, with Mia.

CHAPTER ELEVEN

IT HAD ALWAYS been difficult for Mia to choose which flavour of gelato she preferred. Sometimes, it was strawberry, other times hazelnut, and then there were afternoons when only the richest, most sinfully indulgent chocolate would do. But this was an afternoon for the trifecta, the holy grail of sensations, rich and comforting at the same time.

She dug her spoon into the combination of three heavenly flavours, savouring it as she weaved through the crowded Palermo streets, head bent to avoid meeting the eyes of anyone she might know, or that her parents might know.

Another broken engagement behind her, the news had been announced by the di Angelo family and spread like wildfire.

It was Mia's worst nightmare.

At least, she'd thought it was, until her worst nightmare had morphed into reality and she'd had to endure the offence of Luca's offer followed quickly by the reality of losing him—and knowing a life without him in it.

She'd tossed and turned at night, wondering if she was crazy to have refused his offer.

It was offensive and barbaric and wrong but, just as he'd said, being together was right, and maybe there was even enough rightness between them to justify her accepting his proposal.

But she couldn't.

It would have been impossible to live with herself, and with him.

To be discarded by him when it suited, to know that fate awaited her. How could he have asked it of Mia?

But then, weren't all relationships a gamble? Marrying someone didn't ensure you wouldn't be discarded. Loving someone didn't either—look at his mother. So maybe there really was no hope? Tears, her constant companion since that night, sparkled on her lashes and she didn't bother to check them. Instead, she threw sunglasses on and continued to eat her ice cream, one small scoop at a time, hoping that the sugar rush would do its job any moment now and make Mia feel, for a while at least, a little better.

Her car was parked by a fountain in the square. She scanned for traffic, waiting for a speeding Vespa to pass, then walked over the road, keys held in her hand as she approached. She almost didn't see him at first. Between the hot afternoon sun, the ice cream and trying to unlock her old car without spilling said ice cream, Mia quite literally had her hands full. But then a movement, a familiar shift, caught Mia's attention and she looked across to see Luca Cavallaro standing, feet planted hip-width apart, hands in pockets, eyes watching her. Studying her.

And she was a crying mess.

Great.

Just great.

'Mia.' His voice growled out of him, barrelling towards her, and she flinched, because she wasn't ready for this. She was emotionally exhausted. She still hadn't recovered from their last interaction; she couldn't do this again.

'Luca.' She wrenched open her car door, but Luca was there, his hand on the top of the metal, his body forming a frame around hers, so she was caught between the car and him. He smelled heavenly. She swallowed, wishing her tears would stop, wishing, wishing, wishing a thousand things, all of them impossible.

'I heard about your wedding.'

She blinked. It was the last thing on her mind. Strange how right it had felt to end that engagement, compared to when things finished with Luca.

'It was the right decision.'

Luca's chest moved with the force of his breathing. 'Why didn't you tell me?'

'It wasn't relevant.'

'To us?'

She bit down on her lip and shook her head.

'Do you regret it?'

She blinked, the question strange. Why would he even ask that? 'No.'

'I'm glad.'

She angled her face away, focusing on the fountain with its rapidly falling water splashing over the side onto the footpath.

'I had been torturing myself, you know, imagining you preparing for the wedding, getting ready to become another man's wife. I thought I might stay in Australia. Move there permanently.'

She swallowed hard.

'How could I come back to Italy, to know myself within reach of you, and never touch you again?'

Her heart splintered. 'I'm not getting married, but it doesn't change anything. I'm not for sale, Luca.'

'You never were.' He pressed his thumb to her chin,

drawing her face to meet his. 'I was completely wrong to make that proposition. I was desperate not to lose you, desperate to help you, but it was still one of the dumbest things I've ever said. I'm very, very sorry.'

Until he spoke those words, Mia hadn't realised quite how badly she'd needed to hear them. Thinking he believed her capable of what he'd suggested had been a heavy burden.

'The thing is, until I travelled to the other side of the world, I didn't quite understand why I'd reacted that way.'

A drop of gelato melted over the edge of the cup, landing on her thumb. She lifted it to her mouth without thinking, tasting the sweetness. His eyes dropped to her lips, stared at her there, and her stomach did a thousand somersaults.

'Luca,' she whispered, a plea. 'This has to stop.' A lump formed in her throat. 'You can't keep doing this to me. You keep turning up, and making me think—'

'Think what, *cara*?'

But how could she admit that to him? He wasn't the only one who was afraid of being vulnerable. 'You can't keep acting as if this, us, as if there's something more here. I realised very early on that we want different things in life, so continuing to act as though we're in lockstep or something…it's torture. This has to stop.'

'But what if that's not true, Mia? What if it turns out we both want exactly the same thing?'

She shook her head, the cruelty of the question landing square between her ribs. 'Don't,' she cried, clutching the gelato cup hard, needing to hold onto something.

'I thought I didn't want children. I was adamant on that score. But the truth is, I'd just never met anyone I cared about enough to want to have a family with—the idea of loving terrified me, until I loved and lost. Now? The idea of being with you, of making a family with you, fills me with a joy I've never known before. For you to carry *my* child? It is all I want.' His words burst through Mia with radiant energy. 'Now, the idea of having a family with you is all I care about. We are meant to be together—can't you see that?'

She shook her head, not because she didn't believe him, but because she felt as though she were in some kind of mad dream.

'Mia, listen to me,' he said, with urgency. 'I'm in love with you. That scares the hell out of me, if I'm honest, because I've never been in love before, and all my experience of relationships has shown them to be capable of wrecking a person completely. I've never desired that sort of risk—the reward wasn't there to justify it. Until now. Until I fell in love with you and realised I would walk through the very fires of hell to be with you, to be open about how much I love you, to be loved back by you, even for a short amount of time. It would be worth it. If something goes wrong and I am destroyed by this love, as I fear I would be if you were to leave me, it will still have been worth it. I'm terrified, Mia, of what loving you means, of how dangerous it is to give myself to someone like this, but it turns out, when you're in love—real, life-changing love—it's not a choice, rather than a state of being. I love you. It's that simple.'

She stared at him, completely dumbfounded. 'Luca, stop. It's okay. You don't need to say this. You don't need to do this. I'm going to be okay. I don't need you to save me, to save my family, from financial ruin.'

His response was to lean closer, his face just an inch from hers. 'I am in love with you. Every single part of me loves all the bits of you. For always.' And then, to Mia's continually expanding sense of shock, he got to his knees in the middle of the footpath, the fountain behind him, passers-by pausing to watch. Mia didn't notice any of that, though. She only had eyes for Luca.

'What I should have said, on that afternoon at my house, is that I cannot imagine my life without you in it. This is not about business, it is not about money, it is not about saving you. It is, if anything, about saving me. Do you have any idea what my life was like before you were a part of it? Mia, you are everything to me. You are the first person I think of when I wake up, the last thing I want to see at the end of my day, you are in my thoughts while I work, always. And you have been since I first met you. This last year, I couldn't get you out of my head—why is that? I barely knew you, and yet, on some level, I already loved you.'

She shook her head because it was impossible to believe him. 'Listen to me. I was so angry with you—irrationally so. I hated you for lying to me because I expected so much more of you. I think I had already started to love you, certainly to need you in my life. The second I read of your engagement to another man, I was driven crazy. It wasn't just jealousy, though, it was a need to set things to right. I just…went about it in completely the wrong way.'

She closed her eyes softly. 'Not *completely* the wrong way.'

'I berated you and, hell, I kidnapped you, Mia. I couldn't bear to lose you. I just didn't understand why that was the most fundamentally important thing in my life until I faced a lifetime of living with my mistakes, of living without you.'

'God, Luca,' she said on a half laugh, half sob. 'I have to say, this is the last thing I expected to hear today.'

'But is it something you want to hear?' He stared at her with such hope, such anxious, uncertain vulnerability that Mia could only nod at first, before adding, 'Oh, yes. Very much.'

A smile burst through his features. 'Then you will hear it every single day. Every day. For the rest of our lives.'

Her heart burst.

'You are a part of me, Mia, and I hope, my darling, beautiful love, that you will agree to share your future with mine. Marry me. As soon as we can get a licence, please, marry me.'

Luca being Luca, the licence was expedited and their wedding held only one week later in a small church in the north of Australia, with sweeping views of a stunning tropical rainforest, accompanied by the sound of birds and waves. Unlike their first wedding, which had a guest list comprised of hundreds of Europe's wealthy elite, the church had only a handful of attendees. Mia's parents and a pair of her best friends from high school, Luca's brother and niece, and his father, who, though frail and in a wheelchair, had been flown up from Sydney and sat in the front row with a blanket over his knees despite the heat of the day, an expression on his face that Mia found so incredibly familiar it blew her away.

Luca had said that he was like his father in many ways, and they certainly looked alike—all three of them, for Max had many similarities to Luca, too, and seeing the warmth between the brothers made Mia's heart very happy. But more than that, seeing Luca with Carrick and knowing that her own words had helped bring about a reconciliation made her glow from the inside out. Because the resentment Luca had felt for his father had really only been hurting Luca, and in opening himself to love, to loving his father despite their imperfect past, he'd allowed himself to step into a happier future.

As for Amanda, Max's daughter, Mia was entirely captivated. She was a charming, precocious, intelligent and funny eight-year-old who laughed readily and helped willingly. She went out of her way to care for Mia, sitting with her before the wedding, ferrying her cups of tea, doing everything she could to ensure Mia's happiness. She would be an excellent older cousin, when the time came.

And though Mia had always known she wanted children—and she did—she wasn't in any rush. She was young, and she was, evidently, just a little selfish when it came to Luca. She found the idea of sharing him, just yet, to be something she was not yet ready for.

There'd be plenty of time for that, in due course, but, for now, she simply wanted to enjoy being Mrs Luca Cavallaro.

Their wedding reception was at a Stone family property attached to the 'pearl farm', the most beautiful beach Mia had ever seen. The house itself was nestled in amongst a rainforest with sweeping views of the coastline on one side and ancient trees the other. The wrap-around balcony was adorned with fairy lights, and a long, straight table was set up on one edge, allowing their party to enjoy dinner.

Mia was already in love with Luca, but that night she fell completely in love with this property, his family, with all the parts of him, just as he'd said he felt for her.

And seeing her parents so happy, so relaxed, gave Mia a freedom she'd never thought she'd know. They were imperfect, in many ways, and she would use her mother's style of parenting as a guide of what not to do when she had children of her own, but she was a master at accepting them as they were, for their good, their bad, their mistakes, and loving them despite that. As with Luca and Carrick, letting herself acknowledge a person's faults and then loving them anyway represented a freedom for Mia. Besides, with Luca by her side, nobody in the world had the power to hurt or wound her. She was truly, everlastingly content.

Where the business was concerned, Luca had indeed analysed the strengths and weaknesses of Marini Enterprises, and, once they returned to Palermo after a six-week honeymoon, he set about a significant restructure and rebuilding. It would take years to return the business to its former glory, but within half a year, positive impacts were already being felt.

Eight months after returning to Palermo, Carrick Stone took a turn for the worse, and while there was always grief associated with death, there was happiness here too, because there was love. Both of Carrick's sons were by his side as he slipped from this life. It was a reconciliation none could have foreseen just one year earlier.

But in letting himself love Mia, Luca had opened himself to all kinds of love, to the risks associated with it, but also the confidence that came from being freely honest with yourself.

Mia had truly opened his eyes to a whole different way of living. His love for her grew each day.

The following year, when Mia and Luca travelled to the pearl farm for Amanda's birthday, it was with some news of their own—they gave to Amanda the best gift they could: she was going to be an older cousin.

In the end, they'd conceived quite by accident, and not learned of Mia's pregnancy until she was four months along. The surprise had been a very welcome one—by then, they were both ready. If Mia had entertained any doubts of Luca's sincerity about his desire for children, they were completely wiped away by his reaction.

'Luca, are you crying?'

'No, Mia Cavallaro,' he'd drawled, all alpha male, except for eyes that seemed, to Mia, just the tiniest bit moist. 'Now sit down immediately and prepare to spend the next five months being totally pampered.'

She laughed. 'I'm pregnant, not made of glass.'

'I don't care.' His nostrils flared. 'You are pregnant with my baby and while I cannot physically carry the baby, I can do everything else.'

'Luca?' She pressed a finger to his lips. 'I'm still me— the same person I was yesterday, who went surfing with you. Remember?'

'*Cristo.*' He paled. 'That was stupid.'

'No.' She laughed. 'It's fine. Everything's fine.' She reached for his hand and pressed it to her stomach. 'Everything's going to be fine.'

Nonetheless, Luca barely breathed normally for the next five months. Not only did he want their child desperately, he wanted the baby enough to make deals with God constantly, for the baby's health, for Mia's. He loved excessively, but not without fear. He couldn't bear it if anything were to happen to either of them.

They were blessed, however, with the birth of a healthy baby girl, three weeks ahead of schedule, in the very middle of the night. A year later, a little boy joined their family and only eleven months later, another girl.

Mia had the big, loud family she'd always wanted, and while she was exhausted, she was also deliriously happy. She could never have imagined, on their first, awful wedding day, that her grief and shame could morph into these feelings of such sublime contentment. She couldn't have imagined she'd ever feel happy again, let alone know a happiness like this—and yet she did. Mia Cavallaro was truly, sincerely, blissfully content, and would be ever after...so was Luca.

But all those years earlier, on the night of their wedding, when Luca had known such incredible happiness, he found himself looking beyond his own relief, gratitude and contentment to think of another. Max Stone had been single a long time, since Amanda's mother's death, and there was a jadedness about Max that Luca had only been able to recognise since opening the floodgates to his own happiness.

He found himself looking into the night sky, at the sparkling stars, right as a single light flashed across the sky— shooting past him, inviting him to make a wish. What could a man do, who'd already had all his own wishes fulfilled, but press a request into the heavens for someone else to find their own lasting, meaningful, true happy ending? And so it was that Luca Cavallaro wished upon a star for Max to one day know the same all-consuming love that he, Luca, had finally been blessed with...

* * * * *

PREGNANCY CLAUSE IN THEIR PAPER MARRIAGE

KATE HEWITT

MILLS & BOON

CHAPTER ONE

LANA SMITH MOVED purposefully through the well-heeled crowd, her ice-blue gaze skimming over the elegantly coiffed heads of the top echelons of New York City's business world. Socialites rubbed elbows with bankers, lawyers, and entrepreneurs, while the strains of a seventeen-piece orchestra swelled over the tinkling sound of laughter and the clink of crystal. Among all these rising and shining stars, she could not see the man she was looking for, the man she rarely looked for, but desperately needed right now.

Her husband.

'Lana!' Albert, an aging tech wunderkind who had availed himself of her company's PR services a year ago in order to rehabilitate his somewhat sagging reputation, came towards her, hands outstretched, to air-kiss her on both cheeks. Lana made the requisite kissy noises before leaning back and smiling at him, trying not to appear as distracted as she felt. *Where* was Christos? Earlier that day, he'd texted her that he'd be here tonight. She'd been on the fence about attending at all, because it was her fourth function in the space of a week, but it was always helpful for the two of them to make appearances, short and sweet, together. That wasn't, however, why she was looking for him now.

'I saw your husband just a short while ago,' Albert told her, and Lana's gaze narrowed as her heart leaped.

'You did?' She took a sip from the crystal flute of sparkling water she held in one hand, trying not to sound as eager as she felt. 'Let me guess. Holding court in the whisky bar?'

Albert gave an indulgent chuckle. 'How did you know?'

'Christos always prefers a smaller, more captive audience,' she quipped, although she wasn't sure that was entirely true. Her husband of three years was still something of an enigma to her, and rightly so. She hadn't been particularly interested in getting to know him, beyond the basics, and he'd felt the same. Their convenient marriage had suited them both; they had a healthy respect for one another as well as a pleasant, unthreatening affection and camaraderie, and that was all that was needed for a successful marriage.

Until now.

'I probably should go say hello to him,' Lana told Albert, with a smiling roll of her eyes. 'We've been like ships passing in the night these last few weeks.' Last few years, but nobody actually knew that salient fact, which was, essentially, the point of their marriage.

'Don't be a stranger,' Albert called after her as she began walking towards the ballroom's doors. 'I have a friend whose image needs a little polish…he's young, up and coming, but awkward. You know how it is. I mentioned your name.'

Lana turned back to give him a quick, laughing look. 'You know how to find me,' she replied with a flick of her long, poker-straight strawberry-blonde hair, and then she kept walking, her head held high, a faint smile on her lips as she nodded at the various guests she knew or at least recognised.

She'd been part of this crowd for nearly ten years, first as a wannabe hanger-on when she'd started as a lowly administrative assistant for one of the city's top PR firms, still trying to figure out who she was, then rising to consultant, and then, as much out of painful necessity as ambition or desire, starting her own firm six years ago, having left behind a career—and a heart—that had taken a brutal battering. For a second she let herself remember those years, when she'd been so young, so impressionable, so *broken*, all thanks to one man.

But, she told herself, she could give credit where credit was due—if Anthony Greaves hadn't broken her heart and stamped on her pride, grinding it nearly to dust, she might never have started her own business...or married Christos Diakos.

Marrying Christos three years ago, New York City's enigmatic tech investor and once considered its most eligible bachelor, had been the icing on the cake, cementing her success both in society and business. Not that she needed a man for that, of course, but Lana certainly understood the need to be pragmatic.

Which was what tonight was all about. She'd explain her new plan to Christos in the same businesslike terms in which he'd agreed to their marriage, and that would be that. Yet the clenching of her insides, the sudden speeding up of her heart, told another story.

Somehow Lana didn't think this was going to be as easy or simple as she wanted—and needed—it to be. Even after three years of marriage, she couldn't say she really knew her husband or how he'd react to the proposal she was about to put to him, but she did know that despite his laughing wryness, his easy manner, he had a core of absolute steel. He hadn't swept into this city and taken over business after business, held his nerve with some of the riskiest investments imaginable, and risen to multimillionaire status all within a few years on charm alone, although he had that in spades, as well.

At the imposing double doorway of the ballroom, Lana paused, taking a breath to steady herself, flicking her hair once more behind her shoulders, straightening her spine. The pale blue evening gown she wore, a simple sheath of satin, matched her eyes and made her stand out like a column of ice, which was exactly the image she'd tried to go for when she'd reinvented her broken-hearted self at age twenty-three—sophisticated, a little bit remote but ultimately approachable, determined but also charming, which was why she smiled at everyone she saw, without letting it *quite* meet her eyes. She'd spent a long time cultivating the right image as a PR consultant, someone who had to be both aspirational and approachable, friendly yet always professional. Besides, a sense of reserve came naturally to her, after a turbulent childhood and a single, disastrous romance; it was like a layer of armour against the slings and arrows of the world, one she knew she needed.

Yet she sometimes had the uncomfortable, prickling suspicion that her husband saw through that carefully constructed façade—although to what underneath, she couldn't say. *That* she knew she never gave away, not to anyone, and never would, not even to herself. She'd left that lonely little girl, that broken-hearted woman, behind a long, long time ago.

With her chin tilted at a challenging angle, Lana headed into the hotel's whisky bar, a carefully curated den of masculinity, with deep leather club chairs, a mahogany bar, the amber shades of a hundred different whisky brands glinting in their bottles behind it.

She saw Christos immediately, her gaze instinctively drawn to his magnetic presence, picking him out from half a dozen men with ease. He was that notable, that charismatic, sprawled in a leather chair, a tumbler of whisky dangling carelessly from his fingertips. Dark, rumpled hair, a little too long, a powerfully lithe body well over six feet, so he stood head and shoulders over most men in any room. Golden-green eyes that often looked sleepy, but Lana knew better; he'd be taking in everything. He'd probably leave this so-called social meeting with several business tips, or even a contract in the making. That was one of the things she admired about him. One of the things that had made him, for her, husband material.

She took a step into the bar and waited for him to notice her. Another thing she admired about him—he didn't play games. Didn't pretend not to see her for some stupid ego boost, the way so many men did. The way Anthony had, his gaze skimming over her with something like malice as she'd watched him chat up another woman.

No, Christos turned as soon as she stepped into the room, his gaze training on her like a laser, making an unexpected heat bloom through her body, a quickening of her pulse.

She'd long ago trained herself not to react to that gaze, often seeming sleepy yet so intent, or that powerful body, the muscles of his shoulders rippling under the starched white cotton of his button-down shirt. She didn't react to the bergamot scent of his aftershave, or the long, relaxed stride he had, like a lion who didn't even need to pounce.

Chemistry, never mind actual sex, had never been part of their bargain, and that had been for a very good reason.

And it wasn't going to be part of it now, despite what she was about to ask him. Again, Lana's insides clenched with nerves. Did she really want to do this? Did she dare? She'd had three days to think about it, three days to absorb, accept, grieve. Three days to weigh the pros and cons, to try not to feel emotional, even though she knew, deep down, that this was entirely an emotional decision. One from the heart, the kind she'd learned never to make.

Yet here she was.

'Lana.' Another thing she had learned not to respond to—Christos's voice. Rich and deep, and always with a hint of laughter. Not mean-spirited laughter, the mockery of a man who needed to feel superior—and goodness, but she knew what *that* sounded like—but the genuine humour of someone who found the world a fun place to be. Utterly unlike her in some ways, but Lana liked it about him. He relaxed her, maybe without even meaning to.

She inclined her head, let a smile curve her lips. 'Christos.'

'Sorry, gents, matrimony calls.' Christos rose from his chair in one fluid movement. Despite his height, or perhaps because of it, he was a man who moved with easy grace. He tossed back the last of his drink in a single swallow before handing the glass to the bartender with a fleeting smile of thanks. Yet another thing she liked about him—he was always kind to staff, to the people others would have seen as utterly irrelevant and beneath them.

All evidence, she told herself, that she was making the right decision now.

Christos strolled up to her, stopping close enough so she could breathe in his aftershave, feel his heat. Her stomach contracted again, as much with awareness as with nerves. Lana had steeled herself against a response to him over the years, but occasionally it still came up and surprised her, a sudden wave of longing she did her best to suppress. She didn't need that kind of complication. Now she tilted her head up to meet his laughing gaze.

'You wanted to speak to me?' he asked, his tone turning momentarily serious, his hazel gaze scanning her face with a concern that made something in her soften.

'Sexy and nice,' an acquaintance had once told her with a laugh. *'How did you get so lucky?'*

Of course, that woman hadn't known the truth behind their marriage.

'How did you know?' she asked.

He raised his eyebrows. 'You only look for me at a party when you want something.'

Lana tried not to flinch at that rather matter-of-fact assessment. It was true, but it made her sound a bit like a grasping shrew, not that he'd said it in a mean way, far from it. 'Well,' she said mildly, lowering her voice so others couldn't hear, 'that is the reason for our marriage.'

'Well I know it, my dear.' His tone was teasing, without any spite or malice. Christos had always taken their paper marriage in his stride; he'd been remarkably unfazed when, at an event like this one three years ago, Lana had suggested the idea to him. She'd done so with a calculated sort of recklessness, expecting it to shock or maybe amuse, but Christos had merely raised his eyebrows, smiling, and asked for details.

'Are we meant to be on show,' he asked as he slid his arm through hers, 'or is this a private conversation?'

'Private,' Lana replied as her throat suddenly went

tight. She really had no idea how Christos was going to react to her suggestion.

'Very well,' he replied equably, 'but we might as well take a spin around the room for form's sake, don't you think? I don't believe we've appeared in public together for a couple of weeks. You wouldn't want people to start talking.'

'I'm not sure it matters, after three years,' Lana replied as he gently steered her from the bar, back to the crowded ballroom. 'Surely by now our marriage is an accepted fact in this city.'

'Ah, but people always like to speculate,' he replied, leaning down to murmur in her ear so his breath tickled her cheek. Lana stiffened, doing her best to ignore the tingling sensation that little whisper had caused to spread through her whole body, a spark she forced herself to instantly suppress, before it could ignite. Now, more than ever, she did not want to complicate things between her and Christos with an intense physical reaction. Besides, she was pretty sure she was reacting to him this way, after three years of learning not to, only because of what was on her mind. Her heart.

And she had no idea how Christos Diakos, her *dear husband*, was going to take it.

Beneath his arm, Lana's was as taut and hard as a rod of iron. His lovely wife was often tense, although she did her best not to show it, but tonight the cracks in her usually indefatigable armour were starting to appear, at least to him. Christos doubted anyone else at this party saw beneath Lana's polished and icy façade. She made sure they didn't. She'd done her best to make sure *he* didn't, and for the most part she convinced him that what he saw with her was what he got. But occasionally, like now, when she was clearly trying so hard, he wondered what lay beneath that cool smile and steely gaze.

Hoped, even, that there was something soft and warm underneath? He mused over the possibility before discarding it with deliberate determination. No, not hoped, not at all. Lana might have convinced herself she'd drawn up their terms of marriage, but Christos had been the one to approve the contract. He wouldn't have agreed to anything he didn't want to, and one absolute necessity of their so-called union was that emotion didn't come into it at all. For Lana, certainly, and also, absolutely, for him. So, it didn't matter what was beneath her all-business demeanour, because the truth was he didn't actually care. He would never let himself.

They'd done three sides of the square ballroom before Christos decided he was too curious about what she wanted to bother to complete their stroll. He reached for two flutes of champagne from a circulating tray, only to have Lana shake her head firmly and heft her own glass.

'I've already got a drink.'

He arched an eyebrow as he took in her half-drunk flute of Pellegrino. 'Water?'

'I want to keep a clear head.'

Lana rarely drank alcohol for just that reason, but she was still partial to the occasional sip of champagne. With a shrug, Christos took only one flute. He was becoming more and more curious what his wife needed to speak to him about, because it was clearly something. Something urgent.

Did she want a divorce? Or in actuality, an annulment? He considered the possibility with a necessary dispassion. Part of their agreement had been the understand-

ing that either one of them could end it when they saw
fit—when it no longer suited them, or if they fell in love
with someone else.

Had Lana fallen in love? His stomach tightened rather
unpleasantly at that notion. No, surely not. He would
know. He knew his wife far better than she thought he
did. Even though they saw each other somewhat infrequently, she couldn't keep that kind of thing from him.
Still, it was clearly something, something that would
change things between them in some way, and he wasn't
about to waste any more time figuring out what it was.

With Lana's arm clasped firmly in his and his flute
of champagne in his other hand, he shouldered his way
through the crowded ballroom to one of the hotel's
smaller salons along the corridor—one of those imper-
sonal, elegant side rooms rented out for business meetings or intimate receptions. The one he chose was empty
now, but it had clearly been used for a meeting earlier in
that day, because there was an easel with a whiteboard
propped on it in the corner, with a heading in dry erase
marker half wiped away.

Three Points Regarding...

Lana saw it the same time as he did, and they shared a
small smile, both of them having been in many such in-
terminable meetings. Christos slipped his arm from hers,
tossing down his champagne before discarding the flute
on a side table as he strolled towards the board.

'Have you got three points for this discussion?' he
asked, taking the whiteboard marker and holding it poised
above the board, as if to write them down. Lana looked
startled, and uncharacteristically discomfited.

'Wha—what?'

She really was not on form this evening, he mused,

which was very unlike her. Why not? 'Three points regarding whatever it is you're going to propose.'

'How do you know I'm going to propose something?' she asked, her voice only slightly unsteady.

Christos turned to face her. 'Because you marched into the bar to find me, you want to have a private discussion, and you're nervous.' He smiled faintly. 'There, those are my three points—three points regarding my wife's intent, whatever it is.'

She let out a small, somewhat reluctant laugh. 'Very astutely observed, Christos.'

He inclined his head in wry acknowledgement. 'I try.'

'I know.' She paused, looking straight at him, and Christos felt—something—in him contract. Squeeze. Lana Smith was a stunningly beautiful woman. Tall, elegant, slender, strong. Her hair fell in a gleaming sheet of blonde with a hint of auburn halfway to her waist, not a strand of it out of place. Her eyes were the colour of blue diamonds—pale without being watery, fierce and gleaming in a face that could have graced a Greek statue— of Athena, perhaps, rather than Aphrodite. There was too much strength of character in the clear lines of her face for it to be reduced to some sort of insipid beauty. Her body possessed curves in all the right places—lush yet lithe, supple and graceful. He'd always admired how beautiful she was, as well as how focused and driven, having built her business from nothing six years ago, and worked hard to get it to where it was, one of the city's top PR firms, specialising in the rehabilitation or reinvention of significant figures in the business world.

Christos tossed the marker back on the easel. 'So, what is it you want to discuss with me, Mrs Diakos?'

She looked as if she wanted to protest the name—

she'd stayed with her maiden name of Smith for professional reasons—but then she gave a little shake of her
head instead.

'I do have—a proposal.'

He folded his arms, took a studied stance. 'As I
thought, then.'

'It won't actually affect you that much.'

'Which potentially makes it all the more intriguing.
Or, possibly, completely uninteresting and depressingly
dull, depending on what it is. I assume you're not asking
for a joint credit card?'

She wrinkled her nose, unable to keep the flash of
proud disdain from her face. In the three years of their
marriage, she'd never asked him for money. She'd been
the one to insist on a prenup. 'No.'

'You want my Netflix password?'

She rolled her eyes, a smile tugging at her mouth. He'd
always liked how he was able to amuse her, even when
she was trying not to let him. *'Christos.'*

'Hulu, then? No? Well, it's a good thing, because since
we live in separate residences that's strictly forbidden.'

Her smile deepened, and it felt like a triumph.

'All right, then.' He raised his eyebrows. 'What is it?'
He really was curious now. Why was she so nervous? She
hadn't been this unsure of herself when she'd proposed,
three years ago, while they'd been sitting at a bar much
like the one they'd just left.

He'd been slouched on a stool, minding his own business, ruefully reflecting on the woman who had only just
kept herself from throwing her drink in his face, simply
because he'd decided their liaison had come to an admittedly swift end, as he always did. He never made it past
three dates, never got to the point where emotions could

be engaged. It was a rule that had served him well, despite the histrionics, which were admittedly tiresome. At that point, he'd been ready to swear off women for good, which was why, perhaps, he'd been willing to listen to Lana.

She'd slid next to him on the bar stool, ordered a Snake Bite—whisky and lime juice—and tossed it back in one swallow. Already he'd been impressed—and intrigued.

'Tough night?' he'd asked, and she'd slid him a speculative, sideways glance, looking worldly-wise and weary even though she hadn't yet turned thirty.

'Considering I hate half the human race, you might say so.'

He'd let out a surprised laugh at that. 'Likewise, but I think I hate the other half,' he'd told her. 'What happened to you?'

'Just the usual,' she'd replied, holding up her hand for another drink. She'd shaken her hair over her shoulders, her expression turning to iron. 'Some smarmy man thinking he knows better than me simply because of what he's got in his pants. Condescending to me in business and copping a feel on the way out. What about you?'

He'd been briefly enraged on her behalf, although she'd shrugged it aside as if it happened every day, and maybe it did. Suddenly his own frustration—that a woman had taken a break-up badly—had seemed both petty and arrogant in comparison.

'I can't say likewise this time,' he'd told her ruefully. 'Just that I narrowly avoided having a drink thrown in my face.'

'Well, as long as you avoided it,' she'd replied dryly, and he'd laughed again. He *liked* this woman, he'd realised. He'd never met another woman like her.

A couple of drinks in, her unorthodox proposal—a paper marriage to suit them both—had seemed eminently sensible. She'd wanted a husband to discourage suitors, smarmy men, and endless chat-up lines. He'd wanted a wife to dissuade women from thinking they could be the ones to change his heart. A woman he genuinely liked, who didn't want to love or be loved by him, had made *sense*. Here had been someone he could get along with, who would make no demands, who would be interesting company when he chose to have it. The idea of such a marriage had seemed to suit them both, and he'd never actually regretted it.

But what on earth did his wife want now?

'Well?' he prompted when it seemed as if she wasn't going to say anything. 'What is this oh-so interesting proposal of yours?'

'I want…' Lana took a gulping sort of breath, very unlike her, before she steeled herself and met his gaze with her own, blue eyes bright with determination, chin tilted upwards. 'I want to have your baby.'

CHAPTER TWO

To HIS CREDIT—or not—Christos's expression didn't change. He simply regarded her thoughtfully, his deep green gaze scanning over her slowly, while Lana tensed, waiting for his reaction, his response. She wasn't going to jump in with all her explanations and caveats, her assurances and reassurances, as much as she wanted to. Not until she could gauge his response to what admittedly appeared to be an outrageous suggestion. Although not, she reminded herself, as outrageous as it might first seem, once she'd explained.

'Well, this *is* interesting,' he finally remarked in a low, lazy drawl. 'Definitely more interesting than a joint credit card. Even more so than sharing Netflix. *Much* more, as it happens.'

'I'm serious, Christos.' Her voice trembled and she made herself take a steadying breath. She usually enjoyed and appreciated his ready sense of humour, but she wasn't sure she could bear him joking about this.

'Yes, clearly you are.' His laughing look dropped as he cocked his head, his gaze still sweeping over her in assessment. 'In fact, I don't think I've ever seen you so serious before, Lana. Not even when you first proposed to me.'

'That started out as something of a joke,' she protested,

a bit feebly. They'd both been more than a little drunk at the time, restless and reckless from their recent, disappointing encounters. She'd been bruised from having fended off another thoughtless grope, a typically suggestive innuendo. She'd been dealing with them since she hit puberty, and the one man who she'd actually let breach her defences...well, she wasn't going to think about him. But for her, marrying someone for the sheer convenience of it had seemed like a no-brainer.

But as for Christos...? She hadn't ever truly understood why he'd shown up at her office the next day, with the terms of the marriage outlined in boldfaced type, ready to go over every detail. Seeming enthused about the whole idea, and as reassuringly pragmatic as she'd been. She'd pressed him on the point, and the only information he'd given her was that he preferred to avoid messy emotions, something she could certainly get on board with. And so she'd agreed to it all with alacrity, pushing aside the unease she'd had about why *he* was willing to agree to a marriage made on paper.

And yet...was it really just about fending off would-be Mrs Diakoses? What else could it be? She'd never truly known, but she'd put a prenup in place just in case, even though he made twenty times the amount she did, and she made sure, as ever, to guard her heart, which was far more precious than anything in the bank.

'So, are you going to elaborate on this particular proposal?' Christos asked after a moment, his voice still as relaxed as his stance. 'Because I assume there's a little more to it than what you just said.'

'Yes, there is.' She glanced around the room in all its bland, businesslike impersonality, wishing they were somewhere a little more comfortable. A little *friendlier*, because it was hard enough to go over the practicalities of baby-making while standing in such a sterile room, although maybe she should take advantage of the whiteboard to outline her points.

Number one...you don't need to be involved beyond the obvious.

Christos, as he so often did, immediately picked up on what she was thinking about the room. 'This seems like the sort of discussion we need to have somewhere more comfortable,' he remarked, sliding his phone out of his pocket.

'What are you doing?' she asked as he thumbed a text.

'I have the penthouse suite here on standby,' he explained with a shrug. 'We can go there to talk.'

'Oh, do you?' She couldn't quite keep the telltale sharpness from her voice. Part of their arrangement had been they were free to conduct affairs with other people, as long as they were completely, utterly discreet, but she found she didn't really need or want the reminder right now.

He looked up from his phone, his expression a cross between wry and exasperated. 'For business meetings, Lana. Or VIP clients. Not my...perceived paramours.'

'I don't care about your paramours,' she tossed back at him, and he slid his phone into his pocket.

'I know. I can pick up the key card for the penthouse at Reception.'

Already he was striding forward, sliding his arm under hers, his long fingers resting on her bare wrist, making her pulse jump. Did she really want to go to the penthouse suite with him? In the three years of their marriage, he'd never made a single physical advance, not even a potential innuendo or suggestive remark, and she'd been both glad and grateful. He'd been the perfect gentleman for the entire time, and there was no reason to think he'd change now, simply because she'd told him she wanted his baby.

Right?

'I'm presuming,' he remarked dryly as he guided her towards the lobby, 'that this is just an initial discussion, not a potential act of consummation?'

Lana nearly choked. 'Of *course*—'

'I just wanted to reassure you,' he cut across her, 'because you were looking kind of nervous.'

'I'm—'

'And,' he added imperturbably, 'to tell you the truth, I'm not really in the mood right now. It's been a tough week.' He grinned wickedly at her then, a gleam of teeth and glint of eye that belied what he'd just said and made her body spark to life—again. She'd always known Christos had a keen sense of humour, but she hadn't quite seen—or felt—it like this before, with such a dangerous, exciting edge that ran like a razor along her nerve endings, twanging everything to life. The last thing she needed right now was to feel the zing of attraction for such an impossible man, and yet...

'Good to hear,' she managed, hoping her voice sounded as light as his did. 'Because I'm not in the mood, either.' Frankly, she never was. Not any more. Even if feeling Christos's arm twined with hers was making her achingly aware of him—his body, his heat, his scent.

A few seconds later he'd accepted the key card from the member of staff at the reception desk, and then they were soaring upwards in the penthouse's private lift, towards the sky.

'I've never been in the penthouse of this particular hotel,' Lana remarked as the doors opened to a large living room, all black marble and scattered leather sofas, with floor-to-ceiling windows overlooking Manhattan's glittering skyline on three sides, Central Park a swathe of darkness in the middle.

'I find one penthouse is much like any other,' Christos replied carelessly, tossing the key card onto an ebony console by the elevator as he strolled into the soaring space. 'You really just get them for the view.'

Lana walked to the window, nerves still racing through her body. She'd got this far, she told herself, and at least Christos was interested in what she had to say. 'It is quite a view,' she remarked, nodding towards the lights of the city.

'Yes, it is.' He spoke from right behind her, his breath warm on the nape of her neck, and she jumped a little, whirling around as she let out an unsteady laugh. 'You surprised me,' she said, one hand pressed to her chest.

'I know.' He eyed her thoughtfully, rocking back on his heels, his hands shoved into the pockets of his trousers. 'And you surprised me. Of all the proposals to suggest… what do you mean, Lana, you want my baby?'

Lana tried not to cringe—I want your baby. It sounded like a tabloid headline. Why had she said it like that? And yet it was true, and he'd cut to the chase as always, with no prevarication or pretence. She struggled to know how to answer, to explain. They'd always promised to be honest with one another, the only way their sort of marriage could work. She didn't want to lie now, far from it, but she still felt she had to handle the truth carefully. There was simply too much at stake not to.

'I want a baby,' she stated baldly. 'A child of my own.'

Something flickered in his eyes. 'And my own, presumably.'

'Well, that part seemed to make sense.' She moved past him, towards the trio of sofas scattered across the black marble floor, resisting the urge to wipe her suddenly damp palms on the satin material of her haute couture dress. She had thought through this. At least, she believed she had, although now that she was saying it all out loud, she wasn't quite as sure. But she'd had to do something, after hearing the news. She'd been galvanised into action...but had she been precipitous? 'Considering we're already married,' she explained over her shoulder.

'One of the tenets of our marriage was no children,' Christos reminded her. He shrugged out of his suit jacket, tossing it on a chair before he joined her by the sofas, sitting down in the middle of the one opposite, arms stretched across the back, the cotton stretching across his powerful shoulders and lean yet muscular chest, the epitome of relaxed power.

Lana curled up in the corner of another, kicking off her heels and hiking her dress up around her calves. She couldn't keep from letting out a sigh of relief to have the designer stilettos off her feet.

'Why do you wear those again?' Christos asked, cocking an eyebrow towards the shoes in question.

Lana shrugged. 'They're a power move.'

'And you're all about those,' he acknowledged wryly, while she nodded back. Yes, she was. Projecting power, being confident, never being taken advantage of—or hurt—again. 'So how does a child fit into your business plan, Lana?' Christos asked. 'Because as I recall, that was why you didn't want children. You were admirably career focused.'

'I still am, but I've reached a point in my career where I can afford to hand projects to some trusted deputies,'

Lana replied. She'd thought that part through carefully in these last three days. 'If I had a baby, I'd take three months' maternity leave to start, and then go back part-time for another nine months. After that I'd have to see what was best for both the baby and me.' She wasn't going to have a child just to hand it over to a nanny, not completely, anyway, but neither was she going to completely sacrifice her career. She'd find a balance.

'I see,' Christos replied slowly. His gaze was moving over her again, in thoughtful study, yet revealing nothing. 'So why the change of heart about motherhood?'

Lana hesitated. She needed to be honest, yes, she wanted to be, but she also hated showing weakness. Being vulnerable in any way at all—physically, emotionally, either...both.

'Lana,' Christos said softly, and she knew what he was thinking. *Be honest.* He'd felt her hesitation, had understood what it meant. What else did he understand about her? It was something she wasn't prepared to think about, at least not now.

'I had a doctor's appointment,' she admitted reluctantly. 'And it turns out I'm in the beginning stages of early menopause.'

'Menopause.' Christos looked shocked, that sleepy, thoughtful look dropping away instantly. 'But you're only thirty-two.'

She shrugged, trying to act as if she'd accepted the news when it still felt blisteringly raw. 'One per cent of women experience menopause before forty. I'm one of the unlucky ones, it seems.'

His mouth turned down at the corners, green eyes drooping in sadness as he leaned forward. 'I'm sorry, Lana.' His tone was low and heartfelt. She knew he meant it.

'Thank you.' She drew a breath that hitched revealingly. She hated him knowing almost as much as she hated having it be true. Yes, she'd said she hadn't wanted children—mainly because she hadn't trusted herself as a mother. It wasn't as if she'd had a good example, after all, but claiming her career had been an easy out, so she hadn't had to get into the mess of her childhood—a single mother who had blamed her for her dad's desertion, always resentful, angry, bitter, mean. Lana had grown up learning to brace for the emotional and physical blows, and she'd moved on at just seventeen, working her way through college, living in a series of awful apartment shares, working hard, desperate to prove herself—and to be loved.

So, so desperate. Thankfully she'd moved past that, but now she was going to have to convince Christos she really did want to have a baby, be a mother. 'It was a shock, I can tell you,' she admitted, hearing the slight thickening of her voice before she managed to get herself under control. 'It's true that I always thought I didn't want kids, but I also thought I had all the time in the world to decide for sure. It turns out I didn't. Don't.'

'And so, time is of the essence with this plan of yours,' Christos surmised quietly. He leaned back again, arms folded.

'Well—yes.' She glanced at him from under her lashes, feeling uncertain. He seemed to be taking this all in his stride, but how did he really feel about it? She hadn't even explained what she actually meant yet. Maybe she should do that now. 'But I want you to know,' she told him stiltedly, 'that this wouldn't actually affect you in any way.'

Although he'd been completely still, it felt as if he'd

gone even stiller. 'It won't? Because having a child generally does, you know.'

'Yes, but...you wouldn't have to be involved. At all.' His expression didn't change, not even a muscle twitching, and Lana rushed on to explain, to reassure. 'Nothing about our agreement, our arrangement, would have to change. I'd have the baby by IVF, and you could be completely uninvolved in its—his or her—upbringing. If you didn't want our—our baby to know you were the father, I'd accept that. I mean, naturally, there might be questions later on, so we'd have to figure how to handle that at some point, but, you know, I'd absolutely respect your privacy.'

She gave a little gulp, wishing he'd say something. Show something. His expression was utterly blank, his body completely still. Wasn't this what he wanted to hear? It was the way her dad had been, the way Anthony had been, not that she'd fallen pregnant with him, but he'd made it *very* clear that if she did, he was not interested. Lana knew, intellectually at least, that Christos wasn't anything like Anthony, but since he'd agreed to the no-children clause, had seemed reassured by it even, surely he would consider this good news? 'Christos?' she prompted uncertainly. 'How does that sound?'

How did that sound? Like the most insulting, unbelievable, *absurd* thing he'd ever heard in his entire life.

Christos stretched his arms back along the sofa, taking a moment to keep his expression relaxed, interested. He wasn't ready yet to show the fury—the *hurt*—he felt. He watched as Lana tucked her hair behind her ears, swallowing several times, clearly nervous—and she was someone who was never nervous. She must realise how badly she'd just insulted him, and on so many levels he couldn't even count them. She was asking him, her *husband*, to be an anonymous sperm donor for the child she'd raise on her own, no help needed or wanted. *As if.* As if he would ever let himself be reduced to that, let *her* reduce him to that, a stud for her own convenience.

'Can you expound on some of the particulars?' he asked mildly, and, to both his annoyance and amusement, he saw she looked relieved by the question. As if a few details were going to change his mind, reassure him. Still, he wanted to know what she was thinking, how deeply she'd dived down this rabbit hole of hers.

'Yes, of course.' She smiled, or tried to, but he understood the source of at least some of her strain. Early menopause, and at only thirty-two. Even for a woman who had stated she never intended to have children, it had to be a terrible blow. He thought of his own mother, his three sisters, the big, boisterous family he'd always loved, at least until the heart had been ripped out of it, and he'd chosen to walk away—although it had never truly been a choice. How could he have possibly stayed, considering what he'd done, and more importantly what he hadn't? A failure that reverberated through him all these years later and had been part of the reason why he didn't think he wanted children of his own. They were just little people you could mess up, and yet…

Lana wanted his baby. *His baby.* Those words, that knowledge, *did* something to him.

Having her tell him point-blank she wanted his baby had created a sudden, surprising, seismic shift inside him. He'd been fine with the no-child clause because he'd assumed, on a fundamental level, that he couldn't be a good father. He wouldn't be emotionally available; he couldn't let himself care about someone that much. And then Lana had said she wanted his baby, and something in him had crumbled—or maybe exploded. His first thought had been, quite simply, Yes. Yes, he wanted this. He wanted a child. A family. A second chance, a do-over for all the mistakes he'd made with his own family. He was wiser now; he could handle it, he wouldn't let their baby down the way he had his mother, his sister. And he wouldn't do the dangerous thing of falling in love with Lana.

It was perfect. At least, it could be.

'What,' she asked tentatively, 'do you want to know, exactly?'

'Well, everything, really,' he replied in the same easy voice, although keeping that light tone was taking more effort. Part of him wanted to grab her by the shoulders and demand what on *earth* she was thinking, to suggest something so—so *offensive*. Or did she not even realise it was? Could she be that oblivious, that ridiculous? 'How do you envisage this all working?' he asked.

Again, that look of relief, a gleam of confidence in her eyes and she straightened in her seat. 'Well, it's simple, really,' she said.

The tone she took was one he imagined her using in a business meeting, when she told one of her eager clients how she was going to polish his tarnished image, turn him into someone new and shinily improved, his company into *Fortune 500* material.

'What we're going to do is this…'

No. Way. Not this time. Not with him.

'Yes?' he prompted, his tone scrupulously polite.

'Um…yes, sorry.' She gave a little laugh as she shook her head, tucking a strand of strawberry-blonde hair behind her ear. 'Sorry, I didn't expect you to agree to it quite so quickly.'

'I haven't actually agreed,' he pointed out. 'I just want to hear the details.'

A faint blush touched her porcelain cheeks. 'Yes, of course. Well, like I said, I'd want to go with IVF. According to the consultant, my condition has been caught early enough that I should have a fairly good chance of getting pregnant if I can within the next three months or so.'

'Three months,' he mused, nodding. A relatively short window. 'Go on.'

'Since I have no other, um, fertility issues, IVF has a better chance of being successful.'

'Presumably,' Christos remarked after a moment, 'you'd have an even better chance of getting pregnant the old-fashioned way.'

'Well, yes, I suppose, technically.' Once more a faint blush touched her cheeks with pink, reminding him of a sunrise. 'But obviously that's not something we want to—to consider.'

'Obviously,' he agreed, dryly. When Lana had first proposed their paper marriage, she'd made it very clear, *very* clear, that sex would never be part of their deal.

'I just find it complicates things,' she'd said bluntly, without any emotion, her gaze unflinchingly direct, so much so that he'd wondered what experience she'd had to feel so firm about the subject. 'And there's no need to complicate what is meant to be a very simple solution.' Then she'd suggested he have affairs, as long as they were discreet. At the time, bemused but not entirely opposed since they were both being so open-minded, Christos had chosen to be amenable.

He'd been tired of the rigamarole of relationships, of women expecting things he simply didn't have it in him to give. Every time he'd told a woman he would never love her, marry her, or even see her for a fourth date, she'd chosen to see it as some sort of challenge. But not Lana, not in the least. At the time, the novelty had been refreshing, liberating. Three years on, it wasn't quite so much any more; he was starting to realise he wanted more. How much more, he couldn't yet decide, but he knew it was something. Maybe even this—a child. A family.

'So, IVF,' he resumed as Lana gazed at him, seeming torn between uncertainty and hope. 'And that part for me is, I presume, pretty self-explanatory? Self-induced, as it were?'

Her blush deepened but her chin tilted upwards to that determined notch. 'Yes, that's how it's usually done with IVF.'

'I see.' He was afraid he saw all too clearly. She wanted his sperm in a test tube, and that was it. And what did he get in return? Absolutely nothing.

'And after the baby's born?' he inquired politely. It was difficult now to keep an edge from his voice but he thought he just about managed it. 'No involvement then, either, by the sounds of it? This baby of ours won't know I'm his or her father, you said?'

'Not if you don't want them to.'

He let a pause settle between them for just a few seconds. 'And if I did?'

She hesitated, and he could tell by the confusion that crossed her face she hadn't thought this part through clearly, or even at all. She'd assumed he wouldn't. 'Well… of course, I mean, that would be…that would be…acceptable, I suppose.'

Acceptable, if only just? *Maybe?* What an insult. A surge of rage fired through him, and Christos tamped it down. He wasn't going to get angry. Not yet. 'And if

I wanted to be involved?' he asked. 'As this child's father? What then?'

Lana looked so surprised, he almost laughed. It was as if such a thought had never even crossed her mind. What, he wondered, had ever given her the impression that he would be a willing sperm donor but an absent father? He might have agreed to her no-child clause, but did she really think he was that sort of man? Three years they'd been together, in a manner of speaking anyway, and she didn't have the first clue about who he was as a person. As a man.

'Well, I…' She licked her lips, shifting in her seat, her long, golden legs revealed as the slit in her dress climbed higher.

Christos yanked his gaze away, kept it on her face. 'Yes?' he prompted.

'I didn't think you would,' she admitted. 'You said before that you never wanted children, when we first agreed to the marriage. You made it very clear that children weren't part of your life plan.'

Had he stated it as baldly as that? Probably. He'd known what it was like to love and lose, to be part of a family that was ripped apart and never truly healed, scars running through its centre for ever. He'd never wanted to open himself up to that kind of pain, that kind of loss, and, moreover, he'd never wanted to have the occasion or opportunity to inflict it, unknowingly, or unwillingly even, unable to keep himself from it, just as he had before.

At least, he'd never thought he wanted those things… until now. Now, when he realised he did, and he was, to his own surprise, willing to risk it…for a child. A father's love—and a child's in return—could be a simple thing. A beautiful thing.

'You're right,' he told her, stretching out his legs in front of him and folding his arms. 'I did say that about not wanting to have children. But obviously you've changed your mind, and maybe I've changed mine.'

Her eyes widened, turning a deeper blue shot through with gold as her gaze blazed into his. 'Have you?' she asked, and he shrugged, nonchalant.

'I must admit, it's an intriguing proposition, what you've suggested. I'm more interested than I might have expected myself to be, as it happens.'

Again with that damned relief, passing over her face in a wave. 'I'm glad you think so. As for your…future involvement, I'm sure we could figure that out in time, some kind of arrangement we both were…comfortable with.'

And what, he wondered sourly, would that be? Every other weekend? A monthly get-together? Christmases and birthdays? Considering he hadn't seen his family in well over a year, and that by choice, his determination to be so involved was a little ironic, if not downright hypo-critical. And yet he felt it all the same. Utterly. This was a second chance, a fresh start, and he *wanted* it. 'It's not the sort of thing I'd like to leave to chance,' he told her evenly, and she stilled.

'Not to chance…?'

'Generally speaking, the mother's rights tend to trump the father's in situations involving custody and the like.' It was a general observation more than anything else, but the last thing Christos wanted was some heated battle over their baby. He would never want to subject a child of his to that.

'*Custody...*' She sounded shocked as she shook her head. 'Christos, it wouldn't ever come to that.'

'Is that a promise you can make? On *paper*?' The edge was coming through his voice now, like a stain bleeding into cloth, and Lana noticed.

'Christos...' She shook her head again, now more confused than surprised. 'What exactly are you saying?'

She'd been honest, brutally so, and so, he decided, would he. He leaned forward, his relaxed pose shucked like an old skin, revealing the tension and even the fury pulsating underneath. 'What I'm saying,' he told her, his tone turning soft yet lethal, 'is that there is no way I'd ever consider your absurd, offensive, *hare-brained* proposal. No way in hell.'

CHAPTER THREE

LANA HAD NEVER seen Christos angry. It was this realisation that filtered through her stunned brain first as she stared at him uncomprehendingly, taking in his glittering eyes, the colour that slashed his high, bladed cheekbones, the breaths that came too fast. *What...?* What had just happened?

She realised she had to reframe their entire conversation, and it left her feeling as if she'd been knocked, not just off balance, but flat on her face. She, who excelled at other people's public relations, at presenting their new image and predicting the public's response to it, had just failed utterly with her own PR. She'd presented her case badly, and misread Christos's response and intention, as well.

How had she misjudged it all so horrendously? Because it *was* horrendous, to see him looking so furious with her. She realised she'd taken his benevolence for granted, because she'd always known him to be kind, thoughtful, considerate. They'd shared a certain trust as well as affection, and she'd liked it. She'd trusted it.

But right now, he looked positively enraged, and she felt something in her shut down, the way it had when her mother had used to turn on her as a child, that dangerous glitter in her eyes, or Anthony had frozen her out, ignoring her in public while she tried not to beg and did anyway.

She wouldn't be like that now, yet she knew she didn't have the strength of will to lighten the mood, to offer a wry remark. *Don't sugar-coat it, darling.* The words floated up to the surface of her brain, but she couldn't say them. She simply stared at him, and he stared back, his fury cooling into something icy and hard.

'I didn't mean to make you angry,' she finally said, her tone quiet but firm. She wouldn't back down, not the way she used to, cowering and cringing to her mother, pleading with Anthony. No. She'd never be that person again.

'Yes, I'm aware of that.' He leaned back again, in the same relaxed pose, yet every muscle was taut, tense, his whole body bristling with restrained energy. 'I'm not sure if that makes it better or worse, to be honest.' His tone almost managed to be wry, but still held an edge. 'Why did you think I would be amenable to such an idea, Lana? I know I said I was okay with not having children, but to donate my sperm for a baby I won't even be bringing up? From a purely selfish point of view, what would be in it for me?'

Realisation hollowed her stomach out. 'Nothing,' she admitted after a moment. Why had she not considered that angle before? Of course Christos wanted something from the deal—but what? 'Although I'm not sure what was in our marriage, for you, besides getting some grasping women off your back. Not much of an incentive, really, as far as I could see.'

His expression turned both thoughtful and guarded, like a veil dropping over his eyes. 'Obviously it was enough of an incentive for me to agree to it,' he replied. 'And don't underestimate the convenience of not being besieged by grasping women. But *this*…if I didn't want a child in the first place, I'd hardly be amenable to donating my sperm to my own *wife*. And if I did want a child, I'd want to be involved. Don't you think?'

Misery swamped her and she had to bite her lip to keep from showing how devastated she felt. When he pointed it out like that, it was obvious, unbearably so. She'd been so *stupid*, because she'd been blinded by her own need and fear. Hearing the doctor tell her that her time was running out…realising this would be her only chance at a child, a family… The family she'd never thought she'd dare to have, a baby to love… She'd let that emotion guide her, and not the cool, clear logic that usually did. Head over heart every time, wasn't that her hard and fast rule? Not this time, though. Not when it had mattered the most.

'I mean, why me?' Christos continued, his tone affable yet relentless. 'If you just want a sperm donor, why not just get a sperm donor?'

Another fair and somewhat obvious point. What could she say? The truth, she supposed. She'd been honest so far, and she'd continue to be so, even if it hurt. 'I trust you,' she told him. 'And I… I like you. And…you have good genes.'

'Your three points regarding the conception of our child,' Christos filled in dryly.

Lana gave a soft huff of laughter. Trust Christos to make a joke about it. She liked that about him, too. 'And point four, you have a good sense of humour,' she quipped before adding, 'I suppose I didn't think this through as much as I should have.' She rolled her eyes, trying to laugh at herself, at least a little, even though she still felt as if she were reeling. 'The truth is, I got the news about my—my condition, and I raced to find a solution. And this one seemed…obvious, I suppose. I didn't mean to offend you. I genuinely believed you wouldn't want to be involved, based on what you've said earlier.'

Something flashed across his face, and she realised she'd hurt him with that admission. What kind of man would refuse involvement with his own child? And yet her own father had, and easily so, according to her mother. She'd assumed Christos would be the same without ever thinking it through. Without thinking about what it would say about him, when she realised now that he would never have been like that. 'Obviously, that wasn't a fair assumption to make,' she offered quietly. 'I'm truly sorry.'

He gave a rather terse nod, his jaw still tight. 'Apology accepted.'

She'd made a mess of things, Lana realised, and she hadn't even got what she wanted out of it. A sigh escaped her before she forced herself to rally. To be practical, because that was what she did. There was still a solution to be found here, and that was what she had to focus on. 'Well, if I did go the sperm donor route,' she asked him, 'how would you feel about that? Assuming we remain married, people will no doubt think the baby is yours.'

'They'd have thought that when you were proposing this baby *would* be mine,' Christos pointed out. 'And you still didn't want me involved.'

'It wasn't a question of want—'

'Wasn't it?' he interjected, and now he sounded unexpectedly weary. 'Trust me, Lana, I think I know you pretty well, after three years. You like to be in charge, calling all the shots.'

'Doesn't everyone?' she returned, her tone turning defensive. He talked about it as if it were a bad thing, but who didn't want to be in control of their own life? She knew what it was like *not* to be in control, to let other people call the shots. Of course she was glad she had more agency now.

'The thing with a baby,' he told her, leaning forward a little, 'is it usually involves two parents. Two people calling the shots. Making compromises, working together.'

Briefly she thought of her mother, the bitterness etched on her face for ever, the father who had walked out when she was just six months old, without a single backward glance, never in contact again. 'Not always,' she told Christos quietly.

He knew she'd been raised by a single mother; back when they'd first hammered out the details of their marriage, they'd given each other potted histories of their childhoods. She'd told him how her dad had abandoned her and her mother; he'd disclosed that his mother had died when he was sixteen. Neither of them had either asked for or given further details, and Lana had always supposed the lack of knowledge, of understanding, suited them both fine, although admittedly sometimes she had wondered, wanted to know more.

Now he acknowledged her point with a nod. 'But I'm sure you can agree,' he continued smoothly, 'that it's generally better for a child to be raised by two loving parents.'

'If it's possible,' Lana replied, feeling hesitant even though she did technically agree with what he was saying. She had the feeling she was about to be bounced into something, and she wasn't sure what it was. Christos's expression had turned intent, a small, knowing smile flirting with his lips. If only she knew what he was thinking, but the truth was, she didn't. Despite three years of marriage, she *didn't* know him pretty well. That, it seemed, was where they differed.

'So, when it is possible, it's the ideal?' he surmised, eyebrows raised, attitude expectant. 'The thing to aim for, the gold standard?'

She gave a little shrug, a bit impatient now, edgy, wanting him simply to spit out whatever it was he had to say. 'Yes, the ideal, the ultimate, the paragon, the *epitome* of happy families,' she replied, rolling her eyes again. '*Yes*, fine. What of it?'

'Then why would you mess around with a sperm donor and IVF and all that rigmarole,' Christos returned, 'when you have the ideal, the ultimate, the paragon, the *epitome*, sitting right here?'

She blinked at him. Blinked again. What, exactly, was he trying to say?

'Me, Lana,' he explained, and now she heard the humour in his voice again, and she felt as if something in her had settled, righted. This was the man she knew. Trusted. Liked.

'You.' She raised her eyebrows, smiled a little. She wasn't flirting, absolutely not, but…she liked having him back the way he normally was—funny, wry, affectionate, unthreatening. It made something spark inside her, turn fizzy…although she still hadn't completely cottoned on to what he was suggesting.

'Yes. Me,' he reiterated. 'And you. Having a baby— and a family—the old-fashioned way.'

It genuinely hadn't crossed her mind. Christos could see that right off. The way her eyes widened with shock and her expression turned dazed, her lips parting slightly as she simply stared at him.

'You aren't serious,' she finally said, her voice little more than a whisper.

Christos would have been offended, except he knew Lana too well for that. Attraction wasn't the problem here. He'd always felt it from her, like a live wire they had both made sure never to touch. Lana might not yet have admitted it to herself, but it was there. He wasn't wrong about that.

As for him…well, that definitely wasn't a problem, either. It never had been. Even when he'd agreed to the no-sex rule, he'd known he was attracted to her. He'd even wondered if one day Lana might change her mind, and he'd known, right from the beginning, that he would always be amenable…as well as patient. But now?

'I am absolutely serious,' he told her. 'We're married. You want a baby. It turns out I might, too, somewhat to my surprise, it's true. Why wouldn't we do it the way people have been doing it for millennia?'

'Because…' She shook her head, her eyes flashing with both humour and ire. 'That is far more complicated than what I was suggesting!'

'Is it?' he challenged levelly. 'Really? When Junior asks where Daddy is, you didn't think that was going to be a little complicated? Or when everyone assumes he or she is my baby, and they're *right*, but somehow you haven't mentioned it to the person to whom it matters most, our baby? Lana, that's the *definition* of complicated.'

A blush touched her cheeks again, and she looked down, a strand of strawberry-blonde hair falling against her cheek. 'All right, I may not have thought *every* implication through,' she admitted. 'But getting that…involved…feels complicated to me. Very complicated.'

He studied her for a moment. 'Surely sex is preferable to the IVF route, with all the injections of hormones, the emotional upheaval, the palaver, the uncertainty. From what I've heard about it, and admittedly that's not that much, it sounds pretty difficult.'

Her blush deepened and she kept looking at her lap. In three years, he'd never mentioned the S-word to her. She'd taken it so definitively off the table in their original discussion, and with her reasons being about men forever trying to take advantage of her, he'd felt strongly that he needed to show her he wasn't the same.

And so, for three years his gaze had never strayed below her admittedly lovely face. He'd never made a single suggestive remark. Never touched her except on her arm or occasionally put his own around her shoulders, when they were in company, simply as a gesture of togetherness, solidarity. They'd never even kissed, in all this time, and yet he had no doubts she was attracted to him. Just as he was to her. He felt it like a current in the air, a spark leaping between them, and one he looked forward to fanning into flame.

'Maybe it would be less complicated in the moment,' she finally replied, and it took him a second to recall what she was talking about—sex. Specifically, them having it. 'But in the long term… I don't know.'

'What's making you so uncertain?'

She finally looked up, and her expression was composed, even a little resigned. 'The whole point of our marriage was to simplify things. To not involve emotions or—the physical side. To keep it…transactional.'

'Has it really just been transactional?' Christos countered. He knew he was skating on thin ice by simply asking the question, but he was willing to risk it…for now.

'We've been friends, of a kind, haven't we, Lana? Over the years?' He'd like to think they had. They'd certainly enjoyed a camaraderie, of sorts, when their paths had crossed, at least. He enjoyed her company, and he was pretty sure she enjoyed his. They had interesting discussions; they made each other laugh. That, to him, was a pretty strong basis for a marriage…and a family. The family he knew he now wanted.

She looked startled, but then she smiled, her features softening, suffused with genuine warmth. When she looked like that…well, it was a kick to the gut. As well as to another region. 'Yes,' she agreed, her voice as warm as her expression. 'We're friends, Christos.'

'So, we can stay friends.' He made it sound simple, because it was, wasn't it? At least, it could be. As first she'd spoken, and then he had, it had become clearer in his mind. Their marriage of convenience had had its benefits. Their baby of convenience could, too. It really could be that easy. 'A marriage made on paper,' he clarified, 'with a pregnancy clause.'

She let out a startled laugh. 'That's some merger.'

The smile he gave her was certain rather than suggestive, even as his blood heated and his mind raced with provocative images he did his best to banish—for now. 'Exactly.'

'Christos…' She was blushing again, shaking her head, shifting in her seat, responding to him in a way he loved to see. 'Yes, we're friends,' she stated. 'But I told you before that sex complicates things, and I still believe that. Emotions become involved. Feelings get hurt.'

'Yes, when there are certain expectations,' he agreed, even as he wondered when that had happened to her. Her romantic history was completely unknown to him, but he'd certainly been on the wrong side of that bargain himself, in the past. 'But we know what we do and don't want with this, Lana. We want friendship. Companionship. And frankly, the physical side of things would not go amiss, as far as I'm concerned.'

'I doubt you've been missing that,' she returned dryly. 'With your penthouse suite on standby.'

Little did she know. He'd enlighten her at some point, but he wasn't about to freak her out with that information now. 'I mean it.'

She drew a quick, steadying breath. 'All right, so let me hear your proposal. Three points regarding…?' She trailed off expectantly, eyebrows raised, lips pursed.

Christos met her hesitant gaze with a certain one of his own. He might not have worked out all the details or scoured the fine print, but he was sure about this. About them. 'Here they are,' he told her. 'One, we try for a baby the usual way. Two, we raise him or her together. Three, we stay friends and keep love and all its entanglements out of it. For ever.'

Her lips parted and for a second she didn't speak. 'Can it be that easy?' she finally wondered out loud, sounding almost hopeful.

'It can be if we want it to be,' he replied firmly. He truly believed it. 'You haven't fallen in love with me for the last three years, and I haven't fallen in love with you.' Even if sometimes he'd wondered if he *could*. The glossy, iron-willed woman he'd come to know was someone he respected and admired, but not someone, he'd felt, he could ever love…but was that all there was to Lana? He'd sensed something tender underneath, but he'd never tried to probe those depths…and he wouldn't now. Just like Lana, he wasn't interested in loving anyone, except their baby. A parent's love for their child…that felt simple. Easy. Right.

'That might be, but it's not as if we've spent a ton of time together,' Lana protested, which was true enough. They'd kept separate houses throughout their marriage, although they had guest rooms in each other's homes, which they used on occasion. They appeared together frequently enough not to raise eyebrows or make people wonder—more in the beginning, less so three years on. But they'd never really hung out all that much, or shared real confidences, or spent more than an afternoon, maybe an evening, in each other's presence.

'That's true,' Christos acknowledged, 'but don't you think you would have fallen in love with me already, if you were going to?'

She let out a reluctant laugh. 'Maybe.'

All right, he wasn't going to let that one hurt. It wasn't as if he wanted Lana to fall in love with him. Quite the opposite.

'I don't understand why you suddenly want a baby so much, Christos,' she said quietly. 'When you never did before.'

He shrugged, knowing he would struggle to explain the depth of feeling that had come upon him so suddenly. 'Like you, my biological clock started ticking, I suppose. I didn't realise it until you said something.'

She let out a little laugh. 'Men don't have biological clocks.'

'Now that's just sexist,' he replied, smiling. 'Men can have the desire for children the same way—well, almost the same way—women do. I thought I didn't want to have children because—well, because I didn't want to mess a child up. I still don't.' He smiled wryly, although admitting that much made him feel far too vulnerable. He definitely wasn't going to go any farther with that. 'When you said you wanted my baby, I realised I wanted that, too. I wanted *you* to have my child.'

He let the words linger, so she could absorb the import, the *intent* of them, because he meant every word. Already he was imagining it, in a way he hadn't let himself in three long years. Her body pliant and willing under his, her long, golden limbs splayed and open, handfuls of her sun-kissed hair coursing between his fingers, her lips parted, eyes dazed with desire...

He shut down that line of thought very quickly, before things got out of hand. He shifted in his seat to ease the ache that had started to throb in his groin. Besides, it wasn't just about the sex. He really did want a family. He hadn't expected to want that, hadn't let himself even think about it, not after the disaster he'd made of his own family...but having Lana tell him she wanted a baby had suddenly blown open a door in his mind and heart he'd kept firmly locked for twenty years. A baby of his own, a child they could both love, a family they could create. A new start.

He knew Lana could be coolly pragmatic about most things, but he believed she'd be a good mother. Competent, assured, affectionate, all in, the way she was about everything she cared about. Yes, he was definitely sure about this.

And so, enough with the back and forth, he decided. He'd made his position clear, and frankly he felt it was an offer neither of them should refuse.

'Well, Lana?' he asked, eyebrows raised in gentle challenge. 'What do you say? How about it? Are we going to do this?'

CHAPTER FOUR

LANA STOOD BY the floor-to-ceiling window of her corner office, its view of Rockefeller Plaza beneath her unseeing gaze. She'd paid a fortune for this office, and mainly for the view, but she was blind to it now because all she could think about—all she could see—was Christos Diakos. Her husband.

Well, Lana? What do you say? How about it?

How about *what*? Marriage, in all meaning of the word? Having sex with the man, having a *child* with the man, and yet somehow keeping her head on straight, her heart safe? Last night she'd prevaricated, told him she'd have to think about it for a little while. He'd laughed and said he'd expected no less. He'd risen from the sofa like a man astride the world, totally at ease with himself and the outlandish suggestion he'd just made.

And yet it was what millions of couples embarked on every year. Marriage. Parenthood. Life together, if not love. Why shouldn't she do it? Why did she have to keep herself so apart from everyone?

Because it's what you've learned to do. It's the way, the only way, you know how to stay safe. To be in control.

But maybe safe was overrated. As for control…

And anyway, Lana reminded herself, she would be safe, heart-wise. Christos had been right. If they were going to fall in love with each other, they would surely have done it already. The fact that they hadn't meant they wouldn't. Right? They'd both been successfully inoculated against the dreaded L-word, at least with each other. And the truth was, she both liked and trusted him; she enjoyed his company—his easy humour, his innate kindness, his unapologetic professional ambition. So why not enjoy all the fringe benefits of such a union—a baby and, more immediately, *making* a baby—and not worry about emotions that wouldn't become engaged?

Could it really be that easy? Did she even want it to be? Sex was still scary to her, after her experience with Anthony, the way he'd pour scorn on her in her most vulnerable and needy state. Did she want to go through that with Christos, even if she knew—at least in her head— that he would be different?

A shuddering breath escaped her. She glanced down at the ground forty floors beneath her and felt as if she were about to take a leap right out there, onto the statue of Atlas in the centre of the plaza, his broad shoulders reminding her of Christos's last night, when he'd been stretched out on that sofa, looking relaxed and powerful, potently male and utterly assured of his own charisma. He hadn't had any doubts that she would want to consummate their marriage, had he? And why should he, when he was a man most in demand—or had been, before his marriage?

What women had slept with him since, she tried to never let herself think about. Jealousy was an emotion she definitely did not intend to feel. But if they did do this the old-fashioned way, then fidelity was a must. Wasn't it? It was one of many details they hadn't discussed yet.

'Lana?' Her assistant and most trusted member of

staff, Michelle, came to the doorway of her office. 'You have a call from Bluestone Tech on line two?'

Albert from last night, wanting to refer his awkward friend who needed a rebrand. Lana always welcomed business, although her calendar was completely full for the next six weeks. After that, she might want to clear it completely...a possibility that filled her with fear and excitement in equal measure. Could she even do the motherhood thing, considering the sorry example of her own? She wanted to believe she could, but she struggled with doubts.

'Can you tell him I'll call him back?' Lana asked Michelle, who frowned, glancing around the empty office, before she nodded and retreated back out to the reception area where she had her own desk.

With another gust of breath, Lana walked back to her desk, a single, sculpted piece of walnut, and sat down. She had plenty of work to do—a party to plan, a publicity blitz to launch, calls to return, emails to send, wheels to grease, and yet right now she couldn't focus on anything. Anything but Christos.

She was still staring blankly into space when Michelle came back into her office, armed with a double espresso. 'I thought you needed it,' she said as she set the cup down in front of Lana.

'Thank you.' Lana took a much-needed sip before glancing up at her assistant. 'How did you know?'

'You've been acting distracted all morning, which isn't like you. You've usually ploughed through your inbox twice over by now.' Michelle cocked her head. 'What's up? If you want to tell me, that is?'

Michelle, Lana knew, was the one person she trusted absolutely, more so even than Christos, although that was simply because Christos was a man, and she'd learned never to trust men. From the time she'd hit puberty at age eleven, men had been looking at her, making remarks, innuendos, sometimes even trying to grope or touch her. Whether it was the blonde hair or big boobs Lana didn't know, but something about her physique made men think she welcomed their attention when the exact opposite was true. She'd thought Anthony was different, with the way he'd wined and dined her, but in the end he hadn't been. He'd actually been worse.

Still, she trusted Christos more than she trusted any other man, that was for certain. But Michelle she trusted with the truth. Her assistant knew the truth of her marriage, had even been impressed by Lana's matter-of-factness about it.

'Don't you get lonely, though?' she'd asked when Lana had explained it to her, and Lana had given a short laugh.

'No,' she'd said, which was probably the only time she hadn't been honest with Michelle. Yes, she got lonely, but she'd learned that was far better than the alternative. She'd take loneliness any day over heartbreak, humiliation, hurt. Yes, indeed.

'Christos and I had a discussion,' Lana told Michelle now as she took another sip of coffee. 'We're thinking of having a baby together.'

'What?' Michelle's mouth fell open. 'You want kids?'

'Well, *a* kid, yes.' Lana smiled wryly. 'It turns out I have a biological clock, after all.'

'But what about LS Consultants?' Michelle asked. 'Your life is this place, Lana—'

'I'm not going to walk away from it, don't worry,' Lana assured her. 'But with trusted associates like you, I think I could probably take a couple of months off.'

'Wow.' Michelle shook her head slowly. 'I didn't see that one coming.'

'No?' To be fair, she hadn't seen it coming, either. Not until that doctor's appointment four days ago, when she'd discovered what the night sweats, irritability and irregular periods had really meant—something she still needed to absorb. Accept.

And meanwhile…

'So, what does this mean for you and Christos?' Michelle asked. 'Because this doesn't sound like much of a convenient marriage to me, not any more.'

'Well, it would be, sort of.' Lana gave her assistant a rueful smile. 'We both realised we wanted a family, and it made sense to start one together. But nothing else will change.' Or so she kept telling herself.

Michelle waggled her eyebrows, looking both sceptical and amused. 'I'd say *something* is going to change. Unless you've figured out another way babies come about?'

Lana smiled thinly. She was *not* going to mention the whole IVF debacle to her assistant. Twenty-four hours later and the concept now made her cringe. What *had* she been thinking of, suggesting such a thing? And yet what was Christos thinking of now? Because she was still apprehensive about how it would all actually work. 'All right, maybe that will change,' she allowed. 'But that's just one aspect.'

'Some aspect,' Michelle replied with a grin while Lana tried to get a grip on the panic that was icing her insides. Yes, some aspect, indeed, and one she hadn't considered or engaged in in a *very* long time, for a reason. Not that she particularly wanted Christos knowing that, but…

'So how will it work?' Michelle asked, as if reading Lana's mind. 'Practically, I mean, please don't give me the nitty-gritty.' She held up a hand as she gave a not-so-mock shudder. 'But in terms of your relationship? Will you live together? In whose house? How will you share the parenting responsibilities? Are you going to be a regular married couple now?'

'No, definitely not,' Lana replied to the last question with a firmness she felt absolutely, even if she couldn't yet anchor it in fact. 'We won't love each other, for a start.'

Michelle stared at her, nonplussed. 'What does that even mean?'

'What do you mean, what does it mean?' Lana asked, a bit rattled by the question. 'Wasn't it obvious? It means exactly what it sounds like it means. We. Won't. Love. Each. Other.' Simple, right?

'Ye-es,' Michelle allowed, 'but if you'll be married, living together, parenting together, *sleeping* together...assuming you're doing all this without gritted teeth or bad attitudes... what does it mean you won't love each other? That sounds a lot like love to me, or the facsimile of it, anyway.'

Lana almost laughed at the blithe naiveté of such a question. 'That's not love,' she stated firmly. 'That's friendship. Love is something else entirely.' Love was a sick, hollow feeling at your centre, radiating outward, taking you over. It was a weakness that stole through your body and heart and left you writhing with pain and gasping for air. Love was need, and fear, and disappointment, and shame.

Love was not something she was going to feel for Christos Diakos, or anyone else, ever again. She'd seen her mother grow twisted and bitter, angry and old, all from loving a man. She'd felt her own heart split right in half when the one man she'd dared to give even a *piece* of herself to had walked away without a backward glance, just as her father had. It was what she'd thought all men did...until she'd met Christos.

Could she really trust him—not with her heart, no, never that, but with this much? Her happiness? Her *child*?

'We have some details to work out,' she told Michelle. And she realised she needed to talk to Christos about them asap.

Christos glanced down at the text from Lana on his phone in pleased amusement.

Need to talk details asap.

This was a good sign, he thought as he thumbed a quick text back. A very good sign.

Where and when?

The Metro Club, in twenty?

She'd named the private club for Manhattan's professional elite known for its elegance and discretion, where they occasionally met for a businesslike briefing on the state of their marriage, sharing calendars, planning what events they'd attend together.

He texted back, realising he was smiling.

I'll order you an espresso.

Make it a double.

He let out a little huff of laughter.

Of course.

* * *

Exactly eighteen minutes later, he was seated on a leather sofa in a quiet alcove of the club's lounge overlooking Madison Avenue, sipping his Americano and answering emails on his phone while he waited for Lana to arrive. He felt her presence before he saw her, like an electricity in the air, and he looked up to see her poised in the doorway of the lounge, elegant as ever in an ice-blue silk blouse and form-fitting skirt in navy, her hair swept up into a chignon, a few wisps dancing about her face. She saw him then, and her eyes widened for a second, and it felt as if a jolt passed between them, that live wire twanging to life.

Well, wasn't *that* interesting? For three years they'd managed to exchange glances across crowded rooms and never feel that electric energy, at least no more than a distant pulse of it. Now Christos was sure they both definitely did. Another good sign.

She started walking towards him through the scattered sofas and tables of the lounge, a loose, long-legged stride that made men's heads turn, because she was that beautiful, and not just beautiful, but magnetic. Gazes were drawn, eyes widening in appreciation. Even Christos found he couldn't tear his gaze away. He kept the faint smile on his face as she reached the sofa where he was sitting, dropping her expensive leather bag on the floor before she slid into the leather armchair opposite.

'Thank you for this,' she said as she picked up her espresso and took a sip, eyes lowered so her golden lashes brushed her pale cheeks.

'Of course.' He waited a beat for her to swallow, and then asked in the same amenable voice he'd been using all along, 'So what details did you want to discuss?'

She put her cup down with a slight clatter and took a deep breath before she looked up at him, her gaze as un-flinchingly direct as ever, but with a shadow of…something in it. Something that gave Christos a slight pause, a frisson of unease. He realised he wanted Lana to be the way she normally was—briskly pragmatic, able to laugh at herself, beautiful and funny and smart. Not… *vulnerable*, even just a hint of it lurking in her shadowed gaze, because he really wasn't good at dealing with that.

'I've made a list,' she said, and took her phone out of her bag.

Christos found himself breathing a small sigh of relief. Lists he could do. Lists were what Lana did, and it reassured him. As long as they kept this practical, they'd be fine. He'd be fine. It was when someone said they needed him that he found himself shutting down, walking away. He wished he were different, but he wasn't. He knew that from bitter experience…his mother, his sister. But he wouldn't be like that with Lana, because he wouldn't let himself…and she wouldn't, either. 'All right, tell me what's on it.'

She swiped the screen of her phone a few times and then frowned as she glanced down at her bullet points, her nose wrinkling in a way he'd always found endearing. She had a few golden freckles scattered across her nose that Christos knew she covered with face powder, but when she crinkled her face in thought they always reappeared.

'All right, first point.'

'Are there three?' he interjected, and she looked up, smiling, as she rolled her eyes.

'Three points regarding the details of our union? I suppose I could re-outline.'

'No, just hit me with the first one,' he replied, leaning back. 'I'm ready.'

'Okay.' She took a quick breath. 'Would we share the same house?'

'Yes,' he answered promptly, surprised at just how strongly he felt about that. 'If we have a baby together, we're not going to live separate lives any more. It wouldn't be good for our family.'

'Whose house?'

He shrugged. 'I really don't mind.' He thought of his soaring bachelor loft apartment in Soho, with its retro ironwork and huge skylights, and then her more stately brownstone on the Upper West Side, three stories of carefully curated shabby chic. 'Maybe yours, since it's a bit more family friendly? I don't want Junior to try climbing the spiral stairs to my loft.'

She seemed pleased by that idea, a small, relieved smile curving her lips before she nodded. 'Okay, that makes sense.'

'Next point?' Maybe this would be even easier than he'd thought. Hoped.

She glanced down at her phone. 'After I became pregnant, assuming I did, would we…?' She paused, colouring a little, and Christos filled in, knowing already what she was going to ask.

'Would we continue our state of joyful union?'

Something flashed across her face, a cross, perhaps between amusement and alarm. 'Well, yes.'

He shrugged expansively. 'What would be the reason not to?'

She swallowed. 'I can think of several.'

'Oh?' Now he was curious. 'And what are they?'

'Well, what I said before, about sex complicating

things.' She was definitely blushing now, and she put her phone down and reached for her espresso, mainly, Christos thought, to hide behind her cup.

'I thought we dealt with that last night. We haven't fallen in love with each other, and we're not going to.'

'All right, but...' She put her cup down. 'If we were married—'

'We are married,' he reminded her.

'Properly married. Living together, raising a child together, sleeping together... I'd expect... I'd need you to be faithful.' She spoke as if he would find this difficult, as if it might be a deal-breaker for him, to be faithful to his own wife.

Christos stared at her for a moment, wondering what was going on in her mind. What experiences, what *pain*, had led her to think that he would find such a clause unacceptable?

'Which makes us continuing our joyful union all the more essential,' he replied. 'Of course I'd be faithful to you. And I would expect you to be faithful, as well.'

Relief as well as surprise passed across her face in a wave. 'That wouldn't be a problem, trust me.'

Oh, no? How intriguing. Of course, he'd known her attitude towards sex was a little...*cold*, but now he wondered what made it so. Her seeming reticence didn't alarm him. He was a patient man, and he knew, no matter what Lana liked to believe, that she responded to him physically. He'd seen it, felt it—in her hitched breaths, the flush of her face, the way her gaze found his in a crowded room. Yes, she most certainly responded. And he looked forward to having her respond to him even more.

'So, we've covered two points,' he said as he took a sip of his coffee. 'What's number three?'

CHAPTER FIVE

LANA HESITATED, because number three was one she desperately wanted to know the answer to, but it was also the one that made her feel the most vulnerable, the most emotionally exposed, and that was a state of being she tried never to let herself experience. Not any more. She took another sip of her coffee, while Christos waited. Then she put her cup down, and still didn't speak. How to say it? Frame it, without sounding, well, a little pathetic and needy and *sad*?

'Lana?' he prompted.

The gentleness in his voice compelled her to blurt, 'What makes you believe I'd be a good mother?' The compassion that immediately suffused and softened his face made everything in her inwardly squirm. Oh, she hated that look, even as part of her craved it, craved his understanding. And yet she'd never wanted pity, never ever. She wanted to be strong. To *seem* strong, even when she wasn't.

'I just mean,' she hastened to add, 'I'm assuming you think I would be a good mother, or at least an adequate one, since you seem willing to have a child with me.'

'I do think that,' he replied quietly, without any of his usual wryness.

She forced herself to look up at him, even though it hurt a little, because his expression was still soft with sympathy. 'But why do you? I'm asking because I don't think you could actually know, and, frankly, I haven't exactly given off many maternal vibes, have I?' From the beginning of their relationship, she'd made it very clear that she didn't want children, had no interest in them, even. He'd never even seen her hold a baby, because she never had. Why on earth would he think she was mommy material? *Why would she?*

Christos was regarding her steadily, his compassionate look now replaced by a quiet thoughtfulness. Lana made herself hold his gaze, bracing herself for whatever came next.

Actually, Lana, you're right. Now that you've pointed it out, I realise you'd make a pretty crap mother, so maybe we need to rethink this whole idea.

Then, to her surprise, he took her hand in his, his long, lean fingers sliding across hers, sending sparks of awareness shooting all the way up her arm, through her whole body as she tried not to reveal her instant physical reaction. The last thing she wanted right now was to respond to him in that way, and yet the feel of his hand was both comforting and exciting at the same time.

'I think the real question is,' he asked in a low thrum of a voice that vibrated all the way through her, 'why do *you* think you wouldn't make a good mother?'

Instinctively, without thought, she tried to pull her hand from his, but he tightened his fingers on hers, wrapping around them more securely and holding her in place. The warmth of his palm seeped into her skin, and something even more alarming than those fizzy sparks flooded through her—not just desire, but a deeper emotion, an ache of both longing and acceptance that threatened to undo her completely...all simply from him holding her hand.

This man had the power to affect her...more than she wanted him to. More than he even realised.

She pushed the realisation away, focused on the practicalities. 'I'll be honest,' she told him, glancing down at their twined hands, trying not to feel the warmth of his palm, let it affect her. 'I'm not convinced I will be one, although I'll certainly try my best.'

'I didn't ask that,' Christos replied after a moment. His thumb was now gently stroking her palm, sending shivery bolts of sensation through her, making her feel both sleepy and wide awake at the same time, a yearning unfurling from her centre, radiating outwards, taking her over. Did he realise he was doing it? He must. But why now, when he'd barely touched her in three years?

This was why she'd suggested IVF, Lana thought a little wildly. Because already things had become very, very complicated. For *her*. Not, it seemed, for Christos, and that scared her all the more.

'I didn't ask if,' he told her, 'I asked *why*.'

'I told you why,' Lana replied unsteadily. His thumb was still doing its hypnotising work and she was finding it hard to concentrate. 'Because I haven't ever been maternal. I haven't even *wanted* to be maternal.'

'Why?'

Not another why, for heaven's sake! With what felt like Herculean effort, she managed to pull her hand away from his, but only, she suspected, because he'd let her. She cradled it in her lap, as if it had been injured, hoping he didn't see. 'I told you I grew up with a single mom,' she stated, doing her best to keep her voice brisk. 'Well, *she* wasn't very maternal.' To say the least. 'So, I suppose I never thought I would be.' Had chosen not to be, because she'd seen, she'd felt, how the lack of a mother's love could affect a child. Devastate them emotionally, so they never fully recovered. And she hadn't wanted to take that responsibility, that *risk*, herself with another human being.

Except now, all because of her diagnosis, she was willing to—was she being selfish? What on earth made her think she could actually do it? That she wouldn't mess up her baby's life the way her mom had messed up hers?

Not that she even blamed her mother any more. When her mother had fallen seriously ill five years ago, Lana had forced herself to forgive, to accept, before she had died. It had been important to her to have that reconciliation, and she'd come to realise that her mom had had a very raw deal in life—a husband walking out when she'd had a small baby, a life of hard grind, love affairs with men who had used her and thrown her away. No, Lana no longer blamed her mother for the way she now found herself; she simply accepted it, acknowledged her own weaknesses, tried to work with them.

Maybe this was a bad idea, after all.

'Lana.' Christos's voice was a mixture of stern and gentle. 'Stop freaking out.'

She blinked him back into focus, startled. 'I'm not freaking out.'

'Yes, you are. You're practically hyperventilating.'

To her embarrassment, she realised she was. She'd started breathing faster without even being aware she was doing it. That was what thinking about these kinds of things did to her. She forced herself to let out a long, slow breath and relax in her seat.

'Okay. There.' She managed a smile as Christos cocked his head.

'Do you think you wouldn't love our baby?' he asked,

and she sat bolt upright, her breath coming out in something close to a gasp. So much for relaxation.

'Of course I would!'

He leaned back, smiling a little smugly. 'I think so, too. So, so much for not being maternal, eh?'

She shook her head, horrified to find herself near tears. 'It's not that simple, Christos. It's not just about feelings.'

'I didn't say it was simple.'

'You implied it. I can say I'll love my baby. I can even mean it… But will I? When I don't even know what a mother's love looks like?'

He frowned. 'Was your mother that bad?'

Lana thought of her mother's angry rants, the sudden smacks and slaps, the constant, simmering fury and bitterness. 'Well, she wasn't great,' she said carefully. 'She was tired and strung out, and she resented me for being alive and made sure I always knew it. So, it's made me a little wary of loving people, I suppose.'

She was being more honest than she'd ever been with him before and hating it even as she recognised it was necessary, because she *knew* this about herself. She didn't *like* loving people—the utter weakness of it, the endless opening to humiliation and hurt. Would she feel that way with her own child? She didn't want to, she was hoping she'd be different with her baby, but…what if she wasn't?

'I suppose,' Christos replied after a moment, his tone thoughtful, 'that's a risk every mother—every parent— has to take.'

'It's more of a risk for some than others.'

'And you think it's more of a risk for you?' He sounded more curious than alarmed.

'I—I don't know,' she admitted. 'I'm afraid it might

be.' She glanced down at her hands, now folded on the table. 'The truth is, I don't—I don't like loving people.'

Christos was silent for a moment. 'And yet you were worried that you might fall in love with me.'

A blaze of shock—as well as an unexpected fury—went through her. 'I never said that!'

He shrugged, unfazed by her ire. 'You implied it, don't you think, when you said sex complicates things? Presumably, that was what you meant.'

Yes, it had been, but she still didn't like him saying it as bluntly as that. She didn't like the way it made her feel, all exposed and raw. 'I'm *not* going to fall in love with you,' she stated fiercely, and he gave her a faint smile.

'Good, because I'm not going to fall in love with you.' Amazing how he could say that as if it was a compliment. He leaned across the table. 'But I think we'll both love our baby, don't you?'

Christos watched as emotions chased across his wife's face—surprise, uncertainty, fear, and then, finally, thankfully, hope.

He sat back as he waited for her to process what he'd said. Admittedly, he was a little shaken, not so much by what she'd said, which he'd sort of guessed the gist of anyway, but with the *way* she'd said it. The vulnerability she'd shown, because he didn't know what to do with it. Just as it always had before, it made something in him start to shut down, a door starting to close, and there was nothing he could do about it but try to act as though it weren't happening.

Briefly, painfully, he let himself think of his mother, Marina Diakos, lying in bed, one scrawny hand outstretched towards him in desperate supplication. *'Christos... Please. I love you.'*

And then his sister, years later. *'Christos, please. Come home. I need you.'*

And he'd walked away from them both.

He forced the memories away. He'd failed his family, he knew he had, because they'd shown him their weaknesses, their need, and he hadn't been able to cope with any of it. He'd rejected them utterly, in a way he could never forgive. But he wasn't going to be that way with Lana, because she wasn't going to need him the way his family had.

So really, he realised uncomfortably, the question she should be asking him wasn't whether she'd make a good mother, but whether he'd make a good father.

He hadn't wanted children before, because he'd been unsure of whether he could be a good father or not. So what made him so confident now, that this could work?

'I certainly hope we'd love our child,' Lana replied, drawing him back to the present. 'Since we want to have one in the first place.'

'There you are, then.' He shrugged away the discomfort of his own thoughts. It *was* simple. At least it could be. They could make it so.

She let out a little sigh. 'Maybe I'm overthinking this, but a baby is a big thing. I don't want to mess it—him or her—up.'

'On that we're agreed.'

She eyed him thoughtfully, her head tilted to one side, a strand of strawberry-blonde hair brushing her cheek. 'You seem so sure about this. So...relaxed.'

He shrugged, wishing he felt as relaxed as he was acting. Those old memories, those desperate ghosts, had a habit of rising up and reminding him of just how badly he'd let people down. The people who loved him.

But Lana wouldn't love him.

And as for their child…he'd move heaven and earth to be there for his own little boy or girl. He had to hold onto those truths. 'I try to be. I don't know that there's much point in going over all the things that could go wrong.'

'But it's important to be prepared, Christos. Deliberate.'

'I could never accuse you of not being that.' She smiled faintly, and he smiled back, and in that simple exchange, he felt as if something warm and wonderful were exploding in his chest. 'We can do this, Lana,' he told her. He reached for her hands, clasping them in his own. 'Let's not get bogged down in all the what-ifs. We know where we are. We like and respect each other. Neither of us is going to throw a fit or walk away. Why not just…go for it?' And stop thinking so much, because it made him remember, and that made him nervous.

'Even though twenty-four hours ago the prospect of having a baby had never crossed your mind?' she asked wryly.

He couldn't keep from smiling wolfishly back. 'Well, it had crossed my mind. At least, the *how* of it. I can be honest about that.'

For a second her hands tensed in his, and he watched her carefully, wondering how she would react. Even when she'd been talking about him needing to be faithful, they'd somehow skirted around the actual sex part. 'Yes, about the how,' she said, glancing down at their hands.

'Always glad to talk about the how,' he replied lightly, and she looked up.

'According to my doctor, I should be ovulating next week.'

Okay, maybe not *that* kind of how, but fine. He could deal with a conversation about ovulating, no problem. Christos nodded, businesslike. 'So, we'd best get busy?'

'I'll arrange a hotel,' Lana stated firmly, almost as if she'd already made the reservation. 'I think it's best if this—encounter—takes place on neutral territory.'

Neutral territory? 'It's making love, not war,' he quipped, and for a second she looked annoyed, almost angry.

'*Don't* call it that.'

Jeez, she really had a thing about love, but then so did he, so it was fine. 'It's just a phrase, Lana,' he replied mildly. 'All I meant was you sound like you're planning a military manoeuvre.'

'Well,' she said after a second's pause, 'when it comes to this…it feels as if I am.' She glanced at him from under her lashes, clearly gauging his reaction, and the truth was, he wasn't sure how to react. Was she talking about the whole ovulation thing, getting the timings right, or something bigger? Something more fundamental to who she was, what she'd experienced?

Something he couldn't deal with.

'Well, military manoeuvres can be fun,' he told her with another wolfish smile, and after another second's pause, she smiled back, but there was something almost sorrowful in the curve of her lips, the little nod she gave, and he didn't know if she was disappointed in what had amounted to a brush-off, or relieved.

He didn't want to know.

'Well,' she said after a moment, 'I'm sure you have plenty of experience of such *manoeuvres*.'

He tamped down on the flash of irritation he felt at this. Lana had made several of those remarks recently, and he was starting to feel as though she thought he was something of a man whore, when nothing could be further from the truth. Yes, he'd had his fair share of brief liaisons—he'd made no secret of it when they'd first worked out the details of their marriage—but with every woman he'd always made his expectations clear and, in any case, since they'd been married...

Well, he wasn't going into all that just now.

'So, when will this military manoeuvre happen, exactly?' he asked, and, somewhat to his bemusement, she swiped her phone to check her calendar.

'Next week...the fourth or the fifth of June would be best.' Lana kept her lowered gaze on her phone, and he saw her swallow. Gulp, even. 'A week from tomorrow.' She swallowed again, and then, stiffening her spine, put her phone down and looked up. 'Does that suit you?'

'I don't think I have anything on my calendar.' He'd make sure he didn't. 'Does it suit *you*?' he asked, because she did seem to be taking the idea of them having sex quite seriously, and with more than a little trepidation. He thought of her guarded remarks about men over the years, how they'd taken advantage of her.

Never mind whether he'd been discreet about his alleged affairs during their marriage...had she? Had she had them at all? What did she really think—and feel—about sex?

'Yes, it suits me,' she stated firmly. 'That's when I'm ovulating, after all.'

So romantic, but, he supposed, necessary. 'Are you nervous?' he asked, and immediately she looked wary, tucking that strand of hair that had been brushing her cheek behind her ear in a gesture that seemed nervous, no matter how she chose to answer the question.

'No, of course not.' *Of course not?* 'I mean, it's a… development. And it is bound to change things, at least a little.' She managed a smile, humour lighting her eyes briefly. 'You've never seen me naked, for example.'

No, but he was certainly looking forward to that… along with a lot of other things. 'And you've never seen me naked,' he countered. She blushed, which he liked. 'But that, of course, is just the beginning.' The words seemed to hover in the air between them, along with the images they created, at least in his mind, and, he was pretty sure, in her own. Naked bodies, golden and gleaming under candlelight, twisting and writhing with pleasure…

'Right.' The word came out in the manner of a bullet as Lana slapped both hands on the table, bemusing him, as she started to rise. 'I need to get back to work.'

'Fine.' He stood up, reaching for the suit jacket he'd slung over his chair. 'So, have we covered your three points regarding the new status of our marriage? Any further points you wanted to cover?'

'No,' she said after a moment. 'I think that's it.'

'All right, then.' He raised his eyebrows in expectant query. 'Do we need to meet again before D-Day?'

She let out a little laugh. 'I can tell you're going to have fun with the whole military thing.'

'Well, it *is* fertile ground. Literally.'

She rolled her eyes, laughing again. 'All right, fine. Go ahead with the quips. And I don't think we need to meet again. Not until…you know.' She reached for her bag and slung it over her shoulder. 'I'll make the hotel reservation and send you the details.'

'Right.'

She gave a little nod, clearly pleased, clearly thinking she was in control. She'd make the hotel reservation. She'd call the shots. She'd keep everything neat and ordered and under her authority.

Well, maybe not.

'Good. Great.' Another nod while Christos watched, smiling faintly. 'I know I should have said this before,' she said, 'but…thank you, Christos. You've been more than generous and kind, too, especially considering what I was first suggesting.' She gave a little shake of her head. 'I realise now that the whole IVF thing was a little bit ridiculous, all things considered.'

He raised his eyebrows. 'A little bit?'

'All right, a lot. I just… I suppose I assumed you'd be like all the other men I've known.'

That was an interesting, if sorrowful statement, but one he wasn't about to probe too deeply. 'I look forward to proving otherwise.'

'Thank you.' Another nod. She fiddled with the strap of her bag, and then he saw her professional demeanour come over her like a cloak she drew about herself. Her eyes flashed blue fire and her chin tilted at that determined angle, her lithe body straightening. The only thing she didn't do was click her heels together like a good soldier. 'All right, then,' she said. 'See you next week.'

'See you next week,' Christos echoed as she turned and began to walk out of the club's lounge.

Yes, he thought as he watched her move through the tables and sofas, the admiring glances sent her way, she would see him next week, but not the way she thought she would.

Because if anyone was going to call the shots in their marriage, it was him.

CHAPTER SIX

LANA COULDN'T KEEP a gusty sigh of relief from escaping her as she kicked off her stiletto heels and walked into the living room of her brownstone. She'd had a full day of back-to-back meetings, and her body ached with tension—not from the work meetings, which she'd actually enjoyed, but from the meeting she was going to be having tomorrow night. The *manoeuvre*.

Another sigh escaped her, this one closer to a shudder, and she drew the pins from her hair and shook the tumbled mass down her back as she started to unbutton her blouse. Heading into her bedroom, she shucked off her work outfit and reached for her pyjamas, comfort clothes she never let anyone see her in—old sweats and a T-shirt worn to a paper-thin softness. Her bra went too, tossed into the laundry hamper in the corner. She was going to enjoy this last night of alone time, because tomorrow...

Well, she hadn't actually let herself think that much about tomorrow. She'd made the reservation at one of the city's swankiest hotels, although *not* the penthouse. She'd bought a nightgown, in coffee-coloured silk edged with black lace, not too virginal or romantic or even sexy, but sophisticated, she hoped. She'd booked a morning's worth of spa treatments for tomorrow—waxing pretty much everything, a body wrap, the works. When it came to sex with Christos, she wanted to make sure she was on top form, everything a kind of armour.

Sex with Christos.

A shiver went through Lana, and she thought about how he'd stroked her palm, how she'd responded, that ache opening up inside her. How would she respond when he was touching her far more intimately than that? What if she froze up?

What if she didn't?

It felt like a minefield, and that wasn't even taking into account the emotional side of the whole thing, which clearly didn't bother or even affect Christos, but which she knew she still struggled with. Sex *meant* something to her, which was why she was so scared of having it. Why she hadn't had it in a very, very long time. Should she tell Christos? Prepare him for her own inexperience and inevitable awkwardness? The thought was excruciating.

He viewed sex differently. She knew that. She just had to remind herself from time to time, including now.

Pushing her feet into fluffy slippers—something else she never let anyone see—she headed into the kitchen to make a late dinner. She put a playlist on her phone, hooked up to the surround sound speakers, and the hauntingly melancholy sound of Bach's 'Cello Suite in G Major' floated through the house, one of her favourite pieces of music, for both its sorrow and beauty.

Dinner was a chef-prepped meal she ordered in bulk from a local caterer, something healthy and delicious she could pop in the microwave. As she waited for it to heat, she wondered if she would start cooking when she had a child of her own. Would she make healthy, home-made meals for her family, nurture them with cookies and cakes baked with love?

She wanted to, and yet the thought filled her with something almost like fear. That certainly wasn't how she'd grown up. Did she even know how to do it? She'd never really cooked in all her years; when she'd been young and working her way through college, it had been instant noodles and baked beans. Later, when she'd had the money, it had been meals like this.

But besides the uncertainty about whether she could even manage to make a meal, the thought of her and Christos and their baby seated around a table, bathed in the warm glow of a lamp, eating food she'd made herself...

Well, there was something about that image that terrified her, as well as filled her with a deep and unbearable longing.

She was startled back to reality by the sound of what she thought at first was the microwave dinging, but then realised was actually the chime of the front doorbell. Someone was at her house.

Lana hesitated, caught between wanting to ignore it, in the hope that it was an Amazon delivery, even though she knew she hadn't ordered anything. Her home, three floors of an old brownstone with comfortable furniture in the shabby chic style, was her sacred space, the private sanctuary where she could be safe and alone. She didn't invite people over, and people in Manhattan never just dropped by.

If she ignored it, she thought, whoever it was would probably go away. The microwave dinged, and she opened it and reached for her meal.

The doorbell went again, and then, to her surprise, her phone pinged with a text. Everything, it seemed, was happening at once.

She glanced at her phone, shock icing her insides when she saw it was from Christos.

Open the door. It's me.

What? A ripple of surprise, mixed with both alarm and pleasure, went through her.

She was still staring at the screen when another text appeared.

Seriously, open the door.

What on earth was he doing here? Yes, he'd spent the night sometimes, but in the guest suite on the lower floor, with its own separate basement entrance. And he never came unannounced; that was always one of their rules. Her rules, actually. Visits were always scheduled, because she really didn't do well with these kinds of surprises.

Her phone started ringing.

Warily, Lana swiped to take the call. 'Christos?' she asked cautiously.

'Are you going to open the door?' His voice was rich, velvety, with that hint of humour, and somehow, despite her unease, she found she was smiling.

'How do you even know I'm home?' she asked teasingly.

'I saw you walk up the steps, so that was a clue. Are you going to let me in?'

There was no reason not to, and yet… 'Why didn't you tell me you were coming over?'

'I wanted to surprise you. And we have things to discuss.' His tone managed to seem both playful and firm.

'Do we?' The prospect gave her a deepening sense of alarm. 'I thought we discussed it all already.'

'There are a few salient details I'd like to go over,' he replied easily. 'And after tomorrow, aren't we both living there, anyway?'

'Wh—what? No,' she stammered. 'That was after we had the baby.' How had he not realised that? Of course they wouldn't live together until they needed to. *Right?* 'There's no need to live together *now*, Christos,' she told him, her tone turning almost stern.

'Well, it might help with the baby-making,' he replied dryly. 'Don't you think?'

'We're going to a *hotel*.' It was important to her that their union took place on neutral territory. She still wasn't ready to let him that much into her life, and yet…she was willing to have a baby with him? It didn't make sense, she *knew* that, and yet she felt it all the same.

'Lana,' Christos said gently, 'will you please open the door?'

Underneath the gentle tone, Lana sensed an intractability she realised she had always known he possessed, underneath, but had never actually seen, at least not directed towards her. This was the multimillionaire tech entrepreneur who made unflinching deals, negotiating terms most people would find shocking, even as they were relentlessly fair. This was the man who exuded a quiet authority so powerful he never needed to raise his voice, just an eyebrow. The man so charming people forgot he could also be ruthless, at least in business.

'Lana.' Now, although with the same gentleness in his voice, it was clearly a command.

Lana disconnected the call, too disorientated by the unexpected turn of events to think about what she was doing—or wearing. It wasn't until she'd run down the stairs to the ground floor and unbolted the front door to see Christos standing there, dressed in a charcoal-grey suit, his hair rumpled from the spring breeze, that she remembered she was in her pyjamas, and braless to boot.

Great.

'Good evening.' He smiled and stepped across the threshold, forcing her to scoot out of the way.

Lana crossed her arms across her chest, suddenly, agonisingly conscious of her nipples on display. 'You could have warned me you were coming,' she said. 'I'm in my pyjamas.'

'They're delightful, I must say, especially the slippers.'

'You know I like to be warned about any visits,' she persisted.

'Well, we're ripping up that rule book, aren't we?' he replied easily, shedding his coat and hanging it on the stand in the hall. 'Something smells good. What's for dinner?'

'*I'm* having a warm lentil salad,' Lana replied tartly. 'I don't know what you're having.'

Christos glanced at her, amused. 'Please, don't feel you have to roll the red carpet out for me.'

She let out a reluctant laugh. Christos always managed to amuse her, even when she didn't want to be amused. 'We're supposed to meet up *tomorrow*, Christos,' she reminded him.

'I know,' he replied as he strolled up the stairs towards the living room, 'but I was thinking that it might be a little tough on us both, to go into that kind of meeting stone cold.'

What was *that* supposed to mean? She watched him head up the stairs, his gait easy and relaxed, his body loose-limbed and graceful. 'Cold?' she repeated warily. 'How so?'

Christos had disappeared upstairs, and so Lana followed him up the stairs and into her living room, where he was already sprawled on the deep sofa of cream velvet, feet propped on her cherry-wood coffee table, looking utterly relaxed as well as potently virile. When she drew a breath, she inhaled the scent of his aftershave and it made something warm uncurl inside her, spread outwards. 'Christos?' she prompted.

He raised his eyebrows. 'So, no lentil salad for me?'

'I'm not even hungry any more,' she replied honestly. His arrival had completely thrown her for a loop, which he had to realise.

'That's all right,' he told her with a smile. 'I'm not either.' He patted the seat next to him. 'Why don't you come here?'

Lana was eyeing the seat next to him as if a boa constrictor were curled up on it. What was she so scared of? Well, it didn't matter, because he was determined to allay her fears, whatever they were. That was what this was about. Mostly.

He patted the cushion next to him again. 'Lana, please come sit down.'

She was still eyeing the sofa, looking uncertain, even suspicious. 'What did you mean, go into that—that meeting cold?'

'Come sit down and I'll tell you.'

'Fine.' She tossed her head, bravado back in place, and sat down next to him, her body as taut as a bow, practically quivering. It was hard not to steal a glimpse downward—that T-shirt was so worn it was nearly transparent, and although she kept folding her arms across her chest to hide it, he was pretty sure she wasn't wearing a bra. The sweatpants she wore were baggy and loose, almost falling off her slender hips. Her hair was in loose tumbled waves about her shoulders. He didn't think she'd ever looked so desirable, so *sexy*.

'Tough day at work?' Christos asked and she shrugged.

'No more than usual.'

'How are your feet?'

'What?' She looked startled. 'I saw the stilettos by the door. Killer shoes, quite literally. Do your feet hurt?'

Another shrug. 'No more than usual.'

'Come here.'

'What?'

Smiling a little, he reached for her leg. She was too surprised to resist, and he drew it up, so her foot rested in his lap.

'What…?' Her voice was unsteady, her breathing a little uneven. Already she was responding to him, and he liked it. 'What are you doing?'

'Giving you a foot massage. If you want me to?'

'Well…' She hesitated, and then shrugged her assent. 'I… I guess.'

With his thumb he started to work the muscles in the arch of her foot. After a second's surprise, a small groan of pleasure escaped her, and she let out a little laugh, clearly embarrassed at making such a sound.

'That feels really good,' she admitted, her voice still unsteady.

'Good.' Christos continued to work at her foot, watching her sideways to see how she was responding. Slowly her body began to relax. She leaned back against the sofa cushions with a sigh, and when he reached for her other foot and started on that one as well, her eyes fluttered closed.

'You're really good at this.'

He continued to work his thumbs into the sweep of her foot's arch, applying enough pressure to get at the tense muscles, to feel them relax. It was torture for him, a painful yet exquisite torture. He shifted slightly in his seat, so her foot wasn't brushing a certain part of his anatomy that was tensing even as she became more relaxed. 'Thank you.'

'Have you done it lots of times before?'

He smiled a little, even as he fought a sigh. 'As it happens, yes. But not the way you think.'

Her eyes opened and she lifted her head from the pillows to look at him. 'What do you mean?'

'My sisters used to pay me to give them foot massages. A dollar a pop. It was a nice little earner, when I was young.'

'So, this isn't your way to warm up the ladies?' she asked as she closed her eyes. 'I suppose you don't even need to. They're all willing enough.'

'Well, I certainly wouldn't take anyone to bed who was unwilling,' he replied dryly. Which was what this was about, essentially. He kept working at her feet, as her body became more pliant. He half wondered if she was falling asleep, and that was definitely *not* what he wanted.

A few minutes passed in comfortable quiet, his thumbs rotating circles on the soles of her feet. He glanced down at her, her eyes closed, her golden hair spread across the white pillow, reminding him of Sleeping Beauty. Underneath her thin T-shirt he could see the shape of her breasts, as round as apples, each one a perfect handful. He let himself look, because her eyes were closed, and the truth was he *had* to drink her in. She really had the most *beguiling* body. He ached to touch more than her foot, but that was where he kept his hands. For now.

'So, what did you mean,' she asked sleepily, her eyes still closed, 'when you said it wouldn't be good to go into our…our meeting cold?'

'Well.' He paused reflectively, sliding his hand from her foot to her ankle, curling his fingers around those slender bones, waiting for her response. Her permission. A soft sigh of assent escaped her, and he started to stroke down from her ankle, towards her foot. Wrap his fingers around her foot and then slide back up again, slowly, so slowly, towards her ankle, her skin warm and silky beneath his fingers.

This was *killing* him. He kept doing it.

'Christos?' she prompted, her eyes still closed, her body so very relaxed.

'Right. Yes.' Again, he had to shift in his seat. 'Well,' he said, continuing to stroke from foot to ankle, 'we've been married for three years, and we've barely touched each other. We've never even kissed.'

Lana tensed briefly, her foot flexing beneath his hand, and then she made herself relax. 'That was the point, though.'

'But it's not any more.'

'Tomorrow—'

'Tomorrow, yes, exactly. We go from zero to one hundred in the space of one evening? You might think I'm the king of one-night stands, but that's no way to conduct a marriage. I thought we ought to…get to know each other…a little better tonight, so tomorrow doesn't come as so much of an almighty shock.'

He glanced at her, his hand resting on her ankle, and

saw her eyes wide open, bright with shock as she stared at him. 'Get to know each other?' she repeated.

'Yes.' He smiled and stroked the curve of her ankle with a single fingertip, like the touch of a butterfly. 'Get to know each other.'

She gestured to her feet in his lap. '*That's* what this is?'

'Is that a problem?'

'I thought you were giving me a foot massage!'

'Well, as you can see,' he replied equably, rubbing the arch of her foot again, 'I am.'

A shuddering breath escaped her as she slouched down against the cushions again and he continued to rub. 'What…what do you actually mean by that?' she asked. 'What…?' She licked her lips, making desire dart fiercely through him. 'What is it that you want to do?'

Everything.

His body was raging with desire now, but he kept his voice mild and soft. 'Nothing you don't want to do,' he replied. 'And anything and everything that you do.' He trailed his fingertip from the arch of her foot to her ankle, drawing circles along her skin as a shudder escaped her. 'You're in control of this, Lana, just as you like to be.'

A wobbly laugh escaped her as she slid a little further down on the sofa, so her body was basically splayed before him. 'Funny, but I don't feel in control.'

'Well, I promise you, you are.' And meanwhile he was keeping his own self-control tightly leashed—and it was getting more challenging by the minute. 'Shall I keep rubbing your feet?' he suggested, and wordlessly she nodded.

They had all night, he reminded himself, if that was what she needed. He'd come to her house this evening with no expectations but to touch her and, more importantly, have her want him to touch her. And he'd succeeded in that, but, heaven help him, he wouldn't mind moving on from her feet, lovely as they were.

He kept rubbing, then sliding his hands up to her ankles, back down again. Tormenting himself with this simple touch, never mind her.

Was she feeling it? He thought she was. Her breathing was a little uneven, her eyes still closed, a flush staining her elegant cheekbones. Every so often and she'd slide a little farther down on the sofa, her body becoming a little more open.

He decided to risk a little more, and the next time when he slid his hand from her foot to her ankle, he went a little higher, to her lower calf, her skin warm and supple beneath his questing hand. He waited again, for permission. She went still, and then her breath came out in a little shudder. Her feet relaxed in his lap, toes pushing against him in a way that *really* didn't help with his self-control. He adjusted his position once more, and then started sliding his hand from her calf to her ankle, and then back up again. Wrapping his fingers around her calf as the baggy cuff of her sweatpants slid up towards her knee, and then down again. And again. And again.

His groin throbbed and ached. Her skin was creamily golden, and his fingers slid against her like silk. A soft groan escaped her, and then a little laugh.

'I just realised I haven't even shaved,' she told him. 'I booked a wax for tomorrow morning.'

He laughed softly. 'Trust me, I don't care about that.'

She shook her head, her eyes still closed. 'You've never seen me like this.'

'I know,' he replied softly, and slid his hand up to her knee.

CHAPTER SEVEN

LANA'S BREATH HITCHED audibly as she felt Christos's hand wrap around her knee. Her whole body felt like melted butter, deliciously soft and relaxed even as an ache of longing was radiating out from her core, all the way to the tips of her toes and her fingers, gaining in strength with every passing second. She wanted him to touch her. She *needed* him to touch her. More.

His hand stayed on her knee. Every time he'd moved it, he'd paused, silently asking for her permission, and every time she'd given it, willingly, helplessly, with a little sigh or a shudder. This time was no different. He'd moved from her foot to ankle, ankle to calf and now calf to knee, but it wasn't enough. Silently she willed him to slide it higher. She didn't have the courage to say the words, but, oh, how she wanted him to do it.

Touch me. Touch me.

After several agonisingly wonderful moments, he did. Just two inches up from her knee, his hand splayed against the sensitive skin of her inner thigh, which quivered under his touch. Again, he waited. Lana's blood was pulsing now, her whole body, too, with need.

Touch me.

She scooted herself a little closer to him, her bent leg like an offering, his hand still on her lower thigh. Slowly, so slowly she knew she could make him stop at any time, he slid his hand underneath her sweatpants, along the warm expanse of her thigh, his fingers spread wide, seeking. Higher and higher, each millimetre an endless, exquisite torture, until he stopped so the tips of his fingers were almost, but not quite, brushing her hipbone.

The leg he was touching was still bent, her foot in his lap, and with her breath hitching, she let her knee fall open a little, hoping he sensed the silent invitation, feeling reckless and wanton simply for that one little act.

His hand was still high on her thigh, fingers wide. Lana felt her heart thud.

Slide it upwards, she thought. *A little more. Please. Please.*

He didn't move it. Instinctively she arched her hips just a little, lifting them up in invitation, unable to keep herself from it. She heard a shudder escape him, and she opened her eyes. He was staring straight at her, in a way that made heat and longing flood through her body. Colour slashed his cheekbones, and his breathing was uneven.

'Do you want me to touch you?' he asked in a low voice, and she nodded. 'Tell me,' he said, his tone turning urgent. 'Tell me that you do.'

'I do,' she whispered.

'Where?'

Her heart was racing now, her mind spinning, her whole body both aching and fizzing with a longing she knew she'd never felt before.

'There...' she whispered, and slowly, his gaze still fastened on hers, he moved his hand from her thigh to the warm, pulsing centre of her, his hand slipping under her

panties, his palm pressing against her gently, covering her completely, his gaze not straying from hers.

It felt like the most intimate thing Lana had ever experienced, to have his hand there. Her breath was coming in short pants, and she couldn't look away from him. He continued to press his hand against her, gently, each time sending a fiery bolt of pleasure shooting through her. She wanted more, so much more, and yet she wanted him to keep doing this for ever.

Press. Press.

Her eyes fluttered closed.

'Look at me,' Christos said in a low thrum of a voice, and she made herself open her eyes. His own eyes were glittering, his pupils dilated, his face flushed. Slowly, he slid one fingertip to flex, poised at her entrance.

Lana gulped, her body starting to tense.

'Okay?' he asked, and she wondered how he knew. How had he understood how slowly she would need to go, how in control she would need to feel?

She nodded. 'Yes,' she whispered. 'Okay.'

Slowly, so slowly, he slid his finger inside her, the feel of it shockingly intimate. At first, she didn't feel any pleasure, just the sense of invasion, but then Christos started to stroke her, gently yet with tender persuasion, with such intimate and sure knowledge, finding that little nub of pleasure and stroking it deftly until she felt as if she were being wound tighter and tighter and then suddenly everything burst open.

Her whole body convulsed, and she felt as if she went out of her mind for a few seconds, her muscles banding around his sliding finger, her eyes rolling back as she heard herself moan in a way she never, ever had before, her hips arching against his hand, offering herself up to him as she shuddered from the force of the pleasure he'd evoked in her.

After a few seconds, the waves of pleasure receded in a tide of feeling, and she blinked up at him, her body sated yet still wanting more, shocked at how he'd touched her, how she'd responded.

She'd never, ever responded like that before. She'd never had an intimate experience of pleasure, of surrender, that hadn't involved some kind of humiliation.

'You're lousy in bed, Lana.' How many times had Anthony told her that?

The realisation of what Christos had been able to evoke and reveal in her—and so swiftly and thoroughly—was mind-blowing, and not, she realised, in a good way. She'd been so vulnerable, so exposed, helpless beneath his clever, knowing hands, and he'd *known* it. He could have done *anything* to her, and she would have agreed. Begged him, even, just as she had with Anthony. His finger was still inside her.

She twisted away from him, wincing a little as he withdrew his hand, adjusting her sweatpants as she scrambled up from the sofa, her back to him. She didn't know what the expression on her face was, but she didn't trust it.

'Lana?' he asked, and he sounded both gentle and cautious.

'You must be very proud of yourself,' she told him. She'd meant to sound wry, but her voice came out close to broken.

'Proud?' he repeated, sounding surprised and more than a little disbelieving. 'That's not actually the word I'd use right now, no.'

'You know what I mean, though.' She tucked her tumbled hair behind her ears as she forced herself to turn around and face him. 'Good for you, you've proved you're amazing in bed. Congratulations.' She folded her arms and stared him down as he gazed back, forehead furrowed.

'*That's* what you think this was about?'

'Wasn't it?'

A long, low breath escaped him as he leaned back against the sofa and raked his hands through his hair, so it flopped across his forehead. 'I suppose that's one way of looking at it,' he acknowledged slowly, 'but I meant for it to be about us becoming more comfortable with one another. So that tomorrow wasn't a complete surprise.'

'Comfortable?' she repeated scornfully. 'Comfortable would have been having a *chat*.'

'Comfortable with each other's bodies,' he clarified. There was a slight edge to his voice now, and she wondered why she was pushing him away, almost as if she wanted to make him, not *angry*, no, but not so…persuasive.

Because you're scared. Because when people get close, they hurt you. They use you.

But not Christos. She trusted him, and yet…

'Funny,' she said, 'because I wasn't touching *your* body. You were just touching mine.'

His eyes widened for a second, his irises flaring bright green, before he gestured to himself with one hand. 'Feel free to touch my body, Lana. Any time. *Please.*'

Frustration bit at her. She wasn't handling this right, lashing out in her fear and dismay at being so vulnerable, and yet she couldn't help it. 'That's not what I mean.'

'What do you mean?'

'I… I don't want to be used.'

'*Used?*' He stared at her in absolute incredulity, with

a hint of anger. 'How was I using you, Lana? You were on board with everything I was doing. I made sure of it. I have *always* made sure of it.'

Suddenly she felt near tears. What was *wrong* with her? 'I know,' she whispered. 'I *know*.'

He stared at her for a long moment. 'What's really going on here?' he asked quietly. There was a dejectedness to his tone that tore at her.

I don't want to mess this up, she realised. *I don't want to sabotage this just because I'm scared.*

Slowly, she made herself sit back down on the sofa. She folded her hands in her lap and gazed down at them, trying to organise her jumbled, panicky thoughts. 'I'm sorry,' she said quietly. 'I'm acting like I'm unhinged. I do realise that.'

'Not unhinged,' Christos replied after a moment, his tone turning thoughtful. 'But what's really going on? Because if I were using you, Lana, trust me, I would have got a bit more satisfaction for myself.' He made his tone wry, but she had the sense that it cost him. 'Don't get me wrong,' he continued, 'I loved seeing you come apart under my touch, but, truth be told, I'm a *little* uncomfortable here.' He smiled wryly, and she flushed.

'I'm sorry.'

'Don't be.' His voice was gentle as he reached for her hand, caught it in his own. 'Tell me what's going on. Because if we want even a chance at making this work, I need to know.'

This wasn't part of their deal, Christos thought as he waited for Lana to speak, still holding her hand. He didn't *want* to know what made her tick, that was the whole point. If she'd had a bad experience, if there was some pain or trauma in her past that made her scared of sex, he didn't want to know because he already knew he wouldn't be able to deal with it.

So why was he asking? Why, right now, did he want her to tell him?

'Lana?'

'I've…had a few bad relationships,' she confessed. 'One in particular. I guess it's…affected my perception.'

'Of sex?'

'Yes. Of sex. Of intimacy. Of…everything.'

It wasn't actually, he realised, something he hadn't known, or at least suspected, even if she'd never told him the particulars. Her wary, ice-cold attitude to physical intimacy had been something of a giveaway, after all. 'Tell me about it?' he invited, even as he wondered why he was asking. He didn't want to ask. He didn't want to know. And yet here he was.

She stared at him for a moment, golden brows drawn together, clearly conflicted. 'I didn't think this was part of our deal.'

He raised his eyebrows. 'Knowing our personal histories?'

'Getting close.'

'This isn't falling in love, Lana, this is just being forewarned. I don't want to make any more mistakes, since it seems I did make one tonight.'

To his deep dismay, her eyes filled with tears, one almost slipping down her cheek before she brushed at it with her hand. He was so not good with tears. 'You didn't make any mistakes, Christos.'

'I feel like I did.'

'Well, trust me, you didn't. No one has made me feel the way you did.' She bit her lip, a smile lurking in her

eyes now along with the tears. 'I hope that doesn't freak
you out.'

'It doesn't.' Truth be told, it made him feel like a million bucks. 'But what happened to you?'

A sigh escaped her, long and shuddery. 'All right, I'll
tell you. It's only fair. But I think I need a glass of wine
first.'

'All right.'

She slipped from the sofa and disappeared into the
kitchen, while Christos leaned back against the sofa and
closed his eyes. This had all got a bit intense. He'd come
here with one agenda, and one agenda only—to make
Lana respond to him physically. To open her up like a
flower and let her enjoy the unfurling. But he hadn't intended for it to become emotional at *all*, and yet here
they were.

He couldn't back away now. Not the way he had with
his mother, his sisters—shutting down when they needed
him most, walking away when they'd asked, even begged,
him not to. He'd thought he'd be different with Lana, because his emotions weren't engaged.

And they weren't, he reminded himself, so he could
handle this conversation. He could help her, without feeling anything himself. This was all about the physical,
anyway. Making sure Lana enjoyed sex.

As long as they kept it that way, it would be fine. He
would be.

She came back into the room, a wine bottle in one
hand, a pair of glasses in the other. 'I brought two,' she
said, brandishing the glasses, 'in case you wanted some?'

He shrugged, smiled. 'Sure.'

She must have sensed something a little off about his

tone, because she cocked her head, her blue, blue gaze sweeping slowly over him. 'Are you all right?'

'Yes, of course.' He didn't sound all right. He was starting to get freaked out, although not for the reason Lana thought. He loved knowing he'd been able to make her respond to his touch, but he didn't want her to respond to him like *this*. Telling him her secrets. Sharing her pain. Yet how the hell could he explain that?

I'm fine, but don't talk about your trauma, because you know what? I can't handle it.

'I'm fine,' he said, but Lana did not look convinced. She opened the bottle of wine and poured them both glasses, handing him his before curling up on one end of the sofa with hers.

'Do you want me to tell you about this?' she asked, and he raised his wine glass to his lips.

'Only if you want to.'

She pursed her lips, looking at him hard, and Christos had the sense she knew exactly what was happening, how he was backing away again, unable to keep himself from it, even though he wished he could. 'All right,' she replied finally. 'I'll give you the basics.'

'Okay.' He already knew he wouldn't ask for more.

She took a sip of wine, swallowing it slowly as she composed her thoughts. Christos waited, bracing himself, knowing he had to get his reaction right, and already fearing he wouldn't be able to.

'There was a guy,' she said at last, her gaze on her glass. 'A man. I was young, very young. Twenty-one, just out of university, starting my first internship.' She paused, her lips pursed, her forehead furrowed in thought. For a second Christos let himself simply enjoy how lovely she looked—her hair tumbled about her shoulders in artless waves, not the smooth, gleaming sheet it usually was. Her face devoid of make-up, her T-shirt sliding off one slender, golden shoulder. She was such a beautiful woman, and no more so when she wasn't even thinking about it, using it to her advantage with her power suits, stiletto heels.

'I presume you're going to give me a few more details than that,' he remarked when she hadn't spoken for some time.

'Yes, a few.' She nodded, seeming brisk now, professional, her voice devoid of any of the emotion he'd been fearing.

So why was he disappointed?

His own contrary nature annoyed him, and he pushed the thought away.

'He was my first—lover, I suppose, although I don't even like using that word with him, but I did love him. I was besotted with him, actually.'

She grimaced, and Christos found he didn't like hearing about that. *Besotted?* Really?

'He was ten years older than me, an advertising executive I'd met through work. He was very charming—charismatic, snappy dresser, full of energy. I'm sure you know the type, especially in advertising.' She glanced up at him, smiling wryly, and Christos gave a terse nod.

Yes, he knew the type. Fake, smarmy bastards with their shiny Rolexes and loud laughs.

'Anyway.' A sigh escaped her, her shoulders slumping a little. 'I was…bewitched. That's what it felt like, that's what it was. If he'd told me to jump, I would have asked how high, and then I would have tried to jump higher.'

'You were young,' he said, when it seemed as if a reply was needed. He felt like punching this guy, whoever he was, right in the face.

'Well, that's the background,' Lana told him.

She was looking at him now, her eyes hard, her face like a mask. *No emotion here.*

'And the reality is that sex, intimacy, was something of a weapon to him, one he used to his advantage every time. And the—the bedroom became a place to be humiliated, even to be hurt. And I allowed that to happen.' Her voice, although as hard as his eyes, wavered a little at the last, and she took a quick sip of wine.

Christos stared at her, realisation thudding sickly inside him. He didn't want to punch this smarmy bastard now, he thought. He wanted to kill him.

'Lana…' He didn't actually know what to say. What to do. He wanted to offer her comfort, understanding, take her in his arms and gently kiss the tears he could see gathering in her eyes even as she determinedly blinked them back. He *wanted* to, but he didn't. Couldn't. It was as if he were frozen in place, his mind shutting down, his heart too.

I can't handle this.

He simply stared at her, and he saw understanding gleam in her eyes briefly, like a light being switched on and then just as quickly off. She nodded slowly.

'So now you know,' she said, and it felt like the end of the conversation.

It was the end, because she clambered off the sofa, taking her glass into the kitchen, while he simply sat there, his mind spinning, his heart heavy as a stone. When she came back into the room, she looked composed, calm.

'If you want to stay the night,' she said, 'you can use the guest room downstairs.'

Oof. As if that weren't a brush-off, after what they'd

just shared. Except, he realised, they hadn't actually shared anything. He'd made sure of it.

'All right,' he replied, equably enough, because the last thing he was going to do was insist on anything. Still, he felt duty-bound to ask, 'Tomorrow still good?'

She stared at him for a beat, her expression stony, the smile she gave brittle. 'Oh, yes,' she said. 'Tomorrow's still good.'

CHAPTER EIGHT

LANA SLID ONTO the stool at the hotel's swanky cocktail bar, wriggling a little in the LBD she'd chosen to wear—an elegant sheath of rippling black silk, sleeves, with a square neckline, hitting just above her knee. She'd sometimes worn it to work paired with a blazer, but it could also function as an evening dress, when she was out and about for business.

Which was what tonight was, after all.

'Can I get you something, ma'am?' the bartender asked, and Lana gave him a quick smile.

'Snake Bite, please.'

As ever, a gleam of admiration entered the guy's eyes. Women who drank whisky were always held in high esteem, Lana had noticed, but that wasn't why she ordered the drink. She just liked whisky. 'Coming right up,' he said, and she swivelled on her stool to survey the room.

Christos was due to meet her here in ten minutes. She'd come early, needing the time to compose herself, stake out her ground. She'd already been upstairs to check on the hotel suite, make sure the staff hadn't done anything romantic to it. No champagne chilling in a bucket, no rose petal scattered across satin sheets, thank you very much. Fortunately, the staff had followed her requests and the hotel room looked exactly as she wanted it to look—elegant but functional.

They were *not*, she'd already decided, going to have a repeat of last night. Oh, she wasn't going to go out of her way to avoid any pleasure, even if the idea of exposing herself again, feeling so vulnerable, so helpless under his hands, made her feel more than a little nervous. But the emotional side of things, when she'd talked about Anthony, when she'd told Christos how she'd been hurt—and then had seen the frozen look on his face? Nope. That was definitely not happening again.

Tonight it was all business, and it would be very pleasurable business indeed—but it was still business.

'Here's your drink, ma'am.' The bartender slid the tumbler across the bar, and Lana took it with murmured thanks before tossing it back in one burning swallow. The man whistled softly under his breath. 'You're some sexy lady there.'

She gave him a quick, quelling look. The last thing she needed right now was that sort of comment. She'd been dealing with them all her life, since she'd hit puberty at all of eleven years old, and she'd learned that ignoring such remarks, while not always the most satisfying of choices, usually had the best chance of success.

Fortunately, she'd just seen Christos stride through the hotel's lobby, and so she tossed a twenty onto the bar and walked away. His eyes gleamed as he caught sight of her coming towards him, but she sensed in him a hidden reserve, and she knew it was because of what she'd told him last night. Why on earth had she done that? Well, she certainly wouldn't do it again tonight. Or ever.

'Hello there, husband.' Her smile was playful, her voice light, as she cocked her head. She knew how she wanted to play this now. How it needed to be. 'I've made a dinner reservation in the hotel's restaurant. Apparently, they do an excellent filet mignon.'

'Do they?' He arched an eyebrow, looking far too gorgeous in his navy-blue suit, a paler blue shirt and a silvery-grey tie. His hair was rumpled, his jaw freshly shaven even though it was six o'clock in the evening, and he smelled fantastic. 'Why don't we eat after?'

'What?' The word slipped out, a single syllable of shock and dismay, before she could stop it.

He shrugged, his eyes dancing, his smile slow and sure as his sleepy gaze lingered on hers. 'I'm not that hungry.' *For food.*

He didn't say it, but she felt as if he had. A shiver ran along her skin, and her stomach clenched with both nerves and anticipation. This was not how she'd expected the evening to go. They were supposed to wine and dine each other, talk shop, laugh and chat, and by the time they went upstairs she would feel firmly in control of who she was—and who she wasn't. And she would stay that way even as Christos peeled the clothes from her body, even as he played her body like an instrument, coaxing a tune of pleasure from every inch of her. It would be *business*.

But clearly that was not how this was going to go, because Christos was already turning towards the bank of elevators.

'Wait,' she said, and he turned back, waiting.

'Why the rush?' she asked, forcing her voice to sound light. 'We need to eat.'

'Why not just get on with it?' he challenged with a small shrug. 'Because if we don't, you'll be winding yourself up all evening, getting less and less relaxed, not more so, which I know is what you think will happen, but trust me, it won't. You'll agonise about everything and by the time we're eating dessert, you'll be ready to snap.' His mouth curved into a slow smile. 'Not exactly the best way to start a seduction.'

It was true, Lana knew. She *would* get tense, even tenser than she already was. He knew her so well, better than she knew herself. He started walking towards the elevators, his stride long and sure.

'You don't even know what room it is,' she called after him, 'or what floor.'

He slid a card out of his jacket pocket and held it up. 'I have a key.'

'*What?* How do you have a key?'

'I'm your husband. I asked for one at the desk, and they gave it to me.' He made it sound simple, but Lana suspected he'd had to do some smooth talking to get a key to the room that was reserved in her name only.

Whenever she thought she was in control, Lana realised, whenever she let herself believe that for so much as a second, Christos demonstrated otherwise.

'Why do you need a key?' she half grumbled as she followed him towards the elevators.

He glanced at her, his eyebrows raised. 'Why don't you want me to have one?'

'It's not that.' It was a petty argument, and one she didn't actually care about, except…she was trying to control things. And he wasn't letting her. Why?

'Well?' he asked, eyebrows still raised, as they stood in front of the elevators. 'Are we going to go or not?'

Now, *right* now, upstairs, and then… She tilted her chin, let her gaze flash challenge. 'Why not?'

The answering smile he gave her made her stomach swoop and her toes curl. Why not, indeed.

The ride upwards was utterly silent, an expectation building that felt like a pressure in her chest, a loosening between her thighs. Her heart was starting to race with treacherous excitement, her palms turning damp with nerves.

This was happening. This was actually happening.

Christos stepped aside so she could leave the elevator first, and then he strode down the corridor, to the suite at the end. He didn't just have the key; he knew where the room was. Had he been in there before she had? Or after? She hadn't actually seen him enter the hotel, Lana realised, just in the lobby. What had he done?

'Have you already been in the room?' she asked.

'Maybe,' he replied, and swiped the card, opening the door so she stepped in first. She glanced around the suite, and saw, at least, there were no romantic rose petals on the bed. There *was* a bottle of champagne chilling, so, clearly, he had been here. She didn't know how she felt about that, but before she could so much as think about it, he'd put his hands on her shoulders and was turning her around, slowly but purposefully, so she was facing him, a look of intent darkening his hazel gaze.

Her breath caught in her chest. In the same slow, deliberate way, he backed her up against the wall. She hit it with a gentle thud, surprise slamming through her with far more force. This was not what she'd expected, either.

Christos slid his hands from her bare shoulders to frame her face, fingers splayed across her jawbone, in a caress that felt achingly tender.

'I'm going to kiss you,' he said. 'Okay?'

Wordlessly she nodded. His mouth settled on hers, their first kiss ever, soft as velvet, tender at first but then with demand, with knowledge, with urgency. His tongue traced her lips as he deepened the kiss and she felt as if a hand had plunged right into her chest, shaken everything up, left her both gasping for air and wanting more.

He pressed against her, so her back was flat against the wall, the hard length of his arousal fitting into the juncture of her thighs, thrilling her, shocking her, because already, one kiss in, and he very clearly wanted her. A lot.

And she didn't know what to do with that information.

She put her hands on his shoulders, more to brace herself than anything else, but then he laid his hands on top of hers and drew them up, so they were straight above her head, against the wall. She stared at him with shocked eyes as he pressed the entire length of his body, from fingertip to toe, against her, every inch of her covered by every inch of him.

It felt like a complete physical and emotional overload—once she might have felt trapped by the hard body against hers, but right then she simply felt covered, and not just covered, but shielded. Protected, and even known. And that sensation shook her to her very core. She closed her eyes as he rocked his hips against hers, in the same sort of gentle movement that he'd pressed his hand against her last night, and in the same way she felt herself go boneless with wanting, her breath ragged with need.

Amazingly, his breath was even more ragged than hers. That, she realised, she hadn't expected. At all.

Christos drew his hands down from hers, sliding them all along her body before anchoring them on her hips. Touching her was exquisite agony, and he wanted her to know it. He wanted her to know how much she affected him.

He'd spent several hours last night in her guest room, an ache in his groin as well as his heart as he'd thought about all she'd said—and revealed. She thought she needed to be in control in the bedroom, because she hadn't been before, with that utter jerk of a guy who Christos could hardly bear to think of. Being in control made Lana feel safe, and he understood that. And yet, Christos had realised while lying alone in bed, he'd given her all the control last night. He'd made sure she was calling the shots, giving her consent at absolutely every juncture, and she'd still felt...*used*. It was a word that did not sit well with him. At all.

That was when he'd realised that maybe Lana didn't want so much to feel in control as to see *him* losing it. Not being calculating and cold the way that jerk of a boyfriend had been, but needing and desiring her completely. She needed to see and believe that he wanted her so much it drove him crazy, because it did. Last night he'd kept his own self-control tightly leashed. He'd never shown her how much he desired her, had been entirely focused on her pleasure, thinking, genuinely believing it was the way to make this work between them.

But maybe it wasn't. And tonight, he was trying something else. With his hands on her hips, he slowly drew her dress up to her waist, and a gasp escaped her. She was wearing sheer black stockings and black lace garters, sexy as hell. Christos pushed against her a little more, like a question, and another gasp escaped her, her head falling back against the wall. He kissed her throat, reaching around the back of her dress to drag the zip down. The dress slithered from her shoulders and then with one restless shrug, it pooled at her feet.

He eased back to look at her—black lace bra and pants, those sheer stockings, stilettos, *garters*. 'You're killing me,' he told her on a shaky breath, and she let out an un-steady laugh.

'I was actually going to change. I have a very respect-able negligee—'

'Later.' He was kissing her again, from her mouth to her throat to the delightful vee between her breasts, her skin silken against his lips, his hands still on her hips, anchoring him against her. Her hands roamed across his back, and then slid under his shirt, against his heated skin. That touch alone nearly undid him. A groan es-caped him, and her eyes widened as she looked at him, a silent question.

'I want you so much,' he told her. 'I know this is just the beginning, but I'm not sure how much longer I'm going to hold out, to be honest.'

It was a somewhat humbling admission, but he thought it was one she needed to hear, and in any case it was true. He felt just about ready to explode. 'Really?' she exclaimed dazedly, her face flushed, pupils dilated, and he let out a shaky laugh as he slid his hand along the bare, silky skin between her panties and stocking, pull-ing her leg around his hip and thrusting against her with delicious intent.

'Really.'

Her breath was coming in pants now as she rocked back against him. 'Well, I guess...' she whispered as she continued to move. 'I guess that would be okay.'

'Good.' If he'd wanted to romance her a little more, well, too bad. This was what he needed—to be inside her, hard and hot and fast. He hoped it was what she needed, too.

He guided her hand to his belt. 'Undo it for me,' he managed in a rasp. 'Please.'

Her fingers trembling a little, she fumbled with the buckle, and then, with a snick of leather, he was free. She pushed down his trousers, her fingers barely skimming the length of him, but it was enough to almost make him lose control.

Not yet.

Not quite yet. He pushed aside her panties, positioned himself, pulsing and so very ready, at her core. She arched up and he waited for one agonising second.

'Are you ready?'

'Yes.'

That was all he needed. He drove into her in one smooth stroke, a gasp escaping him as he felt her close around him and they began to move in sync, one stroke after another, each one driving him higher, wilder. He wanted to wait, he *had* to wait until he felt her climax, he knew that much, but, heaven help him, it felt near impossible.

He was close, *so* close, his whole body shuddering, his breath coming in gasps as she folded herself around him, her lips pressed against his throat, her leg around his hip, her hands roaming almost frantically along his back.

And then Lana let out a cry and her body shuddered around his and Christos let himself go. The release was immense, overwhelming his whole body, flooding his senses.

'Lana,' he heard himself saying, over and over. 'Lana. *Lana.*'

Eventually, after what surely was only a few seconds but felt like minutes or even hours, the waves of pleasure receded, leaving them both sticky and sated, their clothing and hair rumpled, their breathing still uneven.

With a self-conscious smile, Lana began to untangle

herself from him, unwinding her leg from around his hip, and then, to his surprise, sliding slowly to the floor.

She shook her head, a trembling laugh escaping her as she slid right down to the ground, still in just her rucked-up underwear, drawing her knees up to her chest, letting her head fall onto them. Christos watched her uneasily, his heart still thudding from the aftershocks of the most incredible orgasm he'd ever had. What if he hadn't handled this right? Had he scared her? Hurt her? He'd never forgive himself, he knew that much.

'Lana...' he began, and then realised he didn't know what to say.

Her head was still resting on her knees. 'I...' she began, and then looked up, her face flushed as she smiled wryly. *'Wow.'*

Christos felt a huge grin spreading over his face.
Success.

'Yeah,' he agreed as he held out a hand to her and helped her up from the floor. 'Wow.'

'I've never...' she began, scrambling to her feet. She reached for her dress, but only to toss it on a chair. He could get used to seeing her in just her bra and pants, and definitely those garters. 'I have *never* felt like that before,' she told him frankly, and warmth bloomed in his chest, along with the pride she'd accused him of last night. But he knew it wasn't the macho pride of another notch on the bedpost; no, it was something deeper and more elemental than that. He'd *reached* her. He'd touched her, in a way nobody else had been able to, and yes, for that, he felt proud. Proud and touched himself.

And, he realised, a little freaked out, but he wasn't going to dwell on that particular emotion now. He just wanted to enjoy this moment, in all of its resounding glory.

'Well,' he told her as he pulled up his trousers with a smile, 'I actually haven't, either.'

'Oh, come on, you have.' She spoke carelessly, but with a sting in the words that he felt.

Not this again.

She stood in front of him, her lithe, golden body resplendent in all that black lace, hands on her hips, her hair tumbled about her shoulders. 'You probably do twice a week, at least.'

'Seriously, Lana?' He didn't want to argue, and certainly not now, but twice a *week*?

'I'm not accusing you of anything,' she replied, even though it sort of felt as if she was. 'Just…let's be realistic. You're good at sex. I mean, own it, Christos. You know your way around a woman.' She smiled and shrugged, and it felt, surprisingly, like a rather brutal brush-off.

This, he realised, was another way she distanced herself, and if he was smart, he would take it, so they could both stick to the terms of their deal. No emotional engagement, but yes, lots of great sex, because, hell, maybe he was good at it. So was she, even if she didn't know it.

This was when he should say, *Why, thank you very much, and let me prove it to you again.*

But the words, so laughing and light, didn't come.

'Actually,' he told her as he tucked his shirt in, his tone more matter-of-fact than wry, 'I may be good at sex, but before tonight I hadn't had it in three years.'

CHAPTER NINE

LANA STARTED TO SMILE, only to see that Christos was utterly serious. She felt the smile slide off her face like a pancake off a plate as she stared at him, incredulous, uncertain, appalled, *hopeful*. The jumble of her emotions felt like too much to process.

'What?' she said finally. 'You're…' She meant to say joking, but at the sight of the almost sombre look on his face, she found she couldn't.

'I'm serious,' he replied in the affable tone he so often used, but she sensed something underneath—an uncertainty, perhaps, or a defensiveness. 'Although admittedly, it wasn't for lack of trying, at least at first.'

She frowned, unsure how she felt about that. 'What is that supposed to mean, exactly?'

He shrugged as he walked into the bedroom, towards the champagne. Lana watched him peel the foil from the cork and realised she was still only in her underwear, and right then it felt a little…exposing. She grabbed the thick, velvety-soft robe off the back of the bathroom door and shrugged into it, the heavy material enveloping her like one of the fur coats from the kids in Narnia.

'Christos?' she prompted when it didn't seem as if he was going to say anything more.

'When we first made our deal,' he explained carefully, his gaze on the bottle of champagne he was opening, 'I thought I'd do exactly what you'd suggested, and have…liaisons. Very discreet, very brief ones. It seemed reasonable, considering our arrangement as well as your own suggestion, and I decided it didn't go against my personal ethics.'

No surprises there, then. Lana folded her arms and waited for more. Christos popped the cork on the champagne and then neatly poured two flutes right to the top, managing to make sure that the fizz didn't overflow.

'Very nicely done,' she murmured, and he gave her a quick, rakish smile before handing her a glass. 'To us,' he said, and Lana clinked glasses.

'To us,' she agreed, although she wondered what aspect of *us* he was referring to. The deal they'd made three years, or three days ago? The incredible sex they'd just had, which she was still reeling from? 'So, you tried to have a…liaison,' she stated after she'd taken a sip of the crisp bubbles, realising she didn't actually like to imagine it in any detail. 'What happened?'

Christos grimaced wryly. 'Well, I won't embarrass myself by going into the specifics, but let's just say it didn't go according to plan.'

'What does that mean?'

His grimaced deepened, although she could tell he was trying to find the humour in it. 'Let's just say I disappointed the lady in question.'

Lana was surprised to find a bubble of laughter rising up in her throat. 'Are you implying what I…think you're implying?'

Christos shrugged, his eyes sparkling over the rim of his glass as he took a sip of his champagne. 'Fortunately, this lady did not take it as a personal insult.'

'I can't believe—'

'I couldn't, either. And I don't intend to find myself in that situation ever again.' His eyes glinted into hers. 'And considering what happened just now, I don't think I will.'

Lana's stomach fizzed as much as the champagne she was drinking. No, she didn't think he would, either. Having Christos want her so much, so obviously, had been the most intoxicating aphrodisiac she'd ever experienced. She'd felt powerful in a way she never had before, powerful and desired. Two things she'd never felt with another man, and especially not Anthony. But she didn't want to think about Anthony now.

'You must have tried again,' she remarked after a moment, her lips pursed. She realised she did not like the thought of it. At all.

Christos shook his head. 'No, trust me, once was enough for that kind of experience.' He gave a not-so-mock shudder. 'In any case, after that… I realised I took my marriage vows more seriously than I'd thought.'

Lana took another sip of champagne, mainly to hide the expression on her face—not that she even knew what it was. She felt extraordinarily touched by his admission, as well as pleased, and also disconcerted. Christos was meant to be the master of no-strings sex and yet he'd abstained for three years because of the vows they'd made, back when they'd barely known each other? There seemed to be a fair amount of emotion in *that*.

'I don't know what to say,' she said at last. 'I never thought… I never expected…'

'I know.' He put his glass down. 'And to be clear, I don't hold you to the same standard, for those three years. Although going into the future is another matter entirely.'

Since he'd been so honest, she felt she had to be, too,

and in truth, to her own surprise, she realised she wanted to be. How novel. How *odd*. 'I'm afraid I'm the winner if you want to play that game, Christos,' she told him with a shaky laugh. 'Because I beat you by a country mile.'

He stilled, his hazel gaze searching hers. 'Oh?'

Lana nodded. 'By quite a few years. Nine, in fact, give or take a few months.' She swallowed hard, toying with the sash of her robe. 'Although I thought you might have guessed that, based on some of my reactions.'

'Well, I suppose I wondered.' He looked down for a moment, his expression thoughtful and maybe even a little sad, and then he glanced up and a smile spread across his face, humour lighting his eyes, giving them a golden sheen. 'What a pair we are, eh? Clearly, we have a lot of lost time to make up for.'

Lana found herself smiling back, suddenly almost dizzy with something that felt like more than relief, closer to joy. 'Clearly we do.'

He closed the space between them in two prowling strides, tugging gently at the sash of her robe, until it came undone, and the robe fell away. His hands slid around her waist, spanning its width and settling there as Lana swayed towards him. Her body was still weak and relaxed from their last bout of lovemaking, but amazingly she felt ready again, and, it seemed, so did he.

'Are you going to take off your clothes this time?' she asked wryly, and his eyebrows lifted.

'Only if you'll do it for me.'

A thrill of wonder—and a little fear—rippled through her. 'I guess I can manage that.' She started to unbutton his shirt, her fingers trembling a little because, as wonderful as this was, she couldn't deny that it felt emotional. Physical intimacy *was* emotional, she realised with a jolt.

How could it not be? She'd known that all along, but she'd tried to deny it—to herself and to Christos. Yet standing here in front of him, she knew she couldn't any longer. She slid her hands along the taut and sculpted muscles of his chest as she parted the folds of his shirt and he shrugged out of it, his eyes now dark with desire, his breath turned uneven once more.

Lana ran a single fingertip along his pectoral muscle and a shudder escaped him. 'You drive me crazy, you know,' he murmured in a husky voice, and she could feel how much he meant it.

'You drive me crazy, too,' she whispered, trailing her fingertip lower, past the ridges of his ribs, to the light sprinkling of hair veeing down below his waistband. Christos sucked in a breath as he wrapped his hand around her own, stilling it.

'I mean it,' he told her in a low voice. 'You really do drive me crazy.' He drew her hand upwards before he cupped her breasts with his hands, flicking his thumbs over her nipples. A shuddery gasp escaped her. 'And I'm glad I drive you crazy, too.'

It felt like a safe sentiment to say, for them both to feel, but Lana knew it wasn't. There was already too much invested in this aspect of their relationship, where they exposed and revealed, not just their bodies, but their very selves. It was too late to remedy that, she knew, and in truth she didn't even want to. Being touched by Christos felt far, far too good. She didn't think she wanted to go without the wonder of it again.

But she *could* keep the emotional side of things confined simply to sex, she decided. They wouldn't talk about their pasts again, they wouldn't share their fears or hurts, their dreams or desires, and they certainly wouldn't ever need or depend on each other in any tangible way.

She'd be able to keep *that* essential part of herself safe still, at least, in a way she hadn't been able to before. Just thinking of Anthony, the sneer that would twist his face when she begged him to listen, to love her... She would never let herself feel so humiliated and exposed again. Ever. No matter what.

'Lana.' Christos framed her face with his hands. 'What are you thinking right now?'

'What?' She glanced up at him, startled, a tremble going through her as he ran his thumb over the fullness of her lower lip.

'You suddenly got a very ferocious look on your face.'

His voice and expression were both so achingly tender that, despite the resolution she'd just made, she found herself blurting, 'I was just thinking how different this is from what I've known before, and how—how it is hard to accept that it truly is different.'

Christos's eyes darkened as he cradled her face so tenderly. 'I won't hurt you,' he said, a promise, a vow, and one she knew he believed he could make.

Lana nodded shakily. 'I know,' she said, compelled to even more honesty. 'Because I won't let you.'

Christos stared at her hard for a long moment, and then he kissed her long and deep, and Lana surrendered herself to it, because that part, at least, was easy.

Because I won't let you.

The words reverberated through Christos as he lost himself in their kiss. What the hell was that supposed to mean? He suspected she'd meant it as reassurance, if not for him then at least for herself, but he hadn't *felt* it that way. It had stung, because if anyone was going to make boundaries, it would be him. Right?

As they fell back on the bed, he told himself to stop thinking about it. He unhooked Lana's bra, drawing it away from her body so her lovely breasts were on full and wondrous display, ready for his touch. There were so many other wonderful things to think about now, after all.

An hour later, they were both sleepily sated, limbs tangled among the sheets, Lana's head resting on Christos's shoulder, her cheek against his chest, which was, he realised, exactly where he wanted her to be. He toyed with the long golden strands of her hair as they both let their breathing settle.

If he'd thought their first encounter had been explosive, their second had been even more so, but in a long and lingering way that had been just as, if not more, satisfying—and emotional.

Yes, emotional. He had to use that word, as wary as he was of it, because he could not deny that what he felt with Lana was different from what he'd felt with any other woman. Every time they came together, he felt as if he were offering a little bit of his soul. He didn't even mean to, but it happened anyway, and he didn't know whether she would accept it or not. Did she even know?

I won't let you.

Lana was clearly going to keep her heart and soul tightly locked away, Christos realised, even as she gave him everything else. And meanwhile he was starting to have the awful, sneaking suspicion that he might not be able to keep from serving his own up on a plate. It was a conundrum, but one that, oddly, wasn't bothering him too much in this moment. He simply felt too happy.

'Do you think we made a baby?' he asked her, and she let out a sleepy laugh.

'*That* would have been quick.'

'But possible.'

'Yes.' She sounded happy too, and he liked that. He liked that a lot.

'Imagine—there might already be a tiny, tiny baby nestled in there.' He slid his hand down to her flat stomach, spreading his fingers wide, feeling a ripple of desire go through him even though he was absolutely spent.

'I don't think it happens that quickly.'

'How long does it take a sperm and egg to do their thing?'

She laughed, a pure, clear sound. 'I don't actually know.'

'Me neither.'

'I could look it up on my phone,' she suggested, and, twisting away from him so he felt the loss, she walked naked to the purse she'd dropped by the door when they'd first arrived and took out her phone. Christos was aching for her to get back into bed with him, but he simply stretched out and acted nonchalant as she walked slowly back towards him, squinting at the screen of her phone.

'It takes up to forty-five minutes for the sperm to reach the egg,' she told him as she scrambled back into bed, and it felt both easy and right to stretch his arm out and draw her back to his chest, her head nestled into his shoulder. She fitted there so very nicely. 'And "up to twenty-four hours for the act of fertilisation to complete",' she read off her phone. 'So not a baby quite yet.'

'Still.'

'"The genetic make-up of the baby is complete at the moment of fertilisation,"' she read, before tossing her phone aside. 'Isn't that *crazy*? As soon as tomorrow there *could* be a tiny, tiny baby, with all its genes and everything, and all it needs to do is grow.'

'A little bit of me, a little bit of you,' Christos said, and she laughed softly, her breath fanning his chest.

'Well, fifty per cent of me, fifty per cent of you.'

'Pedant,' he teased, and she tilted her face up to him, which simply meant he had to kiss her. He'd meant to make it something between a brush and a peck, but it ended up being long and lingering instead, and his hand tightened on her shoulder as hers drifted temptingly lower.

'Lana,' he growled, and she looked at him innocently.

'What?'

'You know what,' he said as her hand went even lower and even though he'd thought he didn't have it in him for another round, he now found that he did.

'Just in case the first two times didn't take,' Lana whispered, and then her lips followed the path of her hands, and Christos found himself closing his eyes as he surrendered to the bliss.

They finished the champagne, ate lobster salad and crusty rolls and sweet, succulent strawberries dipped in chocolate, while sitting naked among the pillows and sheets, careless of crumbs. Christos couldn't remember the last time he'd felt so relaxed, so at ease—with himself, with the woman beside him, with the whole world.

This marriage thing, he decided, had been a *very* good idea. Lana seemed to think so too, even if she hadn't said as much. He'd never seen her so relaxed, either—her hair loose and wavy about her shoulders, her limbs splayed carelessly as she popped a strawberry into her mouth, juice dripping down her chin.

He liked her like this, he realised. Seeing her now, naked in bed, he realised just how tightly held and tense she was, in her normal self. From her stilettos to the gleaming sheet of her hair—it had all been armour, a way for her to face the world down, to conquer it.

But if it was armour, Christos thought with a sudden lurch of understanding, then there was something that needed protecting underneath, and he'd gone into this marriage not wanting there to be. Lana had already showed him some of her vulnerabilities—reluctantly, yes, but they were clearly there. He couldn't pretend, even to himself, that she was nothing more than the image she presented to the world—glossy, self-assured and diamond-hard.

'I think I could sleep for about twelve hours,' Lana said, stretching languorously, making Christos's libido give yet another pulse as she arched her back, lamplight dancing over her golden skin. 'It's a good thing my first meeting isn't till twelve tomorrow.' She gave him a cat-like smile before she rose from the bed and began clearing the dishes away.

After a second's pause, Christos started to help, even though his mind was still spinning. The sleepy, contented satiation he'd been experiencing all evening was stealing away, leaving cold hard truth in its wake.

Their marriage might be a good idea—but it was already also very complicated. And if he wanted to keep his head—and heart—intact, then he needed to think clearly about how he handled himself in the future. Lana seemed to have got the memo; hell, she'd written it. So he definitely needed to get on board.

He was still thinking that way as they got ready for bed a little while later; Lana had changed into the cof-

fee-coloured silk nightgown she'd mentioned earlier, and
that Christos already wanted to slide off her; he liked her
naked. But she had, it seemed, reverted to her usual self,
a stickler for protocol, and their honeymoon, brief as it
was, seemed to be over.

'Goodnight,' she said, and kissed his cheek. They
might as well have been married for fifty years.

Christos let out a growl, a purely instinctive sound,
and then wrapped his hand around the back of her head
so he could kiss her goodnight the way he wanted to—
long and slow and deep.

'Goodnight,' he said, and she looked shaken for a second, before she smiled and turned out the light.

Christos lay on his back, one hand braced behind his
head. As fatigued as he was from all their enjoyable ex-
ertions, sleep felt as if it would be a very long time coming. His feelings—yes, feelings—were a jumbled mess,
and he wanted to sort them out.

Ever since he'd disappointed not just his mother, but
all three of his sisters, he'd avoided any emotion, knowing he couldn't deal with it because he'd just let people
down as he had before, in the worst possible way.

He didn't think he'd ever forget the agonised look on
his dying mother's face. *'Please, Christos. Let me see
you. Let me hug you and say goodbye to you, just one
last time.'*

He'd walked away without a word. What must she
have thought of him? Felt in that agonising moment?
He'd never seen her again; she'd died several hours later.
There were a lot of things he hadn't had a chance to say.

I'm sorry. I miss you. I love you.

And that knowledge was like a wound inside him, a
festering cancer that would never, ever heal. The safest

way he'd discovered of dealing with it was never giving himself an opportunity to need to say those kinds of words again. Never get close enough to someone that they'd be expected to be said. And never letting anyone down when he couldn't say them.

He twisted to look at Lana, who had already fallen asleep, her hair spread out on the pillow, her breathing deep and even. She looked like an elegant angel.

He didn't want to let her down, he thought heavily, most of all, but it might be that he wouldn't be able to keep himself from it…just like before.

CHAPTER TEN

'So, YOU NEED to be someone different.'

Her hands folded on the desk in front of her, Lana gazed at the geeky young tech wizard who was in her office on Albert's recommendation. Thirtysomething, awkward and shy, pushing his glasses up with his forefinger, with a rather endearing stammer and a nervous blink. He'd developed an app that was poised to become huge, and he needed the image to go with it.

'Yeah, that's the plan.' The man, Jack Philips, gave her a quick, uncertain smile. 'Albert said you specialise in helping people make their mark.'

'Well, that's pretty much the point of PR,' she replied with a smile. 'Your company is new, but it's already generating some serious buzz. We can work with that, especially with a digital campaign. A personal element also works—maybe a spotlight feature in one of the newspaper's cultural supplements to highlight who you are?'

'Yeah, that might not work out so well,' Jack said with a grimace. 'My life is pretty boring.'

'Well, we can make it more interesting.' That was what she did—help people to shape their pasts, their whole selves, to be what the world wanted. It was what she'd done for herself, aged twenty-two, after she'd left Anthony and the firm where she'd interned, determined to be different, better, stronger. She knew she could do it for this guy.

He frowned, not understanding. 'How would we make it more interesting?'

'It's all in the information you reveal, the particular slant you find,' she explained.

'I grew up in New Jersey, the third son of a housewife and an insurance salesman,' he said, raising his eyebrows. 'How can you make that more interesting?'

'I can make anything more interesting,' Lana promised him. She loved this part of her job—sculpting and shaping a person's public profile to maximum effect. She didn't deceive or even stretch the truth; she was just judiciously sparing with what details she shared, very precise with the angle she allowed to be used. If she managed to snag him a feature in one of the country's major newspapers, she would be very careful indeed with how he was presented.

'Tech *wunderkinder* are a dime a dozen,' she informed him. 'So, we need to find another angle. Something a little mysterious, enigmatic, maybe.'

He shook his head. 'But I'm really not enigmatic.'

She laughed. 'You will be. Trust me, Jack. I can handle this. I'll get back to you in a couple of days with some initial thoughts and ideas.'

Still looking dubious, he murmured his thanks and rose from in front of her desk. When he'd left her office, Lana spun towards the window to gaze unseeingly down at the view of Rockefeller Plaza. She and Christos had been enjoying their new arrangements for almost two weeks. Two weeks tomorrow, in fact, which was why her stomach was tightening with both anticipation and nerves. If, miraculously, she was pregnant on the first try—well, their *many* tries—then she could potentially take a pregnancy test tomorrow. There were a few tests out there that could be taken even sooner, but Lana hadn't wanted to deal with the painful disappointment of a false negative.

When she and Christos had talked about even the possibility of a baby, that little bundle of cells, she'd felt such an ache of longing, it had nearly made her breathless. She wanted this. She wanted it even more now that she knew what married life—*real* married life—with Christos was like.

The last two weeks had, frankly, been incredible. While her days had remained busy with work, her nights had been spent in bed with Christos, discovering delights she had never known existed, learning his body as well as her own in a new and entirely delightful way.

But it wasn't just those sex-soaked nights, Lana knew. It was everything else, too. It was evenings spent on the sofa, answering emails, her feet in Christos's lap. It was the cup of coffee he handed her when she came downstairs in a rush. It was stepping out of the shower and seeing him wink at her in the mirror or chatting about their workdays over glasses of chilled Chardonnay.

It wasn't, however, anything more than that. It *wasn't* heartfelt conversations, or sharing intimate personal revelations, or saying anything remotely emotional. Yes, Lana could acknowledge that what they did in bed *felt* emotional, or at least intimate. She felt more connected to Christos than to any other human being, ever. But as long as that sense of exposure, a revealing and acceptance of self, stayed in the bedroom, she was fine. *Fine.*

And really, it was all good. She was grateful to Christos for showing her how things could be between a man and a woman when it came to physical intimacy, because when she thought of how Anthony had treated that aspect of a relationship…well, everything in her curdled and cringed with guilt and shame. Sex, for him, had been a way to both dominate and humiliate her. With Christos it had been a shared experience of pleasure, and exploration, and joy.

Yes, she was very grateful to him for teaching her that, over and over again. But not, she thought, of teaching or showing her anything else. Because while she was glad she'd developed in that area, she still wasn't willing to risk her heart. To love someone, to let them in that much, give them the power, not just to humiliate her, as Anthony had done, but to *hurt* her.

Already she sensed Christos could have the power to do that, if she let him, which was why she was standing by her word that she wouldn't. And as long as she held to that line, she'd be fine. Their marriage would be great.

Lana let out a long, slow breath, a smile curving her lips as she turned from the window to get ready for her next meeting.

By six o'clock that evening, she was heading back home with a spring in her step. Amazing how she looked forward to heading back to the house that had always felt, while a haven, an empty one. She'd always liked how she'd been able to let her hair down—literally—and be herself in her own space, but she was starting to realise how much better it was to do that in the company of another person.

Having Christos see and accept her—and even find her sexy and beautiful—in her sweats was far better than simply lounging around in them by herself. It was a discovery that had the power to knock her for six, if she let it. She chose not to. She was gliding on the surface of things, smooth and easy, and she suspected Christos was, too. He certainly hadn't attempted to plumb any emotional depths, far from it. This marriage, as it currently was, suited them both, which was exactly what she wanted. Everything was absolutely great.

So why, sometimes, when she let herself, did she feel a twinge of unease, a flicker of restlessness? Lana chose not to dwell on it. Gift horses and all that. She just wanted to enjoy what so far had been wonderful…and not think any further than that.

'Hello, beautiful.' Christos greeted her at the door with a kiss and a smile; he had made himself at home in her brownstone, which Lana found she liked. He'd only brought his clothes, laptop, and a few books, and yet even so it was nice to see his things scattered around. She'd asked him if he'd minded leaving his loft apartment in Soho—a soaring space of metalwork and glass—and he'd shrugged and said they could hardly raise a family in two separate abodes.

Well, they could, Lana knew, but it wasn't the way they were choosing to do it. Sometimes she wondered if they were a little crazy, to live this normal-seeming life, without any of the emotional attachments. What if it all blew up in their faces?

'Hello,' she replied, and kicked off her usual stilettos with a groan of satisfaction. 'Good day at work?'

'Fair. Made a million dollars.'

It was a joke they'd shared from way back when, when they'd met infrequently, and Lana had started by asking him that question.

'Only a million?' she quipped, and he shrugged.

'It was a slow day.'

She was on her way to the kitchen when she stopped and saw the serious, expectant look on his face. Her stomach felt as if it were curling in on itself. 'What is it?' she asked uncertainly.

'I bought something for you. Technically, for us, but, you know.'

'No, I don't.' It was amazing how quickly her loose-limbed relaxation could turn into tension, to fear. How quickly she expected everything to start to go wrong. 'What are you talking about?'

'This,' Christos said, and withdrew a slim rectangular box from the pocket of his suit jacket.

Lana stared at in uncomprehendingly for a few seconds before she clocked what it was.

A pregnancy test.

Christos watched the colour drain from Lana's face and wondered if he'd just made a big mistake. It was only a test, that was all, but she was looking at him as if he were trying to hand her a snake.

'Lana?'

'It's not even been two weeks yet.'

Was that all that was bothering her? 'Two weeks from tomorrow, but the test is good from ten days after ovulation. I even read the box.' If he was attempting to raise a smile, he failed. She was staring wide-eyed at the box, her face still pale.

'You really want this,' she stated quietly, almost to herself.

Christos felt a frisson of unease, almost annoyance. 'We both want this, Lana. At least I thought we did.' He blew out a breath. 'I was just trying to be helpful.'

She glanced up at his face, a bit of colour coming back to her cheeks. 'I know. I'm sorry. It just threw me. I didn't realise you were counting the days.'

Christos frowned. He wouldn't have said he was counting the days, not *exactly*, but… 'Is there a reason I shouldn't have been?'

'No.' But she sounded unsure, and he didn't know why. He felt as if they'd stepped onto shaky ground without him having realised they'd even moved. It was just a pregnancy test, a matter of expediency, to make sure. Wasn't it?

Because he knew once she took that test, there was a chance its result could change everything. 'You don't have to take it now,' he said, although that had been his hope. 'Just keep it for…whenever.'

She glanced up at him, humour lightening her eyes to the colour of sunlight dancing on the sea. 'Really? You're willing to be that patient?'

He smiled back, relief flooding through him. 'Well…'

'I'll do it now, Christos.' She took the box from him. 'I was just freaked out for a second, because…this is real, isn't it?'

'You'll only know when you take the test.'

She shook her head. 'I don't mean that. Whether it's positive or negative this time…this is the choice we've made. The road we've taken.'

He hesitated, because he knew what she meant, and the import she was giving this moment forced him to give it the same. This wasn't just real, it was serious. Somehow, over the last two weeks, he'd been having so much fun that he'd forgotten that this was all for keeps, that there were lives involved, if not hearts. And if Lana really was pregnant with their child...well, the stakes would then be stratospheric.

He might not only be in danger of letting her down, but of letting their *child* down. How had he not considered this properly before? Realised the inherent danger?

Because, he knew, he hadn't wanted to. And he still wanted a baby. A wife. A *family*. He just didn't want to blow it...with any of those people.

'All right,' Lana said with a small, wry smile, although he could tell she was nervous, 'I'll see you in about three minutes.' And she slipped away from him to the bathroom off the hall.

Christos paced the living room, amazed at how three minutes could feel so long. He was so not good at these crucial moments. If Lana came out and she wasn't pregnant, she might be upset. And he wasn't so good at comforting people.

'Christos, please. Come home. I need you.'

He pictured his sister's tearstained face on the screen of his laptop, and how he'd ended the call, unable to cope with her grief, her need. What kind of unfeeling monster was he? And when he thought of what had happened next... Kristina's taut voice on the call, the news that his baby sister was being rushed to the hospital... Christos never wanted to feel that utter hollowing out of his insides, the realisation of just how terribly he had failed someone he loved. His sister had forgiven him; at least she'd said she had. But he'd never forgiven himself.

But he'd do better now, he promised himself. He would. And if Lana *was* pregnant...

His heart flipped over, although whether in hope or sheer terror Christos wasn't quite sure. He really should have thought all this through a lot more, except...

He knew he wouldn't have changed a thing.

The last two weeks had really been that amazing—and not just the nights, which certainly had been mind-blowing and heaven-sent. But the days too, the little moments. When he woke up and Lana was still snuggled in his arms, soft and warm. When he was working and a sudden text popped up, with a funny gif or link from her, making him smile because her sense of humour, although hidden, rivalled his own. When she plopped her feet in his lap with a knowing, shamefaced grin, and he laughingly started to rub her feet.

There was so much he was enjoying about this marriage, and a baby would only make it better. Right?

The door to the bathroom opened, and Christos whirled around. He realised he didn't actually know what he wanted the test result to be—a baby would be great, yes, but having more time together first would be good, too. And he wasn't sure how Lana would feel about it, either. This had all happened so fast, after all; a month ago she hadn't even known she'd been in menopause. She hadn't even thought she'd wanted a baby.

If she wasn't pregnant, maybe it would be better for them both. Give them a little time to think, to breathe, to be…

'Christos?' Her voice was soft, tentative. She held the test stick in her hand, but he couldn't see its little window—one line or two?

'Did you find out?' Of course she had, but he couldn't tell based on her expression. She looked uncertain, a little afraid, maybe hopeful…

'Is it…?'

'Positive.' She showed him the stick and he saw two pale pink lines. 'I'm pregnant.'

CHAPTER ELEVEN

'I DON'T KNOW about this.'

'It looks great, trust me.' Lana gave Jack Philips a breezily reassuring smile as he dubiously regarded his reflection in the full-length mirror in one of her office's conference rooms. He was trying on different suits for the feature interview she'd bagged him with a major lifestyle magazine. It was a coup for him as well as her, and now he just needed to present the right image—confident, purposeful, assured. The streamlined suit of royal-blue silk was perfect, even if Jack was having his doubts. The glossy image she'd prepared for him was, Lana knew, hard for a fairly shy, geeky guy to step into, but she was confident he could do it…with her help.

Hadn't she done the same thing for herself, when she was just twenty-one, on her own, dirt poor and desperate, on a mission to turn herself into someone glossy and polished and assured? After Anthony had finished with her two years later, she'd been determined to turn herself into the kind of woman who couldn't be hurt, who would stride the world and crush men beneath her heel. She'd wanted to be glossy and hard, distant and strong, and she'd done it. She'd changed herself, at least on the outside if not the inside, because you never could fully escape your past. Still, with the outside she'd succeeded, in spades. So could Jack Philips.

'So,' she asked, her hands on her hips, her eyebrows raised in expectation as she smiled at him. 'What do you think? Does it work?'

'If you say so,' he finally said with a smile. 'Although this isn't something I would normally ever wear.'

'I know.' If he'd been in charge, he'd have shown up to a very important interview in a ragged T-shirt and dirty jeans. But that was why he—and countless others—hired her. To perfect their image, to *create* it, just as she'd done for herself.

Once, that had given Lana a huge sense of satisfaction, of meaning. She knew full well how the longing to be someone different could take over your life, your heart. Only lately, she felt a flicker of—not unease, no, not quite that, but *something*. She was beginning to wonder if she really wanted to change people into something else. If life was really all about the image.

These doubts had started worrying at her ever since Christos had come into her life, her bed, and especially since she'd found out she was pregnant just over a month ago. She'd gone into both those things assuming they wouldn't change who she was, how she acted, what she believed—and yet she was realising more and more how wrong-headed that was. How wrong-hearted. Of course such monumental things would change her. They would have to.

But as for Jack…all they were talking about was a suit.

'So, you're definitely happy with it?' she confirmed, and he nodded, not looking entirely happy but she was pretty sure he could be convinced. The interview wasn't for a few weeks, after all.

After finishing their meeting, Lana went back to her own office, grateful for the mug of ginger tea Michelle had left on her desk. Michelle was the only person besides Christos whom she'd told about her pregnancy; it had been hard to hide, anyway, when the morning sickness had started ten days ago. Michelle had been understanding, not batting an eyelid when Lana had to rapidly excuse herself from a meeting or had a fifteen-minute catnap at her desk.

Christos had been understanding too, and so very sweet. He was always bringing home little treats—saltine crackers from her childhood after she'd mentioned a craving; comfy socks; bubble bath. Anything to make her adjustment to pregnancy easier.

She couldn't fault him at all, Lana thought, and yet... *And yet.*

That flicker of unease she'd been doing her best to ignore burned a little higher inside her. It had started when she'd first told Christos she was pregnant. She'd seen how shocked he'd looked, and that hadn't bothered her, because, heaven knew, she'd been shocked herself. She didn't think either of them had been prepared for how quickly she'd become pregnant, especially considering her condition.

He'd hugged her then, and kissed her, and she would have thought everything was absolutely fine, except for the invisible, paper-thin wall that had gone up between them. Lana could not point to a single thing or even a single moment when she'd seen and recognised that wall. She had no evidence, no reason, *and yet.* And yet. She knew it was there. She *felt* it.

It was in the tiny pause Christos sometimes took before he spoke. It was in the way he smiled at her, his eyes crinkling at the corners the way they always did, but she felt as if he were looking at something else, or maybe even inward. It was in the way he took her into his arms, the way he cherished her body, yet still, somehow, holding some essential part of himself back, so she was left completely and wonderfully sated, and yet still somehow feeling empty, wanting more.

She kept telling herself she was being ridiculous, over-sensitive and maybe even delusional, and then she'd see him and feel it again, and knew she wasn't. But maybe it wasn't Christos who had changed; it was herself. She was aware of something she hadn't been before, because this pregnancy had changed her, along with being with Christos in this new way. Maybe this was the way Christos had always acted with her and she hadn't known, wouldn't have been bothered if she had known, because that was how she'd been operating, too.

Hold yourself back. Keep your heart, that essential part of yourself, back, so you won't get hurt, give someone the power to hurt you.

That had certainly become her MO since Anthony. Anthony, whom she'd felt as if she'd given everything to, even as she now wondered whether she'd truly loved him at all. She'd believed she had, certainly, and she'd certainly let him hurt her. She'd been so dazzled by the advertising exec ten years her senior who had sought her out, seemed to make her the centre of his world, wined and dined her, a girl from the sticks who had never known glamour or attention or interest. Never mind that he'd humiliated her more times than she could count— mocking her at her most exposed and vulnerable, complaining about her performance in bed, telling her she could never please a man. Studying her like a specimen and then squashing her like a bug. That was what she'd thought love was, but now she knew it wasn't. It wasn't anything like it.

But was this?

The question, over the last few weeks, had become more insistent even as she'd done her best to ignore it. She ignored it now as she got ready to go home, looking forward to a weekend of relaxing with Christos. It was so much simpler to focus on what they did together than how they did—or didn't—feel. Because the truth was, whether it was love or not—and really, love was just a word—Lana was starting to fear that she cared more for Christos than he did for her. *That* was what she was feeling…and she didn't like it, not one bit.

She arrived home just after six, surprised to find Christos had already arrived and changed into casual clothes— chinos and an open-necked shirt in a pale green that made his eyes glint like jade. He was in the kitchen, perusing the cupboards with a frown, when she came through the front door.

'I was thinking of cooking you something,' he told her as she came up the stairs, 'but I realised I'd have no idea what you'd be in the mood for.'

'*I* don't know what I'm in the mood for,' Lana replied with a smile. She wasn't even joking. Since the morning sickness had hit, her food cravings changed by the hour, if not the minute, and sometimes she couldn't manage anything at all. Her OB had told her the symptoms should ease soon, but that morning sickness could be a good sign that the baby was healthy and growing. She'd have her first ultrasound in just under a month, and already she couldn't wait.

'Shall I just order something in?' Christos asked, opening the drawer where they kept all the takeaway menus. He wasn't quite looking at her, hadn't actually looked at her properly since she'd come home, and Lana felt it—but not enough to call him on it. She wouldn't know what to say, and the truth was she wasn't sure she wanted to hear his response.

'Sure, let's order something in,' she said. 'I'll just go change.'

'Before you do…' Christos's voice held a certain gravitas that she hadn't heard in a long while, and Lana stilled, her heart already starting to thump. Was this the moment he'd tell her that he'd changed his mind, that he didn't want to do this marriage and baby thing any more? She was braced for it, she realised, expecting it even, ready and yet not ready at all.

'Yes?' she asked, hoping her voice sounded light, mildly inquiring.

'One of my sisters has reached out to me,' Christos told her after one of those tiny pauses. 'I haven't told her or any of my family about the pregnancy yet, but it made me realise that I probably should. And that maybe you should meet them. We could go some time in the next few weeks, if you're amenable. We won't see them that often,' he continued rather hurriedly, 'and in fact, I rarely see them as it is. But…considering they'll be this baby's relatives, well.' He shrugged, his gaze sliding away from hers. Again. 'I want our child to know his or her family.'

'So do I,' Lana replied quietly. Especially as she didn't have any family on her side—never having known her father and her mother dead. No siblings, no grandparents, none of that rambunctious and loving extended family that so many people took for granted, Christos, perhaps, included. 'I'd love to meet them, Christos.'

He let out a breath and nodded slowly, almost in resignation. He didn't look as if he was enjoying the prospect of such a meeting, far from it. He looked like a man who had just been told the date of his execution. Why?

She couldn't, Lana knew, ask, although she wished she could. She wished they had that kind of relationship, that kind of trust, but they didn't, and that much had been clear in the last month. They'd had lots of lovely evenings relaxing together, and even lovelier nights in bed. They'd had long, lazy brunches at restaurants in the city, and long, lazy walks through Central Park in the hazy heat of summer. They'd had enjoyable conversations about work, and life in the city, and had exchanged different sections of the newspapers, chatting about what they'd read. They'd shared so much, and yet in moments like this it felt like nothing at all, because they had not shared their hearts. They'd both made sure not to.

Lana had no idea what her husband was truly thinking or feeling in this moment, and she knew she couldn't ask him, wouldn't dare to. That was the agreement they'd made, after all, right at the beginning. No emotion. No soul-baring. No attachment and certainly no love. It wasn't Christos's fault that somehow, against her own better judgment, she was starting to change her mind. Her heart.

It wasn't his fault at all, and she needed to get herself in line *pronto*, because falling in love with someone who had no interest in loving her was definitely *not* on her agenda…and never would be.

'Be back in a few minutes,' she told him lightly, and walked back towards their shared bedroom. Whatever was going on with Christos and his family, she wouldn't ask about it, Lana promised herself. She wouldn't ask about anything, and she'd stop this pointless examination of her own feelings because she didn't *want* to know how she felt—and she certainly didn't want to feel it.

Christos stared out at the road stretching towards the horizon, his gaze on the hazy blue summer sky, his jaw tight. He rolled back his shoulders, which were also tight. He and Lana were driving to his father's house on Long Island, where his three sisters and his father would be joining them. He hadn't seen his father or Kristina, Sophia, and Thalia in longer than he cared to remember. More than months, probably years. He'd let time drift by without ever going home, even though it was only an hour and a half away. It had just always been easier to stay away. To not have to look in his sisters' eyes and see their disappointment, never mind how his father could never even look at him in the eye at all. Everyone tried to hide it, of course, to pretend it wasn't there, but he knew all the same. He *felt* it.

Not that he intended on telling Lana any of that. He'd enjoyed these last few months with her, in large part because they *hadn't* got into all that stuff. They'd skimmed the surface of their emotions while enjoying the pleasure of each other's company—and bodies. The perfect arrangement, exactly what he wanted, so he really had no idea why he was feeling so restless and antsy now.

Probably because he was going back home, a place that had filled him with only dread and sorrow ever since his mother had died twenty years ago and he'd failed her in the worst way possible.

'Do you know,' Lana said into the silence, and he could

tell by her tone she was trying to sound light, even though she wasn't feeling it, 'I don't know anything about your family? That seems strange, now.'

'Why should it seem strange?' he returned, his tone borderline surly. What was *wrong* with him? 'That's how we both agreed it would be. Should be. I don't know your family, either.'

She was quiet for her moment, and when Christos risked a sideways glance, he saw how thoughtful she looked, how opaque her eyes.

'That's true,' she said finally. 'I know your mother died when you were young, and you knew I grew up without a father.' Something he never had asked about, for a *reason*. 'And that's all we know about each other's families.'

He stayed silent, deciding it was less risky than offering some commentary on her observation, which was making him feel uncomfortable for all sorts of complicated reasons.

'Are you willing,' she asked after another frozen pause, 'to at least tell me their names?'

Guilt flashed through him, chased by irritation. She was making him sound as if he'd been unreasonable, and he hadn't been. He'd simply held to their original agreement. She wasn't going back on it, was she? The possibility filled him with both dread and something else he couldn't name.

'Of course I'll tell you their names,' he replied as mildly as he could. 'I have three younger sisters—Kristina is the oldest, then Sophia, then Thalia.'

'Three sisters! I think you might have told me that before, actually,' she replied musingly. 'When we first met. But I must have forgotten.' He shrugged. Sometimes he tried to forget too, but he never did.

'What are they like?'

What were they *like*? Christos felt his throat going tight. Damn it, he did not want to answer these kinds of questions. But it wasn't particularly unreasonable, he told himself, for Lana to ask them. It wasn't even emotional. It was just that he was feeling pretty raw, now that he was going home, and now that Lana was carrying his own child.

When she'd first told him she was pregnant—a mere three weeks after her initial proposal!—he'd been thrilled. For a millisecond. Following that, he'd been completely terrified, and tried to hide it ever since.

What on earth had made him think he could have a kid without screwing it up? Disappointing and even failing him or her, the way he had his own family? Not that he ever wanted to explain any of that to Lana. And so, he'd been living in this state of paralysis—enjoying their time together, as they had been before she'd taken that test, trying to be as thoughtful and considerate as he could be, without it actually costing him anything. Without thinking about the future.

'What are they like?' he repeated, mainly to stall for time. He wasn't used to talking about his family, or even thinking about them, not if he could help it. 'Kristina is a busybody, if a well-meaning one. That's what she'd call herself, anyway. Always wanting to know about you, always willing to listen.' Even when he refused to talk. 'She'll ask you a million questions the minute you arrive, so consider this fair warning.'

'I will,' Lana replied, a smile in her voice.

Against all odds and expectations, Christos found himself relaxing. A little.

'Sophia is completely different. She's very focused

and direct, but she can also be very private.' After their mother had died, he and Sophia had been similar in their silent grief, unable to connect with anyone, shutting down rather than engaging with the people who loved them most.

'And Thalia?'

'Thalia…' The name escaped him on a sigh. The baby of the family, full of laughter and light…until she hadn't been. And Christos hadn't been there for her, even though she'd asked him. *Begged* him. He'd refused her…with disastrous consequences. 'She's…emotional,' he said at last, and he saw Lana raise her eyebrows. 'When she's happy, she's buzzing and the best to be around, and when she's not…' He trailed off, remembering when she most certainly had not been.

'Help me, Christos.'

'I can't.'

'Christos?' Lana asked softly, and he shook his head to expel the memory.

'That's it.'

'What about your father?'

His father. Christos would have closed his eyes if he hadn't been driving. 'My father loved my mother very much,' he said after a moment. 'And when she died, it was like the life had gone out of him. The…essence.'

'I depend on you, Christos. You're the man of the family now. You have to take care of your sisters.'

Except he hadn't.

'That must have been very hard,' Lana said quietly.

'Yes.' The word was quiet, but Christos heard how heartfelt he sounded. It hadn't been hard; it had been near impossible. Agony, every day, and then worse after, until he'd finally left them all behind, tried to find some freedom, some peace, and thought he hadn't, fooled himself, really, because he knew he never had. Not if he was feeling this way now.

To his surprise, Lana reached over and rested her hand on his thigh, a gesture of comfort, one he hadn't expected. Although they'd certainly been affectionate—and more—with each other in the last few months, they hadn't offered each other *comfort*. Not like this—something quiet and tender and heartfelt.

He had an urge to shrug her hand off, tell her it wasn't needed, and just as strong an urge to grab hold of it and press it to his cheek. He did neither. He just kept driving, his jaw tight, his gaze on the road.

An hour later they were pulling up to the sprawling colonial in one of Brookhaven's gracious streets, the only home he'd known before he'd moved to New York. His father, Niko Diakos, had started life in a tenement on the Lower East Side, worked his way up in the banking business until middle management had allowed him the trappings of respectability. He'd never made the millions Christos had, first with the apps he'd developed and then with more advanced technological investments, but he'd had a solid business, a solid life.

Until his beloved wife Marina had died. Even now, as Christos parked in the driveway, he was picturing the day his mother's body was taken from the house—a sheet to cover her, so Christos hadn't been able to see her face. His father weeping, his sisters huddled together on the stairs. In his memory, that day was dark and grey and stormy, but he knew in reality it had been a sunny summer's day much like this one. Funny, how he couldn't remember the sun shining. Only the terrible, vast numbness he'd felt inside, as if a frozen tundra had claimed him, covered him in snow and ice.

'Christos…should we go in?'

Christos glanced at Lana, who was looking troubled and all too sympathetic, as if she knew how painful these memories were, how hard he tried never to think about them. But she didn't know, he reminded himself, because he'd never told her…and he never would.

'Yes.' He forced the corners of his mouth up in something like a smile. 'Let's go.'

CHAPTER TWELVE

LANA HAD NO idea what to expect as she walked into the foyer of Christos's family home. Based on what he'd said, and really, what he hadn't said, she'd been braced for a frosty welcome, or at least a formal one. Christos clearly had become alienated from his family—after his mother's death? Or later? And why?

What Lana hadn't expected was for one of his sisters to bustle right up to her, her face lit up with a smile, place her hands on either side of her face and give Lana a smacking kiss on each cheek before enveloping her in a bear hug.

Lana submitted to the hug for a second, completely frozen, utterly shocked, before she managed to put her arms around the unknown sister, although she was already suspecting it was Kristina.

'Finally, he brings you!' Kristina exclaimed. She had a strong Long Island accent and was short and round and full of good humour. Lana liked her instantly. Kristina turned to Christos and shook her finger at him. 'What on earth were you hiding her for? She's gorgeous.'

'I wasn't hiding her,' Christos replied mildly. He seemed like his usual laid-back self, his smile wry, his stance relaxed, but Lana sensed some dark emotion pulsing underneath. Was Christos's image—that rueful, smiling, joking entrepreneur—as much of a façade as hers was, that cool, glossy remote persona she donned like armour? Had they both been pretending all along?

It was a surprising and, she realised, actually welcome thought. She wanted there to be more to Christos in the same way there was more to her—and she wanted them to know that about each other.

Now *that* was not an entirely welcome thought. At least, it was a scary one. She'd never wanted to be known before. She'd made sure she wouldn't be. And yet here she was, thinking she wanted to be known—and more— by Christos?

'Come into the kitchen,' Kristina said, taking her by the hand. 'We've got food—so much food!—and coffee. I want to hear all about you. Every single thing.'

Well, Lana thought wryly as she let herself be led into the heart of the house, if she wasn't going to be known by Christos, she certainly was by his sister.

The rest of his sisters were waiting in the kitchen, Sophia dressed in a tailored blouse and trousers, her smile warm but cautious, while Thalia—because it had to be Thalia—catapulted across the room in a cloud of dark hair and threw her arms around Christos with a squeal.

Christos had to take a step back for balance as he hugged his sisters back. Lana couldn't see his face, but she had the sense he hadn't been expecting this.

'Why haven't you come home before now?' Thalia exclaimed, her face pressed into his shoulder. She was small and slender, dressed in a pair of oversized dungarees and a T-shirt. 'It's been years, Christos. *Years.*'

'I've been busy,' he replied as he released Thalia. 'But I'm sorry. I should have come home sooner.'

'Yes, you should have.' She wagged a finger at him,

seeming playful, but Lana could tell how hurt she was by his absence; her large green eyes were glassy, and her lower lip trembled. She couldn't be much more than twenty, Lana thought, much younger than she'd expected. Kristina and Sophia both looked to be in their early thirties.

'Ah, the prodigal son returns.' A man stepped into the room, looking so much like Christos that Lana thought she knew what her husband would look like in thirty years. He had the same long, lanky frame, although a little less muscular, and his shoulders were slightly stooped. His head of thick, wavy hair was liberally peppered with grey, and there were deep creases by his hazel eyes and from nose to mouth. He smiled at Christos, and Christos gave a jerky nod back, not quite looking at him. The older man's welcoming smile drooped along with his shoulders, and then he straightened and turned to Lana with another warm smile.

'I've been so looking forward to meeting you.'

Lana glanced at Christos, because she realised she'd never asked him if he'd told his family about their original arrangement, or their newer one. What did they know about the state of Christos's marriage?

'And I've been looking forward to meeting you,' she replied, shaking his hand. 'All of you. Christos has told me about you, so I think I know who you all are. Kristina?' She glanced at the first sister she'd met, who laughed and clapped her hands. 'And Sophia?' Sophia smiled and nodded. 'And Thalia!'

Thalia nodded, without the smile, and Lana felt a flicker of trepidation. The young woman was looking as if she did not welcome her entry into her brother's life.

'Come sit down, sit down,' Kristina said. 'And tell us

everything. To think, Christos has been married to you for three whole years and never brought you home.'

So, they did know, Lana realised, but how much?

'We're here now,' Christos said, and his tone was just short of brusque, although it didn't seem to put off Kristina.

'So you are, so you are,' she agreed as they all sat down in the adjoining family room, which was comfortable and welcoming, scattered with sofas of cream leather. 'And we're very glad of it. We've been so curious about the woman who managed to get you to the altar, when there hasn't been another who has been able to get you to a third date!' Lana smiled a little at that, and Kristina nodded knowingly. 'He doesn't tell us himself, of course, but Thalia reads all the articles about him in the gossip or business magazines. She even has a scrapbook!'

Which seemed slightly obsessive, Lana thought, but she supposed understandable, especially if Christos never came home...and why not? Right now, his absence from their lives felt like a mystery. His family was showing nothing but love for him, and meanwhile he was sitting on the sofa next to her, looking relaxed, yes, but she could feel the tension emanating from him like a force field. He did not want to be here, she realised. At all. And she had no idea why.

She didn't get any more clues to the answer to that question as they sat and chatted for the next hour, while Kristina plied them with coffee and Greek pastries. She learned that Kristina lived nearby and ran her own bakery in Brookhaven, while Sophia worked remotely for a graphic design company and had a town house in Long Island City, which shocked Lana, because it was only a twenty-minute subway ride from where she and Christos lived. Why had they never had Sophia over? Why had Christos never met up with her in Manhattan?

Thalia, she learned, lived at home with her father Niko, who had retired from banking ten years ago. She was studying online for a degree in art, but Lana got the sense that she wasn't very interested in her studies. She was twenty-two but she seemed younger, losing interest in the conversation, interrupting people, teasing Christos and then pouting if he didn't reply right away. Lana found her somewhat exhausting, although she tried not to show it. Christos humoured her, but she could tell he found it hard.

Something about Thalia caused him pain, she realised; she sensed it, with an instinct she hadn't possessed until recently. She used to never know what Christos was thinking; now she sensed what he was feeling…but she still didn't understand why.

'She's lovely, Christos.'

Christos stiffened as he turned around from the deck railing where he'd been gazing unseeingly out at the yard, mainly to avoid his family after an intense couple of hours. They'd chatted over coffee and cake and every moment had felt like torture. Thalia's endless needs and demands. Sophia's quiet censure. Kristina's determination to make everything seem normal. His father's sorrowful silence.

He couldn't take any of it, not any of it, not when guilt still ate him up every time he came home.

'Christos?' Kristina's voice was gentle as she came out onto the deck, closing the sliding glass door behind her. 'Why did you never bring her home before?'

He shrugged, not looking at her, as usual. 'I don't come home very often, Kristina. You know that.'

'Yes.' She sighed heavily. 'I know.'

'It's better if I'm not here. I set Thalia off. I make Dad remember.'

'We want you here, Christos,' Kristina said quietly, although he noticed she didn't deny what he'd said. How could she? They both knew it was true. Ever since their mother had died, he'd failed his family. He hadn't been there when they'd needed him, when Thalia had *begged* him, and had ended up in a psychiatric ward for three months on suicide watch. That was *his* fault, nobody else's.

Yes, it was better for everyone if he stayed away.

'Tell me about Lana,' Kristina said, and Christos shrugged, unable to keep himself from sounding and feeling defensive. He'd never told his family about Lana; they'd found out from the ridiculous society pages. When Thalia had sent him a text, a few months after he and Lana had embarked on their paper marriage, asking him if he was really married, he'd said yes, because he'd had to, but he'd tried to frame it as more of a business merger than a meeting of minds or hearts, because that was what it had been.

As for what it was now...

'She seems softer than I expected,' Kristian ventured when he hadn't said anything. 'From what little you told us, I thought perhaps she was one of those hard-as-nails businesswomen.'

'She is,' Christos replied, 'in the office. She built up her own business from nothing and is one of the most successful PR people in the whole city.' He realised he sounded proud; he *was* proud. Lana's determination and drive were incredible, just one of the many things he— he *liked* about her. Yes.

'Well, she doesn't look hard as nails to me now,' Kristina said with a hint of a smile in her voice. 'She looks like she absolutely adores you.'

What? Christos turned to face his sister, who was smiling affectionately at him, clearly so pleased by this development…except of course it couldn't be true.

'Why do you say that?' he asked, his voice roughening.

'Because it's obvious. The look in her eyes…it's so tender. Besides, a woman knows, Christos.' She shook her head, still smiling. 'I wish I had a man to look at that way. And I wish a man would look at *me* that way.'

'What are you saying?' He realised he sounded almost panicked, and his sister noticed.

'Usually, a man doesn't mind knowing his wife is in love with him,' she remarked. 'Or that he is in love with her. Unless I'm missing something?'

'It's just…' Christos blew out a breath. 'Lana and I are more friends than…' How to finish that sentence?

'Husband and wife?' Kristina guessed. 'Because you looked like husband and wife to me.'

And they hadn't yet told his family about the baby. That was certainly very husband and wife territory.

'It's complicated,' he told his sister.

'Maybe,' she allowed, 'but maybe it doesn't need to be.' He had no idea how to answer that, so he didn't say anything, and his sister continued gently, 'Can't you leave the past where it belongs, Christos, instead of raking it up every time you go home? I know you do—I see it in your eyes, the torment that doesn't need to be there. It happened. It's over. We all want to move on. We're all trying to, except you.'

Christos found he couldn't speak now; his throat was

too tight. He just shook his head, averting his face, and Kristina sighed.

'Come inside at least,' she said. 'For supper.'

Christos waited until she'd gone inside, needing a moment alone to compose himself. He took a few deep breaths as he gazed out at the lawn, twilit shadows now lengthening along it. Kristina had to be wrong, he thought. Lana didn't *adore* him. If anything, she'd been more insistent about the no-love clause of their paper marriage, right from the beginning. He was the one who'd fooled himself into thinking he was more open about it all, when he now knew he wasn't. He couldn't be.

And yet...what did he actually *want*? If he put aside his fear of hurting Lana, disappointing her and their child, having to live with that disappointment day after day... did he want to love her? Could he? Could she love him, if she knew the truth about what he'd done, and, more importantly, what he *hadn't* done?

A heaviness settled inside him, because he knew the answer. He couldn't. She couldn't. He would disappoint her, eventually, and she would never love him if she knew how badly he'd let people down. People who had counted on him, and needed him, and loved him.

So, what on earth were they doing, having a baby together, especially if what Kristina had said was true, and Lana had somehow fallen in love with him?

What could that possibly mean for their future?

'Christos,' Sophia called, 'come inside before it gets cold!'

Slowly, his heart leaden inside him, Christos walked inside. Everyone was gathered around the dining-room table, which was laden with food, because, he knew, food was love, especially to a Greek woman.

He found himself seeking out Lana instinctively, and as he caught sight of her across the room, he saw she was looking at him in concern, a small, inquiring smile curving her mouth. There was a new lushness to her body, now she was pregnant, and the morning sickness had started to abate. The tiniest of curves to that reed-thin waist, a fullness to her breasts, her body ripe with his child... It filled him with an emotion he wasn't willing to name.

He managed a smile back, and then decided they might as well get giving the news over with.

'Before we eat,' he announced, not quite looking at anyone, 'Lana and I have something to say.' In his peripheral vision, he saw her eyes widen and he wondered if he should have done this differently—hand in hand, perhaps, with beaming smiles. He had, he realised, sounded rather grim about it all.

'What is it, Christos?' Thalia asked, already impatient.

'Lana is expecting,' he said, trying to inject some enthusiasm into his voice. 'A baby. She's due in February.'

A shocked silence followed this announcement and then Kristina clapped her hands and went to hug him, and then Lana, peppering her with questions about how she was feeling, whether she'd tried ginger tea for morning sickness.

Sophia smiled faintly and gave him a quick kiss on the cheek. 'Don't look so terrified,' she murmured as she stepped back. 'It will all be okay.'

'I'm fine,' Christos replied. His middle sister had always understood him the best, and yet he'd pushed her away too, simply because it had been easier. What had once felt like the right thing to do suddenly seemed selfish. Had Sophia been hurt by his distance? She'd always seemed so self-contained, needing no one, but maybe that was as much of a coping mechanism as any of their other reactions to their mother's death had been. Maybe he should have reached out...and yet he couldn't have. It hadn't felt physically possible.

Another way in which he'd failed.

'I can't believe you're going to be a dad,' Thalia said, not sounding entirely pleased about it, and Christos understood why. She had always been the baby of the family, the surprise blessing, only two years old when his mother had died. She'd never managed to truly grow up, and he suspected she was worried about being replaced.

And yet what was there to replace? He hardly ever saw his baby sister. The best he offered was the occasional hurried text. Another way in which he thought he'd been protecting his family but now just felt selfish.

What was wrong with him? Why was he thinking this way?

This was what coming home did to him. It made him doubt himself, his perception of the past, of his family and how they felt. And that made him start to wonder about other things...like Lana.

Did she really love him? Could she, if she knew what he'd done?

Did he even want answers to those questions?

CHAPTER THIRTEEN

CHRISTOS WAS QUIET on the way home, quieter even than he'd been on the journey there, his jaw tight, his brow furrowed as he gazed out at the road. He seemed deep in thought, and Lana found she didn't want to disturb him.

The day had been wonderful in many ways—Sophia and Kristina both warmly welcoming, his father kindly and gentle, the conversation easy with more laughter than Lana had expected. In some ways, Christos's family felt like the family she had never had…big and noisy, warm and loving, yet Christos didn't seem to appreciate or enjoy any of it at all. And Thalia, Lana acknowledged, had been chilly at best, sometimes even rude, ignoring her in a way that felt pointed, or turning away when she had asked a question.

As for Christos… Lana hadn't missed how positively grim he had sounded when he'd made the announcement about her pregnancy. Was he having second thoughts about everything? Did he not want their baby any more? Did he not want *her*?

She wasn't brave enough to ask him. A few weeks ago, she'd given herself a strict talking-to, to get her feelings in line and stop wondering if she could fall in love with Christos. She wanted to enjoy what they had, and while that felt easy enough because what they had was wonderful, she knew she still felt empty inside. Still wanted more…more than she'd ever let herself want before. And the more she wanted, it seemed the more Christos didn't.

Which was exactly the kind of situation she'd been desperate to avoid. But how did you avoid it, when you didn't have control over your own wayward heart?

It was a conundrum that depressed her, even as she couldn't keep from feeling a contrary flicker of hope that somehow, *somehow* it would all work out. Although there wasn't much room for encouragement with Christos looking so grim as they drove in silence.

Neither of them spoke all the way home, parking the car in the private garage down the street before walking in the summery darkness, the air warm and as soft as velvet. Lana unlocked the door to the brownstone and stepped inside, stopping in surprise when she felt Christos move right behind her. She half turned to him in query, only to have his hands come to her shoulders and he backed her against the wall, just as he had on what had felt like their wedding night. He kissed her then, long and deep, with a tenderness that felt deeper than mere passion, a need that was far more than simple lust.

Surprised, because since she'd become pregnant, Christos had always made sure she initiated their lovemaking, wanting to be considering of her fatigue and tiredness, she stilled and so did he, like a question.

And, acting on instinct, Lana answered it, wrapping her arms around him, drawing her closer to him as their kiss continued, a quiet, heartfelt desperation to it that felt as if it could be her entire undoing. Christos moved his lips to her cheek, and then her neck, and then the hollow of her throat. As he did so, a sound escaped him, something more than a gasp but not quite a sob.

Lana slid her hands to his face, tried to tilt it up towards her. 'Christos,' she whispered. 'Look at me.'

But he wouldn't. He just kept kissing her, her throat, her shoulder, the swell of her breasts above her dress, each brush of his lips so exquisitely tender it brought tears to her eyes. And Lana decided that it was enough. He needed her now, she knew with a bone-deep certainty, not just physically, but emotionally. Even if he would never admit it. Even if he couldn't look her in the eye.

And if he needed her that way, Lana knew unequivocally that she wanted to be needed. She wanted to give herself, all of herself, in a way she never had before. And so, she wrapped her arms around him again and opened her body and even her heart to him as he continued to kiss her, stopping only to draw the sundress she'd been wearing over her head and toss it aside.

Lana knew her body looked different than it had even a mere few weeks ago—her breasts were fuller, her belly gently rounded. Christos cupped her belly with his hands, spreading his fingers wide, before he dropped to his knees and kissed her tiny barely there bump with something close to reverence. Pleasure and something far deeper fired through Lana—in all the months they'd been together as man and wife, she'd never felt closer to him than she did now...and yet still so far away.

She had no idea what he was thinking, or even feeling, but she told herself that knowing he needed her was enough. She would let it be enough.

Christos skimmed his hands down the sides of her belly and then tugged her underwear down, his fingers leaving trails of fire wherever they brushed her skin. Something between a gasp and a shudder escaped Lana as she kicked her underwear aside and Christos pressed his mouth to the centre of her, anchoring her with his hands on her hips, lavishing her with tender love and attention in a way that felt wonderfully, agonisingly intimate. She'd never felt so exposed…or so known. It was as frightening as it was wondrous, and she knew she wouldn't exchange it for the safe, sterile world she'd once known. Not in a million years.

A moan escaped her as her hips arched towards him and he continued his loving ministrations, knowing every slick crevice and fold of the most intimate part of her body. She felt a climax building inside her, like a tidal wave poised to crash over her, pull her into its sensuous, swirling undertow, and something in her instinctively resisted it, because she wanted to share this moment with Christos, and yet as he continued, his mouth moving over her with tender insistence, she knew she couldn't.

The pleasure was too intense, too wonderful, and Christos too determined. She drove her fingers through his hair, her hips pushing against his mouth as a jagged cry escaped her and her body went liquid.

She sagged against the wall, held up only by Christos's hands, her own still fisted in his hair. She was reeling with the aftershocks of her climax when he scooped her up in his arms and carried her to their bed. Lana lay sprawled on it, still dazed, her lips swollen, her body flooded with both pleasure and desire.

Christos stood at the foot of the bed, his face flushed, his eyes glittering and his breath coming fast. He stripped off quickly, tossing his clothes aside with an urgent carelessness, before he joined her on the bed, stretching on top of her, braced on his forearms.

She tried to look him in the eye, but he buried his face in her shoulder as he entered her in one smooth, fluid stroke. Lana wrapped her arms around him, her legs around his waist as she accepted him fully, pulling him more deeply inside her, offering him everything she had to give.

And he received it, clutching her to him as they moved in union, stroke after stroke, the most intimate language ever spoken, needing no words.

When his climax came, hers immediately following, Lana knew she had never felt so entirely united with another person, as one flesh, one mind, one heart. She held him to her, her body still wrapped around his, their bodies shuddering in the aftermath. She wanted to say something, but she was afraid to break the spell that had wrapped around them like a bubble, as fragile as glass.

And the words that hovered on her lips felt too precious and sacred to say, to offer, when she wasn't at all sure what Christos's response would be.

And yet she felt them, burning inside her, needing to be said, and knowing the truth of them with a certainty that both shocked and settled her, because she wasn't afraid. Not any more. No matter what happened.

I love you.

She mouthed the words silently as she held Christos in her arms and felt them reverberate through every fibre of her being.

I love you, Christos. I love you.

Lana closed her eyes and smiled as she held the man who held her heart without even knowing he did.

Christos sat slumped in a chair on the little balcony terrace outside the living room. Below him the street was quiet, the city having finally fallen asleep...unlike him.

Lana had fallen into a doze after their lovemaking,

without either of them saying a word, and while she'd slept, curled up on her side, he'd slipped away, pouring himself a generous measure of whisky and bringing it out here, to the dark night, hoping the peace and quiet, the air soft and sultry, would help settle his mind.

He'd been out here an hour and, so far, it wasn't working. He didn't know how he felt, or, at least, he didn't want to think too much about how he felt—and yet at the same time it was consuming him.

Kristina telling him that Lana adored him. The knowledge that these last few months had been the sweetest he'd ever known, and yet he still wanted more. The fear—the terror—that if he told Lana the truth about himself and his failures, she would leave him in a heartbeat. The even greater fear that he would disappoint her or their baby, let them down the way he had so many others.

It was too much to feel. He closed his eyes as he tossed back a burning swallow of whisky.

'Can't sleep?'

Lana's soft voice had Christos tensing in his seat. How had he not heard her come to the doorway? He glanced behind him and saw her standing there like a lovely apparition, swathed in a dressing gown of cream silk, her strawberry-blonde hair tumbled in silken waves about her shoulders.

'No,' he said briefly, and she slipped through the doorway and perched on the chair opposite him. They'd enjoyed many meals out on this terrace, casual conversations, easy laughter.

This wasn't any of those. Already, before she'd said a word, he was bracing himself, knowing what was coming next.

'Talk to me, Christos,' Lana said softly.

He knew, of course, what she meant, and he wasn't going to be so pathetic as to prevaricate or pretend he didn't. He'd always been determined, right from the beginning, to be honest, to be fair, to be kind. He just hadn't realised how hard it would become.

Christos gazed into the amber depths of his glass. 'What do you want me to tell you?' he asked heavily.

'What you're thinking right now would be a good start.'

A sigh escaped him, and he raked a hand through his hair. 'I don't even know, Lana, and that's the truth of it.'

'Why was it so hard to go home?' she asked. 'And why do you go home so rarely?'

'Because it's so hard.'

'Why, though?'

Christos closed his eyes briefly, knowing he was going to tell her and yet dreading it all the same. But maybe it was better she knew. It would, he suspected, keep her from falling any more in love with him, and maybe that was what they both needed—a reminder of how it was supposed to be between them.

'Christos…?'

'It's hard because every time I come home, I'm reminded of how I disappointed and failed my family, back when my mother died. It's hard on me, but it's also hard on them. Seeing me stirs up my father's grief, Thalia's issues.' He glanced at her. 'I presume you saw how high strung and emotionally fragile she seemed at times?'

Lana's expression was both thoughtful and sombre, her head tilted to one side. 'Yes, I did.'

'That's because of me.'

Lana was silent for a moment. 'Surely it can't entirely be down to you, Christos,' she said finally, her voice quiet but holding a certain firm reasonableness. 'You're not the only thing in her life. There have to be other issues affecting her mental health.'

'Maybe, but I trigger them. I know I do, because I caused them at the start.'

Again, Lana was silent, absorbing what he said. He didn't feel any condemnation from her, not yet, but he certainly felt it in himself. He always did when he remembered that agonisingly painful time.

'Tell me,' she said finally, 'what happened when your mother died.'

As she said the words, Christos realised, with a pang of shocked relief, that he actually *wanted* to tell her. He wanted to let it go, and, moreover, he wanted her to know about it. How it might change things between them he had no idea, only that it would, perhaps irrevocably, but it needed to be said.

'My mother was diagnosed with cancer when I was fourteen,' he began slowly, choosing his words with care, each one feeling laborious, laid down like an offering. 'It was difficult. Thalia was only a baby, Kristina twelve and Sophia ten. My father was loving, but he worked all the time and he struggled to cope with the demands... not just physically, but emotionally. I wanted to be there for him, for them all, but it was hard.'

'I'm sure it was,' Lana murmured, her voice soft with compassion.

'At first my mother tried to go on as normal. She wouldn't talk about her chemotherapy, or how sick she was, and she was always there to greet us with a smile.' Already he felt his throat thickening. 'She was so strong, and I suppose that's why it came as a shock when suddenly she wasn't. When I was sixteen, she stopped treatment. There had been a few months of seeming remission, and I think we were all hopeful. Then the cancer came back, as it often does, more aggressive than ever before. She wanted to go into a hospice, but my father insisted she come home. He wanted to be with her. He loved her very, very much.' His voice almost broke and he drew a quick, steadying breath.

Seeing his father absolutely overcome with grief, barely able to function as his mother had withered away, had cemented in him a certainty that he never wanted to love someone that much. Need them so desperately.

Yet what if you already do?

Christos pushed that thought aside. 'Those weeks she was at home were awful,' he said quietly. 'She was so weak, so…different. And we had no help, because my father didn't want anyone to see her like that. He wanted everyone to remember my mother as she used to be—a laughing, lovely, beautiful woman. And she wasn't any more. I didn't even like seeing her…she'd lost so much weight, and her face looked…it looked like a skull.' He pictured her eyes, burning into him, begging him. 'In all truth, I could barely stand to sit with her.' He bowed his head, the words coming faster now, the confession like a bloodletting. 'And so, I wouldn't. I avoided her, and she knew I was, and I know it hurt her. Kristina and Sophia could both handle it, they sat with her for hours. Kristina would come in with Thalia, who was just two, put her in my mother's arms, and help her to hold her. And I… I stayed away.'

'That's understandable, Christos,' Lana said quietly, and he let out a hard, almost wild laugh.

'Is it? Is it understandable that the day before she died, she asked me to sit with her? She knew she was dying, that she would die soon. *I* knew she would die soon. Her strength was seeping away…you could practically see it happening, minute by minute. She begged me, Lana. *Begged* me, with tears in her eyes, her voice. "Please, Christos, let me see you. Let me hug you and say good-bye to you." And you know what I did?' He drew another breath, his voice turning jagged with pain. 'I pretended I hadn't heard her. I walked right by her bedroom—she was sitting up in bed, even though she had no strength, her arms outstretched to me, calling. And I didn't go in. I didn't even answer her. I never saw her again. She died that night.' He dropped his head into his hands as a shudder ripped through him, and then, in surprise, he felt Lana's arms, soft and accepting, fold around him.

'Oh, Christos.' Her voice was soft, sad, and so very tender. *'Christos.'* As she held him, he felt the sobs building in his chest and he wanted to keep them there. He *needed* to, and yet he couldn't. He couldn't, and they escaped him in choked gasps as she held him and he cried for the mother he'd disappointed, the mistakes he'd made, the grief he'd repressed, the regret that had been eating away at him for two decades.

'I'm sorry,' he finally managed, wiping his eyes, half ashamed, half relieved by his emotional display, the kind of histrionics he'd never let himself indulge in, ever. Yet here he was.

'Don't be sorry.' She pressed her hand against his damp cheek, looking fiercely into his eyes. 'Never be sorry, Christos, for showing me your heart.'

The words pierced him like a sword. His heart? Yes, he had, but…but it went against their agreements, their instincts. 'Lana…'

'Don't say anything,' she said quietly, briefly laying a

finger against his lips. 'I know it's not what we agreed. And it may not be what you want—'

'I don't know what I want,' he admitted in a low voice. 'Not any more.'

'Then don't say anything,' she said again, her voice fierce and determined. 'Let's just be.' She pressed a kiss to his lips, and he clasped the back of her head, holding her to him, needing her more than ever.

'There's more I haven't told you,' he confessed when they had broken apart. Now that he'd begun, he wanted to say all of it. 'It wasn't just that one time. I failed in so many ways…after my mother's death, my father asked me to be there for my sisters, because he was so broken by grief, and I wasn't. I *wasn't.* I ignored them, I got irritated by them, I shut down in every way possible.'

He searched her face for signs of disappointment, of judgment, but found none. 'And then that just became the way I operated, and they accepted it, but I always saw their disappointment. My father, too…he's never been able to look me in the eye since my mother died. He's more disappointed than angry, but that feels worse.' He drew a breath, gazing straight at her, seeing only empathy. 'When I left for university at eighteen, I was glad to get away. I tried to come back as little as possible, even though it added to Kristina and Sophia's burdens, especially with Thalia being so little…for some reason, she'd latched onto me, the big brother, and made me a role model when I was anything but.' He paused, steeling himself for what came next.

'When she was fifteen, she had her first depressive episode. She called me, begged me to come see her. She was in such a state, crying, pleading…and it reminded me of my mother. Of her begging me to sit with her.

And I couldn't… I just couldn't…' He stopped, composed himself, and started again. 'So, I told her no. I texted Kristina, to tell her to look after her, but I didn't answer any of Thalia's other messages. I turned off my phone and acted like it hadn't happened. That night…' His voice choked again. 'That night Thalia tried to kill herself—cut her wrists, almost bled out. It was touch and go for days, but thankfully she survived. She spent three months in a secure psychiatric unit, on suicide watch. That was my fault, Lana. All my fault. And you can't tell me I was young, that I can be forgiven, because I wasn't. I was nearly *thirty*. It was only three years before I met you.' He stopped then, waited for the judgment that would surely come.

'And you've clearly been paying for it ever since,' Lana told him quietly. She didn't sound condemning, but her voice was firm and level. 'I can see that full well, Christos, and I won't excuse what you did, because it *was* wrong. It was a terrible mistake. But how long must you pay for your sins? Will you ever forgive yourself? Will you allow yourself to be forgiven?'

He shook his head. 'My family doesn't forgive me.'

'I'm not sure about that,' Lana replied. 'But I know you don't forgive yourself.'

'And you think I should?' He couldn't keep from sounding incredulous.

'What benefit is there in raking yourself over the coals for it, again and again?' she challenged quietly. 'After a certain point, regret isn't helpful. It just festers like a wound, like a poison. Torturing yourself with guilt doesn't help you. It doesn't help your family. And it won't help our family.' She took his hand and pressed it to her middle. 'Our baby needs a father who isn't wracked with guilt, determined to be distant in case he messes up. He or she needs a dad who is there, who is involved and invested and fully present. You can be that father, Christos. I know you can.'

He stared at her, desperately wanting to believe her, and yet also so afraid to. He'd already failed too many times. Even if he could forgive himself for that—and with Lana's help, maybe he could—he knew he would not be able to forgive himself if he let down Lana and their child. Never.

And with his track record, it felt as if it was only a matter of time.

'Christos?' Lana prompted softly, and because he couldn't tell her all that, he simply took her in his arms. She came willingly, wrapping herself around him, her cheek tucked into his chest, and Christos closed his eyes, letting himself savour the moment, because heaven only knew what the future held.

CHAPTER FOURTEEN

'I FEEL LIKE a monkey in dressing-up clothes.'

Jack Philips was staring at Lana, dressed in his narrow-legged royal-blue silk suit, looking dapper and handsome and very unhappy.

Lana rested one hand on her burgeoning baby bump. It was November, the ochre and russet leaves fluttering from the trees in Central Park, the air holding a decided crisp chilliness. She was twenty-six weeks along and she was *finally* blooming. After the morning sickness had abated and her bump had begun to show, she'd felt an unequivocal excitement for this next stage of life.

That, she acknowledged wryly, had maybe less to do with her burgeoning bump and more to do with her relationship with Christos. Since that night on the terrace, when he'd shared so much of his story, his heart, their relationship had grown both stronger and deeper. They hadn't said it in words, but Lana had felt it. The emotion. The *love*. Admittedly, those three little words hadn't crossed either of their lips, and Lana tried not to wonder or worry about why not. She wanted to be content with what they had, reminding herself of what Michelle had said—'*That sounds a lot like love to me.*'

Did it really matter if they hadn't said the words? If

they never did, even? Lana knew she felt them every day, and she hoped, she *hoped* Christos did, too.

But right now, she needed to think of Jack. His interview had been bumped several times, but the photographer and journalist were now coming to her office in just fifteen minutes, and Jack looked great…but also not so great.

Lana was well used to last-minutes jitters from her clients, whether they were about to give an interview, or a speech or host a party. Part of her job was talking them down, building them up. Giving them that shot in the arm of confidence that helped them step into the image she'd created for them.

But right now, she realised she wasn't sure she wanted to do that. If Jack was unhappy with his look, the lacquer of sophistication she'd painted on him with smart clothes and styled hair, chunky glasses, and a practised script, why bother with it at all? For ten years she'd been all about the gloss, but in the last few months it had started to flake away, and she hadn't even minded.

She'd started wearing her hair in its natural waves rather than straightened to a gleaming sheet, and she'd worn less make-up, too. Power suits didn't go well with pregnancy and so she'd had to make do with tailored maternity dresses. All in all, her look was softer, and she felt softer, as well as more approachable, more herself. Her real self, the self she'd hidden when she'd walked away from a broken relationship, determined to be different, because that had to be what people wanted, since Anthony certainly hadn't wanted the real her.

But Christos seemed to.

If she could trust it and not question anything. Live in the moment and not worry about the future…

'If you really don't like the suit, Jack,' she told him, 'then change back into your old clothes.'

His eyes widened as he stared at her uncertainly. 'But I came here in a ripped T-shirt and dirty jeans.'

'I know.' She smiled conspiratorially at him. 'But so what? These journalists and photographers see slick, sophisticated people all day, every day. They are all about the curated image, the so-called authentic self that is absolutely anything but. Maybe you need to give them the real deal—who you truly are, warts and all.'

'Thankfully, I don't have any warts, but I take your meaning,' Jack replied, and she laughed.

'Well, phew, I guess.'

'Albert told me you'd give me a whole new image,' he told her thoughtfully. 'And you did, but now you're saying to scrap it?'

'Essentially, yes. I'm not trying to talk myself out of a job, but what's the point of being fake?'

'Well, it's a form of self-protection, I suppose,' Jack replied seriously. 'If you're fake, you can't be truly rejected, because the real you is never seen.'

'Exactly,' Lana answered, heartened that he got it— and, amazingly, finally, so did she. 'And what's the point of that? If you can't be real, what are you?'

'You are not,' Jack told her, 'sounding like a PR person.'

'I know.' Lana couldn't keep from laughing again. 'Maybe I need a rebranding. "Authentic PR" or something.'

Jack nodded slowly. 'That's not a bad idea.' Already he was shimmying out of the tight-fitting blazer. 'Now let me get out of this straitjacket.'

Lana was still smiling as she took a cab home later that evening. Jack had changed back into his old clothes, and given a very candid, very geeky interview that had completely surprised and charmed the journalist. The photographer had taken ruefully ironic photos of Jack, not looking smart and sleek, a superstar in the making, but doing goofy things, balancing a pencil on his nose or playing trashcan basketball. It was different and whimsical, and Lana was pretty sure he was going to be a huge hit with the public…and it had nothing to do with her.

'Why are you smiling like the cat who has the cream?' Christos asked when she came home. They had an evening charity gala to attend, and, while Lana usually looked forward to such events, she realised tonight she'd rather curl up at home with Christos and Netflix.

'I did something different today,' she said, and then told him all about Jack Philips. 'I'm afraid I may be talking myself out of a career.'

'Or into an even better one, at least for a little while,' Christos replied as he pressed a kiss to her bump. They'd had the twenty-week scan six weeks ago, and the baby was healthy and growing; they'd decided not to find out whether it was a girl or boy.

'Some things,' Christos had said, 'are meant to be a surprise.'

'How's Junior today?' he asked as he straightened from greeting their baby to press a kiss on her lips.

'Fine. Making me a bit achy, so he or she must be growing.' She rubbed her bump ruefully; now that she wasn't working, she was conscious of the twinges in her back, along her belly. They'd been bothering her all day, but her OB had told her it was to be expected as the baby grew, and her muscles were forced to stretch.

Christos frowned in concern. 'We can skip tonight, if you'd rather.'

She would rather, but she knew it was an important event for him; he was about to close on a deal with a tech start-up he was interested in. 'No, let's go,' she told him. 'But maybe leave early.'

He caught her in his arms for another kiss and a devilish wag of his eyebrows. 'I'm always up for leaving early.'

Christos watched their limo pull to the kerb from the brownstone's balcony as he waited for Lana to emerge. He felt almost buoyant with happiness—as he had, amazingly, since that night when he'd confessed everything to her and she'd taken it in her stride, offered him acceptance and love in return.

Wait, *love*?

Christos let the knowledge spread inside him, as warm and golden as honey. Yes, *love*. In the end, it was just a word. He thought he'd probably loved Lana for a while—maybe even since she'd first slid onto the stool next to him and ordered a Snake Bite, and he'd been so impressed with her attitude, grit, and determination. That initial feeling had only grown in strength and certainty since then.

That first feeling was, perhaps, why he had been willing to agree to the paper marriage at the start, and then the pregnancy clause made three years later. It was why he hadn't been willing to embark on affairs, and why he wanted nothing more now than her in his arms, by his side, for ever.

The knowledge, surprisingly, didn't scare him. Was that what love did to you? Changed you? Made you into a better, stronger version of yourself?

But what if you let her down?

Admittedly, in the last three months, since that heartbroken confession, they hadn't engaged in that much emotional heavy lifting. Lana had told him a little bit about her childhood, the mother who had always been angry and distant, but she'd also said she'd made peace with it and forgiven her mother before she'd died. Telling him hadn't been so much about showing vulnerability as demonstrating how it was possible to move on from hard and painful things, and yet the fact that she had showed such vulnerability had made him love her *more*, not less.

But what about when the rubber hit the road? When life got hard, when things became uncertain or risky or dangerous? Would he be strong enough to love her then, the way he knew he wanted to?

Because he didn't have a great track record.

'I'm ready.'

Lana's voice floated from the living room and Christos turned, catching his breath at the sight of her. She looked glorious, in a floaty gown of emerald-green satin that draped over her bump and swirled about her calves and ankles. Her hair was drawn up in a loose bun, with tendrils curling about her face.

'I don't look like a tank in this, do I?' she asked with an uncertain laugh, and he strode forward to take her in his arms.

'You look like a goddess. Athena, as I once thought.'

She gave a little laugh back before he kissed her. 'Athena and not bodacious Venus?'

'Athena, goddess of wisdom. Smart and strong and a little bit intimidating but also incredibly lovely.' He kissed her again and for a second she rested in his arms, her head tucked beneath his chin.

'I'm so happy,' she said quietly, almost as if she was afraid of his response, or at least cautious of it. They'd skated on the surface these last few months, enjoying everything in a way that had felt easy, but after his confession on the balcony they hadn't gone any deeper. Was it because they hadn't needed to, or because they hadn't dared?

'I'm happy, too,' Christos replied in the same quiet tone.

Lana eased back to gaze up at him, her eyes wide and clear. 'I'm glad.'

It felt as if they were saying so much more than they actually were, and the import of the moment wasn't lost on him.

I can't disappoint her, he thought with a frisson of panic. *I can't let this lovely woman down, the way I did my own mother and sister. I have to be strong enough this time.*

Was it enough to want that, he wondered, even if he still wasn't sure he could?

An hour later they were circulating through the ballroom of one of the city's finest hotels, in fact the same hotel where Lana had first suggested the pregnancy clause to their marriage. Christos smiled to think of her then, so nervous and determined, and with that outrageous suggestion of IVF! He could laugh about it, now that he was gazing at her across the ballroom, laughing and chatting to someone, ripe with his child. Pride and, yes, *love* swelled within him. He loved her. He loved her. And he needed to tell her so.

'Hello, Christos.'

Christos turned at the sound of the quiet voice, his mouth dropping open when he saw who was standing in front of him, smiling sadly. His sister Sophia.

'Sophia…what are you doing here?'

'I came with a date. I don't often go to these big events, but occasionally I do.'

'I've never seen you…'

'No, but then you weren't looking.' She spoke pragmatically but Christos felt shame pierce him all the same. Sophia had lived just outside the city for years and he'd never made the effort, because it had always been easier not to. Not to face the memories, feel the guilt.

'I'm sorry,' he said, and she raised her eyebrows, her smile turning wry.

'What for?'

A gusty breath escaped him. 'For everything, I suppose. Not being there back…then, and not really since, either.' He shook his head. 'It was just always easier. For me, but also, I convinced myself, for you.' He paused, realising he'd never spoken so honestly to his sister before. 'But maybe it wasn't.'

She nodded slowly. 'We always wanted you there, Christos.'

'I know.' He realised as he said the words that he *did* know. It was all part of the guilt he'd felt, all the while trying not to feel it. Doing his best to believe that it was better for his family for him not to be around, when all the time it had been better for him. Although no, not better, just easier.

Except there had been nothing easy about it.

'I just couldn't bear to see your disappointment,' he confessed to Sophia in a low voice. 'And Dad… I know he still can't look me in the eye.'

Surprise flashed across his sister's face. 'Christos, it's you who can't look him in the eye. Dad doesn't blame you for anything.'

Christos shook his head, the movement visceral and instinctive. 'No, he does. Of course he does. I didn't—I didn't say goodbye to Mom. And I didn't look after all of you.'

'You were sixteen. He never should have asked you that, and he knows it, trust me.' She laid a hand on his arm. 'Talk to him, Christos. Talk to all of us.'

'Thalia…' Her name came thickly from his throat, tears stinging his eyes. He'd let down Thalia worst of all.

'Thalia has always had her issues,' Sophia told him. 'I know you've torn yourself into shreds over not coming when she asked you to, but, Christos, there was always going to be something with Thalia. That's how she's wired.'

'But if I had come when she—'

'You can't be sure of that,' Sophia cut across him. 'And in any case, you need to let it go. Think of the future, not the past.'

Christos smiled faintly. 'That's more or less what Lana told me.'

'I like her,' Sophie replied frankly. 'I think she has the strength of spirit to take you on.'

He laughed then, with genuine humour. 'Touché.'

Sophia smiled. 'I mean it.'

'I know you do.' He smiled back, and for a moment, things between them felt normal, warm. This, Christos realised, was easy. It was the easiest of all, and it gave him a glimpse of what the past could have been, but, more importantly, *far* more importantly, what the future could be.

A ripple of alarm travelled over the crowd, intermingled with gasps. Christos turned to look, as did Sophia, both of them frowning in consternation.

'Is there a doctor here?' someone cried out, and some-one else asked for somebody to call 911.

'What's going on?' Sophia exclaimed, but suddenly, instinctively, Christos knew. He pushed his way through the crowd, his heart starting to thud, until he caught sight of her, and froze, transfixed by the terrible sight, a thousand terrible memories tumbling through his mind.

Lana was crumpled on the ground, her beautiful gown stained with blood.

CHAPTER FIFTEEN

EVERYTHING WAS A BLUR—the lights, the people, the sounds of concern and alarm. All Lana could feel was the intense, excruciating pain, banding her stomach, screaming in her back, obliterating all rational thought.

She'd been feeling twinges on and off all evening and had been determined to ignore them. Stretching pains, she'd told herself. They were natural, her OB had said. She'd had a check-up just three weeks ago and everything had been absolutely fine. Everything *would* be absolutely fine, she insisted to herself, because nothing could go wrong now that she was so happy—and so was Christos. He'd told her so, and it had been the next best thing to the words she was trying not to be too eager to hear. *I love you.* They'd been singing out of her heart every day, but they'd never passed her lips, nor Christos's. But it didn't matter, Lana had told herself, because she *knew* Christos loved her, even if he couldn't articulate it.

In any case, the pain had grown worse, harder to ignore, and then, in the middle of a conversation, she'd felt a sudden gush of liquid and she'd doubled over, gasping with the pain that had banded her middle, more intense than ever before.

She'd heard gasps and cries from the people around her before she'd crumpled to the floor. She'd felt liquid be-

tween her thighs, seeping into her dress, and when she'd
put her hand to it, her palm had come away smeared with
bright red blood.

She'd let out a cry, and then a doctor was there, and
they were loading her onto a stretcher, and there were the
blurred faces of so many people surrounding her, looking scared and concerned, but no one looked familiar.

No one was Christos.

He would hate this, she realised as they carried her to the
ambulance. This was his worst nightmare come to life—
having to be fully present and available emotionally in a
situation as painful and dangerous as this. Facing his deep-
est fear again, with higher stakes than ever before. This was
when love was tested, refined by fire, and what Christos
had always been afraid of. Why he'd avoided it…until now.

Why he wasn't here, by her side, caring for her and
their baby?

Because Lana didn't see him among the faces in the
crowd, and she rode in the ambulance alone, passing out
halfway through the journey, coming to in an operating
theatre, a surgeon peering at her closely.

'Lana Smith?'

'Yes…'

'Your baby is in distress, due to a placental abruption.
We need to perform an emergency Caesarean section. Do
you give your consent?'

She'd blinked up at him, too woozy to fully understand what he was saying. 'But…but I'm only twenty-
six weeks along…'

'This is the only way to save your baby.' The doctor
sounded grimly certain, and Lana tried to grab his hand,
but found she was too weak.

'Where's my husband?' she asked, her voice a desperate, plaintive thread of sound. 'Where is Christos Diakos?'

The doctor shook his head. 'I'm sorry, I don't know where your husband is.' She let out a choked cry and he continued, 'Do you give your consent?'

'Yes...*yes.*'

That was the last thing she remembered.

Lana didn't know how much time had passed when she woke next, to a hazy blur of light and sound. She tried to blink the world into focus and found she couldn't. She tried to reach down to feel the reassuring bump of her baby, but she wasn't strong enough to move her hand. Terror gripped her hard, but then she fell back into unconsciousness, grateful to let the world slide away again.

When she woke again, the world was a little clearer— she saw she was in a hospital room, everything white and sterile, and she was completely alone. An array of monitors and machines were positioned next to her, a steady beeping from one of them the only sound in the room. Tears gathered in her eyes as she looked around for Christos, but she couldn't see him anywhere.

She opened her mouth to call for him, but her lips were cracked and dry and no sound came out. And what about her baby? With what felt like superhuman effort, Lana reached down to touch her bump—and found, to her shocked horror, that it wasn't there. She felt nothing but sagging, empty flesh, and she let out a moan, a sound of raw grief, utter terror. Where was her baby?

Where was Christos?

Lying there, in that bright, sterile room, with no baby or husband, she didn't think she'd ever felt more alone.

This is why you don't let yourself love people, she thought, closing her eyes against the room, the world. *Because it hurts so much when they let you down. They walk away.*

Just as Christos had been afraid he would.

The next time Lana awoke, a nurse was in the room, bustling about by her bed. She must have made some sound, for the woman turned to glance at her, smiling when she saw her eyes were open.

'You're awake! Well, isn't that good news?'

'What…?' Lana's voice was paper-thin, and she had to lick her lips to moisten them, except her mouth was so dry she couldn't.

'Here, honey,' the woman said kindly. 'Let me give you a sip of water.'

She helped Lana lift her head to sip from a straw, the cool liquid wetting her lips and sliding down her throat, providing immediate relief.

Lana sagged against the pillows with a groan. 'Where…where is my baby?' she asked in a croak.

'Your baby is fine,' the nurse assured her. 'She's in the neonatal unit, since she was born so early. She's tiny, just two pounds seven ounces, but she's a fighter. The doctors feel she's got a very good chance indeed.'

Lana closed her eyes in both relief and sorrow. *Two pounds…!* The tiniest scrap of humanity, and yet so very precious. A little girl. A tiny, tiny, precious girl.

'When you're a little stronger, someone can take you to see her,' the woman promised. 'But you've been in a bad way, I'm afraid, for over a week. You lost a lot of blood, and for a while…' She shook her head and Lana felt fear clutch at her.

Had she been that close to death? Christos would have been out of his mind with worry and fear…

Or maybe he hadn't been. Maybe he'd just walked away.

She didn't want to believe it, she couldn't, and yet the reality was stark, staring at her straight in her face. He wasn't here.

'Have you...?' Her voice rasped painfully in her throat, and she swallowed, determined to get the words out. 'Have you seen my husband?'

The nurse gave her a confused look, her forehead furrowed. 'Your husband? What does he look like?'

'Tall...dark hair...hazel eyes...'

The most handsome man in the world.

The nurse shook her head, sympathy now softening her features. 'I'm sorry, I don't think I've seen him. That doesn't mean he hasn't been here, though. I'm only on shift a couple of times a week...'

And she hadn't seen him about at all? No dutiful husband sitting by the bedside, then. Tears silently slipped down Lana's cheeks as she realised Christos must not have been there at all. Had he left her, left their daughter, just as he had his own family? And what did that say about *her*? Her father had left her when she'd been only a baby, her mother had resented her for her whole life, the one man she'd convinced herself she'd loved before had walked away without a single care.

Why should Christos be any different? Why should she? They'd both just been conforming to their true selves. Lana would always be left...and Christos would always do the leaving.

'I'm sure he's here somewhere,' the nurse told her, patting her hand. 'It's a busy hospital...maybe he's with your daughter...' She trailed off, rather feebly, Lana thought, because if she'd been so ill for so long, surely Christos would have been there at some point. The nurse would have recognised the description, at least. 'I'll ask around,' the nurse said, and Lana let out a choked sound, something between a laugh and a sob.

'Don't bother,' she said. 'I don't want to see him.' And then she closed her eyes, trying to shut out the grim truth that she couldn't avoid; it screamed in her ears, seeped into every pore. Christos had left her.

'She doesn't want to see you.'

The nurse's expression was implacable as Christos stared at her in incredulity that quickly morphed into fury—and fear.

'What? What on earth do you mean?'

'I'm sorry, sir. Your wife made it very clear she didn't want to see you.'

Frustration burned in his chest, along with a far deeper hurt. Lana didn't want to see him?

Yet was he even that surprised?

He'd failed her, back at the ballroom. He'd failed her so badly. When he'd seen her lying there, crumpled on the ground, everything in him had shut down. He'd been incapable of thought, of movement, frozen in place by the memories that had tormented him for so many years— his mother in her bed, calling out to him. Thalia's broken voice on the phone. The way he'd failed before, and the utter terror that it was happening again.

He would let Lana down.

He already had. And yet he still couldn't make himself move.

He'd stood there, completely frozen with terror, with memory, while she'd been bundled onto a stretcher, taken away. Then Sophia had touched his shoulder, squeezed.

'Christos, it's going to be okay. We'll go to the hospital.'

He'd stared at his sister blankly, and then it was as if he'd had an injection of adrenaline, of realisation. He had to get to Lana. He wouldn't fail her any more than he already had. By the time he'd made it outside of the hotel, she'd already been on the way to the hospital.

What must she have thought, when she'd looked around in those frightening moments, and hadn't seen him?

He'd known he would hate the fact that he'd disappointed her in those crucial moments, but he'd also known he had to look forward…for the sake of their marriage, their child. By the time he had arrived at the hospital with Sophia, having been told Lana was taken to a different one, she was already in the operating theatre, having an emergency C-section. Christos had been powerless to do anything but wait.

And then he'd received the news that Lana had had a little girl, a tiny baby girl who had been fighting for her life…as Lana had been fighting for her own. He'd stared at the surgeon in blank shock as he'd removed his surgical mask, looking weary and almost as hopeless as Christos had felt.

'It was a placental abruption. These are very rare, happening in less than one per cent of all pregnancies, but when they do happen, they're sudden and very dangerous.'

Christos had felt his stomach hollowing out while Sophia had stood next to him, a steadying presence. 'What…?' He'd had to make himself start again. 'What are you saying?'

'Your wife lost a lot of blood, Mr Diakos. A *lot* of blood. She's being given a transfusion, but when a patient has lost as much blood as she has, it's always a cause for concern. A grave cause for concern.'

'Are you saying her life is in danger?' Christos had demanded hoarsely.

The surgeon had nodded grimly. 'That's exactly what I'm saying.'

Christos's reaction had been visceral and immediate. 'Let me see her. I have to see her.'

'I'm sorry, but that won't be possible just now. When she's more stable, yes. But until then...'

'I have to see her,' Christos had insisted, his voice rising, his fists clenching. 'You don't understand—'

'Mr Diakos, I understand completely,' the surgeon had replied wearily. 'But until the transfusion is complete and we can be sure that her body has accepted the new blood, seeing her could put her in danger. I promise you, as soon as it is safe, you will see her.'

Safe had been an endless eighteen hours. He'd insisted Sophia go home; she'd promised to return in the morning. She'd been there for him in a way he hadn't been for her, in the past, and he'd been painfully grateful for it. Meanwhile, Christos hadn't slept, hadn't eaten, hadn't done anything but panic and pray. He'd also seen their daughter, their tiny baby girl, so perfect and pink and small, the most beautiful baby that had ever lived. If he'd been allowed, he could have held her in the palm of one hand. As it was, he'd had to make do with peering at her through the glass, his heart aching and aching. He could lose the two people he loved most in the world...and what he knew most of all was he was going to be there for them. This time, he was going to be there for both of them.

When they'd finally let him see Lana, she'd been unconscious, her beautiful face so very pale, her body so terribly still. He'd held her hand and talked to her, tried to make her laugh even though he'd known she couldn't hear him.

'That first time you sat next to me in that bar, Lana? I fell for you then.' He'd almost been able to hear her scoff, and he'd continued as if they were actually having a conversation. 'I'm serious. I didn't realise it, of course. I'm not that sentimental. But I fell for you—for your strength and your spirit, but also because of the vulnerability I glimpsed underneath, although if someone had told me as much, I would have run a mile. You know I would have, don't you? You always sensed that about me, even before I told you as much. But not now, Lana.' His voice had choked, and he'd stroked her hand, trying to keep the tears at bay. 'I'm not running now. I never will again.'

At other times, he'd spoken to her of their daughter. 'She's the most beautiful thing you've ever seen. Tiny but fierce. She certainly has your spirit, thank goodness. All the doctors and nurses say she's a fighter. She's going to fight for her life, Lana, and so are you.' Again, his voice had broken and this time he'd had to pass a hand over his face, exhausted, overwhelmed, *emotional*. 'You are,' he'd insisted. 'I know you are. You have to, Lana, for our baby girl, and—and for me. Because I love you. I should have said those words before, because heaven knows I've felt them for so long. But I love you. *I love you.*'

With every fibre of his being, he'd willed her to open her eyes, to hear him, but she'd slept on, as beautiful as an angel, as still as a statue. Then their baby girl had developed a fever, and for two days he'd gone between their bedsides, afraid for both of their lives, while Sophia had supplied him with takeaway meals and decent cups of coffee from a nearby café.

When their daughter was finally out of the danger zone—for now—he'd gone back to Lana, only to be told by this stony-faced nurse that his wife didn't want to see him.

For a second, Christos hadn't been able to process it, because he'd just been so glad that Lana was finally awake and able to speak. But what the hell did she mean, she didn't want to see him?

And yet was he even surprised?

'There must be a mistake,' he insisted, trying his best to keep his voice level when in truth he felt like shouting, swearing, storming into Lana's room, and yet at the same time weeping from his own guilt and grief. 'My wife will want to see me,' he said, wanting to believe it. 'I know she will.'

'She said she didn't.'

'Look,' Christos said, and now his voice was wavering, trembling. 'It's been an incredibly intense week. Lana—my wife—was in danger of losing her life, and our baby girl was, as well. Whatever she's saying…it might be she doesn't realise what's going on. What's happened. I need to see her.'

The nurse's expression softened briefly. 'She did ask for you,' she admitted. 'And seemed disappointed when you weren't there.'

Which was a knife to the heart if anything was. Christos practically staggered. So Lana knew he'd let her down. How could he possibly make it up to her? 'Please let me see her,' he said quietly, a plea, and thankfully, *thankfully*, the nurse finally nodded.

Seconds later he was opening the door to Lana's room, holding his breath as he saw his wife half sitting up in bed, still looking so pale, her eyes closed. They opened when he closed the door, awareness flaring in their crystalline depths, and then, to his surprise, to his sorrow, Lana began to cry.

He'd never seen her cry before, not like this. Her expression seemed to collapse in on itself and her shoulders shook as she held her hands up to her face, as if to hide her tears, her pain.

'Lana. Lana. My darling Lana.'

He went to the bed and took her gently in his arms, kissing her hair, her hands, and then her damp cheeks when she let him. He didn't even hear what he was saying, over and over again, until Lana, through her tears, asked, 'Do you really mean that?'

Then he realised he'd been saying, over and over, *I love you.*

'Yes,' he told her. 'I love you. I love you. You've given me the biggest scare of my life this last week, but I love you so much. So, so much. More than anything, except perhaps our baby daughter, who is the most gorgeous thing in the world, save you.' He kissed her again as she laughed brokenly, through her tears.

'Is she all right?'

'She's going to be all right,' he stated firmly. 'And I'll take you to see her as soon as they let me. She has your spirit, Lana, and your blue eyes.'

She laughed again, a hiccup of sound. 'Christos, every baby has blue eyes.'

'Not as blue as yours,' he returned, and she smiled, although she still looked tearful, and that made him ache, because he knew it was his doing, and he'd never wanted to be the one to hurt her.

'I thought you'd gone,' she said quietly, a confession. 'I thought… I thought you'd left me. For good.'

'Never.' He held her face in his hands as he gazed into her eyes, wanting to imbue her with his certainty, his strength of feeling. 'Never, Lana. When you first… collapsed, back at the hotel, I wasn't able to get to you in time. I'm so, so sorry. You were in the ambulance, being whisked away, before I could.' He paused, knowing he needed to be completely honest. 'I froze,' he said in a low voice. 'For just a few seconds. It all came rushing back—with my mother, with Thalia, my *fear*, and I couldn't move. I couldn't do anything. But only for a moment, Lana, I swear.' But a terrible moment too long. He knew that. 'I'm sorry,' he whispered. 'So sorry.'

'Oh, Christos—'

'By the time I ran towards you, you were in the ambulance. And then they told me the wrong hospital, and by the time I got to you, you were in Theatre. But as soon as I could see you, sit with you, I did. I was. I swear, Lana.' He squeezed her hands, desperate for her to believe him, for her sake as well as his own. 'I let you down. I know I did, and I'm sorry. But I swear I never will again.'

'A nurse told me she hadn't seen you,' Lana whispered. 'And when I woke up, you weren't there.'

'I'm so sorry—'

'It's not your fault.' She shook her head, squeezing his hands back. 'It was just…for a moment, it felt like all my old fears came to the fore. All the insecurities I never let myself think about, never mind admit to anyone else. I thought about my mother, my father, the man I…' She gulped. 'And I wondered why I was even surprised that you would leave me, when everyone I'd cared about had left me before—'

He couldn't bear to hear her say such things, and yet he knew she'd needed to say them. 'Oh, Lana.'

'I should have been more honest before, about how… vulnerable I felt, I suppose. I didn't even realise quite how much until you were gone. But even so, I should have trusted you, Christos.' Her eyes were wide, filled with both pain and regret. 'I should have believed you would be there, if you could. It was just for a little while it felt as if I couldn't even think—'

'I understand,' he whispered, because of course he did. 'And I'm so sorry.'

'It doesn't matter.' She smiled, although her eyes still held the pearly sheen of tears. 'You're here now. I'm so sorry I doubted you, even for a moment.'

He shook his head, his throat thick with emotion. 'And I'm so sorry I gave you reason to doubt.'

'You didn't, Christos. It was me…my fear and insecurity.'

'Still.'

'No more looking back at the past,' she reminded him. 'Only to the future…a future where we're together.'

He nodded almost fiercely. 'Always.'

Her expression became serious as she continued, 'I should have said those words earlier too, Christos, because I love you. I love you so much. I didn't want to, I fought against it, but it happened anyway.' She laughed, wiping the last of her tears, as he took her in his arms again.

'I'm glad,' he told her. 'I am very, very glad.'

With a small, impish smile curving her lips, Lana leaned back to look up at him. 'Three points regarding our marriage,' she stated, eyebrows lifted in query.

Christos grinned, before making a show of frowning in thought. 'Let's see…first point, I love you.'

'Second point, I love you,' she fired back.

'And third point, we love our daughter.'

Her smile turned satisfied as she nodded slowly. 'I like the sound of those points,' she said, and Christos kissed her again.

'Me too,' he replied as he took her in his arms, and she nestled against him. 'Me too.'

EPILOGUE

Three years later

'LOOK AT ME, Mama, look at me!'

'I'm looking, darling, I'm looking,' Lana replied with a laugh as her daughter, Charis Marina, ran down the hill, blonde curls flying. They had named her Charis, the Greek word for grace, because it had felt fitting. So much grace had been shown, in the midst of all the heartache and healing. And Marina, for Christos's mother, so she would always be remembered.

Those first few months after Charis's birth had been challenging, to say the least. She'd stayed in the hospital for four months, and Lana had gone there every day to hold her daughter, to drip-feed her from an eye dropper, to make sure her daughter, tiny as she was, knew she was loved. Christos had come in the evenings, and sometimes during his lunch hour, and somehow, they'd survived—two fevers, a bout of pneumonia, and some serious jaundice, but Charis had come home when she was four and a half months old, weighing just over four pounds.

Since then, she'd continued to grow and strengthen, a little behind her peers in terms of physical development, and definitely on the petite side, but the paediatrician had said that was normal. She was their little sprite, with her blue eyes—the same colour as Lana's, just as Christos had predicted—and her wild blonde locks.

She'd brought Christos's family together in a way they never had been before; this new life had created a new life for the family—one of forgiveness and acceptance. Now she and Christos regularly made the trip out to Brookhaven to see his father and sisters; Thalia, although still fragile, adored her little niece, and Kristina delighted in being an auntie, sneaking Charis treats from her bakery whenever she could. Sophia, living so close to the city, had become a regular visitor to their home there, as well as here, the sprawling, relaxed house they'd bought out in the Hamptons, for weekends and summers. Lana loved nothing more than running through the long grass with her daughter, or looking for shells on the beach, or baking—something she'd never done before—with Charis dipping her finger into whatever she was mixing, no matter Lana's gentle reprimands.

'But it's so good, Mama,' she'd protest, making Lana smile.

She'd taken to motherhood in a way she'd never thought possible, in part because the nature of Charis's birth had made her daughter all the more precious. Her condition meant she wouldn't have any more children, although she and Christos had spoken about adoption, and they'd had their first meeting with a caseworker just last week. It felt as if all things were possible, because they'd already seen and survived so much.

They were here, after all.

'Careful, sprite!' In one easy armful, Christos scooped up a squealing Charis and tossed her over his shoulder as he strolled towards Lana, lying on a picnic blanket on the grass. It was a beautiful summer's day, the sky the colour of a robin's egg, the sunshine lemony and warm. A day that felt like a blessing, like so much in their lives.

'There you go.' He deposited Charis onto the blanket, and their daughter scrambled up and threw herself into Lana's arms, who accepted her with a startled *oof* before drawing her into a hug.

'Hello, pumpkin,' she murmured against her hair. Her gaze met Christos's over their daughter's head and they shared a loving, tender smile. Lana knew what he was thinking without him having to say it, because she was thinking it, too.

Are you as happy as I am? As thankful? As blessed?

The three points regarding their family.

With a smile, Lana settled their daughter between them and leaned over to kiss her husband. Yes, the three points of their family, and the only ones she needed to remember. As she met Christos's smiling gaze once more, she knew he was thinking it, too.

* * * * *

COMING
SOON!

We really hope you enjoyed reading this book.
If you're looking for more romance
be sure to head to the shops when
new books are available on

Thursday 14th
March

To see which titles are coming soon, please visit
millsandboon.co.uk/nextmonth

MILLS & BOON

MILLS & BOON ®

Coming next month

THE KING'S HIDDEN HEIR
Sharon Kendrick

'Look... I should have told you sooner.' Emmy swallowed.

She was biting her lip in a way which was making warning bells ring loudly inside his head when suddenly she sat up, all that hair streaming down over her shoulders, like liquid gold. She looked like a goddess, he thought achingly when her next words drove every other thought from his head.

'You have a son, Kostandin.'

What she said didn't compute. In fact, she'd taken him so completely by surprise that Kostandin almost told her the truth. That he'd never had a child, nor wanted one. His determination never to procreate was his get-out-of-jail-free card. He felt the beat of a pulse at his temple. Because what good was a king, without an heir?

Continue reading
THE KING'S HIDDEN HEIR
Sharon Kendrick

Available next month
millsandboon.co.uk

afterglow BOOKS

Introducing our newest series, Afterglow.

From showing up to glowing up, Afterglow characters are on the path to leading their best lives and finding romance along the way – with a dash of sizzling spice!

Follow characters from all walks of life as they chase their dreams and find that true love is only the beginning...

OUT NOW

millsandboon.co.uk

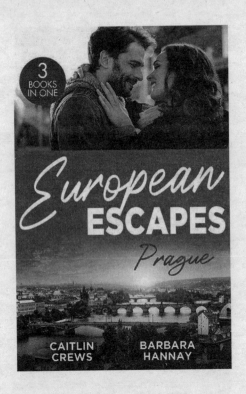

LET'S TALK

Romance

For exclusive extracts, competitions and special offers, find us online:

- **f** MillsandBoon
- **X** @MillsandBoon
- **⊙** @MillsandBoonUK
- **♪** @MillsandBoonUK

Get in touch on 01413 063 232

MILLS & BOON

THE HEART OF ROMANCE

A ROMANCE FOR EVERY READER

MODERN

Prepare to be swept off your feet by sophisticated, sexy and seductive heroes, in some of the world's most glamourous and romantic locations, where power and passion collide.

HISTORICAL

Escape with historical heroes from time gone by. Whether your passion is for wicked Regency Rakes, muscled Vikings or rugged Highlanders, awaken the romance of the past.

MEDICAL

Set your pulse racing with dedicated, delectable doctors in the high-pressure world of medicine, where emotions run high and passion, comfort and love are the best medicine.

True Love

Celebrate true love with tender stories of heartfelt romance, from the rush of falling in love to the joy a new baby can bring, and a focus on the emotional heart of a relationship.

HEROES

The excitement of a gripping thriller, with intense romance at its heart. Resourceful, true-to-life women and strong, fearless men face danger and desire - a killer combination!

From showing up to glowing up, these characters are on the path to leading their best lives and finding romance along the way – with plenty of sizzling spice!

To see which titles are coming soon, please visit

millsandboon.co.uk/nextmonth